DOCUMENTS CONCERNING
RUBASHOV THE GAMBLER

Carl-Johan Vallgren was born in 1964. He is the
author of eight books, of which *The Horrific
Sufferings of the Mind-Reading Monster Hercules
Barefoot* . . . was the first to appear in English. His
novels have been translated into eleven languages.
He lives in Stockholm.

CARL-JOHAN VALLGREN

Documents Concerning Rubashov the Gambler

A Novel

TRANSLATED FROM THE SWEDISH BY
Sarah Death

VINTAGE BOOKS
London

Published by Vintage 2008

2 4 6 8 10 9 7 5 3 1

Copyright © Carl-Johan Vallgren 1996
English translation copyright © Sarah Death 2007

Carl-Johan Vallgren has asserted his right under the Copyright, Designs
and Patents Act 1988 to be identified as the author of this work

First published with the title *Dokument rörande spelaren Rubashov*
by Albert Bonniers Förlag, Stockholm, 1996

First published in Great Britain in 2007 by Harvill Secker

Vintage
Random House, 20 Vauxhall Bridge Road,
London SW1V 2SA

www.vintage-books.co.uk

Addresses for companies within The Random House Group Limited
can be found at: www.randomhouse.co.uk/offices.htm

The Random House Group Limited Reg. No. 954009

A CIP catalogue record for this book
is available from the British Library

ISBN 9780099498247

The Random House Group Limited supports The Forest
Stewardship Council (FSC), the leading international forest
certification organisation. All our titles that are printed on
Greenpeace approved FSC certified paper carry the FSC logo.
Our paper procurement policy can be found at:
www.rbooks.co.uk/environment

Printed in the UK by CPI Bookmarque, Croydon, CR0 4TD

Once upon a time there was . . . *No, that won't work* . . . It all happened in the time of . . . *Good God, what do you mean by 'in the time of?' Try again* . . . Long ago there lived in . . . *How can you say long ago? It wasn't long ago, it was just now, you idiot, just the other day!* . . . It so happened, not so long ago, that a man in the city of . . . *Hopeless, completely hopeless! We give up!*

In Iroquois cosmology, Earth's daughter gives birth to twin sons. One is born in the usual way and shortly thereafter his brother, Flint, is born from his mother's armpit. This proves the death of her. Flint brings ill fortune with him from the very start.

His brother (whose name we have forgotten) is of a quite different calibre. He invents cattle, fire, houses and all manner of practical things for the good of humankind. Flint tries to imitate him, but is nowhere near as gifted. He tries very hard, but fails in everything. Then he loses patience. He hurls mountains around, to destroy the unity and harmony his brother has devised for humankind. And the mountains divide all the peoples and tribes of the Earth; they begin to speak their own languages and dialects and a host of misunderstandings arise, leading to war and barbarism. Flint can only cry. He cannot bear being his brother's unsuccessful shadow.

El, the chief god of the Canaanites, also had a son: Baal. Baal was

1

the god of growth and fertility; he was green, with horns, and could hardly be heard when he spoke, for his mouth was full of leaves on which he sucked and ruminated. His foremost enemy was Mot, the god of sterility and death. They had a great number of disputes as the millennia passed, and one overcast afternoon Baal, who was by nature weak and sickly and preferred to walk alone in the forest, communing with the birds, lost a major clash about the winter solstice. As a result he was degraded and enslaved, then executed and dispatched to the realm of the dead, where he vegetated in the dead matter and gnawed on stones and earth, crying and utterly alone.

Seven years passed on Earth. Every harvest failed, rotted, washed away in the rain, froze or was devoured by locusts. The people starved. They died like flies. And as the eighth year approached they were quite desperate and turned to bloody animal sacrifices to draw the attention of the gods to their misery. As luck would have it, Anath, Baal's sister, responded to their plea. As the goddess of love and war, she was not to be trifled with, and she had invested a good deal of emotion in humankind. What rejoicing there was in the villages when the message reached them that she had found Mot. First, she split him with a sword, then she burned him with a flaming brand, and finally she ground him in a mill. What remained of him became seed-corn, which she caused to be sown in the fields, and Baal was released into the bargain. In triumph he returned to the Earth; and when the Earth saw him, she became verdant, more dazzling than ever, for Earth had missed Baal more than anyone else had . . . This drama of early agriculture gradually became the basis of a legend about an eternal battle between life and death, fertility and infertility, between Baal and Mot, good and evil. But somehow the attributes of the antagonists become muddled. The colour green, for example, and who wore the horns.

The view until not so long ago was that God was originally both good and evil. With his right hand he busied himself with love and mercy, and kneaded forth the right side of the human soul, yetser ha-tob, the good side, while his left hand dispensed anger and destruction and shaped the left half of the soul, yetser ha-ra, the evil side. Right and left, we think, from our as-yet-undefined position; right and wrong; it sounds far too abstract to be entirely credible.

2

As for the story of Yeshu the Nazarene, we can immediately put aside the theory of the sacrificial lamb, since it is quite conventional and leaves no room for wild speculation, which we love. Let us instead take a closer look at what Irenaeus has to say about complications:

According to Irenaeus, an evil angel held the human race hostage for its sins. He punished them thoroughly, and with every justification, for they were an undependable lot, stealing and lying and fighting and deceiving and breaking all manner of commandments, and that sort of behaviour needs to be held in check. But God was sentimental about his seed and found it hard to sleep at nights because the tortured cries of humankind were simply frightful, and their prayers for help and mercy more heart-rending than ever. He decided to take action. It wasn't easy. Legal obstacles presented themselves. Didn't the evil angel have justice on his side in holding the humans hostage for their sins? He did, and could therefore lay down conditions. God, he said, must personally pay the ransom to set them free. That seemed sensible, since the Almighty was the only one around with any free will. Human beings certainly had neither the power to choose nor the means to pay, and therefore God offered his only son as ransom. The evil angel accepted the offer, which proved to be ill judged, for with the son of God as his hostage he was overstepping the boundaries of justice. The son of God was, after all, entirely without sin, and it conflicted with eternal order to hold a sinless creature captive. At a stroke, says Irenaeus, the evil angel thus lost humankind and God's son, and was banished to a dismal realm of shadows.

Watch out for him at the race track, Tertullian warns us, that's where you'll find him. And in the astrologists' towers, the magicians' tents, at the bathhouses, taverns and theatres. Especially at the theatres you'll find him. The theatre is his favourite haunt. You can see him there in the front row of the audience, sucking on his silver stick with the toad's head, and sometimes on stage wearing a terracotta mask, playing the choleric bard in a Greek tragedy.

Nothing is for ever in the cosmic order, claims Origenes a short time later. An archangel can fall and become a demon, a human being can rise and become an angel. An angel can be devalued into a human

*being. And the fallen archangel can confess his sins and be taken up
to the throne of heaven once more.*

*This is the story. Full of paradox, misunderstanding, legend and
incomplete documents. But we've got to start somewhere.*

And so . . .

Once upon a time there was . . .

No, that won't work.

It all happened in the time of . . .

Good God, you must be joking!

Try: At the end of the last century . . .

I

Prologue in St Petersburg

(New Year's Eve 1899)

At the end of the nineteenth century there lived in St Petersburg a man named Josef Nikolai Dimitrievich Rubashov, son of a Kirghiz merchant and an Estonian woman, in whose veins ran the blood of the Swedish populations of Pärnu and Haapsalu. Josef Nikolai – or Kolya as he was also known – was thus a fairly typical representative of holy Russia, that vast embroidery of peoples and languages, of enlightened fools, pious and ungodly, who since the dawn of time had intermixed and spread out over almost one-sixth of the surface of the Earth, from Odessa in the west to Yakutsk in the east.

Of the years he spent growing up in one corner of this mighty continent there is little to tell: of his childhood on Tverskaya, in the shadow of the domes of Smolny Cathedral; of his summers in Narva, where the family once owned a little country retreat; of his love for his mother Tatiana Rubashova, who now lay ill with a severe epileptic condition; or of his passion for the actress Nina Fourier, prima donna and *belle de jour* at the new Théâtre Française; not to mention his poisonous relationship with his elder brother, the correct and tetchy Mikhail Rubashov, head of the family.

One could give an account of this period of his life, present it by means of letters and notes written in his own unmistakable hand, or of communications concerning his education by governesses. One could refer, moreover, to documents still in our possession. We lack nothing in this regard. On the contrary. Our filing cabinets are full of dossiers, papers and neatly completed forms, of photographs and newspaper cuttings, stuck into dusty albums, all painstakingly numbered and catalogued.

But we do not. Our interest lies in quite different matters. Josef's childhood and adolescence, you see, will soon belong to another era.

His story only assumes any importance on a particular stroke of the clock, a stroke at which things will change for him absolutely. And we shall reach that point soon, since time is now, at this moment, carrying us ever closer to the first, trembling second of the twentieth century.

Only two things are of interest to us before the church bells of the city ring in the new century, and the crowd on Nevsky Prospekt, many thousand strong, breaks into a cheer: the black charabanc that, wheels skidding in the snow and slush, is nearing the house in Sadovaya Street where Josef Nikolai rents a fourth-floor room from an officer's widow; and the Lombardic playing cards laid out ready for shuffling and cutting on the table in his room. The carriage is bearing his fate, a fate determined from the outset by those cards. For Josef Nikolai is a gambler of the most inveterate kind, possessed by the demon of gaming, a sybarite of suspense. And as a consequence, as a final link in the chain of continuously raised stakes, very soon – any moment now – his remarkable fate will be sealed . . .

He was an addict of cards and dice, a slave to odds and stakes, permanently high on the belladonna of expectation, and had been so ever since losing his first game of dice at the age of eighteen to a French lieutenant who was passing through. Twelve years had elapsed since that day, a decade of paltry winnings and dizzying losses, a marathon dance through the underworld gambling clubs of the imperial city. Possessed by the demon, he had seen his inheritance go up in smoke, family heirlooms pawned, credit withdrawn. And now, finally, in the last breath of the nineteenth century, he was pauperised, up to his eyes in repayment demands, ripe for the debtors' prison.

8

There was not a single game of chance invented at which he had not lost. He had tried them all: poker, pontoon, whist, gin rummy, scopone, cassino, polignac and auction cribbage. Dice and draughts, tossed coins and drawn straws. For hours he had stood at roulette tables, seeing the chip piles slowly shrink and disappear into the banks' insatiable maw. His brow aglow with gambling fever, he had stood in queues outside betting shops. He was an institution at St Petersburg's racecourses, a standing joke in its skittle alleys; he had lost on horses and dogs, at baccarat, in imperial charity raffles; and in the cellar at the house of a Mexican freight-shipping agent he had lost his confirmation ring on a bloody cockfight.

Maybe it was such matters he was pondering as he sat alone in his room while fireworks illuminated the night sky beyond; plus the fact that, in spite of all his losses, in spite of standing now on the brink of ruin and having even gambled away all his mother's annuity, in spite of all this he had taken pleasure in it.

For it was true. He had taken a pleasure beyond all reason, and perhaps that fact should have made his shame all the deeper – but he felt no shame whatsoever. It was a new world that had opened up to him when the Frenchman put the dice into his open hand and in a strange, drunken voice asked him to throw; a world of chancing and cool calculation, guessing and algebra, intuition, cheating and probability theory; of fever and cold sweats, and the vaguely ecstatic loosening of the bowels that never fails to make itself felt every time you see your opponent's hand when the kitty is ten thousand roubles.

Now he got to his feet and went over to the window. The house was quiet, but from the centre of the city came the hum of the celebrating crowds. Nina, he thought. Was she out there too? The little actress with the big, crimson mouth and the gap between her teeth, the woman he had loved insanely for almost ten years? He had lost her as well, with the same carelessness as he had gambled away his diamond tie-pin or the marten-fur coat once worn by his father, the late Dimitri Rubashov. Not so long ago she had been at his side, when as a young heir he had invited her to the city's most elegant restaurants, and sent her jewels and love poems by Lermontov written on Chinese paper and liberally splashed with Dutch perfume. Now she no longer wanted to see him, a fact he found as natural as knowing that snow is cold or that birds fly. Why should she want to? He, Josef Nikolai, a poor lodger, ruined, with the threat of the debtors' prison hanging over him like the great branch of a menacing tree. In this, too, he took a kind of pleasure, the same shameless arousal he had found in his interminable succession of losses.

Another pyrotechnic set piece exploded, covering the sky in flowing tresses of sparks. Kolya stiffened. For in the sudden light he could see the carriage slithering through the snow, less than half a block away.

'Can it be possible?' he thought. 'Can it really be possible? By God. He's coming . . .'

The knock on the door was loud and clear, like a lottery ticket seller's, thought Josef, or a debt collector's. He hesitated for a moment, feeling a shiver of fear, before taking the lamp and going out into the unlit hallway. His landlady, Mrs Orlova the officer's widow, was not at home, and nor were the other lodgers: neither the German Herr Zweig, a lawyer's clerk; nor Waida, the batman, who lived in the room facing the inner courtyard. Every last person was out celebrating the start of the new century, everyone but himself, he assumed, as he went to the door in trepidation.

He opened it, and stopped. A sudden gust of wind blew through the stairwell, and as his lamp began to flicker and cast long, pointed shadows across the walls, he could not distinguish the features of his guest. Only a strange smell. A vague aroma of vinegar and rotten eggs, a hint of brown coal dust, and a scarcely discernible note of ammonia and sour milk, crowned with the somewhat eruptive odour of green cheese.

'Josef Nikolai Rubashov?' said a reedy, slightly childish voice. 'We have an appointment.'

'That's me,' said Kolya.

'Good. No time to lose. My diary is full.'

So saying, the guest stepped into the hall and closed the door behind him. He took off his overcoat, made of silvery, shimmering fur that Josef Nikolai could not recall ever having seen before. He held out his hand and Kolya shook it, feeling rather as if he were in a dream.

'I didn't think . . .' he said. 'I mean, I wasn't quite sure . . .'

'Sure I would turn up, you mean?' his guest offered. 'What were you expecting, Kolya, that my arrival would be heralded by a shower of toads? *Mon frère, quelle folie.* Haven't you seen the rockets out there? In case it has somehow escaped your notice, allow me to remind you that we will soon be entering the twentieth century. According to the Gregorian calendar, in a quarter of an hour from now, to be precise.'

The guest folded his fur coat over his arm and Josef gave an awkward smile. He could distinguish him more clearly now. He was a man of his own age, to judge by external appearance, which would naturally be a mistake. Short of stature, quite thin, with a hairline receding at the temples, and a snub nose with a droplet that was about to fall from its cavities, like a melted pearl. He wore round glasses and had a fresh shaving cut on one cheek. He was carrying a brown, calfskin briefcase. There was a pen stuck behind his ear.

'What are we waiting for?' he asked. 'I can't stay beyond midnight. Writing a contract doesn't take long, Josef Nikolai, but there are certain formalities to be observed.'

Kolya smiled, feeling awkward once more, and led his guest across widow Orlova's hall floor, covered with worn rugs from distant Samarkand, and into his room on Sadovaya Street, four flights up.

Outside, against the St Petersburg sky, the full range of pyrotechnic art was on display: showers of light, mushrooms, flowers, signs of the zodiac – all in the colours of the Russian flag. Josef stopped by the table where the pack of cards lay ready for cutting. This encounter was making him feel slightly giddy, a little lightheaded, as if he had stood up too quickly.

'What are you staring at, Kolya?' asked the guest. 'My clothes . . .

aren't they, to coin a phrase, *à la mode?* Let me tell you, I do my best, but there's hardly time to acquire an item of clothing before it's dreadfully out of fashion, and one has to get another. I do as well as I can, considering the lack of time and this constant running around from person to person, all of them demanding meetings for one reason or another.'

The visitor laid his coat aside on the chaise longue and pulled off his chamois-leather gloves, finger by finger, with the nonchalance of a woman. He glanced over at the window.

'Chiortrograd,' he mumbled. 'The Devil's City. That's what they call it. The fools. One may well wonder what virus it is that has infected all these people. We will soon be entering the twentieth century, but do you think anything will change? Hardly. And if anything does, it will only be for the worse.'

He took off his glasses, de-misted them with a rub on his shirt cuff, perched them back on his nose and turned to Josef again:

'And you, Kolya?' he said, smiling. 'What are you after? A woman? Several women perhaps, a whole harem to dribble wine into your mouth and feed you candied pears? Or is it money you want? Gold, jewels, three wishes? Revenge on an enemy, a cure for chronic syphilis, a formula for brewing a love potion? Own up, it's nothing to be ashamed of. I've heard it all before.'

Kolya was once again aware of his guest's strange smell, this time intermingled with something else: a cheap, unsophisticated cologne. 'No,' he said. 'In my case, it's the thrill.'

The guest frowned, mumbled something inaudible and began a tour of the room. He stopped at Josef's wardrobe, opened it and looked inside.

'Not much here,' he said. 'A bag of mothballs, two waistcoats, a dead fly, and your best suit worn thin in the sleeves. Financial difficulties, I see. Which of the vices has it been, Kolya? Absinthe?'

He closed the wardrobe again, went over to the card table and ran a beautifully manicured fingernail lightly over the pack of cards.

'And what have we here? Marseilles. Fifteenth century. They're copies. I played with the original once, exquisite . . . it's vanished now, of course, in some insane war.'

12

He abruptly fell silent, folded his arms on his chest and stared at Josef.

'Are you joking?' he enquired wryly. 'What sort of thrill? Now tell me what it is you're really after.'

The guest fell silent and looked Kolya up and down, chewing his lip slightly as he did so.

'Is it a woman?' he said finally. 'A broken heart, Kolya? The symptoms, I may say, are unmistakable.'

'No, it's a question of the thrill. I have heard that Monsignor is fond of games of chance.'

The guest began to laugh, a very attractive, chiming laugh that reminded Kolya of tokens, delicate little silver tokens falling one by one into a winner's pocket.

'Poker?' he said. 'I see. One more in the long line of crazy gamblers. You're in a worse state than I thought. Just move my gloves, and we'll make a start. Good God: *it's the thrill*. Well, I never!'

Kolya picked up the gloves and put them on the shelf by the window. More fireworks were going off, lighting up the street below, and as his eyes were spontaneously drawn downwards, he saw the carriage, which had now turned and was parked on the other side of the road, outside the baker's.

'What about your coachman?' Kolya said. 'You could have asked him to come up with you, sir. It's cold out there.'

'He's not much of a talker,' the other man said with a yawn. 'And he doesn't feel the cold at all.'

Kolya looked down into the street again, at the figure hunched in the driver's seat, dressed in a thin black coat that appeared slightly glazed in the light from the rockets and the snow, which had begun to fall once more in fine, jagged flakes. He could see him clearly now: the pale face, the dark, all-too-sunken eyes; and the fact that, despite the cold, there was no frosted breath rising from his mouth.

Heart pounding, he returned to the table.

'Your cut,' the guest said.

And they sat down to play.

*

Basically, thought Josef Nikolai as he sat with his opponent on Sadovaya Street and cut the pack in preparation for the first deal, there's only one way people react to the completely unexpected: with shock, of a milder or more severe variety. If it doesn't paralyse us with its force, it leaves us at the very least with a feeling of unreality, or is happening in an existence separate from the usual one, and the latter certainly applies to me at this moment . . . He surreptitiously observed his guest, who was glumly examining his cuticles, apparently quite unconcerned about the coming game. For what did he convey, this man, this character, this creature, with his peculiar manner and gruff cynicisms, with his round glasses and the pen behind his ear, if not precisely that: a dreamlike sensation? The reality was not coinciding with Kolya's mental image of this meeting. If he had visualised anything at all, without going into detail, it was something quite different; something more frightening. But the guest was not in the least frightening. Apart from that slightly odd smell, he generally put one in mind of some local-government clerk – in fact, he was not entirely dissimilar to Waida, the batman who lived at the end of the corridor.

Kolya felt a sudden sense of shame as he recalled his guest's words about the shoeblack: 'All your exertions with that ridiculous castrato, you surely don't think they were what brought me here?' The Skoptsist monk, the little castrato Iliodor, who in his squeaky voice had dictated the letter for him, burned an incense of aloe and ground amber and read a piece from *Solomon's Key*. Iliodor claimed to have made provision for his own spiritual future decades earlier, producing as proof a yellowing contract, written in magpie blood, he said, with a quill pen made from the wing feather of a gander, on a bit of parchment stolen from a monastery; and later – at least two bottles of Madeira later – in his cell at the Skoptsist monastery, in the gleam of a tallow candle, he had even bared his shaven head to let Josef Nikolai see with his own eyes the number branded into the skin behind one of his big, red ears. He hadn't taken it seriously at the time. Now he thought perhaps he should have done.

'What's the matter, Kolya?' asked his guest kindly. He had taken

14

off his glasses to adjust one of the sidepieces, and was now replacing them on his nose. 'Are you not quite well? Perhaps you are having second thoughts. Don't for God's sake imagine I find this amusing. I've plenty of other things to do. I can go if you wish.'

'No,' said Kolya. 'Stay.'

The guest patted the pen that was stuck behind his ear.

'As you wish,' he said. 'But despite your personal assurances that you have no demands beyond the so-called *thrill*, we must none-theless have something to play for. It goes without saying. You stake your soul, of course, and put it entirely at my disposal. But what do you want if, against all the odds, you happen to win?'

He thought of all the hundreds, nay thousands, of gamblers he had encountered: those who fell on their knees in tears after losing their last possession; those who, jubilant and dancing, left a gambling table twenty thousand roubles richer; the destitute and the elevated; or Captain Petrovich of the cavalry whom he had seen with his own eyes, after losing a game of dice, take up a small-bore revolver and blow his brains out in front of his wife . . . Yes, he thought, I have seen them all, farmers and soldiers, cripples and earls; Bakuninites and Decembrists. They were all members of the brotherhood of gambling, and he, pulled taut like them by the bow-string of unfathomable suspense, loved them as dearly as the game itself . . . There was but one of them he had never had occasion to meet before. And that was why he was here now. This was the gamble of his life. This was the ultimate in stakes and choice of opposition: playing for his immortal soul without asking for anything but the thrill in return.

'Well, Kolya,' said his guest with some urgency. 'What do you wish me to stake? A pot of gold ducats, raymondines, florins? The heart of an unfaithful woman? The choice is yours!'

'No, it is enough to have the honour of facing you as my opponent.'

'Honour?' The guest stared at him. 'That's no answer in matters as delicate as this *affaire*. Consider a moment, Josef Nikolai: is it really worth it? Are you following the voice of your conscience? I don't play with people who, in states of temporary confusion, act in

15

conflict with their deepest convictions. One must play for something substantial and of value. That's fundamental. Those are the rules.'

The visitor extracted a cigarillo from the inner pocket of his waistcoat, lit it, blew out smoke and coughed twice.

'Let me tell you, Kolya, that for me this whole business . . . how shall I put it . . . means nothing. What difference is it to me: one more or less? So think it over carefully. What do you really think you stand to gain by it? Undying fame? A juicy memory? A good story to tell by the fire in the autumn of your years? I can't make you out. So I'm giving you a chance to reconsider. Be sensible!'

And Josef hesitated. He thought of his mother, Tatiana Rubashova, of her sad, nut-brown eyes staring at him from her hospital bed at the Holy Synod Hospital. Of her fragile body and the little heart fluttering beneath the lavender-scented sheets; of the much-thumbed calendar of saints and the bunch of everlasting flowers on the bedside table. If she could see him now, her heart would burst like an overripe fruit and she would die before she could manage to raise her frail hand in one last sign of the cross.

He looked at the playing cards and then at his guest, who was anxiously winding his pocket watch, shaking it and raising it to his ear with an expression of concern. The image of Kolya's mother faded and was replaced by another, of his brother Mikhail Rubashov, who with a look of sheer hatred pointed a trembling index finger, threatening him . . . A wave of self-contempt washed over Kolya. What was the point? Wasn't he already lost? Wasn't he hopelessly destined for perdition for all time? Yes, he was expecting it and he deserved it. So why shouldn't he, one last time, just once . . . The temptation was too great. He said:

'I don't want to be sensible. We'll play for nothing but my soul. If you've no objection, we'll begin at once.'

'I really do regret your pig-headedness, Josef Nikolai. But since you insist, let it be as you wish. Just a few formalities first.'

The guest leaned over and picked up his briefcase from the floor. He opened it, reached a pale hand deep inside and drew out a document.

It was an unremarkable, pre-printed form – not wholly unlike those used for the intermittent imperial censuses. A few section-marks and explanatory footnotes, a few ruled feint lines with pre-printed text. A perforated section with brief details about himself, completed in a scrawled hand. Date and place of birth, something about his certificate of baptism, a quotation from the letter he had written with Iliodor. The date had already been filled in: it was tomorrow's; the first day of the new century, by the Russian calendar.

'What are you waiting for?' asked the guest. He had taken the pen from behind his ear and was holding it out, across the table. 'This is an IOU, I suppose you could say. To avoid legal misunderstandings in the future, if you should lose. The pen is filled with nothing but ink. Contracts signed in blood are the stuff of pure legend. I detest blood; quite simply, I can't stand it; sometimes I even pass out.' He lowered his voice. 'You can still change your mind, Kolya. But time is short, very short. I have another appointment in less than half an hour.'

Josef, however, was no longer listening. He put pen to paper and signed, as a faint vertiginous feeling suffused him and the last vestiges of his doubt vanished like a volatile gas out into widow Orlova's dreary apartment.

'And now,' said the guest. 'One last thing: the money.'

And from the same briefcase he extracted ten bundles of notes, as thick as cutlets and tied with coarse twine, gave five to Kolya and kept the others himself.

'We must create a certain ambience, you know,' he said with a smile. 'For if we are to play, Josef Nikolai, then we will do it in earnest, as gamblers do, and whoever is the first to find himself with two empty pockets will have lost.'

Much later, when the church bells of St Petersburg had stopped ringing and Josef was sitting alone in the silent apartment, it would dawn on him that something had gone wrong with time that evening; that his opponent had somehow suspended it. For the game of poker, which by the clock had lasted scarcely ten minutes, had felt like hours, long-drawn-out, eventful hours.

They had played straight poker with no open cards, with free betting, and as is usual when two players meet for the first time, their positions had kept changing drastically. At one point, after taking a particularly large pot, the guest had almost three-quarters of the money in a neat pile beside him, but Josef had fought his way back in with some sequences of three of a kind and some high-value pairs. Much to his astonishment, the guest was a far worse player than he had expected. His face could be read, revealing on more than one occasion that he had a bad hand. He complained of the irritating light from the fireworks, sweated in the poorly heated room, grunted, muttered out loud, and even swore in fury after making the obvious mistake of discarding an ace of clubs in the hope of a hearts flush. No, his guest was not a true player. He did not belong to that company of lost soul-searchers for whom only the intoxication of the game sharpened the eye as they applied their misguided knowledge of human nature to reading the characters of their fellow players, and thus their hands, just as in an open book.

But the game had continued. Josef was later to recall his disappointment at missing a straight, and losing a pot despite holding three aces. Everything was strangely clear: the guest's face and grunts, the rustle of the banknotes, the mildly intoxicating suspense he felt at every new deal. The money on the table, he later realised, must have amounted to more than two hundred thousand roubles, a sum he had only dreamed of since that day twelve years before when he came into his inheritance. But the value of the money as anything but the stuff of the game, the bricks for building this transient temple of suspense, had simply not occurred to him.

They reached the finale. They were evenly matched, and soon found themselves sitting with an enormous pot untouched before them. Josef had long since stopped counting the deals; hours seemed to have passed, but he didn't feel remotely tired.

The guest shuffled and dealt. Josef's first hand was worrying;

from the mixed colours and denominations he kept his two best cards, a queen of spades and a jack of hearts. The guest, whose hand was clearly even worse, exchanged all his . . . Josef took three new cards, placed them behind the other two, fanned them out and restrained himself from the slightest twitch that could have betrayed his triumphant delight; it was a full house of jacks and queens.

Against the night sky, so many rockets were now exploding that it seemed as bright as day. The buzz from Nevsky seemed to have intensified, and from a nearby street came the sound of bellowing and sporadic cheers. But Josef was oblivious to it all. He stared at his guest, who in turn stared at his new hand and wiped a few drops of perspiration from his brow. He was aware once more of the slightly sour smell emanating from him, and with that smell tickling his nostrils like a musty feather, with a feigned, scarcely discernible expression of uncertainty, he added half his remaining notes to the pot – virtually convinced that his opponent would throw in his hand.

The guest regarded him in bewilderment, scratched his neck and appeared to be hesitating. 'Remarkable,' he heard him mumble. 'Very strange.' But then he shrugged his shoulders and, with a crooked smile, made a counter-bid – and raised the stake.

They had reached the end. There was no chance of Kolya throwing in his cards. Why should he? The win was as good as his, the whole enormous pot. With a full house of queens and jacks in his hand. All he had to do was put the rest of his money on the table and then see his opponent. In front of him, the guest stifled a yawn, took out his pocket watch again, shook it and looked at the time. It was quite impossible for his cards to be any better than Kolya's own, since he had exchanged his entire hand: a full house of aces and kings, a four or a flush – the chance of things like that happening were only one in a thousand.

Josef put the last of his bundle of notes in the pot.

'You'll see me, then?' said the guest. 'I warned you, my good Kolya.'

And with a slight shrug of his shoulders, his face not betraying any emotion, he put his cards on the table: four kings.

'You've lost,' was all he said.

And at that very second, the New Year bells began to ring.

There would soon be silence. The hubbub from the main boulevards was dying away. The glare of the rockets was gone. Against the window, the snow was falling; thin white flakes, celestial dust. Widow Orlova's Swiss wall clock ticked slowly from the far reaches of her apartment; time seemed to have reverted to its normal rhythm, five minutes into the new century. Josef heard the chair creak under him. He felt nothing in particular. It was like any other loss, apart from the fact that he had lost no money, because it had all belonged to his guest in the first place. Outside the window the sky was dark once more, with only a few stars to be seen through the falling snow; a faintly luminous cipher of light.

He heard the guest clearing his throat:

'I really am sorry you lost, Kolya. It was as unexpected for me as for you. I was lucky. Unbelievably lucky. A four of a picture card? I couldn't believe my eyes.'

Kolya looked down at the floor, where the worn calfskin briefcase stood. It didn't even feel absurd, he thought, just unreal, like some story he had been told long ago, and then had almost forgotten.

'A new century,' the guest said, 'and everything's suddenly so quiet. I really shouldn't be sitting here . . . I ought to go. I'm late already.'

Kolya nodded. He wondered what to do next. Thank his guest for coming? Wish him bon voyage? What was the proper etiquette in cases such as this?

He said:

'What happens now?'

'Another appointment, on Morskaya. Then I have to go south. A certain bishop in Cherson has asked for an appointment, and after that I've a general in Minsk. It just goes on and on, I tell you, and there are times when I wish somebody would put an end it all, with one big, annihilating explosion, so I could finally have a bit of rest.'

'No, I mean to me. I mean, will I . . . ?'

20

'End up in the hotter regions, you mean? Dear Kolya, hell is a metaphor, a theological sophism. What century do you think we're living in?' The guest let his finger glide over his lips, as if he had already said too much. 'What's more,' he added, 'it's full. Overflowing. Has been for centuries.'

He leaned forward from his sitting position and pulled the briefcase up onto his lap.

'It's complete chaos in my spheres. Truly. Total anarchy. And that's why, because of the crowding, I've had to adapt my methods. Punishment by immortality. Earthly life becomes the eternal prison of the soul, as it were. Patience, my good Kolya, patience will be the watchword in your case.'

Muttering something to himself under his breath, he tied the banknotes into bundles, stowed them in his briefcase and got to his feet.

'You must forgive my abrupt departure,' he said, 'but my coachman is waiting, new clients are waiting, everyone's waiting, the world is the waiting room for the soul.'

'I don't believe it,' said Josef Nikolai.

'Believe what?'

'Any of this. How can I believe it? Good God, just look at yourself, you look like . . .'

An ordinary bookkeeper, he was about to say, or a batman. But then he shut up, as if he had transgressed the boundary to the private sphere.

'Josef,' said the guest. 'What is it you want of me? What is it you all want of me? What does it take to make you believe? Miracles? Certainly not a contemporary look. But what am I to do with cloven hooves and a ridiculous pair of horns? I couldn't bear the shame of it. What do you expect . . . smoke and flames? Visions and illusions. Is that what you want? Very well.'

And at that moment Josef Rubashov saw something that would etch itself into his memory and dispel for ever all his doubts about the true identity of his guest. For where that being had been, two metres from him on the floor, the actress Nina Fourier was now standing, or at least a copy of her, a doppelgänger so terrifyingly

21

identical he could never have distinguished between this one and the original, had it not been for the slight sour smell and the guest's spectacles, perched on the tip of the doppelgänger's nose.

'Josef,' said Nina in her own, highly individual voice with a trace of French accent. 'Don't you believe me . . . Josef?'

It was a shock so grave that for a moment he was on the verge of fainting, but before he reached unconsciousness he was hurled through a second shock, a sequence of shocks, back to a clarity so intense that it burned him like ice; for Nina's place was now taken by his mother, wearing the gown of a patient at the Holy Synod Hospital with the monogram of the Archbishop on the collar, holding her dog-eared calendar of saints in one hand and a blurred zinc etching portraying Josef Rubashov as a child in the other. She said, in her usual, tired voice, rendered more pitiful by the effects of the falling sickness on her teeth and tongue over the years: 'Josef Nikolai, I do not understand why you cannot believe.'

And now, in a succession so rapid that Kolya could hardly register it, one transformation followed another: his mother turned into Mikhail Rubashov, who became his father Dimitri Rubashov, who turned into a black hen, a limping donkey, a shaggy dog, a hunchbacked dwarf, a local drunkard, a holy fool, a lame Turk, followed by a host of other animal and human figures, all of whom addressed him in their respective languages and voices, until the guest stood there once more in his previous form, not entirely unlike the batman Waida.

'I must ask you,' he said matter-of-factly, 'not to speak in too much detail of what you have just seen. It could damage your reputation. People have certain notions of reality, and they are ready to leap to their defence.'

So saying, and with a brief nod to Josef Rubashov, he took up his fur coat and his gloves, his pen and his worn calfskin briefcase, and left the apartment on Sadovaya Street.

Kolya remained seated where he was for quite some time, incapable of getting up. The smell of sour milk and brown coal dust still lingered in the room. His gaze flickered between the playing cards, the kerosene lamp and the bare, dismal walls of the room.

Finally, on legs that trembled a little, he made his way to the window.

Down below, in the lightly falling snow, the guest was walking across to the charabanc. The coachman must have fallen asleep, for he gave him a shake, raised a hand as if to deliver a blow and shouted something, presumably a reproach, which Kolya could not hear. The coachman seemed remorseful as he sat hunched over the reins. He was quivering beneath his cowl, and from the empty eye sockets of his skull shone a faint glimmer of shame.

In his dazed condition, Rubashov wondered whether the dead could really sleep. And the immortal, he thought, how was it for them?

New Year's Resolutions

(New Year's Day 1900)

But Josef could sleep. All that night, the first night of the twentieth century, he slept a very deep sleep with his head sunk like a big, hairy egg into his pillow on Sadovaya Street in the imperial capital. He dreamed of a clock, and himself somehow trapped in its mechanical works, and every hour on the hour a door opened in the clock face and he was forced to stick his head out, like a cuckoo, and chant a nursery rhyme in Latin, before the door shut again and he was trapped once more among cogs, springs and weights.

And while Josef slept, St Petersburg was waking up to the first morning of the century, a morning that stank of vomit and excrement, half-empty beer tankards, rancid fat and costly champagne; for the celebration had been lavish in both palaces and hovels. Softly, like a drowsy millipede, the city began to move. Beggars came creeping from coal cellars and doorways. Menservants with aching heads tiptoed between piles of refuse and pools of vomit, on their way to the bakers' shops to buy fresh, butter-rich loaves for their moaning, hung-over masters, who on this day would not rise from their beds and cosy mistresses for many hours, if at all.

Drunks fortified themselves with the dregs from discarded bottles, red-eyed priests hurried to monasteries and churches. The snow on the streets was stained with urine. The house fronts bore spatters of gunpowder from the rockets of the night before. Crêpe paper was blowing in the wind. Animals were bleating, barking, whinnying and lowing.

And eventually, widow Orlova's furious banging on the door roused Josef Nikolai, too. Sweaty, jolted from sleep, he sat up and ran his hands over his legs to smooth out the creases in the last pair of everyday trousers he possessed. With a shudder, he recalled his dream. It had been spiced by a number of extra variations: there had been a black cat sitting in front of the clock face, and every time the door had opened and he had been thrust out to chant his rhyme, it had lunged to bite him with its sharp teeth. His brother Mikhail Rubashov, hanging from the minute hand, had screamed at him to take his own life, ruined as it was by the most odious of sins; and in the dream Josef, filled with shame, had wondered whether he in fact had a point . . .

But outside in the corridor, the voice of the officer's widow was growing ever more shrill:

'Josef Nikolai! There are two gentlemen waiting for you in the hall. Josef Nikolai, are you awake? Can you hear me?'

He could hear, but had no wish to reply; he was no sooner released from his dream than he became aware of the strange scent that was still, like a diaphanous veil, an olfactory echo of the night's events, lingering in the room. He looked over to the table, where the cards still lay. And beside the pack, two open hands, one a full house and the other a four. With a dim sense of unreality, he recalled what had happened the night before. The guest. The coachman. The succession of transformations.

Out in the hall, the widow was whispering with someone, and then her voice came again:

'I demand you answer, Josef Rubashov! Can you hear me? You will have to take responsibility for your actions. The gentlemen are out here waiting, they say it's important, very important, to do with a promissory note. And I must talk to you about the rent.' She rattled the door, but it was locked. 'Four months is more than I can take. I'm a kind-hearted person, Mr Kolya, but there are limits. Can you hear me?!'

Josef got up. Beside the pack of cards he had spotted a sheet of paper, and to his amazement he saw it was a carbon copy of the so-called contract, or promissory note, that he had signed just before midnight. He held it up to the light, which was streaming in through the window like a thick grey juice. He wondered how it came to be there; he had no memory of the guest having left it on his departure.

At the bottom, beside his own signature, was another, illegible one, just a scrawl, and across it a stamp in some indecipherable script, possibly Hebrew . . . He folded it once across the middle, then again, and proceeded to tear it into pieces the size of his fingernail, which he tossed into the waste-paper basket.

From outside the door, the widow called again, 'Josef Nikolai, I can hear you! What are you doing? Why aren't you answering? Let me in so we can talk this over like adults. Four months, and not so much as a rouble from you. The lot's gone on gaming, and not all of it legal . . . Open the door, the gentlemen are impatient!'

But Josef had no plans to open the door. He pulled the chair out from the table, sat down, rested his head in his hands, and to his surprise discovered yet another contract, another copy of what he had just torn to shreds. Frowning, he crumpled it into a ball and threw it over his shoulder. But when he looked back down at the table, it was there again – and finally the truth hit him.

Outside the door, the widow had given up. He could hear her dusting her ikons in the corridor, then slamming a door, presumably in rage. In the room of Zweig, the lawyer's clerk, all was silent, but from Waida's room came the sound of someone throwing up, severely and repeatedly, followed by a complaining mumble, probably a prayer . . . Kolya had by then double-checked his theory by looking in the waste-paper basket. It contained no torn-up contract, and the one he had crumpled into a ball and thrown onto the floor had also vanished. Muttering absent-mindedly, he paced back and forth across the room with the document in his hand.

Reaching the tiled stove, he took out a match and set fire to the contract. It was remarkable: the flames did not seem to touch it, simply flaring round it like a hot red film. He wondered what sort of material it was made of. Some kind of oilcloth, perhaps? Or maybe it was impregnated with some sort of fireproof chemical?

Next he fetched his last bottle of Dutch genever and poured the spirit onto the floor in a little puddle. He dipped the paper into the liquid, first one side, then the other. Again he set fire to it, but it remained unscathed. Instead, his old bedside slippers and an empty hat box made of papier mâché caught fire, and the flames spread to the waste paper basket. The fire developed rapidly, smoke rising in cumulus-like clouds. Kolya rushed over to the bed, picked up the full chamber pot, threw the contents over the flames and then stamped wildly in the basket.

When he had finished he looked up, his face blackened with soot, and saw through the smoke the widow Orlova, who had let herself into the room with her spare key. She stared at him, coughed, and choked out the words:

'Josef Nikolai . . . I'm throwing you out.'

Scarcely a minute later he was standing in a gateway on Sadovaya Street. In a bundle over his shoulder he carried his last remaining possessions: a few clothes, a pack of cards and an odd piece of paper. As he had disappeared out of the widow's back door he had heard the agitated cries of a certain Armenian pawnbroker and an investor, discovering he had fled.

Out of sight of his creditors, he set his course to a new point of the compass and headed up towards Nevsky. A few cabs with red-eyed drivers passed him, then a horsedrawn tram. On the other side of the street, a little band of beggar children were building a snowman: Father Frost with a broad belt of cardboard, a burned-out rocket in one hand and an empty aquavit bottle in the other.

Josef Rubashov considered his situation. Viewed objectively, his position was not ideal. Destitute and no roof over his head. But as so often with things viewed objectively, this was only the beginning. Josef had something greater than the security of money or a home: he had plans.

He crossed the bridge over the Fotanka Canal and passed by the meat-red palace of Prince Beloselsky-Belozersky. The snow had once again begun to fall. People were huddled against the cold. A drunk lost his footing on a patch of ice and, in the distance, the clock of Kazan Cathedral struck.

At Moscow Station he stopped again and felt in his bundle to make sure the contract was still there. He folded it in two and put it in the inside pocket of his coat. The snow lashed his face, but he did not recoil. With a feeling of invincibility, of owning the whole world and being able to defend it against all comers, he continued along the wide boulevard, across Alexander Nevsky Square and the River Neva, its foul, stinking waters bearing away rubbish, frozen vomit, ice-floes and the occasional drowned corpse to an unknown fate.

He was in the south-eastern part of the city. Along the street came two kaftan-clad men pulling a cartload of fresh horse hides. The building he sought was wedged between a bakery selling unleavened bread and a rabbinical seminary, where a bearded man in a skull-cap was reading prayers on the front steps. With a sudden rush of excitement, he spied the sign that hung on the door: 'Surgery. Dr Mordechai Isaak.'

He gave his name to a cross-eyed housekeeper and was shown into a dark waiting room. He sat down in an armchair. The walls were adorned with large anatomical diagrams; transparencies of the human body, cross-sections of brains, circulatory systems, neural pathways, muscles and intestines. On a table there was a glass case containing a human skull. In one corner stood a yellowed skeleton. On the walls hung pincers for blood-letting, a ventouse and other old-fashioned surgical instruments. Josef's thoughts went to the guest and his sleeping coachman. But the night's events were blurred round the edges, as if he were remembering them through a drunken haze. Contract . . . transformations . . . immortality? These were concepts that meant nothing to him. But he was certain that the strange sheet of paper he had in his pocket was not made from any common material.

After a little while he was shown into the doctor's consulting room.

'Kolya?' said the doctor brusquely. 'What's the reason for your visit?'

The reason for his visit was the remarkable document, naturally, plus the fact that Dr Isaak was as incurable a gambler as Josef himself. And since Josef knew the psychology of every true player as thoroughly as he knew his own, he knew that Dr Isaak wouldn't be able to resist a wager – the stranger, the better. After a few initial pleasantries, he therefore produced his suggestion. The wager was to be two hundred roubles (a sum, he reasoned, large enough to capture the doctor's attention, but still small enough for him not to insist on seeing Josef's money first) on whether the doctor could destroy the small, insignificant sheet of paper with a whiff of sour milk about it, which he was now holding up in front of him with a very earnest expression.

The doctor took it, looked at it without reading it, sniffed it and wrinkled his nose.

'Are you serious?' he said. 'Destroy a piece of paper?'

'Two hundred roubles if you can.'

'You're not sick, are you, Josef Nikolai?'

Kolya didn't even need to deny the accusation, for he could see in the doctor's eyes that the bait had been swallowed . . .

What followed resulted within an hour in his leaving the doctor's surgery two hundred roubles and a good few memories richer. The money would soon be history, he thought, but he would keep the memories for his distant old age, when he might need to retrieve them to enjoy a good laugh. The doctor tried absolutely everything. First, burning it in his iron stove, then mincing it in his hand-cranked shredding machine, and when neither of those methods worked he had taken it into his laboratory and there, through a stream of invective in Yiddish and Sephardic Spanish, tried to expunge it from the surface of the Earth. But nothing made any impact on the paper. Neither ether nor sulphur, saltpetre nor the pure alcohol in which the doctor preserved old kidneys and ovaries for the purposes of research. In the end the doctor had broken down and sobbed, for he was, besides his other eccentricities, a very bad loser.

Seeing Josef to the door, he said in pleading tone:

'I hope this will remain between the two of us, Josef Rubashov, and not leak out to any of our mutual acquaintances.'

Josef swore to remain silent. The doctor was so caught up in the wager that he never thought to ask any questions about the remarkable sheet of paper, where it came from or what it meant. For in the psychology of a gambler, the world was ordered according to the higher principle of suspense and thrill, and the choice of objects on which one might observe was limited by that same principle.

St Petersburg was now seriously starting to emerge from the worst hangover it had endured for a century or more. The streets were populated not only by servants, drunkards and beggars; the more elegant ladies and gentlemen of the city had also ventured out for a breath of air. A forgiving layer of new snow had settled over the rubbish. A northerly wind had blown away the worst of the stench from the streets and squares. The streets were packed with trams, hansom cabs and even the odd automobile.

Josef Nikolai looked out through the steamed-up windows of a tram on the way back into the centre, at the churches with their spires and golden onion domes. Inside the tram, a poor invalid with no legs was dragging himself along the floor with a begging bowl in his mouth. One soldier was loudly telling another of his exploits the night before with a gypsy woman of ill repute . . . Kolya thought of the two hundred roubles secreted in his inner pocket. The amount was not negligible; he could live on it for a couple of months if he was careful. He could rent a room under a false name to get his creditors off his tail, drink at places where he wasn't known, lie low until things calmed down.

He ran through his plans. With a little luck he'd be able to bet on the contract with a couple of other people, but not many more than that because word would get round. An extra few hundred roubles was all he was likely to earn, and that wouldn't cover even a tiny fraction of his debts. The thought suddenly depressed him. When it came down to it, everything would be the same as before; nothing would really change for the better.

The tram went over Fotanka, and in the distance over the rooftops he saw the tower of the Admiralty building sticking up, like the pointed yellow beak of some fallen wading bird. His mood was sombre. He had almost forgotten the events of the night; maybe they were interconnected with his dream? He hadn't been feeling entirely compos mentis of late. No wonder. Too much debt. Unlucky in love. And his mother, who lay dying. Somehow, he realised now, he had gone through his endless succession of losses still cherishing the hope that one day some kind of fortune, some whim of the gods, would change everything for the better. That he would get back his good life, a certain amount of wealth, a certain level of freedom, his love – not necessarily for Nina, but for people in general, for the city, for existence. But now, sitting on the tram on his way down the boulevard, as the beggar with no legs slithered along the floor like some sinewy toboggan, he knew it would not be so. It would never be so. The Day of Judgement would come first. The sky would fall in first.

For the first time he realised the full extent of the fiasco of his life, and the thought was so strong and vivid it distressed him. What had he left, for which anyone would give even a kopek? Wasn't it in fact true, what his brother Mikhail Rubashov had screamed at him, hanging from the minute hand in his nightmare? 'Take your own life! Go hang yourself! Throw yourself in the Neva or shoot yourself in the head with Father's old blunderbuss! You were born with a silver spoon in your mouth, people looked after you, cared about you, loved you. But now, look around you. Where are your friends? Where's your family? Apart from our mother Tatiana Rubashova, whose senses are so enfeebled by her falling sickness, apart from this dying, mentally debilitated woman, there is no one who cares about you. You are lost, damned, already dead. So why not do it? Just try! You know you want to! Deep inside, you want to . . .'

His brother was right, he thought. There was no longer any point carrying on with this life already ruined, this course tormented by the gravest of sins. Everything his brother had screamed at him was true.

The tram halted at a stop and he got off. The snow was falling in flakes the size of walnuts. The cloud made the sky almost black. He was in the depths of the darkest regions of his consciousness, on poisoned ground, a great, desolate plain of the soul, a salt marsh of pain, above which a black moon dripping with venom was suspended on a string of putrid phlegm, with no hope in sight on the horizon . . . A steam-driven tram was approaching at high speed from the other direction. Its bells clanged. People scrambled onto the traffic island. Someone shouted: Watch out there! But Kolya wasn't listening. He stepped straight onto the track, and the next moment everything went black.

He felt nothing. Nothing at all, except a faint, dull headache, like waking up after drinking a few glasses of bad Moldovan champagne. Nothing more. No pain in his torso or his limbs. No ragged tongue or smashed teeth. No taste of blood, no particular fear. Perhaps he was dead? Perhaps death was like a hangover from third-rate champagne? But clearly he was alive, for he was surrounded by a circle of people, addressing him as you do the living.

'A miracle from God,' he heard somebody say. 'A true miracle.'

A toothless old woman made the sign of the cross. Someone bent down and helped him to his feet. 'Unbelievable,' said someone else. 'He should have been split down the middle like a bit of firewood. Two carriages, twelve pairs of wheels, he should have been mincemeat.'

Someone passed him his bundle, another slapped him on the back. The beggar with no legs, who had dragged himself off at the same stop, offered him a swig from his bottle. Kolya drank. The spirit burned his empty stomach. He was hungry; therefore he was alive.

'I'm a doctor,' came a voice. 'Make way.'

So they had sent for a doctor. If they had sent for a doctor, it meant he was alive. Otherwise, a hearse would have come. Snow was falling. He could feel it on the back of his neck, where his coat had been torn apart at the seams. A policeman shouted to the crowd to disperse. A St Petersburg policeman. St Petersburg policemen didn't feature in what you read about the hereafter. But maybe this one was an exception. Was he breathing? Yes, he was breathing. And people were touching him, straightening out his clothes, even embracing him. Somewhat dazed, he allowed himself to be led away to a cab.

'Where are you taking me?' he asked.

'To the nearest hospital. You'll need to be examined, sir. You may have internal injuries. Run over by a tram. Good God!'

They helped him into the cab. The constable stank of rotten teeth. A hint of antiseptic rose from the doctor's clothes. From a bakery came the aroma of *pirozhki*. He could smell it all. So he must be alive.

At the hospital they could detect no injuries: no fractures, no burst spleen, not the minutest bump or scrape. The surgeon who had examined him shook his head.

'It's incomprehensible' was all he could say. 'Utterly incomprehensible.'

The hospital priest, summoned in the expectation of administering the last rites, was similarly moved. He set down his censer with a clatter and shook Kolya by the hand.

'In view of the power of this miracle,' he said solemnly, 'I can only recommend a pilgrimage to Athos.'

And once the doctor had listened to his chest with the stethoscope one final time, he was allowed to get dressed again. They bade him farewell, advised him to be more careful in traffic in future, and a nurse saw him to the door.

Standing in the street outside the hospital, with the red sign of the Aquarium gambling club winking like a mad nebula just a stone's throw away, the full realisation dawned on him. It moved within him like some physical object, a truth so fantastical that it surpassed all other feeling and extended to every nerve ending. He fingered the contract in his pocket. He remembered the words of his guest before the big transformation display: '. . . Immortality.

33

Patience, my good Kolya, patience will be the watchword in your case . . .'

So there it was. What had happened last night was true. What had happened just now was true as well. He, Josef Nikolai Rubashov, could not die.

In holy Mother Russia at this time they played two kinds of roulette without counterpart anywhere else in the world. In one of these, the selected number of bullets was placed in the cylinder of a revolver, which was then spun by a special inspector, after which the player himself put the muzzle of the revolver in his mouth and fired. The other, less well known but just as common, had grown out of the cloth duel, a cherished part of the mythology surrounding the Romantic poets of the nineteenth century. Here, two players stood one each side of a horse blanket hanging from floor to ceiling, and shot through the fabric at a given signal until someone was hit. An imperial decree of 1827 outlawed the game, but as so often with imperial laws and ukases, it was ignored.

Cartoons in the *St Petersburg Gazette* at the turn of the century show the participants attired in monocles and frock-coats, their revolvers in one gloved hand and their cigars in the other. In the background stands a servant, chilling the bottles of champagne. And it was indeed mostly young noblemen who thus added exotic spice to the lives of luxury and security of which they had long since tired. But there were also ordinary gamblers, so far gone in their hunt for ever higher stakes that they willingly saw their own deaths reduced to a figure in a set of odds.

In the first of these forms of roulette, there were two kinds of bet. The participants could themselves put a sum on the outcome of the game, straightforward odds in converse proportion to the number of bullets in the revolver cylinder. But the real profit lay in the sums circulated by the public, a sort of provision for their contempt, by proxy, for death. Here, the betting system was different and the odds could vary wildly. For the gambling public, death was reduced to cold statistics and, with a set probability curve, the risk of a shot being fired could no longer be six to one if a number of players had already escaped unharmed. At a given moment, death advanced its mathematical position, and the odds of surviving shortened.

In St Petersburg in those days there were some ten illegal venues for this form of roulette, and the most renowned of them all was in the basement of the Aquarium gambling club. That was where Josef had now arrived on this first afternoon of the century, absolutely determined to change the course of his fate . . .

Having paid an entrance fee of twenty roubles to a uniformed doorman, he went downstairs to the club. The room, the size of a hospital ward, was full. A lieutenant from a Cossack regiment had just seated himself in the armchair that went by the name of the Throne of Death, positioned on a platform at one end of the room. Thousands of roubles were already changing hands. The book-maker, a German in a black calico suit, walked among the audience to collect their stakes.

The Cossack had already placed a bullet in the cylinder, and a man in a waistcoat and an embroidered silk shirt was spinning it round and round before locking it in place with a sudden flick of the wrist. He laid the gun on a handkerchief in the palm of his hand and passed it to the player. The stakes collected, a ghostly hush settled over the room. The Cossack stared at the revolver, raised it slowly and put the muzzle in his mouth. He was breathing heavily through his nose, and his hand was trembling so violently that the man in the embroidered shirt had to squat down and help him hold it still. His eyes flickered over the room. Finally they came to rest on a point a few metres away, where two other Cossack officers were standing, presumably his friends. Someone swore under their breath. And he fired.

It was all over in a moment. Death had shown its face for a fraction of a second, but then vanished equally swiftly, for statistical reasons. Just a brief click, and then the air was once more filled with ear-splitting cries as the bookmaker went round handing out the winnings . . .

Four rounds later, it was Kolya's turn. An even larger crowd had gathered. The odds, he thought, should have changed considerably

35

since the Cossack played, since the revolver had clicked in the four subsequent rounds as well.

He sat down in the armchair. Someone put a cushion at the back of his neck. He was aware of a smell of sweat and terror, left behind in the chair by those who had preceded him. The red damask was stained with darker patches. He wondered how often it got new covers.

'How many cartridges?' the bookmaker asked.

'Five,' he said.

'Five?' The man stared at him for a moment. 'Do you really mean five cartridges?'

'A madman,' he heard somebody say. 'Trying to commit suicide. There are simpler ways of killing yourself.' More disjointed phrases reached him through the uproar: 'desperate . . .', 'we'll see, he might get away with it . . .'

Then the man handed him the revolver, served on the handkerchief like some kind of sandwich.

Silence had descended again. Kolya stared at the gun, an American model with a sealed cylinder so you couldn't see how it was loaded. He held it loosely in his hand. It weighed next to nothing. Death was light, he thought, and life so much heavier.

He looked around him. Reflected in the eyes of the others, he was nothing but an outcome. This could break the bank, he thought. Most of them have bet a lot of money on me surviving, but they know it will be a miracle if I do. He could hear his own thoughts with perfect clarity, as if he had spoken them out loud. Perhaps he really had? He didn't know. He raised the revolver and inserted the muzzle in his mouth. The metal had a cold taste, like snow . . . *The silence. The audience. Gentlemen in top hats. Noblemen, blue-blooded. That one there is bright red in the face. Ought to drink less. In our country, alcohol claims more victims than the famine. My holy Russia. The empire is swimming in spirits. Good for the health, the doctor claims. Load of rubbish. The Cossacks are still here, but not the one who gambled with his life. Had he soiled himself? Cossacks. They drink, too. Brave soldiers. The Tsar's pride and joy. But such funny names. People from the south. Nina? Alive. Mama? Dead before long.*

I must have been sitting here staring for ages, because they're starting to buzz like flies. Gamblers, the lot of them. Know their thoughts like the back of my hand. The fellow in the frock-coat. Recognise him from Adlon's roulette table. Only ever bets on odd numbers and red. Some kind of obsession. Professor of civil law. Myshkin, he's called. An acquaintance. Drank beer with him after a few wins. An acquaintance. Holding his betting receipt in his hand. Wonder how much he staked. Two hundred? Gambling on my death. Strange acquaintance. Smell of sweat. The German's staring. Ought to do something about his accent. Dnieper German. Bound to be a Mennonite. Why are they here? The Empress's fault. Catherine. Should never have lured them here. Ukraine is for Ukrainians . . .

The muzzle was still in his mouth; he almost gagged as the end of it touched his soft palate. And if it doesn't work, he thought. If nothing is as I believe it to be? Death makes no allowances. It has no favourites. Strikes and is gone. Quite at random, pure blind man's buff. And you're left sitting here with your brains all over the cushion cover.

He tried to swallow, but it was as impossible as at the dentist's. Very slowly, hesitating to the last, he applied pressure to the trigger. Now! he thought. Any second now.

Then there was a click.

The room erupted. Everyone was shouting, no one listening. The winners were jubilant, and the bookmaker was checking betting slips. There'll be nothing left in the bank, thought Kolya, and some of the money is mine.

But others were less elated. Those who had gambled on the side of caution and lost. And as a counterpoint to the jubilation, a few cries could be heard alleging that cheating had gone on, the revolver had been tampered with. Silence descended again. A tall aristocrat pushed his way through to Kolya.

'Give me the revolver!' he demanded.

He let him take it. The guest, he thought. The contract? He had escaped the tram and now this. The tall aristocrat bundled him aside. The room was silent as he aimed the revolver at the armchair. An enormous bang deafened the onlookers, and the whole backrest of the chair was blown away.

Those stains, thought Kolya with a lucidity that amazed him, those stains aren't blood as I first thought. They never re-cover the chair. They just replace it!

That afternoon Josef Nikolai Rubashov repeated his macabre act of bravado at no fewer than seven of St Petersburg's illegal gambling clubs. At all of these he asked for five bullets to be put in the cylinder of the revolver before he fired. And, just as at the Aquarium, his actions generated huge excitement. Banks were emptied and revolvers test-fired with the same result, and long before the moon had time to rise above the imperial capital, Josef Nikolai was a rich man again. His profit that afternoon amounted to no fewer than a hundred and eighty thousand roubles, an almost incredible sum in fin-de-siècle Russia.

He felt happy. Happy with his sudden wealth, happy that his luck had turned, like a capricious mistral, but perhaps just as happy with the decision he took as the afternoon drew to a close, namely: never again to play for money.

It was a choice that grew inside him with the intensity of a religious vision. Never again, he knew now, would he set foot in a casino. Never again in this life would he queue in a betting office. Enough was enough.

A heavy burden was lifted from his shoulders. He felt several metres taller. His world looked wider. Less than halfway to the horizon he could see his new life waiting; a life with stakes in the form of virtues, a life with human winnings, a love lottery that was bound to make him happy, sooner or later. He was free at last. The demon of gambling had been driven from his body by the click of eight revolvers. For the first time in many years he could breathe . . .

He must tell his mother about his sensational decision. It was a little past seven when he got to the Holy Synod Hospital. A nurse, a nun who was sitting in the corridor knitting tea cosies, nodded in the direction of his mother's room.

He entered the room and found Tatiana lying sunken in torpor. He stood by the bed and looked at her with the misty-eyed gaze of a prodigal son. On the bedside table lay her well-worn calendar of saints, open at a picture of the virgin of Kazan. Everything was just the same as the last time he had seen her, four weeks previously.

'Mama,' he said. 'Are you asleep?'

The old woman opened her eyes.

'Dimitri, Dimitri?' she mumbled. 'Is it you?'

'No, it's me, Kolya.'

It seemed to take her a few seconds to digest this fact. Then she smiled.

'Kolya! I didn't hear you. Have I been asleep?'

'You've had a fit, the nurse told me.'

'A fit? What sort of fit?'

'Falling sickness. You don't remember anything afterwards.'

He glanced over at the calendar of saints. 'Dimitri' she had written on the cover in angular, childish letters, her dead husband's name. As her illness had worsened, the old woman had also grown somewhat senile.

'Mama!' he said again. 'I've given up gambling.'

His mother regarded him tearfully. Saliva bubbled at the corners of her mouth.

'But Kolya dear,' she said. 'You've never gambled, have you?'

'Yes, I have, Mama. I've gambled for twelve years. But now I've done with it for good.'

'Not you, Kolya,' Tatiana Rubashova persisted. 'Gambling and women have never been for you. Dimitri says you would make a good priest.'

Papa's dead, for God's sake, he felt like saying. But he didn't say it. Instead he said:

'Well, I have, Mama. I've been a gambler. Don't you remember, I even gambled away your annuity?'

'Annuity? I simply can't believe that of you, Kolya. You were the kindest child this side of the Urals. I remember when your brother

39

stole your tadpoles in Narva and put them in cook's fish stew. You didn't breathe a word, though you loved those tadpoles more than your own soul. They had just started growing little legs, remember, and your brother had them cooked. Not a word from you. Just a few tears, then you went out to play with your tin soldiers.'

'But don't you remember, Mama?' he tried again. 'Your annuity, I blew the lot.'

'Annuity! What do I need one of those for? Not even thirty yet.'

'Sixty-five, Mama, you're almost sixty-five.'

'Sixty-five? Me? Good Lord, how the time goes.'

'Anyway, that's all over now,' he said. 'You needn't worry any more. And I shall pay back every kopek I took from you.'

Unable to suppress a certain amount of pride, Kolya took out a bundle of notes from his pack and waved it like a fan in front of the woman in the bed.

'Do you understand, Mama!' he said. 'I'm back where I started. Don't look so sad about it. I shall have you moved from here. To a select private clinic on Morskaya. Trips to health resorts on the Black Sea at Christmas and New Year.'

'I'm fine here,' his mother said. 'And you should be careful with your money and not wave it around like that. You're too young to realise how many robbers go about their business on our Russian soil. You have always been a gullible lad, Kolya, it's the Swedish blood in you.'

'But, Mama,' he ventured again.

'Trips to the Black Sea! What would I do among all those negroes? But sit yourself down, boy. Sit yourself down on the bed by me and we'll ask the housekeeper to bring some beef tea. Sixty-five, you say? I'd never have thought it.'

The conversation between mother and son continued for a while in this rather muddled vein on the first evening of the century. They were each living and speaking in their own separate worlds, thought Kolya, and neither of them could get an entry ticket to the other's. His mother's world – or rather, her time – had coagulated somewhere around 1880. It was a world of Gogol evenings and tea parties, and an unforgettable court ball at the Winter Palace in 1881, when Dimitri Rubashov was at the very peak of his career and it was whispered that he lent money even to the Nicolayevich family. That was long ago, and now it was quite the opposite: his mother's consciousness was shrouded in a darkness of the same intensity as the light once cast by the chandeliers of the imperial palace.

He looked down at her; she had sunk back into her stupor. She resembled an angel, he thought, in her white nightdress with her silvery hair forming a halo around the pale moon of her face. He would take her away from here. He had money now. He had stopped gambling, and he was happy. Maybe, he thought, the hospital priest was right: he should give thanks for his good fortune with a pilgrimage to Athos.

Sitting by his mother's sickbed, he visualised himself with ashes in his hair, on his way up the holy mountain, singing some appropriate hymn. But the thought ended in a religious cul-de-sac, for the path of his imagination was suddenly blocked by the guest, waving the indestructible contract. A shudder ran through him. When all was said and done, this was he whom he had played against and lost to, the great scourge, the prosecutor, the tempter, king of shadows and duke of sins. He was the one Kolya had challenged. And he had performed marvels, transformations, and sentenced him to . . .

His mind was in conflict with regard to the preceding hours. Good and bad consciences battled against each other; witnesses stepped forward in his defence, others with gross accusations. Both sides delivered dazzling summings up, with supporting evidence reaching back to his tenderest years. And to preserve his sanity he finally sided with the faction that declared he had been living in sin, with a feeling of already being lost, maintaining moreover that there was a loophole: he had played, after all, without demanding anything in return. He had not sold his soul in exchange for riches and earthly happiness, he had played only for the thrill, and he had earned the money now wrapped in his bundle for himself, honourably, at Russian roulette. There was no case to answer.

With an effort of will he put these thoughts from his mind and touched his mother's limp hand. He breathed deeply and took

41

heart. Matters would resolve themselves, he thought, for that was the way of the world, at least for those with a little money; everything was resolved in the end. Everything.

Later that evening he found himself outside the house of his brother Mikhail Rubashov. It had stopped snowing, and high above the house the stars were making lace, weaving their brocade of light. The ground floor was in darkness, but lights were shining from the drawing room on the first floor. He hesitated, his hand on the door knocker. Six months had elapsed since they had last parted, after an acrimonious argument about Tatiana Rubashova's annuity. Mikhail had threatened to involve the police, and Kolya had replied darkly that he knew things about his brother's shady dealings in the grain business that would undoubtedly keep him from exposing the affair to legal scrutiny. They had been blackmailing each other since they were in short trousers. It was hardly credible that they were brothers.

He knocked at the door, which was opened by Olga, the maid.

'I'm not to let you in,' she said. 'The master's forbidden it, as you well know, sir.'

'Tell him it's about Mother. I want to have her moved.'

'I'll try. But the master's in a bad mood.'

She shut the door in his face, only to reopen it shortly afterwards and ask him to go up to the drawing room.

His brother, a cigar protruding from the corner of his mouth, was standing by an oil painting of the late Dimitri Rubashov, also smoking a cigar. Mikhail looked haggard, thought Kolya, after a wild New Year's night, perhaps. Or something he knew nothing about. Their contact never extended beyond the limited sphere of insults.

'Little Alexandra has been ill,' he said. 'Scarlet fever. Father Vasili was here and read from the breviary, but the crisis is over now. I haven't slept for a week.' He gave a start, as if he had caught himself using too friendly a tone. 'If you think you can beg money off me,' he said irately, 'you can get straight out of here.'

'Quite the reverse,' said Kolya. 'It's to do with Mother. I want to have her moved to a private clinic. I'll bear all the expense.'

His brother stared at him. 'Good God, what a sight you are!' he said. 'Aren't you ashamed to be seen in that coat of rags?'

'I had an accident.'

'Your creditors? They'll be able to set up their own guild soon, there are so many of them. Two of them were here this morning. If I refused to offer guarantees, they said, the debtors' prison would be expecting you. Excellent, I said. That's where he belongs. He's caused nothing but misery since he came into his inheritance. He's left our poor mother with scarcely the clothes on her back, and virtually sent her to the grave. Go ahead, lock him up and throw the keys down a well. It's no more than he deserves.'

Mikhail puffed away furiously on his cigar. 'And they said you'd been thrown out of the kind widow's house. I can understand that, I said. I'd rather have the devil himself for a lodger than my brother Josef Nikolai. I would personally throw him out of my house, even if it were forty degrees below and he had no shoes on his feet . . .' A coughing fit interrupted him, and he sat down in a chintz-covered armchair. 'And what you want with Mother I cannot fathom. Haven't you tormented the poor woman enough?'

Josef did not reply. He had opened his bundle and placed a pile of notes on the side table. He counted them. Ten thousand roubles.

'Where did you get those?' his brother demanded. 'Are you in league with the Bakuninites? Good God, Kolya, if Father could see you now.'

'I want her moved to a private clinic. There's a good one on Morskaya.' He counted out five thousand more roubles and put them in a pile beside the first. 'This is for you. You've paid all her costs this past year. It's to make amends, Mikhail. I've given up gambling.'

His brother was struck dumb. Somewhere in the house Kolya heard a cough, perhaps the little girl.

'You've given up gambling? And you expect me to believe that?'

'Believe what you like, but it's over. I regret it. I regret every single second. There'll be no more of it.'

43

Mikhail got to his feet. With little mincing steps, as if he were afraid that any violent movement might make the money vanish, he went over to the table. He wetted his thumb on his brown tongue and counted the notes.

'And this is for me?' he said. 'It's not possible.'

'I told you, I've given up. There'll be no more of it.'

A tear came into his brother's eye. He blinked it away and tugged awkwardly at his bow tie.

'Kolya,' he exclaimed. 'My brother.'

So saying, he threw his arms around Josef Nikolai, hugged him to his cigar-reeking shirt front and burst loudly into tears, his face turned to the wall, from where Dimitri Rubashov looked down with amazement on his ill-matched offspring . . .

That was an unexpected finale to the first evening of the century, Kolya thought later, to be reconciled with his brother after half a lifetime of animosity. But it fitted the pattern. The last twenty-four hours had been full of remarkable events, wild changes of direction and extraordinary paradoxes. He had been given some cast-off clothes of his brother's to wear, a coral-coloured frock-coat and an Austrian-style hat. Mikhail had summoned his wife, the nervous Natasha Rubashova, who on hearing the news that Josef had given up gambling, offered him a room in the house. He politely declined. His plan was to take a hotel room for the night, and as soon as he had arranged a place for his mother at a private clinic, to look round for an apartment of his own. He drank one last glass of liqueur, left thirty roubles to buy presents for the children, kissed Natasha's hand, thanked them for the clothes and apologised for having to leave so soon. Mikhail himself showed him down the stairs.

As he stood in the hall, Kolya heard agitated muttering from the maid's room next door. It sounded like a prayer.

'That's Olga,' said his brother. 'The simpleton believes the Day of Judgement is upon us. The devil was seen on Nevsky last night. A beggar saw him drive past in a black charabanc with a corpse for a coachman. He was wearing spectacles!'

Mikhail Rubashov tapped his temple lightly with his fingertip.

'Tell me one thing, Kolya. How can Mother Russia ever rise up out of her backwardness with subjects like that? We might just as well bring back serfdom.'

He shook Kolya by the hand and kissed him on the lips. And in an unctuous voice he whispered: 'There's a place for you in the firm if you're interested. The old bookkeeper died a month or so back. It's an excellent position for anyone who wants to get to know the business from the inside. You'll have worked your way up within a year. I could even see myself offering to take you into partnership.'

Josef thanked him and promised to think it over. And with the maid's mutterings like some ghastly buzzing in his head, he left Mikhail Rubashov's house.

Midnight that same evening found him standing in the bar at the Hotel Adlon, drinking champagne. From the next room came the cold ticking sound of a roulette wheel as it slowed to a halt, but he felt no urge – not the slightest hint of an urge – to play. The chandeliers cast a soft light over the gathering. There was a quiet rustle of silk and taffeta. The after-effects of the previous night's festivities had muted the atmosphere. People sat in small groups around the marbled tables, sipping mint liqueur and curaçao.

He listened to the background chatter. A circus dwarf was arguing with one of the waiters. Along one wall, decorated with painted columns, a gypsy orchestra was playing waltzes. The notes fell like mild rain onto his tired thoughts. A whole day and night would soon have elapsed since the visit, and he wondered whether any rational standards could be used to measure that event, or all that had followed it. It seemed incomprehensible. Ten years of constantly dropping temperatures on the thermometer of his luck, and now this. He thought of Olga's prayer and the beggar who had seen the guest drive past in a black charabanc. But he no longer felt any fear. He felt gratitude. His guest was not a bad creature, he thought, but he was vilified, prey to the prejudices of humankind.

Immortal? It was too incomprehensible by far, beyond the

45

bounds of his understanding. Even so, a new life had begun for him, and if he played his cards right he would never again need to live in poverty.

He pondered on what the immediate future might hold; limitless opportunities lay before him. He saw himself as a partner in his brother's firm, or perhaps a moneylender with solid property as security. He would abstain from gambling, of course, and drink only in moderation, for experience had taught him that one vice gave birth to another and together they bred like rabbits. He was engrossed in these thoughts when the waiter handed him a bergamot-scented note.

He unfolded it and read:

Dear Kolya,
   From my lookout post five tables away I can see that your luck has turned. New clothes, a comical hat, expensive champagne, etc. My latest lieutenant has left me for a winter manoeuvre. Would you do me the honour?
   Your Nina Fourier

Many years later, when everything was different, he was to think that of all the surprises sprung on him that first day of the century, this had perhaps been the greatest.

He turned. She smiled at him, and he knew that smile was the promise of a future . . .

The Good Years
(1900–14)

In a photograph in the *St Petersburg Church Journal* of 1905 we see Josef Rubashov with Semion, Vice-Chairman of the Welfare Committee. The picture was taken on the occasion of the opening of a new home for widows on Vasilievsky Island. Josef Nikolai is in top hat and tails and wearing a gold signet ring the size of a large beetle on his finger. Enthroned at his side is the portly churchman, and in the background we see the dreary brick building with its first residents posing on the front step.

It's a revealing picture: the poverty, the emaciated old women in their headscarves and patched woollen skirts; but we are also witnessing a new spirit of enterprise, the barons of industry and public benefactors such as Josef Rubashov . . .

He never took up that offer to become a partner in his brother's firm. Maybe it was pride, maybe stubbornness, but probably it was because he was afraid their old enmity could flare up again and put family harmony at risk. Instead, he invested his fortune in the wood-pulp industry, which was now flourishing along with the new freedom of speech. From wood pulp, he first went one stage back in the production process and bought a Finnish forest, then one stage forward with the reckless purchase of a newspaper in Kiev. From forests and newspapers he moved on to matches and sulphur production, and by the outbreak of the Russo-Japanese War in 1904 he was part-owner of a group of chemical factories that supplied gunpowder to no fewer than four army corps. He had soon laid the foundations of a whole business empire. He owned properties in the Crimea, a copper mine in the Urals, a soap factory in Königsberg and a chicken slaughterhouse in Reval. He dealt in steel engravings and antique ikons, and ran a workshop producing chasubles and processional crosses. He invested in war bonds and foreign securities; and caused a minor sensation on the stock exchange by selling shares in the arms industry and investing in a network of companies producing wooden goods, with cheap coffins as its speciality. As he said, 'Once the gunpowder's sold, there's nothing left to do but dig graves.'

He was only thirty-five, but his name was respected, inspiring as much terror in his enemies as it did gratitude amongst the needy he had helped. He was the chairman of a consortium for the development of Russian airships. And as part-owner of a Galician plant-breeding company, he kept a watchful eye on new root-vegetable crosses that might help keep the Polish provinces from starvation. One day when he went out to buy the *St Petersburg Gazette*, he was addressed by a girl selling violets. He bought a bunch to take to Nina Rubashova, and on the way home he had the inspiration of introducing organised door-to-door flower selling. It proved a success, for out of the doorstep sales grew St Petersburg's first floral greetings company, and in due course five huge glasshouses with a monopoly on the sale of Christmas roses. Everything he touched turned to gold. Within a decade, he was a millionaire.

He made himself known as a patron of young poets and a sponsor of experimental opera, with the world-famous bass Shaliapin in the leading role. In consultation with the Bishop of St Petersburg, he donated tens of thousands of roubles to charitable causes. A heated day shelter for war widows bore his name, as did a holiday centre for consumptive farmgirls. No beggar left his door empty-handed, and for a whole winter he ran a soup kitchen in his own back yard. He became more and more the philanthropist and felt inexplicably drawn to the Quakers.

In the summer of 1902 he married Nina Fourier, who to gratify Tatiana Rubashova converted to the Orthodox faith and took

Kolya's family name. She went on working at the Théâtre Française for a few years, but once Josef's empire began to grow in earnest, she handed in her notice and took charge of the household. She was the perfect hostess when his business associates came to dinner: choreographed the staff with scarcely perceptible glances, quoted passages from *Madame Bovary* by heart and sang Muscovite couplets to the accompaniment of a German pianola. The love between man and wife was ardent and passionate, without being destructive in any way. There was only one thing missing to make their happiness complete: children.

After trying in vain for almost five years, they went to consult an East Prussian specialist, who pronounced Nina Rubashova sterile as the result of a uterine infection. They mourned the diagnosis as one might mourn the death of a close relative, but their shared grief made their love even stronger. They talked of adoption without reaching a final decision, and for one summer they took in a girl from distant Sverdlovsk. The girl was blind and they engaged a governess to teach her Braille, but when she returned home they felt so bereft that they decided never again to receive anyone else's offspring in their home.

Throughout this period Josef went nowhere near a roulette table. He kept his promise to himself and never gambled – not even buying tickets in the charity draws organised by his own wife. Nor did he ever give a thought, engrossed as he was in his worldly happiness, to what had happened on the first night of the century. The whole story seemed so far removed, like something he had dreamed, something his imagination had hauled out of the deep cellars of his subconscious. He kept the contract in a desk drawer in his office; sometimes he would take it out and, with a mixture of scepticism and sentiment, study it under the glare of the office lamp. Amazed but not in the least frightened, he would regard his face in the bathroom mirror each morning. Remarkably, not a wrinkle, not one line was to be seen; and when Nina Rubashova turned to him one morning in the huge four-poster bed and burst out, 'You haven't aged a day since we met,' he took it as a compliment.

Tatiana Rubashova's condition gradually improved, thanks to advances in medical science. Her illness was no longer referred to as falling sickness, but as epilepsy, which to Kolya's ears sounded even more serious, but which could now be eased by hypnosis and new medicines. Her attacks decreased in both frequency and duration, but unfortunately her senility was progressing in inverse proportion. After entrusting her care to private clinics for several years, they brought her home and engaged a nurse trained in Freudian techniques in Vienna and Krakow. Nina Rubashova and Tatiana got on well, although the latter became increasingly convinced as time went by that the former was her own mother, on one occasion even asking to be put to the breast. But gradually, lulled in the cradle of old age, she sank into a dusty silence, broken only by her rustlings with the calendar of saints – and apparently happy, since a dream-like smile was constantly on her lips . . .

With his brother, he maintained the status quo. Their contacts were formal, coloured by the sort of suspicion that is the consequence of half a lifetime's antagonism. But Kolya did help his brother, without his knowledge, when his little business was threatened with bankruptcy after several years of stock-market falls in grain prices as the result of cheap American imports. They seldom met, except on family occasions or in connection with the big religious festivals of the year, when Mikhail always had a few drinks too many and started telling stories about Jews, which he'd heard from business associates from the Ukraine. Josef detested his cheap musk perfumes and his greedy way of staring down Nina Rubashova's corseted cleavage, but he was also aware that his brother envied him and therefore avoided any sort of bragging that might intensify those feelings. For the same reason he refrained from buying another pony for little Alexandra Rubashova, who had been begging for one ever since he had gone into the stud-farm business. He intuitively realised that a single obsessive enemy could do more harm than a recession or a national strike. He was cautious, and caution made him strong. In this way, ten years passed – largely under a star of good fortune.

*

But when he was out for a solitary autumn walk along the Fotanka Canal in 1909, something happened to remind him of the origin of his good fortune: he saw the little castrato Iliodor begging money by the Anichkov Bridge. He took refuge in a doorway to avoid discovery. His reaction was a puzzle: he was hyperventilating and had broken out in a cold sweat, the perspiration running down between his buttocks. He watched the castrato, who with a fixed smile was holding out a dirty cap to passers-by. Iliodor's eyes were quite empty, as if a light inside him had been snuffed out; and when a little later he got up and left, Kolya followed him.

Their walk took them deep into the poor quarters of the city. Shouts and drunken singing could be heard through the thin wooden walls of the houses; the streets narrowed to alleys where daylight could hardly penetrate from above. It all smelt of rotting cabbage and bad drains, and barefoot urchins ran after him, begging for money.

From a back courtyard he heard the voice of the Skoptsist monk, clear and melodic. Kolya crept after him and, concealed behind the thick trunk of a maple, saw Iliodor standing cap in hand, singing an old hymn. Somebody opened a cracked window and threw him a few kopeks, which he skilfully caught in his cap. Then he stopped singing, and his face distorted into a hideous grimace.

Slowly the castrato descended to his knees and burst out into curses and prophecies of the end of the world; then, at the height of his delirium, he took a dagger from under his cowl and drew it across his hand. The wound bled profusely, but the castrato merely laughed, the high, hysterical laugh of a child. It was quite apparent that he had lost his mind.

Darkness began to fall, and there were no street lights in that district. The castrato made his way back out into the street, turned right down a side alley and was swallowed up in the darkness.

Josef Rubashov leaned against the wall of a house. The rats were rustling in the dark, and some way off a drunk was singing a verse from a lewd song. He was beset anew by all the old thoughts. He was overwhelmed by the feeling that his happiness had been bought on credit, and that sooner or later he would be forced to repay it with interest wholly disproportionate to what he had borrowed. This was the direction in which his dark and uneasy thoughts were straying, when someone tugged so violently at his coat tails that he almost overbalanced.

'What do you want of me?' the castrato demanded.

'Don't you recognise me? It's me, Josef.'

'I've never seen you before. Why are you following me?'

'Don't you remember? You helped me once.'

Iliodor smiled.

'I don't remember doing that,' he said. 'I don't remember anything. Look . . .'

He held out his clenched hand, and opened it. In his palm lay a finger: crooked and bloody, already yellowed where the skin had rolled itself round the cut surface.

'It's for him,' he whispered. 'For my prince. A gift. It didn't even hurt; he helps me not to feel the pain.'

Then the little man held up his other hand to show: there was nothing left of the thumb but a little stump of flesh and cartilage and a few scraps of skin.

'It didn't hurt,' he assured Josef. 'I do it out of love. My soul belongs to him.'

'Iliodor,' Josef said, but then stopped for he suddenly had no idea what to say next.

And with another hysterical laugh, the castrato left him in the dark and disappeared out of sight down the stinking tunnel of the alley.

At the end of that year, 1909, the family bought a house near Haapsalu, on the Estonian coast. It was an old manor house with assorted outbuildings, and had once been owned by a German baron, a Knight of the Order of the Sword. With his wife, Josef Rubashov had the dilapidated buildings renovated and began to spend most of his spare time there.

His fortieth birthday was approaching, and he considered it was now time for the development of some leisure interests. He began collecting antique coins, and within a short space of time became a minor authority on Byzantine conscript coinage and Greek tetradrachmas. He tried hunting, but quickly found he detested the cold-blooded murder of creatures that were wild and free. In the company of his stablemaster Fyodor, who was deaf and dumb, he went for long walks in the forest, and devoted a whole spring to cataloguing the Estonian marsh flora in the spirit of Linnaeus.

He loved seeing his wife embroidering coasters for the china in the shade of a two-hundred-year-old apple tree; and now that a tearful and emotional Tatiana Rubashova was able to breathe in from her sickbed the scents of the place where she was born and raised, he knew she could die in peace.

It was a happy time. His love for Nina was as colourful and untamed as the sweet peas the peasant farmers planted against the whitewashed walls of their houses. He had forgotten Iliodor, or at any rate sent him off to some far-away enclave of his mind. His fortune took care of itself, 'a sort of financial perpetuum mobile', as he put it in letters to his acquaintances.

At night, the very sensation of happiness sometimes woke him from his sleep. Then he would lie awake, looking out into the Baltic night with Nina Rubashova's little face buried in the crook of his arm like a jewel in a box.

Nothing could threaten him. He was strong. Happiness made him strong, it was perpetual virtuous circle . . .

In the autumn of 1911 Josef Rubashov was invited in his capacity as patron of the opera to a ball in the Winter Palace. It was November, the season when the autumn storms raged over the north Russian plains, and Nina, who was susceptible to changes in the weather, was in bed with mild influenza. After some hesitation, he decided to go alone.

He did not recall much of the dinner itself; the speeches all sounded the same, as did the tributes to the imperial couple, who were not even in attendance. The family was represented by a Muscovite grand duke, nephew of the murdered Sergei.

After the dinner, the festivities moved to the Malachite Drawing Room, a state room that had once been used as an audience chamber for foreign ambassadors. Its splendour overwhelmed even Josef Nikolai: the sea of gold and marble, the huge columns of green malachite, the doors of pure gold and the Bohemian crystal chandeliers, hovering up by the ceiling like great airships armed with prisms the size of ostrich eggs. A portrait by Goya of the actress Antonia Zárate put him in mind of his wife.

He was standing by himself, contemplating this extravagance, when someone touched him on the shoulder. It was Grigori Efimovich Rasputin.

'You seem in low spirits, sir,' he said. 'Is anything troubling you?'

The man wore peasant clothes: a simple embroidered shirt and tall boots. His beard extended well down his chest. In this sea of ballgowns and tail-coats, of wealth and scholarly conversations in French, he was a personification of the true Russia, of Asia cross-fertilised with Europe.

'I do not think so.'

Rasputin stared at him. The man's eyes were incredibly sharp and blue.

'I'm seldom mistaken. Would you like to unburden yourself to me, sir?'

Kolya smiled uncertainly, but Rasputin was earnest.

'Everyone is weighed down by something. Be they emperors or beggars. You are no exception. Let me guess. Childlessness is tormenting you. You need not worry, sir: there is a surprise in store for you.'

Kolya stiffened. But Rasputin merely regarded him with a smile, letting his tongue run over his rusty brown teeth and giving a series of little belches that smelt of onions.

'And your mother is ill, if I'm not mistaken?'

He must have heard others speak of me, Kolya thought. But before he had finished thinking the thought, Rasputin the *staretz*, the holy man, interrupted him:

'No, never. I don't even know your name.'

Without Kolya noticing, they had begun to walk across the room.

54

Small groups of people turned to watch them and whispered. They passed a painting by Titian of Mary Magdalene, breasts bared, gazing orgiastically into a cobalt blue sky. Rasputin burped again, quite unselfconsciously, and then they were out of the crush.

'It's true,' said Josef. 'I'm childless and my mother is ill. How could you know?'

'Don't concern yourself with that,' Rasputin said. 'They will leave you soon enough, anyway. That's the way of the world: an endless cycle of meetings and partings.'

He's mad, thought Kolya. The imperial couple surround themselves with holy fools. An indiscriminate mixture of prophecies and drivel. Nina wouldn't leave me . . . But once again, his train of thought was interrupted:

'Not mad. Prophetic, perhaps. But I pay a high price for the words the angels whisper in my ear. People shun me on the same grounds. Men are more afraid of what is to come than of the past, for some reason. This clinging to chronology is our joy and our curse. For what would we do without it? After all, guilt is determined by time; without causality there is no sense of right or wrong. And what use would God be to us if we never felt guilt?'

They had come to a halt by one of the windows. The guests' conversations in the state room sounded like the surge of a distant sea. Below them the Neva flowed by. Dark pontoons rocked on the dull surface.

'You seem to be reading my thoughts,' Josef said.

Rasputin looked out at the river.

'I would prefer not to express it that way. I don't hear them. I feel them. Every individual has an aura. That aura emits movements, violent tremors of thoughts and memories. And I am a seismograph.'

Falling silent, he put a hand on Josef's shoulder.

'What is your name?' he asked.

'Josef Rubashov.'

'Well, Mr Rubashov. I've got to go. The sirens are calling. Can't you hear their song? The ladies of the imperial city. But we shall meet again, believe me.'

He gave a brief nod and turned to go. With dignity he made his way through the crowd. And then he was lost from view . . .

In the July of the following year, 1912, the first of the events prophesied by Rasputin came to pass: Nina Rubashov gave birth to a son.

Her pregnancy was medically inexplicable. It was a miracle, a physiological aberration, a whim of sympathetic Providence. She had a difficult labour that lasted almost four days and nights. The boy's first cries were heard one Sunday, under the sign of Leo. He came into the world blessed with a caul and fully formed milk teeth, and was baptised Leopold.

They lived in an ecstatic whirl, a heaven on Earth, and their love reached spheres they had thought barred to mortals. A Finnish wet-nurse was engaged, and the child suckled her with the strength of a calf. With his mother's sea-coloured eyes and his father's golden hair, the boy appeared to Kolya a miracle of beauty and anatomical harmony. He loved him with an intensity he had not believed possible.

They remained in Haapsalu for the summer. They took long walks, the boy cosily tucked into a perambulator. The natural world paid homage to their happiness: the trees bending in the wind, the sunflowers smiling, the corn steaming in the heat. In the baby's nursery, the wet-nurse hung up an amulet as a protection against the evil eye. Kolya laughed. Nina Rubashova laughed. They did a lot of laughing that summer . . .

In the autumn of that year, new disturbances erupted in the Balkans and the fall of an American commercial bank destabilised the stock market. It was nothing to worry about, but Josef Nikolai felt obliged to keep a discreet eye on his interests, so the family returned to St Petersburg. With a few deft option moves, he strengthened his position on the front line of the stock exchange, and the wellspring of their happiness continued to ripple. Their boy was a quiet child, who by the winter solstice had learned to crawl like a grass snake and gurgle 'Mama' in St Petersburg dialect. In

Tatiana Rubashova's sickroom, sitting on the lap of a father moved to tears, the little one looked down at his senile grandmother and gave her the name 'Vava'.

At Christmas, they opened their doors to the beggars of the district. Hordes of old folk and children were served soup in the kitchen. Christmas presents were distributed to the young, and cast-off clothes to those in rags. Fifty pairs of children's shoes had been bought as a job lot by Nina Rubashova. It was most moving to see the faces of the poor illuminated with the glow of repletion. Josef Rubashov recalled the reports that had been streaming in from the provinces of mothers who had let their children suckle a sow when their own breast milk dried up; or of families so destitute that they could never all leave the house at the same time, because there weren't enough clothes to go round. He not only understood the importance of charity in such times, but also valued his riches as a gift. He knew how it felt to be in free-fall. He had been in the depths of poverty before his luck turned, and it was a fate he would not wish on his worst enemy.

But among the crowd thronging their kitchen that Christmas there was a woman named Sonia Filipova. She lived in a hovel in an inner courtyard nearby, earning a few kopeks telling fortunes in egg yolks, and revealing the fates of dead people in the hereafter with the help of items that had belonged to them. When times were bad for prophecies and psychometry, she went out begging with an orphan boy called Gavrila. One evening when Nina Rubashova was standing as usual with her son on her arm, supervising the serving of the soup, this woman grabbed her by the sleeve.

'Young mother,' she said. 'Your house is cursed. The curse of your husband rests on your house.'

The woman's eyes rolled wildly and she collapsed onto the floor in convulsions, not wholly unlike those suffered by Tatiana Rubashova during her increasingly rare fits. Nina Rubashova was quite at a loss until Josef came rushing out of the drawing room. Trembling, he waved a vinegar-soaked handkerchief under the woman's nose until she came round and stared at him with a look so terrified he would never forget it.

'You are damned,' she whispered. 'God help you, good sir, but you are damned.'

On Twelfth Night their lives changed utterly and abruptly: the little boy suddenly fell ill. He refused to eat, and what little they got down him soon came out again. The attacks of diarrhoea were followed by fever and muscular cramps, and large, pus-filled blisters erupted on his body.

Doctors were called. They gave him camphor injections and opium drops on a sugar lump, but weeks passed and there was no improvement. The boils burst and disfigured his face beyond recognition. His body dehydrated, and extended bouts of high fever made his little brain boil in the cauldron of his cranium. In March, when the illness loosened its grip, the boy was left retarded. He had been reduced to an idiot.

The shock to Nina Rubashova was so great that she took to her bed and stayed there all spring. Many years later Kolya would remember her face with photographic clarity as she lay apathetically stretched out on the sheets, repeating to herself: 'My God, why did you not let it happen to me?' He feared she would lose her mind, and that fear turned into hatred of his own offspring. He could no longer bear to see the boy, still less touch him, as he sat in his cot, smeared with excrement and staring into mid-air with the opaque gaze of an idiot . . .

Summer was approaching and Josef Nikolai tried to forget by immersing himself in his work. But if he had previously monitored his interests out of the corner of his eye and found intuition his trustiest weapon among documents and figures, fortune deserted him now that he was, so to speak, staring his empire straight in the face. He started making mistakes, and a new outbreak of jitters on the stock market shook his dominant position. On a single day in May 1913, he lost two million roubles as the price of government bonds plummeted, and by midsummer that year several of his factories were facing grave liquidity problems. His floral greetings firm went bankrupt when the bulbs rotted in the soil of his glasshouses, and a landslip at his copper mine killed thirty-six miners. Predatory speculators forced him to sell his real estate at below the market price, and in an effort to save his plant-breeding company he sold the house at Haapsalu.

By August only a fraction of his former empire remained: a fish-salting works, a small area of forest and the sulphur factory. He had even had to sell the apartment. The family were now living in four rooms in eastern St Petersburg, and of the servants only the wet-nurse remained.

Every night Nina Rubashova sobbed herself to sleep, and her cries of mourning were so desolate he could no longer lie beside her. He moved to a camp bed in his mother's room. The old woman was blessedly oblivious to the misfortunes that had afflicted the family. She would cluck in delight as he prayed at her breast, and wake him at night by singing in her sleep.

He never looked at the boy. He closed his heart to him, and when the wet-nurse reproached him for his lack of paternal instinct, he simply sneered, as if at a tasteless joke.

He avoided home. With the moon as his only lamp, he would sit in his office staring at the accountant's ever gloomier monthly reports. Now the sulphur factory, too, was making a loss, and a commercial bank was threatening to seize his forest in Finland. He smoked cigars and wrote incoherent blank verse on the backs of yellowing IOUs. But strangely enough, he never looked for ways to console himself. Somehow he took a perverse pleasure in the misfortunes befalling him. He assumed he was doing penance for old sins and undeserved happiness, but could remember no crime proportionate to such punishment.

One night on returning home from the office he found Nina Rubashova in the bathroom with a glass full to the brim with arsenic solution.

'Drink it if you like,' he said. 'It's all the same to me.'

He saw her red-rimmed eyes in the mirror as she poured the poison down the sink, and without a word she returned to the bedroom. Plagued with feelings of guilt, he wandered the darkened rooms. He prayed to God, but the God to whom he appealed in his despair would not listen. He paused in the kitchen, where the embers had gone out in the tiled stove. He put in more wood and coal briquettes, lit the fire and opened the damper to make it burn up. From the bedroom he could hear Nina Rubashova's desperate lament. Numb with grief, he left the flat, forgetting to close the damper before he did so.

He took a hansom cab out to Novaya Derevnya, the gypsy quarter. He sat in a tavern until dawn, drinking cheap vodka with lemonade. The image of his wife with the glass of arsenic before her tormented him. He loved her. She was his everything, the jewel in the crown that was now crumbling before his eyes. A hare-lipped gypsy fiddler played at his table. An old woman in patched clothes put a comforting hand on his shoulder. His grief was so palpable that the waiter refused to accept payment for his drinks.

The sun was already coming up when he took a cab back home. The trees' fingers clawed at the grey dawn. He felt extremely lucid, as if the alcohol had washed his thoughts clean of months of layered deposits and dirt. Once again he prayed to God, and in the silence that followed he thought he heard a voice telling him not to lose his trust. He twined his fingers together and hoped. Perhaps everything would resolve itself somehow? With the aid of faith, nothing was impossible. With the aid of faith, you could move mountains. Images of saints came into his mind, holy men and women who had suffered and died for their faith; and he asked them all for guidance in this dark hour.

A glimmer of hope was born inside him. If he couldn't rescue his empire, they would learn to live in more straitened circumstances. The nourishment of love would sustain them. He wanted a happy marriage: maybe he could learn to love his child again; maybe they could have other children?

But even before the cab reached the front entrance he knew. The smoke hanging over the street; the people shouting and running; the clanging bells of the approaching fire brigade. It was a horrific blow. Long before anyone told him he knew.

They had burned to death in the fire.

*

60

He wanted to die. Nothing else. Just to be extinguished by death.

Death was his dream. Death was his aim, his deliverer, the mighty hand that with a single tug would shatter the chains of his torment. He wanted to leave the memories, the obsessions, the wreckage of his life and love. There was nothing else in his thoughts, only that. Deliverance. Death.

He wandered like a spectre through St Petersburg. He saw nothing, heard nothing, just walked, walked in circles round the ghastly hub that was his grief. He couldn't even cry.

In the steadily falling autumn rain he burbled like a madman, shouted, sang, and finally fell into a silence broken only by the irregular beating of his heart. When thirst came upon him, he lapped water from the gutter. He ate whatever was in his path: refuse, horse droppings, leaves and gravel. He slept wherever sleep happened to overtake him.

On the fifth night, he found his way quite by chance back to his office. There was almost nothing left; his employees had looted the premises.

A family portrait stood on his desk. He kissed it, then threw it to the floor, stamped on it and tore it to pieces.

In a cleaner's cupboard he found a tin of rat poison. He mixed it with rainwater to a thick gruel and ate it with tears of relief. As he threw it all up again, he beat his head against the wall with frustration.

Dizzy with his longing to be snuffed out, he went up to the attic. He made a noose out of some old rope and fastened it to a roof beam. With the aid of a stepladder he climbed up and placed the noose around his neck. He let go and dropped. He shut his eyes and waited for death, beaming with joy. The rope creaked as he slowly swung there, a metre from the floor. His neck was as tightly tied as the end of a sausage; his head felt like an overripe fruit, ready to burst.

But when nothing had happened by the end of half an hour, he grew tired of it and cut himself down. He went across to the gable end of the attic and opened the low window. He didn't even take a run at it. Just leaned out over the window sill until his centre of gravity shifted and his body fell. It felt like an eternity before he reached the ground, but he didn't see his life passing before his eyes. The attic was six storeys up, and he roared and sang as he fell the last few metres. He landed on the cobbles with a dull thud. For a moment he felt a stupefying pain at the back of his head, and from some point inside him came a fiery red light. Deliverance, he thought, deliverance has arrived . . .

But nothing happened. He lay still, eyes closed. The rain beat into his face, he shivered with cold. In the end, with a crazed laugh, he got to his feet and went back to the office.

He found the contract at the very bottom of a desk drawer. It was years since he had so much as spared it a thought. Now he stared at it: its perforations, endorsements, stamps and signatures. There was an almighty howl inside him, but however he struggled to let it out, it would not come . . .

In mid-February he moved into a boarding house for the impoverished on Sadovaya Street. Seeing himself in a mirror for the first time in weeks gave him a shock. He had lost thirty kilos in weight. The skin hung like some leathery fabric from the coat-hanger of his shoulders.

He remembered that he had stepped out in front of trams and automobiles, had been run over, but got up again and continued along the street laughing, to the unspeakable horror of any bystanders. No one had come near him; his suffering was of such vast proportions that people fled at the very sight of him.

He slept in parks among drunks and superannuated whores, and woke from ochre-tinted nightmares where demons were howling his name. On one occasion he swallowed glass. On another he walked through a burning warehouse at the harbour. He had memories of a night in a basement room where he had mixed quinine with chemist's alcohol and drained the glass, spluttering. He had leaped at dawn from a water tower and then from high scaffolding on one of the new boulevards.

In the end he had given up. There was no point. The curse lay upon him. Though he wished it with his whole soul, he could not die.

From the balcony, through the screen of snowflakes, he could see the widow Orlova's house, and the windows of the room where he had played cards with the guest, fourteen years before. He remembered everything clearly now, everything that had been said and done that night, and realised he was now suffering the expected punishment for his crime. He knew what lay ahead. There was only one way out. To locate the being who had condemned him; to seek him out and plead for mercy. It was the dark side's court of appeal he had to find; the appellate court of fallen souls. Only there could he get a return match. Only there could he be granted an amnesty.

But the only lead he had was the little castrato Iliodor. He remembered the letter they had written together, which the Skoptsist monk had undertaken to deliver in person to the highest quarters of darkness. And he remembered how contemptuously his guest had spoken of Iliodor, fourteen years before. With a shudder he recalled shadowing him; the demented laughter of the castrato; and the severed finger he had shown him in the alley . . .

He went to the monastery where they first met. There was a service in progress and the chapel was full of castrati with shaven heads and nut-brown cassocks. Before the altar stood a priest, swinging a censer made of alabaster; small boys, novices of the order, processed down the aisle with ikons held aloft. A prayer was said, and a hundred high voices mumbled amen.

He sat in a pew, empty except for one old castrato wearing a giant crucifix on his breast.

'Is there an Iliodor here?' he whispered.

'Iliodor?' The monk looked at him in surprise. 'Iliodor is in hell . . .'

They walked through a monastery garden with frozen fountains and great drifts of snow, like pregnant whales, and came through an entrance into the main building, and long winding passages led them to the heart of the monastery. In a dank room, lit by flaming torches, a little boy lay chained hand and foot to a wooden bench.

'He's going to be initiated into the brotherhood,' whispered the old monk. 'With the great seal.'

Ten or so Skoptsi gathered round the boy; they poured vodka down his throat from an earthenware jug and prayed to the patron saint of castrati. The boy whimpered while they heated the surgical instruments to red-hot in the flames of the torches. As their murmured hymn grew louder, they parted his legs. Fear had given the boy an erection. With strong thread they tied and stitched his scrotum like some engorged bouquet. A scalpel was raised, and with a single cut they sliced off his manhood. One of them held up the organ in the flickering light; a few bloody sinews dangled from it like roots from a plant.

He followed the monk through passages lined with cells and portraits of eminent priests. Finally they reached some steps, which led them down into a cellar. There, naked in a glass coffin against the wall, lay Iliodor.

'We embalmed him,' the monk said. 'We show him to the novices as a dreadful warning.'

He lifted the coffin lid and touched the top of the little man's head.

'Look,' he said. But Kolya had already seen it: the number branded into the skin behind the ear.

'That's the devil's mark,' said the monk. 'It's two years since he died. He'd sold his soul and in the end it drove him mad. He assaulted young boys. He did worse than that: killed two of them. He cooked and ate them, limb by limb . . . Look!'

He parted Iliodor's lips with his fingers.

'He filed his teeth until they were as sharp as a wild animal's. We know who gave him the idea. Such evil can't come from a single human being. We keep him here as a terrible reminder.'

He stayed at the boarding house for another month. With the yellowing contract in his hand, he stared out at the falling snow and listened to the silence within him. He went over the events of the last years, detail by detail, teasing them apart like the components of a delicate piece of machinery, and fitting them back together again in a vast jigsaw of memory. The labyrinths of love where he had once sauntered and strayed in such happiness. The money he had amassed like so much hunted game at his feet, million upon million, without effort. The miracle that had been the coming of their child, that gift of biblical proportions, against which he in his arrogant pride had turned his face.

He thought of his mother, the queenly woman he had loved as much as his wife; a love that had grown as she had declined, watered by feelings of guilt from his time as a gambler. With a sharp pang he remembered the house in Haapsalu, the travels, the lovemaking and the unforgettable evening at the Bolshoi when he had proposed to Nina Rubashova and she had replied with a silvery, chiming 'Yes' before fainting from sheer joy for one dramatic second. Or the plans they had had, the dreams they had cherished through those bright, starlit nights when they had stayed up whispering to one another in love's always imperfect language. But nothing had turned out as he once hoped; he had miscalculated everything.

He slept lightly and woke often. He dreamed of a strange smell of brown coal dust and vinegar, and of his guest from the dawn of the century appearing just for a moment, to see his distress and be tempted to have pity on him.

Everything lay in the hands of that being. He, Josef Rubashov, was under the jurisdiction of darkness.

Knockings

(1914–15)

'The imperial family will be here any minute! For God's sake, Kolya, have you filled the samovar? I don't pay you to stand there asleep. What's the use of servants who can't think for themselves? And dust the ikons. Take down that tapestry. He doesn't like rustic scenes any more. Too inoffensive, he says; the people need potent symbols in these extreme times. And the biscuits, the ones with the raisins, put them out. And the table! Heavens! I almost forgot the table. It's in the hall cupboard; a folding table decorated with esoteric symbols: a cross, an hourglass, and Solomon's six-pointed Seal. Knockings on the table, Kolya! Have you never been to a seance before, despite your – how shall I put it – little occult experiences? No, I know. Quiet as a mouse. It's our secret. Light the incense to create a bit of atmosphere. Nothing attracts gossipy spirits like oriental incenses. Two bottles of Madeira; they're in the pantry, a little gift from . . . what's her name, the one who was here yesterday? Katya Ivanova on heat! God help me. You need only taste one of them. I don't trust anybody any longer. Friend one day, foe the next. Not impossible for her to have laced that nectar with belladonna. How is the Doctor, by the way, our last hope? Asleep, of course. Make sure you take him something to eat on your way past. How can he ever be any use if we don't take care of his nutritional intake? Food is alpha and omega for old people. Kolya, do you hear me? Get a move on . . .' Rasputin said.

Josef went out into the kitchen and opened a bottle of Madeira. He poured the contents into a carafe and put some other bottles in the cold room to chill. It was hard to credit that they drank cheap dessert wine; the little woman wearing the insignia of her order on a sash, and her husband with two kilos of medals on his chest. They paid too much attention to Grigori Rasputin, that was clear, if he had got them to replace French champagne with Russian liqueurs. He wondered if it had anything to do with the war. Nationalism was the order of the day. It was making them hurl themselves into mass graves from Antwerp in the west to Königsberg in the east. It was true what Grigori the *staretz* was always saying: you have to find a higher principle in whose name you can let yourself be slaughtered. War and song. Gunpowder and prayer. For the Tsar and Holy Mother Russia!

He poured himself a small sample of the wine. A taste of iron. It was like sucking on a scab, only sweeter. But no poison. Grigori had good reason to be on his guard. Hardly a week passed without some enemy sending a doctored food parcel. The whole world knew he had a weakness for liqueurs and sweet things. It was all the same to Josef Rubashov. He simply threw it up: everything from rat poison to razor blades. 'There's no better taster to be had,' Rasputin had said when they had gone on their first journeys together. 'Not even a pound of dynamite primed for the stomach could do him any harm.'

That had been almost six months ago, when they were mapping the extent of the Russians' obsession with myths. Folk had told them the most incredible stories; showers of snakes, witchcraft, signs and dark omens, dilettantes, charlatans and clouded crystal balls. Not even Ouspensky had been able to do anything for them, and Gurdjieff was now living abroad . . . Then at a stroke, everything changed. They found the Doctor.

He put his ear to the door of the dressing room. Not a sound could be heard from the creature within. He assumed the Doctor was sleeping. What did a few hours' sleep here and there matter in a case like this? And it was thanks to Grigori that this treasure, the Doctor, was in St Petersburg. One might wonder why he was taking an interest. The imperial family needed him as never before. Little Alexei wanted to play with his sisters and their skipping rope. Not a hope. Haemophilia. One little scrape and he'd be bleeding to death between his silken sheets. And Papa was having a meeting at the front. He should never have listened to Nikolai Nikolayevich. The war party forced us into this. Fourth of August. The dog days. They should have sent each other ice cream instead of ultimatums. It was inconceivable. First the Archduke in Sarajevo, then the Austrians using it as an excuse to have a go at little Serbia. What a farce in the corridors of diplomacy. Kaiser Wilhelm fishing for salmon trout in the north of Norway, holiday time in Berlin, not a soul in a position of responsibility. A few junior lawyers, sitting playing with paperclips in the Foreign Ministry. The Austrians negotiated their way to a green light, so of course we had to mobilise. Couldn't let them wipe out a nation we've had under our protection for twenty years. Long live pan-Slavism! Free from Nikolai Nikolayevich's martial speeches in the Duma.

But the Tsar had favoured restraint, you had to credit him with that: 'We'll only mobilise against Austria-Hungary, not annoy old Wilhelm in Berlin.'

'It can't be done!'

'Why not?'

'You must see, your Majesty, that with our gigantic army, with our enormous borders and time-consuming transportation, it would be chaos. Full mobilisation is the only option.'

Lord Jesus in heaven, any idiot could have worked that out, and then of course the Germans and Austrians had to do the same. All in thirty-four degrees of heat. The milk was turning sour in every country named in an atlas. Dog days. People behaving as if they're mad. A hundred thousand fell to their knees as soon as the Tsar appeared at a window of the Winter Palace. For the mother country! For the true faith! The fellow had never been so popular. The whole continent ran amok. The jubilation knew no bounds. Vienna, Paris, Berlin; the biggest public party in the world. People ran off to the mass slaughter laughing. The war will be over in a month, said Grand Duke Nikolayevich, and took communion in Kazan Cathedral. We head straight for Brandenburg. And what happens? Ludendorff tricks him and beats him hollow in Masuria. Then you have to resort to knockings on the table for help . . .

There came a ring at the door. It was a woman; he recognised her from one of Rasputin's dinners.

'I must speak to Grigori. It's important.'

Good God, it isn't them. Luckily. He didn't know how he should behave in front of royalty. Fall on his knees, perhaps, crawl in the dust and sing the Imperial Anthem in E major.

'Don't you hear what I say? I want to speak to Grigori.'

He recognised her; she had been there a few evenings back. Little Katya Ivanova, daughter of the field marshal. The Doctor had moaned in the dressing room and Miss Ivanova had wrinkled her nose so the powder flew: *'Have you got a sick cat in the house, Father Grigori?'*

'You had better wait here while I go and fetch him.'

He went to Grigori's bedroom and knocked on the door.

'It's Katya Ivanova. She says it's important.'

'For God's sake get her out of here, they'll be arriving any minute. Have you got the table ready?'

Grigori appeared before him in the doorway, carrying with him a faint smell of manure and onions, like an invisible shadow. Like a throne behind him stood the enormous love-boat on whose sheets half of St Petersburg's female aristocracy had passed inspection. The man with the marvellous eyes, the man with the look of a holy lunatic, who would set the standard for the coming century's gurus and court intriguers; dressed in unlikely peasant garb: tall, unpolished boots, baggy trousers and a long shirt of rough homespun, with Siberian designs, soiled with smears of jam, biscuit crumbs, vanilla sauces, jellies, mousses, crème caramels, cloudberry puddings and hundreds of other little delicacies on which he had gorged with the delight of a child and the greed of a convict.

'Katya Ivanova? Tell her to come again tomorrow, to my dinner.' There was a knowing twinkle in his eye. 'Something for your ears only, Kolya. Between the two of us, I rather like her. What do you say? Love is a gift from God. The union of the body gives us a foretaste of paradise.'

But he wasn't listening. He was on his way back, to deliver the message.

'Grigori says you must come back tomorrow when he's giving a dinner.'

'But doesn't he understand? I need to speak to him now.'

'You must come back tomorrow, Miss Ivanova.'

She started to cry and tried to fend him off, but with a resolute shove he got her out onto the landing and shut the door. *Staretz*, he thought, and behaving like that! If the Empress could hear him: 'We must sin in order to receive forgiveness.' Or: 'God's mercy is accorded to those who show their carnal weakness.' And those women hanging in clusters from him, like a bunch of grapes. He had had them all, every sort. Lustful women, hysterical women, religious women, old, young, ugly and beautiful, the crippled and the lame, and one who bellowed like a cow. A strange morality indeed for a man who called himself God's chosen one and had a wife and children in Pokrovskoe.

He lit the censer in the drawing room and brought in the plate of biscuits and the mystical table. Was this what symbolised Rasputin's power of attraction? A tin plate of peasant biscuits and a table for spiritualists? The simple and the occult, the real Russia in a nutshell . . . The room, he noted, smelt like old sheep's cheese preserved in vinegar. A pair of Grigori's woollen socks was hanging over the arm of a chair. He removed them and opened the window to air the place. That man really was the limit. Black under the nails. Giving off an indeterminate smell of dung, however much he washed, and that was often. Women with their eyes raised orgiastically to heaven would soap him in the bathhouse round the corner, and he would smack them on the bottom and cry: 'Enough of your groping, you little strumpet!' Father Grigori, he thought as he poured water for the tea into the samovar; the *staretz* with the unerring nose, who could find his way to the oyster through seven layers of petticoats; the man was clearly amphibious, and equally happy under water.

On a serving table he set out glasses and cups, and a jar of pickled cucumbers. The doorbell rang again, and he ran his hand over his hair to check his parting. Knees trembling, he opened the door, but it wasn't them this time, either.

'Can I speak to Father Grigori, if it's convenient? The guards downstairs let me in once they'd searched me. I showed them my references from the ministry.'

A bureaucrat. Junior civil servant from some distant *guberniya*. Presumably he'd come all this way to St Petersburg for an audience with the highest authority. To ask Rasputin to put in a good word with the Tsar. A new project for efficient broiler production, maybe, in some little dump in the provinces whose name nobody could even pronounce. To supply the army. Noodles and chicken soup. A stroke of genius. Wanted to get rich, no doubt. Poor man, what are riches compared to mortality?

'One moment. I'll see what I can do.'

Again he went in to see Grigori, who was now standing half-naked in front of the full-length mirror, massaging linseed oil into his beard.

'Send the fellow packing. Tell him to come back at Christmas.'

He went back, sent the man away and shut the door behind him. It went on and on, this never-ending stream of knocks at the door, beggars, fools, adventurers and agitated women washing through the apartment on Gorokhovaya Street. He had seen them thrusting envelopes of thousand-rouble notes into Rasputin's pockets, asking him in humble voices to put in a word with the Minister of the Interior. And the *staretz* would give away the lot to the next beggar who rang to ask for a crust of bread. Here you are, five thousand! Go and buy a *dacha* somewhere!

Back in the drawing room, he closed the window and drew the curtains. There was a sound from the dressing room. He opened the door and peeped in. The food still stood untouched. The Doctor was still asleep, a snoring bundle on the mattress . . . This bodily decay. Those empty eyes, in whose depths oblivion gleamed and memories – how many years' worth? – faded. And yet, this man was his only hope.

'Doctor?' he whispered. 'Can you hear me? Are you awake? Do you remember anything? Do you know where you are?'

A gurgling noise, like the last eddy of water disappearing down a drain, issued from the old man's throat. He had been sleeping for several weeks now. Maybe all hope was already lost? He wondered if Rasputin intended mentioning the Doctor to the imperial couple.

There was a sound from behind him. He closed the door and turned round.

'No, Kolya. Why should I? It's a private matter between us. Stop worrying and go and get ready. Put on your uniform and try to look subservient. They're on their way. They'll be coming incognito, escorted by a marshal of the court.'

Rasputin smiled. It had happened again: he had read Kolya's thoughts as if they had been printed on a piece of paper. He would have to be on his guard. Over the last month he had developed a method for being left in peace with his consciousness: he wrapped his most intimate thoughts in a jumble of whims and fancies, ramblings and nonsense, which more than once had caused Rasputin to burst out: 'Stop it, Kolya, for God's sake, you're giving me a headache with all that rubbish!' Poor Grigori. The Sibyl's fate. Not easy being clairvoyant. But he still can't help showing off. Can't drive him half a block in the car without him telling me what's round the next street corner: 'Hundred to one there's a drunk in a red knitted cap lying on the ground begging, round that corner!' Quite right. A drunk. In a red cap. And Grigori chuckles . . .

Now, just as the church clocks of St Petersburg struck seven, he locked the Doctor's door.

'Forget him for now,' said Rasputin. 'And put on an apron for serving. They're here. And Prince Yusupov is with them.'

Kolya opened the door and gave a deep bow. He felt unsettled at the prospect of the encounter. He had only ever seen them in pictures before; the Emperor in uniform or his regal costume with the full regalia of state; the Empress with a crown and the ceremonial sash across her breast. Now they had materialised in the doorway before him, in ordinary bourgeois garb. He didn't know what etiquette prescribed for him; perhaps he was supposed to kneel to them. But before he could decide what to do, Rasputin came to the rescue:

'Little Father. Little Mother. God bless you. Welcome. And whom have we here? Your Grace, Prince Yusupov.'

Yusupov, a relation of the Tsar, bowed stiffly behind the imperial couple.

They went into the drawing room. Grigori bade them take a seat on the simple wooden settle. The incense had impregnated the air, and Kolya took his place at the serving table.

Taking care to remain unobtrusive, he studied the imperial couple. He could not escape the slight sense of unreality and silent submission that inevitably comes over a man of the people at the sight of royalty. Was that really Alexandra? The myth, the subject of constant slander. She spoke with an accent, for she had grown up at the English court, but by birth she was a German princess. The republican politicians disliked her because she was the Tsarina, and the nationalists because she was German. There was a perception that the dynasty was nourishing a viper in its bosom who whispered stratagems to the Kaiser in Berlin. Beside her on the settee sat the slender Tsar, his beard trimmed short. He had already smoked three cigarettes. He was said to be a chain smoker, a nervous habit he had inherited from his Danish mother. To think that this weak, coughing body could bear the fate of the Russian people on its shoulders . . .

'How goes the war, Little Father?' asked Rasputin. 'You look pale.'

'A disaster, Grigori. Seen in the light of our original strategy, that is. The Grand Duke allowed two army corps to fall in East Prussia. Half a million men. Rennenkampf was preparing to attack Königsberg. They were to join up afterwards and march straight on Berlin.' He tapped the ash off his cigarette into a china dish in the shape of a Latin cross and gave an audible sigh. 'I don't know what happened after that, no one seems to have any idea. The general staff is in chaos. Samsonov was beaten at Neidenburg. The Germans took a hundred thousand prisoners. And last month Hindenburg attacked Rennenkampf's northern army. The whole left flank fell.

Our boys were mown down in their tens of thousands at the Masurian Lakes. We're back where we started, or worse. In some places, the enemy has even made camp inside Russian lines.

He fell silent and stubbed out his cigarette.

'Your Majesty is forgetting the Polish front,' said Yusupov. 'We have driven the enemy out of Lodz. And what are a hundred thousand prisoners? We will send a hundred thousand more, and then another hundred thousand. We are prepared. Let us drown the enemy in the blood of our fallen men.'

'Why must you always be so dramatic, Yusupov? Pray to God instead. And let Father Grigori say a prayer for our good fortune in battle.'

'God helps those who help themselves, your Majesty. What we need is the spirit of self-sacrifice.'

Kolya pushed the serving trolley closer to the table. Yusupov gave him a suspicious look.

'I did warn you, Little Father,' Rasputin said. 'You should never have listened to the warmongers in the Duma. What can this war achieve?'

'You know more than most people about eternal bliss, Grigori,' countered Yusupov. 'But war is something you don't understand. For God's sake, see your limitations. You're talking like a traitor to your country, in front of our Emperor.'

The Prince got to his feet, visibly annoyed. Now he crossed to the window and looked out through the crack in the curtains: 'By the way, Father Grigori, how is the security here? Those guards downstairs doing a good job? The bloodhounds?'

'I didn't ask for all this attention. It was the Minister of the Interior and the chief of the St Petersburg police who insisted.' Rasputin turned to the Tsar again: 'A hundred thousand prisoners, Little Father. You must hope the censors do their job.'

'The censors seem to be the only things that work in my country. As for the will to go to war, we shall just have to hope our subjects are loyal. The Minister of the Interior has suggested we stick to the capital's new name. Petrograd. What do you think about that, Grigori? St Petersburg is too German.'

He looked hopefully at Rasputin, but the *staretz* looked extremely grave.

'You don't seem to realise that this war could very well bring you down. You should have heeded my advice from the outset and kept the empire out of this mass slaughter. What can it achieve? Let the Europeans destroy themselves. I know the Russian soul; it has had enough; it will soon be turning on you, on your wife and your children, perhaps on the whole aristocracy.'

The Tsar pondered Rasputin's words. The Empress sat in silence, twisting a simple silver ring on her finger. Only Yusupov appeared unmoved . . . It was incredible, Josef thought, that he was in the same room as these people. But the war brought the most diverse destinies together. It was on everyone's lips now. On the Emperor's, on Rasputin's, on the peasants' and the beggars'. Even his brother, he thought . . . and the memory brought a sting of pain with it . . . Mikhail Rubashov was a lieutenant in the reserve. Maybe he was one of those who had perished over there in East Prussia.

'Kolya!'

Rasputin's voice roused him.

'Don't stand there dreaming. Serve us the wine and biscuits. Have you sampled them for me? The raisins too?'

With an embarrassed bow, he put a biscuit in his mouth and chewed, slowly. A taste of oats and burned sugar reached his palate, then the sweet sourness of the raisins. But no suspicious undertones; none of the light bitterness of strychnine, none of the pungency of potassium cyanide or the floweriness of thorn-apple.

'My taster,' Rasputin explained. 'One can't be too careful in times like these. And Kolya is a phenomenon. There isn't a single poison that has any effect on him. Believe me!'

'A taster, good God,' said Yusupov. 'You should think more of your reputation than of what you stuff into your stomach, Father Grigori. The whole of St Petersburg is talking about your activities. Too great an influence on affairs of state, they say. Especially on the Tsarina.'

The Empress silenced him with a look.

'Grigori,' she said, 'I'm so worried about Alexei. We can't keep him shut up like a wild animal. He needs to get out and play. It oppresses his soul, especially now Nikolai is away at the front so often.'

'Let the boy play. I have prayed for him and the illness is loosening its grip. Take him south to the monasteries while Father is at the front. God will give him strength. He will find new fuel for his faith.'

Kolya had begun going round with the serving trolley. The Emperor nodded kindly and took a biscuit. The Empress smiled and took two. Yusupov took a glass of Madeira and waved him away.

'What concerns me more than monastery visits,' Yusupov said, 'without in any way belittling the great suffering of the heir to the throne, is the Ukraine. Your Majesty ought to advise the Grand Duke to send a battalion to Kiev to counter any disturbances. We can't afford a civil war on top of all these other setbacks. There's a Stenka Rasin in every tavern down there. And a Pugachev for every loyal Tsarist. Opportunities will arise for the socialists to spread their pro-independence propaganda. We have a Trojan horse at the heart of our empire. Hang it all, we must make sure we assert the primacy of Greater Russia over the minority states!'

'Now now, Yusupov, take it easy,' said the Tsar.

'I'm sorry, your Majesty, but it never hurts to take a cautious approach. In wars, you have to take care of the home front, too. And we mustn't commit any faux pas while our allies look on. It would be a miserable performance if separatists and Socialists were seen to get the better of us. What would the French say?'

Kolya positioned himself a little way from them, waiting. Yusupov, he thought. The Prince belonged to the war party. Related to Nikolai Nikolayevich, and hadn't been a *verst* outside St Petersburg since the war broke out. He didn't understand what business the man had with the imperial couple. He seemed untrustworthy. But appearances could be deceptive. As with the Doctor. Every last hope lay with him. That is, if he was who he claimed to be. Ancient. Eternal . . .

Once more he was interrupted by Rasputin:

'For God's sake, Kolya, how many times do I have to tell you, your droning makes me dizzy!'

The *staretz* stared at him, and the guests stared in their turn at the *staretz*.

'Forgive me. It's a private matter between me and my taster. I sometimes get the idea he's talking aloud to himself, all manner of drivel.'

'Exactly. That just about sums up what people think of your prophecies, Grigori,' said Yusupov. 'You talk too loud. All manner of drivel.' He gave Rasputin a hostile look and turned to the Tsar. 'Before I lose the thread, your Majesty. A battalion to Kiev. After all, it can also double as a force in readiness against the doomed Saracens. We can expect a Turkish front to open up at any moment.'

The Tsar lit another cigarette from the glowing end of the previous one.

'You can save your advice for later, Prince,' he said curtly. 'Father Grigori, I suggest we consult the table . . .'

The seance commenced. Rasputin and the three members of the royal family sat around the elliptical table. They were holding hands and their eyes were closed. Rasputin was on his way to falling into a trance. The scent of incense was stronger now, and somewhere above it, coiling like a second voice, you could smell Rasputin's unwashed woollen socks. The silk in Yusupov's expensive suit rustled. He had turned to look over towards the dressing room. A sound could be heard from within: a faint cough.

There came a few knockings from the table, and then, after a pause, a longer sequence.

'What are they saying?' whispered the Tsar. 'You must ask about the war, Grigori. Ask what we ought to do at Lodz?'

'I do not know who it is communicating with us,' said Rasputin. 'A woman, I think. Yes, a woman. A woman of your family, Little Father.'

'Catherine, it must be Catherine. Ask her if we need more men on the Austrian front. Ask her if we can get over the Carpathians before Christmas!'

New knockings were heard, but in such quick succession that they were more like triplets played on a drum.

'She's saying, I think she's saying . . . keep an eye on Ulyanov. She doesn't know who Ulyanov is, but you should keep an eye on a man named Ulyanov. Prepare yourselves for a long war, she says, a war that will cost millions of lives, for no territorial gains.'

'Who in God's name is Ulyanov? An anarchist? My empire is vast. Ask her if it's anything to do with the war. How can she expect me to take decisions on such flimsy grounds. Ask her to be more specific.'

There was a new sound, but this time it was more like a banging, and it came not from the table, but from the Doctor's room.

'Are you expecting visitors, Grigori?' asked Yusupov. 'The back way? At this hour?'

He let go of the imperial couple's hands and turned to the door of the dressing room, but at the same instant the knockings from the table began again.

'Don't break the circle, Yusupov,' said the Tsar. 'That's an order!'

'But didn't your Majesty hear that noise?'

'An order, I said!'

Yusupov reluctantly obeyed.

'Now,' said Rasputin. 'She will soon be back with us.'

New knockings ensued, even more rapid than before. The Tsar was in such suspense that he sat there with his tongue hanging out, like a dog.

'What does she say? For God's sake, Grigori, what does she say?'

'She says: among the people . . . widespread famine, trench warfare in the west, protection against gas, wear blue on Mondays, a German is a human being too, take two parts sugar to one part black radish . . .' Rasputin frowned. 'She seems confused,' he said. 'Now it's mostly nonsense.'

He fell silent and listened attentively. From the dressing room the banging was heard again, the violent pounding of someone trying to get out, but the sound was drowned by a rattling from the table.

'Now,' said Rasputin. 'Now. Wait! Most remarkable. Really most remarkable.'

The Tsar's lower lip quivered; he moistened it with his tongue.

'What is it now? What is it now, Father Grigori?'

'It's for you, Josef,' said Rasputin.

He turned to Kolya and raised his eyebrows in two crescents, and Josef suddenly remembered how he had looked outside the Doctor's hermit lair in Vitebsk a month earlier.

'It's the spirits,' he said. 'They claim he's getting well again. They claim he's woken up and can help you, Kolya: our friend Doctor Suscarapel.'

Dr Suscarapel

In November that year, and as predicted in a dream, they undertook a long journey by train and sleigh, and finally found themselves in a forest in the *guberniya* of Vitebsk, standing in a clearing by a frozen spring. Before them was a ramshackle hovel. A roof of branches and turf had been laid across stone walls on a rock base. The walls had been weatherproofed with mud. From the branches of an ancient oak hung a strange, rusty sword. A crow cawed from a stone. An open pit stank of excrement.

Not without astonishment, Josef Rubashov stared at a hermit dwelling deep in the wilds of Russia, having been in ignorance of their destination until now. A lifetime of religious quest had made Rasputin enigmatic about everything.

Half a year had passed since their second meeting, in June 1914, a month before the outbreak of war. It was the memory of the ball at the Winter Palace that had made Josef Rubashov seek him out; the evening when Rasputin had predicted the birth of the child and Nina Rubashova's death.

Rasputin remembered him very well from their meeting three years before, and he listened without a single interruption to Josef's story, which included every significant event since that night at the turn of the century.

'What makes you think I can help you?' he asked once Josef had finished.

'You, if anyone,' Josef Rubashov replied, 'have the necessary gifts.'

Rasputin sighed. A year before he had had a highly detailed vision of Russia being destroyed by a mighty fire. There could be no misinterpreting this sign, he said; it portended a great war, and he wanted at any price to stop the Tsar from leading Russia into a bloodbath. With a look so melancholy that Josef would never forget it, he blew the dust from a facsimile of the prophecies of the medieval monk Tostov and, quivering with suppressed emotion, interpreted the text so that it uncannily resembled the dangers which the country now faced, and one of the symbolic figures bore a striking resemblance to himself. Then he asked to be left alone.

Josef Rubashov waited for two days in the monastery lodgings where he was staying temporarily. His instinct told him Rasputin was the only person who could help him, but he also realised that the *staretz* was a man for whom fate had larger tasks than this. He was therefore surprised when the *staretz* appeared on the third morning. He had consulted his conscience, he said. And it forbade him to abandon a human being in need . . .

They set off the same afternoon. Dusty clumps of birches lined the road, while in the fields priests were walking in procession with ikons to bless the harvest. When Josef asked where they were going, Rasputin told him about a country church where the devil was said to have spoken from the pulpit on the morning of St John the Baptist's Day, after which the congregation had gone mad, slaughtered their animals and got drunk on the blood of a black lamb. Perhaps it was yet another portent of approaching misfortune, he said, or perhaps it was just a rumour. He admitted the story wasn't worth investing too much hope in, but their enquiries had to start somewhere . . .

They reached the village late in the afternoon. In the heat, the square and streets lay deserted, and it took them over an hour to locate a living soul, a farmer, who recognised Rasputin from the newspapers posted up on the village walls, and then kissed the hem of his long shirt. He confirmed that a slaughter had indeed taken place, but said it had been a protest against the new taxes. He admitted, too, that a stranger had preached to them in the chapel, a devil in a way, for he was one of the band of Mensheviks and had preached conscientious objection among the peasant farmers. And as the farmer delivered an incoherent monologue on Russia's dismal future prospects, Rasputin turned to Rubashov and whispered: 'As you see, Kolya, our task will not be an easy one.'

This meeting set the tone for the weeks that followed. They visited a place where it was said a shower of snakes had rained down, but all that remained were a few cast-off grass-snake skins and two feeble-minded shepherds who claimed it was a punishment for having intercourse with their cows. From a village near Novgorod came a rumour that an exhausted parish clerk had taken a dozen ghosts to the court of death for disturbing his night-time sleep for a month or more: those who had died by drowning had wrung out their clothes; others had flicked churchyard earth around; a third group had sat gloomily staring into the fire. In his despair, the clerk had appealed to the devil, and eventually received a sacred promise that the dead would walk no more. Rasputin and Rubashov made their way there, exchanged a few words with yet another lunatic, and returned to the capital as short of leads as when they left.

But Rasputin refused to give up. In the middle of the month he contacted his monastical friends. They were part of the network of contacts he had built up in the countryside over more than half a lifetime's pilgrimage, a network extending way over the Urals into far-off Siberia.

Answers arrived by letter and telegram. No one had seen Josef's guest in action, but they had the most fantastical events to relate. One letter described a man possessed by nine demons of sickness, each of which blasphemed in seven different languages. Another told of a calf born with three heads, the middle one able to forecast the weather and predict deaths several months ahead. In Cherson, a smith had eaten red-hot coals and quenched his thirst with molten lead without scalding himself. And in a forest outside Minsk, a deranged gamekeeper had declared himself the bride of Christ, nailed himself to a cross and sunk through the earth like a stone in quicksand.

A woman had developed pus-filled boils from holy water, and another had been kidnapped by a flock of witches flying over a cathedral in Georgia, and the same witches had later been discovered by a choirboy with second sight during an Orthodox mass in Karelia, in which they, invisible to the rest of the congregation, had sat back-to-front in the gallery, gnawing on the tender parts of a suicide's corpse.

It all seemed improbable, said Rasputin; these stories were more likely to be different ways of describing the approaching catastrophe, the war drawing inexorably closer.

And the war was indeed drawing closer. Hardly a day went by now without the Emperor making an inflammatory speech to the nation. Even boys were being mobilised. The reserve troops had been called up. On the streets of St Petersburg, the Cossack regiments were parading.

One morning he saw his brother, Mikhail Rubashov. It was in the market hall on Apothecary Island. The reservists had set up a base in a warehouse. Mikhail was standing on the pavement in his lieutenant's uniform, facing a platoon of new young recruits. They were barefoot and shouldering dummy weapons made of wood. In the heat, from a distance, Josef Rubashov observed the exercise. He could hear his brother's voice, gentle, much gentler than he had ever heard it before . . . No more than fifty metres divided them, but distance, he realised, was irrelevant. His brother believed him dead. In Mikhail Rubashov's life he, Josef Nikolai, had perished in the flames along with his wife and his mother. A mass had already been said for their souls. Tears had been shed, curses uttered. He knew his brother was grieving for them deeply. No one had been spared from Josef's punishment.

He pushed aside an impulse to go up to him. What purpose would he serve by admitting his sin, the fact that everything had been his fault from the very start? He turned away and buried his face in his hands. He was already dead, he thought. And the dead had no right to haunt the living.

83

A short time after this episode, at the start of August, they had word from a priory near Volchov. The prior, an acquaintance of Rasputin's, said he had something important to impart.

It was evening when they arrived. The prior met them at the front gate. He was very pale, as if suffering from shock, and without saying a word he showed them up to a tower room where visiting pilgrims were accommodated.

'A while ago,' he said, 'an old man came on foot from the south. A small man, hardly any bigger than a boy. He introduced himself as a physician. He was the oldest human being I had ever seen.'

The prior sat down on the bunk in the cell and took a rosary from the pocket that hung from his girdle.

'For two days he went among the novices, muttering and laughing by turns. He seemed confused, to say the least . . . The second night he was here, I could not sleep. I was going to the chapel to pray, but on the way I heard a sound from the staircase that leads up here . . . It was him, the pilgrim. He seemed to be talking to somebody. I waited outside the door until he went quiet. Then I peeped in. And he had gone. It was if he had dissolved into thin air. There wasn't a sign of him. Except this . . .'

The prior fell silent, and from the same pocket from which he had produced the rosary he drew a sheet of paper, a yellowed old page with a few ruled lines, perforations and blocks of writing. Josef could see what it was: a contract like the one he himself had signed fourteen years before. At the top of the sheet, a name had been filled in: 'Doctor Suscarapel.'

'I know what kind of contract this is, Father Grigori,' said the prior. 'I have seen one before. When I came to the priory as a novice, there were still Bogomils living in the mountains. Several of them had entered into pacts with the devil . . .'

The prior stopped speaking and looked down at the floor.

'It bodes ill,' he said in a whisper. 'There's a catastrophe waiting to happen, Grigori . . . a catastrophe that will be the ruin of Russia.'

The evening they got back to St Petersburg, a thunderstorm was raging over the city. Great flashes of lightning lit up the sky. Up in his apartment, Rasputin asked Rubashov to sit down on the couch used for hypnosis experiments, and declared that he had finally begun to see a pattern; that now, gradually, they could start putting two and two together. It would make things easier, he said, if they could live under the same roof from now on, for as Josef must realise, they were now very close to finding a creature who could help them. When Josef asked who he meant, Rasputin shook his head. Later he said: there's a time for everything, and time is something you have plenty of, Josef Nikolai . . .

The world war broke out on the day Josef Rubashov moved into Gorokhovaya Street. St Petersburg was abuzz with rumour all morning. The newspapers ran special editions. The headlines announced victories. Rennenkampf's armies had met no opposition as they penetrated deep into East Prussian territory. There was a wild, carnival mood. A spontaneous torchlit procession paraded through the centre of the city. Champagne corks were popping in all the restaurants. But Rasputin locked himself in his room, and through the door Josef could hear him cursing the army and offering prayers for a swift end to the war.

Late at night through that first summer of the war, he would go up to his attic room above Rasputin's apartment. Exhausted by all the impressions saturating him after a day in the company of this man, he was incapable of thinking a complete thought until the day drew to a close. The prior, he wondered, the pilgrim? The abandoned contract? And Suscarapel . . . who was Doctor Suscarapel?

He had to wait until November for an answer. By then, a year had passed since catastrophe had hit him with its full force. Not a day had gone by in the meantime without him thinking of his wife and son. His grief was still a primeval force under whose laws he was a marionette, a leaf tossed to and fro by the wind. Not a day went by without him sending up a prayer to God for success in his search.

The world is a playground for mysteries, Rasputin had said once, when despair had him in its grip; it is large enough to accommodate all God's miracles. Humankind only discovers them gradually. A few thousand years ago it was colour-blind. And just as colours have been revealed to us over time, other mysteries will now be revealed. So you must have hope, Kolya.

Shortly thereafter, he received a directive in a dream: here, in Vitebsk, was a being who could help them . . .

The forest lay white and silent around them. Snow had fallen. The sleigh driver stood by his sleigh a little way off, shivering. They had travelled for hours along snowed-up roads to get here. And now, very slowly, a door opened.

'Allow me to introduce,' whispered Rasputin, 'Lord Philipp Aureolus Theophrast Bombast von Hohenheim, doctor of medicine from Basle, inventor of the elixir of life, disciple of Fugger, equal of Celsus, the great Paracelsus, also known by his anagram: Doctor Suscarapel.'

Decades later Josef Rubashov would remember this day for giving him his first insight into the nature of ageing, for the man now appearing at the door to the hovel defied all his preconceptions of time's wear and tear on the human body.

This was physiognomic decay without parallel. He was an album of all the pains and symptoms of old age. His height was that of a ten-year-old child, and he was moreover so emaciated that he must have lived in fear of the wind blowing him away. His face was criss-crossed with lines and disfigured by big scars. His nails were like chips of stone and his teeth like splinters of rusty metal. In places around his chest and arms, the skin was so worn that you could almost see straight through him. Even his shadow seemed ancient: yellowish and full of holes, like a cheese. And his back was adorned with an enormous hump . . .

Many centuries earlier, as a controversial natural healer, Paracelsus had given death the slip. He had still not reached fifty, but by the standards of his time the course of his life was virtually at an end. Years of feuds about the healing effect for plague victims of the minerals in marble, and whether his sensational lectures on popular medicine should be given in Latin or German, had left him bitter and broken. He dreamed of his happy youth, when he had studied under the abbot Johan Tritheim and the alchemist Fugger, with whose help he had developed a method for calling forth demons of sickness and keeping them in check with magical pentagrams. He had wanted to don a monk's habit, but to his disappointment had not been accepted into any order. So he had taken to the road instead.

Extensive journeys in Asia and Europe had taught him to speak and read sixteen languages, but driven by his restlessness, he had never stayed longer than a few months in any place. He had served as personal physician to eccentric princes and caused a scandal by running away with ministers' daughters. In 1520 he was among the plundering hordes following the Danish king Kristian on his warlike advance on Stockholm. After the great bloodbath on the square at Stora Torget, he managed to appropriate the executioner's sword, the only artefact apart from his barber-surgeon's equipment that he then preserved and kept with him. The sword was considered to possess unheard-of power as a result of having severed eighty heads from their bodies.

According to the chronicles, he departed this life in the year 1541 in Salzburg, but the devil came to the graveyard by night and dug him up. One apocryphal source described the event as the result of an agreement entered into when he was a young man one night in Paris when, under the influence of a salve of henbane rubbed inside his anus, he had summoned up the ruler of the underworld and sold his soul in exchange for an elixir of life. A contract had been signed to prevent any legal doubts arising in the future. He had thanked his helper with a kiss, talked him into revealing a few epoch-making alchemical formulae and the key to the riddle of numerology, then cursed the Habsburg dynasty and left Austria for good . . .

Throughout his first century as an immortal, he had kept his distance from Europe. Its people disgusted him. Their constant bickering and pettiness. Their grunting copulation and grisly wars. He was obsessed with the idea of finding the lost Eden. In the company of a black cat, he had made his way on foot across the

87

most rugged terrain. He had stormed snow-clad mountains and rafted up unknown rivers. He had been to the wastes of India, where the fakirs lived on dew and carried three kilo weights on their erect penises. He had viewed the Himalayas, the roof of the world, from Kanchenjunga and crossed the Gobi Desert by camel. He had lived in ice huts on northerly islands and in African palaces whose walls were crowned with human jawbones. Later, as a stowaway on an English schooner, he had crossed the Atlantic to seek the Philosopher's Stone in the Spanish colonies, married a mulatto woman and stayed there until she died of sleeping sickness at the age of a hundred and six.

Decades passed, and gave way to centuries. Driven by a nameless longing, he had continued his travels. After a year of plague in the Low Countries, the stench of corpses had made him turn his face to the east. He had gone to Russia, where he had scraped a living as an itinerant faith-healer under the anagram of Doctor Suscarapel. Decade had succeeded decade. Eventually he had reached Vitebsk, where he had thrown in his lot with a wise woman. The relationship had been purely a business one: they had bought and sold relics and established a monopoly in the sale of medicinal herbs.

But during a year of famine in the mid-nineteenth century they had been accused of having made the harvest fail, and been stoned as for witchcraft. The wise woman, whose name was long ago forgotten, had died, but Paracelsus, though buried under a small mountain of slate and granite, had dug his way out and slipped away under cover of darkness. A year or so later he was recaptured and burned at the stake, but he stepped from the flames without singeing a single hair on his head. The terror-stricken peasant farmers set their dogs on him in the belief that he was Napoleon, returning on the orders of the Antichrist – a widespread fear at that time – and Paracelsus, to be on the safe side, fled into the forest . . . For several months he wandered aimlessly around in the wilds. He walked in circles until he lost all sense of direction. Finally he found his way to a glade with a spring, where he paused for a few days to calculate his position with the help of the stars and the height of the sun. But he was tired and lethargic, and for lack of any imaginative plans the days had turned into years. Apart from a few pilgrimages and monastery visits in Volchov, he had remained in the wilds for almost a century. Gradually his presence had give rise to folk tales about an ancient pixie of the forest, who could speak the language of the birds.

Rasputin related all this as they stood outside Paracelsus's hut. Grimly he regarded the old man squatting by the old oak tree, who poked at the ground with his rusty sword, mumbled something incomprehensible and stared empty-eyed into the forest. When he had seen him in his dream, Rasputin said, the Doctor had been hale and hearty, full of energy, very keen to talk. But now, strangely enough, he seemed senile and hard of hearing.

They took him that very afternoon to a hotel in a nearby village. Wrapped in a horse blanket, the Doctor seemed lost in the mists of old age. When they bathed him in the inn's copper, he seemed unaware of what was going on around him. When the *staretz* shouted his name into his ear at top volume, he merely gave his hump a listless scratch. His old pores emitted a fearful stench. They peeled layers of mouldy skin off his back and burned his louse-infested clothes in the wood stove. They had to change the water in the copper seven times before they could see its verdigrised bottom through the dirt.

Exhausted by the suspense of it all, Josef observed his brother-in-misfortune. The thought of not being alone in his fate raised the skin on his arms into goose pimples. There was more than one of his kind. Knowing that this man might be able to help him made him feel light-headed. This mystic and alchemist, this veteran in the tribe of the immortal.

That night, the sky cleared and a moon lit the room with its cold gleam. Josef looked over to the bed where Paracelsus lay curled up, his sword beside him. From the hotel maids' room came a woman's giggle and the sound of Rasputin mumbling an excited prayer. Outside, a lamplighter worked his way along the street and back.

In the moonlight, Rubashov fell on his knees by the bed of the ancient man:

'Tell me where I can find him,' he whispered. 'Tell me, for goodness sake, and redeem my soul.'

But Paracelsus slept for four weeks in the dressing room they had prepared for his use. On the evening of the imperial couple's visit, he regained consciousness and showed signs of life, but it took him until New Year to recover fully. After gurgling like a baby for weeks, reminding Josef Rubashov of his mother, the old doctor one morning had clear eyes and asked in a slightly quavering voice where he was. They gave him some explanation and he took their replies with composure. Apart from a degree of deafness, he now seemed normal in every way. He was pleased, he said, to be in St Petersburg, a city he had never visited before.

He looked round Rasputin's apartment and asked them their names, then anxiously enquired after his sword, which they gave him. Next he asked what year it was, and when they said 1915 he scratched his hunched back in astonishment and mumbled:

'Good grief, I seem to have been asleep for fifty years!'

They gave him some broad orientation in the world situation, the kings and princes of the age, recent technological advances, and the war which in less than six months had claimed as many lives as all previous conflicts combined. And after a short pause in which Paracelsus appeared to be digesting this news, Rasputin got out the old contract he had left behind at the priory in Volchov and explained why he had been brought here.

The Doctor regarded them in silence for a long time, before telling them in a whisper that he hadn't seen the one they were seeking for almost four hundred years. Their relationship, he said, was entirely businesslike, and he had never had reason to regret the agreement they had made in the time of Charles V. He had enjoyed his perpetual travels and the special sort of freedom that stems from never having to fear designs on your life. For that reason, he had never made any effort to locate him. In answer to Josef's respectful appeal for help, he asked for time to think it over.

Paracelsus's thinking turned out to take all winter, a period of convalescence in which the last symptoms of his senility vanished and he regained some physical strength. Rasputin, on the other hand, went downhill. All the indications were that he was slipping into depression.

He was beset daily by visions and nightmares. He was convinced that he was going to be murdered, and that Russia's fate stood or fell with his own. The signs were unambivalent, in his view. The world was heading for destruction. The war was escalating, and several times a week Josef Rubashov would have to drive him out to Tsarskoe Selo, the imperial country residence, where he tried to persuade the Tsar to take Russia out of the war. On the way home he would often break down in tears.

In the February of that year rumours began circulating that he had started an affair with the Tsarina, and at the Press Club a notorious royalist made an impassioned speech against his influence in national affairs. The newspapers openly accused him of being a spy, and one night leaflets were distributed, in which he was said to have sold state secrets to the Austrians . . . That was the final blow. He sat sleepless in his room at nights, engrossed in the Book of Revelations. Sometimes he would wake Josef and ask him to sit up with him. Mortal dread drove its spear into his breast. He sweated and muttered incoherent prayers. He turned his ikons to the wall so the saints would not witness his despair.

When rumours of German invasion plans started going round, he ordered whole barrels of Madeira from a wine merchant on Morskaja, and disappeared ever more frequently to the brothels with little-known acquaintances.

But at that time, Easter 1915, Josef noticed nothing of Rasputin's torment. He was preoccupied with Paracelsus . . .

That remarkable old doctor lay for the most part stretched out on his mattress in the dressing room, smoking a pipe. He was biding his time, as he put it, waiting for the compass to set a new course, and what were a few months more or less when eternity was at his feet. He had turned out to be easily distracted, inclined to day-dreams and, unfortunately, the greatest of liars.

In his symphony of lies and half-truths, Paracelsus blended the high and the low, the ridiculous and the sublime, the possible and the impossible. He was totally without inhibition, not prioritising any one thing over another. He lied as blatantly about small details as about world events, and often got embroiled in a tangle of internal contradictions from which he had great trouble extracting himself. He claimed to have cured Erasmus of Rotterdam of gout, but strangely enough had simultaneously served as a barber-surgeon in the sixth Levantine punitive expedition, where he had lost a toe in battle against a Turkish pirate. He had discussed concordat issues with Luther long after the latter's death, and made pioneering contributions to research into tapeworms by secretly inoculating the worms into groups of gypsies, although gypsies were in fact still unknown in western Europe at that time. He had been rich and poor, elevated and humbled; in short, everything remotely permissible within the bounds of his imagination.

Alone with his thoughts, Josef wondered if this was perhaps what time did to them; perhaps it was time itself which through the power of its eternal flow distorted the truth, which used the filing tool of the centuries to grind and polish it beyond recognition, or repeatedly recalculated it until the copies bore no likeness to the original.

Perhaps there was in fact no truth at all? Perhaps there was only the indifferent rhythm of the years and moments?

But a week before Annunciation Day something occurred to rekindle his hopes. He took Paracelsus down with him to the store-room in the cellar, to look out a statue of the virgin that Rasputin needed for a dinner. In the musty half-light, Paracelsus happened to trip over one of the packing cases containing Rasputin's old alchemy laboratory, and at the sight of a cracked eighteenth-century retort, the Doctor's eyes blurred with tears. He solemnly announced that he had come to a decision: he would help Josef lure forth the one he was seeking, and heavenly alchemy was the method he would employ . . .

They started that very night. Josef was amazed by the sudden energy of the old man who shared his fate; for among funnels and retorts, distilling apparatus and invocations gabbled backwards, Paracelsus appeared in his true element, several hundred years younger, back in the half-heathen century of his youth, guided by the invisible hand of Master Flugge. Before morning came, he had transformed the cellar into a seething laboratory. Vessels steamed. Liquids bubbled. Bunsen burners hissed. An acrid smell of quicksilver hung in the air.

They didn't sleep a wink for two days and nights. Suffused with feelings of blood brotherhood, they navigated their way through a sea full of submerged occult rocks, and by dinner time on the first day Paracelsus succeeded by means of irreverent incantations, an incense of gold cyanuret and woody nightshade, all manner of decoctions, plus calculations of planetary conjunctions and the day's prognosis for necromancy read in a rotten egg yolk, in summoning up a dozen semi-materialised demons. At least, that was what he assured his companion they were. And Josef, for once, had no reason to doubt him.

It was a pitiful collection of misty apparitions that writhed within the prison of the magic circle that day, sighing dismally and pleading for mercy in unintelligible languages. There was the seven-headed Ornias, demon of nightmares; there was Tephras, lover of darkness; Akephalos, lord of jealousy; the Pleiads, seven malevolent sisters who spat slime and threatened to roast them over an open fire, larded with the Host; there was Obizuth, who consisted only of eyes and whose task was to terrify babies, but who at the sight of Paracelsus broke down and cried; there were the Decani, the demons of sickness, fluid and wrestling: Kurtael who afflicted people with colic, and Lyrus, lord of scabies; there was Asmodeus, preventer of marriages, now looking introverted and anaemic; Onesklis, instigator of patricide; and the lizardlike Xerphatos, who licked inside the farmhands' ears at night, urging them to bestiality and drunkenness.

Paracelsus was like a man possessed. Eyes glowing, he muttered and shouted and burst into hysterical laughter. Standing safely outside the magic circle, he taunted the apparitions in Latin, trying with a combination of threats and promises to make them reveal where Josef's judge was to be found. But whether because of his own lack of ability, or ignorance on the part of the creatures he had managed to conjure forth, he got no answers out of them. And gradually, despite intense invocations on the Doctor's part, they dissolved and vanished.

Two days and nights passed thus, with declining levels of success. No more demons showed themselves, and those things that were made to materialise inside the magic circle were puzzling: a cracked hourglass from Roman times, a verdigrised suit of armour from Spain, a silver coin bearing the head of the Pharaoh Rameses, and a semi-calcified skeleton with a poorly knitted fontanelle. With many a heavy sigh, Paracelsus dredged his memory for an alchemical key to get them back on the right track. But none of this helped; neither the guest nor the demons appeared, and in the end the circle lay empty . . .

In early April 1915 the Doctor asked to be left alone in the laboratory. He wanted to work undisturbed, he said, and Josef suspected he was planning to undertake some particularly hazardous experiment demanding great concentration, for which solitude was an absolute prerequisite. In actual fact, Paracelsus was simply trying to refresh his worn-out memory.

To his horror, he had discovered that many of his hard-won skills had managed to escape via the back door of forgetfulness. It plagued him. It drove him to the brink of insanity. And seated on a dusty pile of books, amidst an indescribable muddle of vessels and pans, test tubes, siphons and pipettes spoilt by quicksilver solutions, and small lumps of lead that when molten had run into the shape of hairy spiders, he made a desperate attempt to win back the knowledge that amnesia had stolen from him in an unguarded moment.

He rehearsed what he knew of the Sephiroth. He recalculated the conjunction of the planets. He practised Geber's Moorish formulae and went through his own symposia from the distant time when he held Basle University's secret Chair of Magia Naturalis. But nothing helped, no rehearsals, no exercises in mental gymnastics, not even any of the handbooks for conjuring up the devil, written by Swedenborgians and German pneumatologists, which he surreptitiously ordered from the Rosicrucians' book shop. The most vital esoteric learning was lost to him; the most advanced alchemical insights and the subtle intuition that distinguished a true magician from a circus trickster and charlatan.

In the dank cellar he cried for a while over the poetic riches of the Secret of Secrets before, as he thought, putting aside his books for good. He was on the verge of giving up. He felt done for. Consumed by forgetting . . .

Even so, just after Easter he turned up in Rasputin's kitchen with a tearful look and a sheaf of graphic representations of the seven metals under his arm. He seemed to have aged again; his hearing, at the very least, seemed worse than ever; and his breath smelt bad as he explained there was one option left: to follow in minutest detail the secret rituals of Aaron the Copt.

They made careful preparations for this last experiment. Paracelsus sent for a magic fork – that is, a forked hazel twig cut with a single stroke of a silver knife, hardened in rotten magpie's blood. And with this tied round his neck as a powerful amulet, he set to work with Josef, beginning with a seven-day fast.

They kept to the cellar. They sat before an altar mounted with two black mass candles and a censer spreading the scent of storax and camphor. Only after sunset did they take a little food, consisting of sacramental wafers and black pudding, seasoned with spices but no salt. And as the ritual prescribed, they also got drunk every other evening, on red wine in which the corollae of five black poppies and one hundred and forty grams of pulverised hemp seed had been steeped, after which it had been strained through a cloth woven by a prostitute. So the days and nights passed, in darkness, hunger and intoxication . . .

Many years later Josef would remember the Doctor passing the time by embroidering on his adventures through the centuries. As usual, what he had to tell were tall stories too fantastical to believe, but Paracelsus never let lack of credibility get in his way. On the whole, he seemed indifferent to whether he had a listener or not. Perhaps his voice was addressed only to himself? Perhaps lies and truth no longer mattered after so many lifetimes spent wandering the world?

In the gleam of the sputtering mass candles, he told Josef about the vast occult library he had built up at the court of the gypsy autocrat Ramiro Ramires in Sierra de Gredos; about the first editions of *Grimorium Verum* and the laws of Honorius; about the magical book of Lemegeton, which despite its seventeen hundred pages weighed only nine grams; about Henok's revelations, written in invisible ink distilled from something the Byzantine medicine vendors called angels' tears; and about the manuscripts, bound in gold, by Albertus Magnus, Roger Bacon and Arnold of Villanova. The Doctor had amassed four million volumes there in under a decade. Among them had been Abbott Johan Tritheim's original three-volume work on telekinesis and the art of communicating over many hundreds of kilometres without sending messengers or writing letters; an early draft of *De Occulta Philosophia*, and the most secret formulae and works on the interpretation of dreams by Tertullian and Dr Faustus. There was also a huge collection of scrolls of hieroglyphs, invisible to the naked eye, and a hundred and forty bags of cabalistic scripts, arranged in the order laid down by Enoch of Egypt, everything from Sephir Jezirah to beginners' introductions to the mystical interpretation of numbers, written on the tanned hides of extinct animals.

Paracelsus's eyes gleamed in the dark as he meandered through the centuries. If he were to be believed, he had been everywhere: at Wallenstein's first defeat, and at Napoleon's retreat from Moscow. He had drunk cider with Robespierre and cleaned brushes for Velázquez. At various points, he seemed to have been in half a dozen places at once. But such contradictions did not worry him. Oblivious to the darkness and the strange-smelling incenses, he continued his tale. His worn old body rattled whenever he shifted position. He laughed and slapped his hump each time some particularly amusing memory came to him . . .

The ceremony itself, Paracelsus had decided, would take place on the Catholics' Walpurgis Night, a time that was also warmly recommended by Aaron the Copt. So one evening at the end of their week of fasting, he went out to look for a suitable place. On this point, the ritual made very specific demands. It prescribed a cemetery haunted by evil spirits, a gruesome ruin out in the countryside, a place where a murderer had been exalted, or an abandoned convent where a nun had lost her faith. No other setting, Aaron wrote, should be considered.

He was back just before dawn. Full of excitement, he described the Armenian cemetery, and a duel with a seven-headed ghoul, a patriarch, which he had won by the skin of his teeth after blood had been shed on both sides. Josef felt dejected once more. Once again the thermometer of his hope fell by several degrees. But he decided to accompany Paracelsus nonetheless . . .

It was a night on which fruit trees were budding and migratory birds returning, despite it being unusually cool for the time of year. Paracelsus was in cheerful mood. He carried a bag over his shoulder, containing four nails from the coffin of an executed criminal. That was child's play, he said, compared to what some other rituals demanded: the head of a cat that had eaten its fill of human flesh for five days, for example, or candles made from the melted fat of unbaptised infants, or the collarbone of a patricide and double bigamist. But the power of such black relics, he assured Josef, was easily matched by his magic sword, and the magic fork . . .

That night they followed Aaron the Copt's ritual in the minutest detail. Muttering special invocations, they went three times anti-clockwise round the cemetery, and then the same number of times clockwise, but this time backwards. Paracelsus gabbled strange strings of words. He shuffled through sheets of parchment, made visual estimates using the zodiac and seemed transported into controlled ecstasy. Then he asked Josef to take a seat on the first gravestone he could find, and shut his eyes.

In the dark, he could hear the Doctor whistling an old tune and then opening his bag, busying himself with the nails, and after that, presumably with his sword, absent-mindedly starting to hack at the ground.

It all went quiet. The cold flowed up from the gravestone where Josef sat. He shivered in the raw air. And the minutes passed. Ten minutes. Then ten more. And after a silence, which by Josef's reckoning must have lasted a good half-hour, he opened his eyes.

'Paracelsus?' he said.

But the Doctor . . . the old Doctor was gone.

He hunted for him for several hours. He looked inside the huge marble mausoleums erected to rich Armenian businessmen. He looked behind the crumbling gravestones of the poor, ornamented with little heaps of gravel and dried flowers. He searched in unlocked toolsheds and in the hollow of an old oak, whose wind-swept crown looked as though it were imitating a pair of hands clasped in prayer. Initially he called the Doctor's name timidly, but then ever louder, until someone at a distance in the darkness opened a window and shouted to him to be quiet.

He went back to the place where he had sat with his eyes closed while the Doctor had carried out the great ritual of Aaron the Copt. He sat down on the gravestone. Night contracted its black muscle around him. High above, the stars winked out their mighty cipher.

The Doctor was gone. Rasputin, Josef realised, was no longer in a condition to be of any further help. He knew he must continue the search, but alone . . .

Thus we see him sitting there, in the moonlight, under the stars. We see him clearly in our documents. We see him yearning, eyes shut. We see him very clearly . . .

Variations on a Theme of Hell

(Western front, 1915–17)

1st Bavarian Infantry Regiment, 'Liszt' Regiment
Battalion Staff
From: Lieutenant-Colonel Pieck
Regarding: Commendation for decoration: Iron Cross, 1st Class,
and Bar (posthumous)
Name: Joseph N. Rushbov
Rank: Private

Citation:
Private Rushbov enrolled as a volunteer during the recruitment
campaign in East Prussia in May. After summer training in
Chemnitz and Gera, he was attached in July via the Fourth
Volunteer Corps to the Liszt Regiment, 1st Company Recon-
naissance Unit at the 'Longwy' section of the front. Rushbov first
distinguished himself for particular bravery in the field during
'Operation Clementin', in which two hundred metres of front
around fortification 5 were captured from the enemy at a cost of
10,000 lives. The night before the attack, Rushbov had volun-
teered to go over to the enemy's forward posts, and was able to
report extensive preparations for an artillery barrage, informa-
tion that was invaluable at the staffs' planning meeting on the
19th. Between June and November he carried out no less than 14
further voluntary scouting missions along the enemy's front lines.

He disappeared while reconnoitring hostile batteries in the early hours of 16th November. Sergeant Wisch, who was in command of the redoubt at the time, reported enemy fire and 'shouts in French' at the post opposite, some 10 minutes after Rushbov crossed between the lines (see report).

Rushbov did not return. Herzog, leader of the reconnaissance unit, reported the company's cat missing the same night. A rumour is circulating among the men that it followed Rushbov to its death, for Germany and the Kaiser.

Boulay, October 17th, 1917
F. Pieck. Lieutenant-Colonel

He was lying at the corner of a bulwark with a view over a cratered quagmire. Where was he? At Longwy, some said, while others claimed it was the town of Thionville they could see on the horizon on clear days. Time, he thought, geography – it was all ground down into mud in this trench war.

'Can you see anything?' asked the sergeant from behind him.

He scanned no-man's-land with the binoculars, but all he saw were the usual things: bodies, rusty shell casings, craters full of mud and scrap metal; a Frenchman hanging over a barbed-wire barricade twenty metres away. The body was in an advanced state of decay. The belly was bloated. One arm was almost off. Of his face, nothing remained; the flies had eaten down to the bone.

'Nothing,' he said. 'All quiet.'

The sergeant nodded.

'Stick your head out a bit. Can you see their supplies?'

He propped himself on his elbows and slithered forward. The surface layer of the ground glinted in the last light of dusk: white bones worn smooth, uniform buttons, the skeletons of men and horses.

'Anything new?' the sergeant asked again. 'I want to know what they're up to at their forward post. It's too quiet here, far too quiet.'

The sergeant was right, he thought; it was too quiet. Usually you could hear the calls from the French redoubts on the other side: '*Ils ne passeront pas . . . Ils ne passeront pas . . .* They won't pass!' But over the last twenty-four hours, the voices had died away, like the shooting. It portended something.

'They're cooking. Only the machine gunner left at his post,' reported Rubashov.

The sergeant smiled.

'They fancy their luck, those Frenchmen. *Très chanceux.* Here we are living on cold porridge and what we find in the pockets of fallen comrades. By the way, do you know the big difference between them and us? Well, the French wage war to be able to eat, and the Germans eat to be able to wage war. But we, Rubashov, which side are we really on, since we're neither Germans nor Frenchmen?'

The sergeant gently scratched a louse bite. He was a volunteer, too. He'd been out here since the start of the war. Italian, somebody said. Spanish, according to someone else, but he never mentioned his origins.

'Can't you hear what they're saying?' he asked. 'I want to know what they're up to.'

'They're sixty metres away. I can't hear a thing.'

'I've got to have more than this to take back to the company commander. Can you see any new guns? Are they bringing up new artillery?'

'Not as far as I can see.'

His thoughts turned again to corpses. The war was being fought on a foundation of bodies: they provided humus for nettles and low bushes; they merged with the ruined buildings, the junk and scrap metal and shell casings; they were piled up with everything else when they were constructing new earthworks or strengthening the old ones. In the reconnaissance unit's redoubt there'd been a blackened hand sticking out of the trench wall. The men had hung their helmets on it for over a month before an inspector from the battalion staff had given orders that it be removed. It was a composting process, he thought, making use of nature's eternal cycle; everything rotted into food for worms.

'It's getting dark,' he said. 'I can't see anything any more.'

'Can't see anything? That's no answer. What d'you think we're here for? To play with the company cat?'

'Maybe you'd like to try tracers, sergeant?'

Wisch shrugged his shoulders.

'Answer me one thing, Rubashov. What will they do with peace in Russia?'

'I don't know, sergeant.'

'Will they try to build something new? Will they try to change the world? Or will everything be like it was before: a pause until the next hell's let loose?'

'I don't know, sergeant.'

'And Rasputin, the prophet. They say he made a will in which he foresaw oppression far worse than that under the Tsars. Do you know, Rubashov, when the war's over I'm thinking of going there to see for myself.'

The sergeant spat in the mud and took a report book from the pocket of his uniform.

'What do you think of Wrangel?' he asked.

'I've no particular view, sergeant.'

'He claims he's waging a battle for freedom. Against the Reds, he says, against a worse oppression than the old one. Did you notice any of the old oppression, Rubashov? Or did you belong to the privileged classes? They're hanging the priests now, Wrangel says. And the nobility. The Bolsheviks have made peace so they can murder everyone they can find on the home front.'

The sergeant gave him a look of displeasure.

'War or peace,' he said. 'Socialism or capitalism. Does it really make any difference?'

Sergeant Wisch got up and crept across to the alcove. He pushed aside the barbed wire and wriggled out on his belly to Josef Rubashov. He was soon lying beside him, report book in hand, and his dirty uniform gave off a faint scent of perfume.

'Rubashov,' he said earnestly, 'what are you doing here, really? Can you give me an honest answer to that question? *Pourquoi?*'

'I'm looking for someone.'

'And you imagine this is the right place? Believe me, nobody finds what he's looking for in this war. The only thing you find is human evil, and that's completely useless because it doesn't teach us anything we don't already know.'

'What're you doing here yourself, sergeant? You're a volunteer too, sir, after all.'

'What am I doing here? Making notes, Rubashov. Making notes of what I see and hear. What you say, for example, or what other people say. I'm trying to document this cursed war so it will never be forgotten.'

The sergeant gave a sad smile.

'And when the war's over,' he said, 'I'm going to Russia. And I shall note down what I see and hear there.'

Visibility was now zero. They crawled back behind the defences. The sergeant lit a pipe. His eyes glinted a little in the darkness. Josef smelt another waft of his perfume.

'There are six hours left before I have to deliver this report to the staff tent. I suggest you sneak over under cover of darkness and find out what they're up to. There's something in the air.'

He looked along the stretch of defensive wall, towards the alcoves where the rats scurried, intoxicated by the smell of corpses.

'My God,' he said, 'where's the cat got to? We got the damned company cat to get rid of the vermin on our section. Rubashov . . . have you seen the cat?'

The moon had gone behind a cloud as he negotiated the barbed wire. He crept off across the compost of the dead and was swallowed up into the darkness. There were no shouts to be heard any longer; no echo of a stray bullet.

He knew his way round no-man's-land as if it were his own pocket. He picked his way carefully between craters and unexploded shells. He stepped over corpses and bloated carcasses. Rats ran from under his feet. Maggots swarmed in rotting chest cavities. For death, he thought dully, the uniform was irrelevant; like termites, it consumed everything in its path, and all it left behind was earth and maggots.

The men had lost all emotion out here. They no longer felt any sympathy, or grief, or even disgust. Only a cold hunger, a hollow feeling in their stomachs that could never be assuaged. That was war, Sergeant Wisch would say: a soulless machine demanding its quota of death, as fuel to keep its belts, cogwheels and pistons in motion. And on the western front, it never paused. Neither side was trying to economise on the fuel of human bodies. Twenty thousand men could be sacrificed on a single day to gain a few square kilometres. Then both sides would lie still and listen to the faint rumble of the machine ticking over, and the officers would have time to report in their losses and make commendations for medals for bravery every forty-eight hours.

Year group after year group had been swallowed by this invention, and now they had reached the boys born in 1901. Of the older ones, only the veterans remained, like the sergeant, crafty fellows who had managed to get through the first years and had somehow grown resistant to death's virus. They had developed a peculiar talent for this existence: for slithering and crawling, for constantly hunting food, for killing with the same indifference with which any ordinary person would stifle a yawn.

He stopped, right in the middle of no-man's-land. Fifty metres away, he could see the lights in the Frenchmen's redoubts. He caught it again, that scent. And somewhere very close, he heard the cat mew.

In August one of the snipers brought a cat into the company. It was a tabby, a farm cat they had found on a reconnaissance mission in one of the abandoned villages. The sergeant had suggested they use it to keep the trenches clear of rats. They put it on a leash attached to a running line. In less than a week, the trench was free of rats. In another week, the explosions had made the cat deaf. After that, they didn't need to keep it tied up any more.

One night, when Josef was on watch in the redoubt, the cat began to mew. This surprised him, for it had not uttered a sound since its arrival. He saw it huddled there, staring out into the dark. He heard its mewing, shrill and uncontrolled, and it was at that moment, completely unprepared, that he caught a whiff of something.

There was no doubt. It was that smell from the start of the century. The shock had numbed him for a long while. It had taken him unawares; it had crept up on the trench from some point in no-man's-land. When he turned round, he saw that the cat had left the fortifications. He saw it leap up onto the sandbags and creep through the barbed wire. Without thinking, he went after it.

They had wandered around no-man's-land for more than an hour. Mewing, the cat had tried to cross the quagmire, and each time the smell briefly vanished or faded the cat had stopped, waiting, motionless, until it caught the scent again. The cat wandered in circles between the front lines. Then, just as suddenly as it had come, the smell was gone.

In the weeks that followed, this happened a dozen times. That was when he had started volunteering for scouting missions. It gave him a good excuse for being in no-man's-land. The cat went with him. It was as though it realised they were both hunting the same being and could be of use to each other.

The smell of the local government clerk, as Josef tended to think of him, was stronger now than it had ever been. He could sense it very keenly: every nuance, every degree on the olfactory scale. He stumbled on through the darkness. The cat walked in front of him, alternately purring and mewing. He could see its yellow eyes flashing like little lighthouses.

They followed an abandoned trench until they came to the battered foundations of a house. Then, as if very sure of what it was doing, the animal turned left, down towards a pond, and disappeared from view.

It was darker now. New layers of cloud hid the moon. He had to feel his way forward. The smell intoxicated him. It tore and pulled at him and made his eyes water. He stumbled over unexploded shells and tattered standards. Once he trod on a corpse. He felt a belly burst and give way beneath his foot, there was the buzz of millions of insects and the stench of putrefaction almost made him vomit.

He located the cat by one of the barbed-wire barricades on the French forward line. It was sitting still, watching something straight ahead. Josef could hear his own breathing very clearly. He was amazed they hadn't spotted him and raised the alarm.

Ten metres in front of him, crouching in the trench, were four boys from a Russian volunteer regiment. He could hear them talking quietly. They were offspring of the nobility, he assumed, who had fled with their families after the events of March. They had gone to stay with relations in Paris, and were fighting for the French while they waited for a chance to return home. They were only boys, he thought, but the war had robbed them of their right to a childhood. They put on hoarse voices to give a manly impression, but deep in their eyes the terror glittered.

A sound made him look over to the trench leading to the rear fortifications. There, bent over a map, sat another man. He was older, and had the rank of captain. Josef saw him stand up and go over to the boys. He heard him issue watch duties, then he handed out ammunition. The man shone a torch onto the map and pointed to a spot on the German line. The light illuminated his face. Josef Rubashov gave a start. The face was familiar.

Somewhere from no-man's-land came a new and powerful waft of the government clerk's smell. The cat mewed again, and at that moment the men noticed him. They stared at him in complete silence for two minutes before firing a hail of bullets, accompanied by roars of mortal fear; and when they saw him still standing there, shocked but smiling, they tossed aside their weapons and fled into the labyrinth of trenches . . .

The scent had gone. The cat had vanished, too.

He crept into the redoubt. Their mess-tins still lay in the mud. He took one of them and filled it to the top from a pot on the fire. He ate in a dream, and when he shut his eyes he could see the captain's face in front of him, bearded and dirty, yet very familiar.

So there he sat in the abandoned redoubt at the western extremity of the war and waited for another waft of the smell. Hours passed, but he didn't notice. Nor did he notice the group of French front-line veterans creeping along behind the defensive line from four directions. All he was aware of was the sudden pitch blackness and the smell of jute as they put a sack over his head.

He was held captive for three weeks. Every night they interrogated him, but he didn't say a word. At dawn they would leave him in a chicken coop, exhausted from lack of sleep, his eyes strained by the spotlights they had shone in his face, hour after hour. Sometimes a guard would come and shove something edible through the wire mesh, but his hands were tied behind his back and he had to eat the food like an animal. The rain chilled him. All he could see as people passed were their boots, sometimes kicking his cage with a crash that roused him from his torpor, or sending a stream of stinking urine squirting down the back of his neck. It was hate, he thought, that brutal, impersonal hate which infected everything in its path, year after year with equal intensity, so they didn't even think twice about calling up children to the slaughter.

One morning in the third week they dragged him out and tied him to a tree at the edge of their camp. There were military police everywhere; a brass band took their seats on a balustrade and began tuning their instruments. He was convinced he was about to face a firing squad, and at the thought of the havoc that would ensue when the gunpowder smoke cleared and they saw him standing there unscathed, he laughed. But he soon fell silent as it dawned on him that his only part in the proceedings was as a witness.

Straight ahead of him, through the sea of officers and policemen and shining brass instruments, he saw five posts, and tied to them were the boys he had frightened away from the redoubt.

The military band began to play, and the crowd gave way in front of him so that his line of sight was clear. On a podium, a colonel got to his feet and read out the sentences: '. . . desertion . . . execution by firing squad . . . leaving a lookout post crucial to the Republic in the face of a single enemy combatant'. At the word enemy, all eyes turned in his direction, but he was oblivious to them because of the cold sweat running down his face; he was looking at the condemned men with the sort of tunnel vision that only afflicts someone feeling boundless guilt. It had become clear to him that he was the one responsible for their fate.

He shook as he faced their terror; their fear and their immense longing for the life of which they were about to be deprived. They were whimpering and begging for mercy; and over to the left, to one side of the execution ground, stood the captain. As the commanding officer, he was presumably to be shot last of all.

On the podium the colonel reached the end of what he had to say, and four guardsmen shouldered their arms. A fanfare sounded, and amid the din, one of the boys called for his mother. Then he caught sight of Josef Rubashov and his voice turned into a scream of terror, rising ever higher into the cloudy sky of the front until it was cut off, as if by invisible scissors, and the bodies slumped.

He would never forget their death-throes, the foam and blood issuing from their mouths, the eyes detaching from their sockets. He did not take his eyes off them for an instant. He neither could, nor wanted to. For it was he who had condemned them to death, and as their judge he was obliged to witness it.

Another fanfare rang out, and the captain was led forward. For a moment their eyes met, and the man's look was so familiar, so very well known. They tied him to one of the wooden posts, and the field chaplain made a final sign of the cross.

Josef Rubashov was crying now, crying like a child; he cried and cursed and spat in the direction of the judging officer's podium. He was screaming like a baby as the bullets hit the captain's chest and a rose of blood bloomed on his shirt. It was his brother, Mikhail Rubashov.

All that night, he lay awake. The executed men had been laid out on stretchers just outside his prison; a moon illuminated their white faces and made their bodies seem to float in soft light. He couldn't stop looking at his brother; he wanted the image of him dead imprinted on his mind, his lifeless eyes and familiar features; he wanted him as fuel for his hatred. For it was hatred he felt now: hatred for his former guest, the government clerk.

And with every minute he lay staring out into the darkness, his hatred grew stronger. It grew in him until it encompassed everything he was. He would find the guest, he knew that now, but not to beg for mercy. His own fate no longer moved him. This was about something else: about creating a single opportunity for standing face-to-face with that inhuman creature and just having him there long enough to spit on him and curse his name.

Thus the night passed, and anyone who had happened to squat down and look into the cage where Josef Rubashov lay huddled would have seen on his face the bloodthirsty smile of a beast of prey. For he was smiling grimly and could feel the hatred pounding inside him like a pulse, a current, an emotion so powerful it seemed to be living a life of its own, as a great, dark, stinking poem. And perhaps it was because he had given himself up to it with such concentrated rancour, such an avalanche of human fury, that his attention lapsed. Because it took him a while to notice the smell that once again, slowly, like invisible smoke, like a quiet whisper, drifted in over the French staff base at Longwy. And when he finally became aware of it, he felt about in front of him, as if expecting his hands to be able to grab hold of some invisible body part of the clerk – his neck maybe – to strangle him. In doing so he happened to touch the door of the cage, and realised the lock had come undone . . .

Again the odour surrounded him, again it seemed to be teasing him and luring him first in one direction, then in another. But it was no longer the thought of salvation that prompted him to follow it in circles; hate was driving him now, though not the hate he had seen shining in the eyes of the soldiers, not the hate that descended like a plague on everything in its path, leaving behind it a primeval forest of crosses with coffins for roots, drawing its nutriment from composted heaps of corpses. It was a different sort of hate that impelled him now: a concentrated, focused hate: a blaze of blue light, a beacon of cruel desire for revenge, a moon of lust for retribution, lighting his route northwards. Nothing else existed but this violent, seething, concentrated rage. He would not rest until he had found him. And there was no time for hesitation; somewhere

here, he realised, the clerk must be concealing himself and inciting people to fight each other; somewhere in this filth.

When the French gave the order for a creeping barrage, he was standing in the eye of the storm. He saw the troops advance at a precisely regulated pace, and the artillery aimed its precision fire to land immediately in front of them, creeping slowly along ahead of their steps, like a curtain of death being pushed forward by their bayonets. It was one vast inferno of cries and fire. In the trenches, whole regiments were buried alive; blown-off limbs and broken corpses were littered over hundreds of square kilometres. But Josef Rubashov no longer saw the human suffering. He only followed the smell, he only saw the light beam of hate, and all he could think about was how he would spit in the face of the clerk, curse him, get his hands round his throat and strangle him . . .

One day on the flat meadowlands north of the Somme, he stopped. It was very quiet, eerily quiet. The sun was burning his face and a breeze was rattling the barbed wire. The leaves were starting to fall from the trees, to yellow and fall, as if autumn was arriving in the course of a single minute. The flies died on the carcasses in no-man's-land. The frogs stopped croaking and birds fell from the trees.

It was impossible to see with the eye, you merely sensed it: something suffocating that filled the lungs and made the phlegm come away in clots from inside your throat and your eyes run. Half-blinded, he walked in the direction the wind was blowing. He stopped at a German trench. There, around a canteen wagon, the steaming mess-tins still on their laps, was a platoon of gassed Germans. Death had taken them as they ate, and some had died with their forks in their mouths.

So the weeks passed in a world of invisible death, a world where death came on the wind. But Josef was oblivious to it, for another smell was leading him on: the smell of the guest, the scent to which his rage was tethered like a beast of the field. At nights it took him zigzagging between the forward posts of the two front lines. He would find himself standing listening to the soldiers' prayers and moans, to their dreamy voices, distorted by the rubber of their gas masks, as they spoke of their home towns and their girls, in Saarland, Cornwall and Gascony. But they never seemed to notice him standing there, as if frozen to the edge of the trench. Only when he involuntarily let slip a whisper of sheer hatred would they look up at him with the phosphorescent eyes of terror, and he would run from them with the bullets bouncing off his back.

Finally, in the early autumn, he reached Flanders. He surveyed its lunar landscape in amazement. It was a world of craters in red sand and ash, where nothing could grow. You never saw the sun or the stars, for here, in this area, more than a million shells were fired every day.

Somewhere between Bixshoote and Passchendaele, in no-man's-land, he found a house that the artillery had missed. He was now deaf as a result of the constant shellbursts, and the only sound in his head was a faint ringing. But the smell was intense. He had not smelt it so strongly since the day he saw his brother shot by the firing squad in Lorraine.

Eyes closed, he entered the house and followed the scent down into the cellar. It was everywhere in him and around him now, and so strong that it made him quite light-headed. He opened his eyes. Before him in the dull light of his hatred sat the cat, the tabby cat from the front at Longwy. He looked into its eyes, and what he saw there was a sorrow of proportions sufficient for the entire human race. A great darkness filled him then, but as he took a step forward, the creature dissolved, and at the same moment the smell, too, disappeared.

A sudden fatigue came over him. The darkness wrapped him in a quilt of air, and in his mind's eye he saw the cat once again, its paw extended as if in some sort of entreaty he did not understand.

When he awoke, all was quiet. He climbed the steps. The sky was blue and the dense clouds of dust had settled. Grass had grown up through the barbed-wire barricades. Paper and rubbish were blowing in the wind, and from a distant field he could hear cows lowing. At that point, he realised the war was over.

II

Tract for the Immortal

Andante in G minor

1. *Remain in one place. Find an uninhabited forest or damp cave, a dark room, a gloomy cellar or solitary monk's cell. Alone you must await the end of all time.*
2. *Love is your first enemy.*
3. *Friendship is your second enemy.*
4. *Avoid the living, for they will desert you. Faithless are the living. To dust they shall return, to earth and ashes. Your tears shall water their graves.*
5. *Your brothers and sisters are dead matter. Make for yourself an idol of stone. To this shall you speak when your loneliness oppresses you.*
6. *Memory is your third enemy. Expunge clear thought, eradicate recollection, lay waste to consciousness. Make a barren desert of the past. Extinguish the light of reason.*
7. *Do not speak. Words breed consciousness.*
8. *Do not listen. Sounds are the white cane of mortals. Blind and deaf shall you live.*
9. *Let your body be a shell encasing emptiness.*
10. *Heed no clocks. Your time is outside time, your life a Fata Morgana, for you shall have no life before death.*

In saecula saeculorum

Charleston for Immortals

(1920–30)

Our documents concerning Josef Nikolai Rubashov are not comprehensive. There are gaps. In the years 1918 to 1920, for example, we lose track of him. We do not know what he is doing during this time. Perhaps he is resting? Perhaps he has temporarily given up his search? It is the autumn of the latter year before we encounter him again, in Graf von Braun's diary, kept during a stay in the Sanctuary of the New Aeon, to which we will have cause to return.

A lesser document, but of interest nonetheless, dates from 1922, the year Mussolini leads the great march on Rome. It originates from gambling circles in Monte Carlo.

In police interrogations in connection with gambling irregularities, a Count Orloff, a Russian exile, names 'Mr Niko Rashbulov', who is said to have swindled the Russian and Polish expatriates of a considerable sum of money 'with the help of a strange, indestructible document'. The transcript of the interview gives the impression of someone desperate. He is described as poor, 'with no shoes on his feet'.

Similar information reaches us at about the same time from Austria, where an internal memorandum circulating within the fraud squad of the Vienna police refers to 'a White Russian or Ukrainian who within a short space of time spread alarm in the gambling circles round Meidling Station'. Once again a mysterious piece of paper is mentioned, along with rumours of Russian roulette. Here, too, we have cause to suspect Josef Rubashov.

In Berlin in the early 1920s, the first mountain films were made at Universum Film's newly built film factory in Tempelhof. These were the prototypes of the silent-film melodramas in alpine settings later perfected by such directors as Leni Riefenstahl. There is a remarkable entry in the company's annual report of 1923. The appendix 'Additional expenditure for trick filming and stuntmen' refers to an extra, a Russian immigrant, who during the filming of a climbing scene is said to have fallen from a piece of scenery twenty metres high, painted to look like the almost impassable southern side of the Jungfrau. The man, one of the hundreds of unemployed people who queued daily at the film company's office for work as extras, had miraculously survived the fall without a scratch, been compensated with a cheque and vanished from the studios, limping.

But on the next day of filming, the anonymous account in the annual report continues, the man again reported for work as an extra, and was given the same stunt role as before. Again he fell from a height of twenty metres without suffering anything worse than a headache, and again he received monetary recompense. Only on the third occasion did the suspicion of 'some kind of deception' arise. The police were called and the man was questioned. The extra allegedly remained throughout 'silent and sullen in the Russian way'.

In the February of the following year, news reaches us from London. At that time, the advertising hoardings were covered with posters for the Apollo Theatre. Bright-red posters, topped with a logo of a skimpily clad ballerina embracing a circus bear, advertised not only the standard variety show numbers, but also the Kirghiz escapologist Josafar, whose water act in the theatre's small auditorium was described as a world sensation in the same class as Houdini's bravura performances. The legendary escape artist was at that very time travelling in Europe.

The events of February that year are described by Edgar E.

Hoeffler, Houdini's first biographer, himself the grandson of the renowned Jack Hoeffler in whose circus the king of escapology had made his debut forty years earlier:

At the end of the month, Houdini and his wife Bess arrived at Victoria Station in order to discuss terms with an impresario, a Mr Moore, for a British edition of a planned book of memoirs. The agent met them on the platform. He told them about a sensational new escape artist who was to perform that evening at a variety theatre in the dockland area of the city. The three of them set off to attend the performance . . .

It was a full house, Hoeffler writes, but they found seats in a box high above the sea of people, shielded from curious eyes. Houdini rubbed his hands and whispered excitedly to his wife. He was looking forward to his encounter with the Kirghiz escapologist, for he had cut down on his own performances in recent years and devoted his time instead to explaining the tricks of other illusionists, exposing false mediums and charlatans who, in his words, 'like a contagious plague, unleashed by the Fox sisters of Hydesville, had spread across the world'.

A brass sextet played a fanfare, then a tail-coated master of ceremonies came on stage. He introduced the artiste: the mysterious Josafar who had turned up in the theatre's cheaper restaurant one day in the middle of a snowstorm, wearing nothing but a torn army tunic of standard wartime issue, and begging to be auditioned by the manager. After some hesitation, the manager allowed him to demonstrate his act, and realised instantly that he had a sensation on his hands . . .

The curtain went up, Hoeffler writes, to reveal in the spotlight a man of about thirty, wearing an old-fashioned, striped bathing costume. Behind him, Houdini was to note, stood an aquarium on four legs, 'about the size of a coffin, and full to the brim with water'.

Josafar bowed to the audience and asked for a volunteer willing to come on stage to inspect the tank. In a whisper, Houdini asked his wife to volunteer, which she did. When she returned, writes

Hoeffler, she assured her husband that the tank was completely full of water; and that the glass was very thin and could not possibly contain any pockets of air.

Then Josafar bowed once more, allowed himself to be tied up with rope by a scantily attired assistant, Miss Vera Winkel, and at once lay down on the bottom of the tank, expelling the air from his lungs with such force that the bubbling could be heard even in the back row of the stalls. Thus commenced the display of escapology that was to perplex Houdini for the rest of his life.

According to Hoeffler, Miss Vera Winkel placed a glass lid on the tank, and the lights were dimmed so that the man was illuminated by a single spot. He looked like a chloroformed giant baby, writes the biographer, 'an exhibit in a natural science institute', lying utterly immobile as the minutes ticked by.

After about ten minutes had passed, there was an uneasy murmur from the audience, and all at once a woman shouted that he was about to drown and needed help. But just as her voice rose from the stalls, Josafar turned in the tank with the agility of a fish and waved to the audience from his watery prison as a final bubble rose from his mouth like a silver pearl.

Infinitely slowly and painstakingly, he began to loosen his bonds with his teeth, but by the time his hands were free, a further ten minutes had passed. It took *another half-hour*, writes Hoeffler in italics, meaning that *fully fifty minutes* had elapsed since he entered the tank, for Josafar to untie the last of Miss Vera's knots, at which point he lifted the lid and stood up, dripping. Bess clapped hysterically, but Houdini was ashen-faced and cried to Moore: 'This goes against all known laws of human ability to survive without oxygen!' Josafar himself did not even seem out of breath. He smiled wearily, absent-mindedly wringing water from the braces of his bathing costume.

In the village of Cefalù i Sicily there lived at this same time a man with an ever-growing reputation. He was known as a mountaineer, a notorious womaniser and provocateur, and as the author of a large number of occult manuals with content so sadistic as to arouse public disgust. He had once held a leading position within the Order of the Golden Dawn, but had been expelled after a schism with another famous member of that fraternity, William Butler Yeats.

Under the name of Prince Chiva Kahn, this man had travelled in Asia for many years, amassing an amazing knowledge of Vedic healing and popular magic. But his life was tinged with tragedy. His first wife, Rose Kelly, went mad, and a newborn daughter died of typhus in Rangoon.

During the first decade of the century he founded his own order in London, Argenteum Astrum, the Silver Star; egged on by the gossip magazines, which called him the most evil man in the world, he had his teeth sharpened to fangs like those of a wild beast, so that he could give his mistresses snake bites. He experimented with drugs and devised complex blood rites, based on the Book of Revelations, in the course of which he had himself baptised The Great Beast 666.

Spoilt daughters of upper-class families were attracted to his seances, and his female disciples were instructed to go about clad in scarlet, like the woman riding the beast in Revelations in the final hour of the Apocalypse. He was indicted for obscenity and boasted of his executions of dumb animals.

On the outbreak of war, he went to the USA, where he was widely hated for his pro-German propaganda. The papers were full of indignant letters from readers, but he took every insult as a compliment and donned a devil's mask to marry his great love, Leah Hirsig. Then, at the start of the Twenties, the couple returned to Europe and settled in Sicily. The man now had dreams of founding the biggest spiritualist church in the world, and to lay the foundations for this vast construction he set up the Sanctuary of the New Aeon in the village of Cefalù. Within a short time he had a functioning monastery there, and a library crammed with hermetic literature. He was now calling himself Lord Boleskin, but his real name was Aleister Crowley.

*

The life of this man – Lord Boleskin, Prince Chiva Khan, the Beast, Aleister Crowley – is recorded in minute detail from his childhood years in Stratford to his death from drug addiction in Hastings. Only one short period is shrouded in darkness. The time in question is the autumn of 1920.

One of the few sources for this part of Crowley's life is a certain Graf von Braun, a Swiss theosophist who lived in the Sanctuary for several months, studying pneumatology under Crowley's tutelage. In his sporadic diary entries between September and New Year, we can read of the poor economy of the monastery and of the water situation, which was so unsatisfactory that several of the guests went down with dysentery. There are also detailed descriptions of seances and black masses, and of experiments with mescalin carried out by Hirsig and an English disciple under clinical conditions.

But some of the entries also refer to the mysterious Russian vagabond who turned up in the monastery garden one day, carrying a dirty bundle over his shoulder. We can safely assume it is Josef Rubashov.

'He had the eyes of an older man,' von Braun writes, 'although he looked no more than thirty. He asked to speak to the person in charge, and I showed him into the library, where Crowley was sitting, poring over an Eliphas Levy manuscript. I retired to a distance and could hear the two of them start talking, in whispers, with the intimacy of two people who had known each other some time. Then they disappeared upstairs to Crowley's office.'

We can only guess at what happened in the course of the autumn; von Braun seems to take only a reluctant interest in the visitor, and his diary entries, written while still under the influence of narcotics, cast a veil of mystery over the object of our interest . . .

On one occasion, he relates, the Russian locked himself and Crowley inside the laboratory. It was about the time of the full moon, and they only emerged four days later. Crowley was very pale, 'as if he had suffered a severe shock'. That evening von Braun overhears snatches of an exchange between Crowley and Leah Hirsig in their bedroom. 'Agitated voices!' he writes. 'And then

Hirsig shouting, "I don't believe it, it's impossible!"' The subject of their conversation remains obscure.

The next entry is dated October 5th. Crowley's circle is paying a brief visit to the Alps to make preparations for mountain-climbing expeditions the following spring. On the train, the Russian shares a compartment with Crowley, Leah Hirsig, von Braun and Ninette Shumway, Crowley's mistress. Shumway reads aloud from Geraldine Cummins's *Scripts of Cleophas*, automatic writings in six volumes. Crowley is writing a letter to Gerald Brosseau Gardner, with whom he has begun corresponding that year. They converse quietly about Gardner's ceremonies, 'The Cauldron of Rebirth' and 'The Dance of the Wheel', and Crowley can't conceal his pride at the younger celebrity being influenced by his own cosmology. Von Braun provides the background: 'According to Crowley, there were in the past two ages of the world: the age of Isis, which was the era of matriarchy, and the age of Osiris, which was the era of the man. In 1904, the world slipped into the age of Horus, the era of the child. This is characterised by "Thelema", the will, or the human being as God. Crowley teaches us to act in accordance with "Thelema" and do precisely as we wish. Away with all authority. Every human being follows the path of his or her own redemption. Do not protect the weak and depraved from the results of their own inferiority.'

After travelling for two days and nights, the party reaches Geneva. It is evening and they book into a hotel by the railway station. Over a relaxed dinner, notes von Braun, Crowley recites sonnets by Shakespeare: 'the second great personality of Stratford, after himself'. They smoke cigars and drink cognac. They discuss the Plymouth Brethren, and Hirsig maintains that Crowley bears the hallmarks of his upbringing in such an environment. After a few lively exchanges, they move on through other, related topics: the revivalists, the Swedish shouter movement, Madame Blavatsky.

Von Braun relates that at one point the Russian falls asleep, and is soon 'sounding like a sawmill'. But Crowley wakes him 'and asks him to tell the story of old Rasputin'. In broken French, the Russian proceeds to give 'a disjointed account of his time as the Siberian charlatan's food taster' – 'I don't believe a word of it!!' adds Brown with double exclamation marks.

But that night, after everyone has gone to bed, pandemonium erupts in the Crowleys' suite. There is a pounding as if someone were trying to knock a hole in the wall. The whole top floor is awoken and von Braun rushes to the Crowleys' room in his night-shirt. 'The chandeliers were swinging,' he writes, 'the paintings fell from the walls, a whisky tumbler slid along the table top as if guided by an invisible hand. I even saw a coat hook unscrew itself from its mounting on the wall.' A terrified Leah Hirsig flees into the night, but Crowley remains seated in an armchair, smilingly explaining the episode as a simple poltergeist phenomenon. The Russian, too, appears on the scene. He stands in the doorway and 'sniffs the air, first expectantly, then with disappointment'.

At the end of November that year Crowley organises a seminar for spiritualists at the Sanctuary of the New Aeon. Some forty partici-pants assemble. The nights are spent in a nearby cemetery. High on drugs, they participate in seances. Hirsig is trying to develop a new method for necromancy, but the experiment fails when a female medium gives way to hysterics and has to be taken to hospital. The Russian is frequently engaged in whispered discussions with Lord Boleskin. Things grow ever weirder. Tombstones inexplicably fall over. Strange sighs are heard in the darkness, and there is a mysterious glow inside a boarded-up chapel. One night Crowley falls into a trance and writhes in agony on the ground. He foams at the mouth and cries hysterically for help. When he is himself again, he accuses the Russian of plotting against his life.

Around Christmas 1920, the atmosphere at the monastery grows increasingly strained. There is something strange about their Russian guest, von Braun notes. When they are climbing alpine-style in the mountains, he is stung by a fat-tailed scorpion but displays no toxic symptoms, and when the contaminated water causes an epidemic, he is the only one unaffected. Crowley grows increasingly nervous and suspects him of being an envoy from dark powers.

On New Year's Eve, Crowley attempts with Shumway's assistance to poison the man, but their concoction of privet berries and cyanide fails to work. In a whisper, Crowley confides to von Braun his theory that the visitor is a demon, come to create chaos in the Sanctuary. But von Braun notes that the Russian seems oblivious to the atmosphere: he plays with the baby goats and stares vacantly out at the sunset, and at nights sits in Crowley's library reading everything about Paracelsus he can lay his hands on.

One day, high on mescalin, Crowley draws a small-bore pistol and fires several shots at him, without causing him any injury. Von Braun, also under the influence of the drug, is present throughout and assumes Crowley has aimed poorly. As if sleepwalking, he begins to inspect the wall for bullet holes. He finds none, at which point Crowley breaks down. The Russian sits in a rocking chair, munches on an apple and gives a guilty smile.

The final diary entry is dated January 3rd. On that day Lord Boleskin's circle celebrates a black mass at an abandoned Carmelite monastery outside Palermo. A black lamb is slaughtered and Crowley appears in a mask made out of a pumpkin. Naked female disciples perform a dance symbolising the eight phases of the moon. Everyone gets drunk on communion wine.

Von Braun's notes, which appear to have been made straight after the event, are fragmentary. He mentions a smell, 'something sour, like old milk', and then 'the face of a bespectacled man, floating above the fire'. The Russian is said to have got to his feet at this point, 'scented the air like an animal' and stared out into the darkness. Overcome by a sudden feeling of melancholy, the company watches the strange visitor. Without a word, he melts into the night – 'as if', writes von Braun, 'heeding a call the rest of us could not hear' . . .

We are not able to relocate Josef Rubashov until the autumn of 1926. Then we see him in a picture. The Belgian trade-union paper *Liberté* carries a report of a mining disaster in the brown coal district of the Ardennes. In all the chaos at the accident site, only one survivor has been found, a Russian pit inspector by the name of 'Ruslov'.

We see him posing for the camera in his helmet and miner's gear, a broken lamp in his hand. We see the familiar facial features, the eyes caught in the middle of their restless darting. Behind him we can just make out the stretchers on which the dead have been laid, covered by blankets. Ruslov looks exhausted and the newspaper reporter writes that 'the inspector was not disposed to comment'. When they try to find him a week later for a follow-up interview, he has disappeared . . .

The Twenties approaches its end to the rhythm of the Charleston, and the camera image becomes a more important contemporary document than artists' sketches. Films, too, are gaining ground, and the documentary genre is in its infancy. That is why, in the spring of 1927, we again see him in a picture, but this time as a moving image, in a silent-film reportage about the daughter of Grigori Rasputin, who is making a career for herself under the name of Gala as an actress in France. In the film caption his name is properly written out: Josef Nikolai Rubashov, 'a close friend of the prima donna's legendary father'. The two of them are seen together at a film premiere and a dinner laid on by the Odeon cinema, at which Charlie Chaplin is also present. Josef Rubashov, in tails and white gloves and feverishly smoking his cigar, moves nervously among the partygoers. We do not know what has made him seek her out, merely that the visit is a short one.

In the summer of 1927 he is to be found in the circle of a well-known Canadian medium on the French Riviera, Madame Craigh. We know this through Felix Yusupov, who has been living in exile in France since the revolution. Yusupov mentions his name in a letter to a fellow exile, ex-minister Baron Morell in Brittany. He claims to have met Rubashov on several occasions in the company of Madame Craigh at a nightclub in Antibes. 'Grigori's taster,' he notes in amazement, 'doesn't look a day older!'

Perhaps the encounter with Yusupov, or a suggestion from Mrs Craigh, makes him think of the east again, for he returns to Russia the same year.

In a blurred photograph taken at the 15th Party Congress, we discover him in uniform among the Red Guard. It is the day on which Trotsky's fate is sealed and real power over the Soviet population is handed over to one man: Stalin. Josef Rubashov's nostrils, we see, are flared; his face is distorted in a grimace, as if a terrible thought, or a painful memory, or conceivably a fearful stench, were tormenting him. He is staring at the delegates at the far end of the hall, and if we were to have the picture enlarged, we would see among them the back of a figure who may perhaps seem vaguely familiar to us, but the distance is too great and the picture too grainy for us to say with any certainty . . .

In the winter of 1928 we pick him up again, this time in a film made by the secret police, OGPU. The film shows the expulsion of the *kulaks* from Smolensk. We find him dressed in rags in the never-ending column of freezing, starving human beings. Corpses lie piled on carts, and some of the bodies have had their buttocks cut off; hunger has driven people to cannibalism. Josef Rubashov is carrying an emaciated little girl in his arms. The light in her eyes grows dimmer and dimmer until it fades and goes out as we look on, and her soul flies away. We see the tears running down his face.

This is how he seems to move: from one eruption of human or superhuman evil to the next. He is witness to natural disasters and terrible misfortunes. He turns up among mediums and occultists. We know he is on the spot when an anarchist bomb explodes outside the Carlist headquarters in Madrid, and that he is even imprisoned for a time on suspicion of the crime. We also observe him keeping track of the political situation in Italy, and withdrawing for a time into solitude in the Scottish highlands. But he seems distracted, almost confused, as if acting without a plan.

On New Year's night 1930 we see him in another photograph, taken by an unknown photographer in Paris. It is an indoor shot, from a brothel in Montparnasse. Josef Rubashov is wearing a pasteboard party hat and on his knee sits a consumptive prostitute. Their smiles are identically false, their eyes equally dead and joyless. Josef Rubashov is holding a bottle of cheap champagne in one hand. With the other he is gripping the edge of a table, to keep his balance. He has an air of desperation about him. Intoxication makes him look older, and something in his deportment reveals him now as an old man who has seen too much.

Thus on New Year's night 1930 he vanishes from our horizon again. He leaves a taste of mystery behind him; and a new lacuna, which we can only fill by guesswork.

As previously stated, our documentation is not comprehensive. But we will hear from him again. A few years later we are on his tail once more. By then he is far from France and its *maisons de joie*.

The place is Berlin. The year: 1933.

Scenting

(Berlin 1933)

. . . a medical colleague, Soellers, a gerontologist, later told me of an interesting case. At a clinic in Pankow, a Russian patient presented clear indications of old age, although in terms of appearance, physiognomy, posture, etc., he gave the impression of being thirty-five at most. He had come in for a general examination.

A consultant, a specialist in geriatric complaints, later listed what he had found: the man was displaying symptoms of presbyopia with characteristic stiffening of the lens in the eye, and yet a sight test confirmed that he had excellent vision. It was the same with the hearing test. When the doctor examined the ear, he found reduction in hearing of a neurological type in the eardrum and lateral semicircular canal. But there was no indication that the man's hearing was in any way defective. The doctor, not wishing to worry the patient who had otherwise been pronounced healthy ('fit as a fiddle', as Soellers put it), and as far as could be judged had come to the clinic purely because he felt a need for some company, as is often the case in Berlin, asked for his teeth to be examined, too. The dental wear and tear were of the kind normally found in a male of sixty or sixty-five. Soellers, not a poetic soul, could find no better metaphor than that of the bumblebee, flying gaily on although it is really too heavy and should drop to the ground . . .

Gottfried Benn, diary entry 1932

From our concealed position in a doorway, where the brick walls are plastered with black and red election posters with unforgettable slogans about justice and race, we register him marching past in a procession, singing with all the rest, on his way to the Prinz Albrecht district. He was wearing short lederhosen, although it was winter, with braces pulled taut, and a helmet with a chin strap, and a brown shirt with an armband, decorated with a sign that put our knowledge of inscriptions to the test (Persian, perhaps?). He was moved to tears, for in this gathering nobody was alone. You were one unified tramp of boots and one voice in a vast collective choir singing a song of a better future, never left alone to sink into the mire of memory, into your own futile little story, into the petty redoubt of private hardships. You could revel in dissolving into the community. You loved the comradeship, the beer and sausage evenings, the marches and parades, singing 'Heili Heilo' or the Horst Wessel Song with all the power your lungs could muster. It was in tune with the age, wasn't it, to belong to a party, a club, an association, a fighting group, a coterie? Every single person had their own volunteer corps these days: the Freikorps, the Stahlhelm, the Communist Red Front. The whole of Germany divided up into private armies.

Gone were the crisis years, the dark middle ages of inflation and the stock-market crash. People weren't stupid. They knew better times when they saw them. The treasury printing presses rolling to feed the strikers in the Ruhr. Inflation and bankruptcies. People had needed wheelbarrows if they wanted to go to the post office to buy a stamp. They turned on the gas taps in despair. They hanged and shot themselves, took poison and threw themselves out of windows. They gave up everything they owned and drowned their starving children.

Back then, after the Great War, the cripples had lined Friedrich-strasse. Men with no noses or eyes, no jaws or legs or arms or ears; or even worse. Beggars, war invalids whose pensions didn't cover so much as the striking strip on a box of matches. And people had hardly recovered from that free fall of poverty before the stock market crashed. Housewives who'd had to prostitute themselves for gruel to feed their babies. Men in soup-kitchen queues, fighting over the last helpings from the bottom of the pot, where the greasy dumplings lurked.

But that was all over now, was it not? Friedrichstrasse was lined with the flags of the movement. Communist or Nationalist, they surely all wanted the same thing? Weren't they all members of the marching brotherhood of well-pressed uniforms, shiny boots and singing voices? The year before they'd worked together in the Reichstag, and during the big transport strike in Berlin. Some of Josef Rubashov's brigade called themselves beefsteaks: brown outside, but red inside.

'Heilii heiloo,' sang the massed participants. People on the pavement gave them the salute, youngsters waved, even the dogs barked in greeting as the massed ranks stamped by in their iron-heeled boots.

You couldn't help it, you were suddenly caught up in it. All at once, there you were at a mass rally at the palace of sport, shouting with the full force of your lungs, and then you shed a tear or two as the orchestra played the Badenweiler March. Then Goebbels stepped up and gave a speech, and sometimes Walter Ulbricht the Communist was there too, and everyone was touchingly united, but at the same time incredibly disunited; and afterwards you'd go and drink beer together, Communists and Nazis in one blissful brotherly union, where the only way to tell the difference was the shirts, and scarcely that. And you'd all round off the evening with a tremendous punch-up, mostly for old times' sake.

The young people joined the Artaman League; they revered the soil and lived in communes in the countryside, drinking nothing stronger than nettle tea. The children joined the youth movement, cute little *Hitlermädels* and *Hitlerpimpfes*, girls and boys who made collections for the poor and sang lovely songs about comradeship round the campfire.

Kraft durch Freude was the organisation for their leisure time, providing cheap holidays in the Alps for the workers and bathing cures in the Sudeten spa resorts for gouty old ladies. There was a society for everybody: the Nazi Kennel Club, Hitler's Riding Club, the SA Stamp Collectors' Association and the *Deutsche Frauenorden*, consisting mainly of old nurses who ministered to the warriors after the great brawls in the beer tents.

He had worked miracles on the Germans, this Führer, that was undeniable, and now he hung behind glass and in frames on every man's wall, looking out over the living rooms of the nation, his hair slicked down and his expression earnest, gazing his strange, dark gaze. They saluted him with arms outstretched, as a sign of reverence and power of endurance, and in reply he flung his hand back towards to his shoulder, which sometimes seemed a bit casual, given the effort everyone else had to put in, and the stiff arm muscles they suffered the morning after a mass rally; but it was only fair he should enjoy a few perks as Germany's newly appointed Chancellor.

No more truck with the crazy demands for compensation, he'd promised that, and for the unemployed, work in a vast road-building scheme, and a decent army so at least you could defend yourself; but no more war, he was keen to stress, or at any rate only if the other side started it.

They passed the Potsdamer Bahnhof and turned down Nieder-kirchenerstrasse. People cheered and shook their clenched fists, and Josef Rubashov smiled. He smiled because he realised this was something he had secretly been longing for; something he had secretly yearned for and dreamed of, for decades. To be able to enter into some higher spirit of solidarity, to forget his curse, to be among the living again, to bury his dreadful fate in the great name of the cause. He no longer cared about the bespectacled clerk. He didn't even hate him any longer. What was his trifling curse to a million people's dreams of a better world?

Outside the Prinz Albrecht Hotel, they came to a halt. In the surrounding streets the *Sturmabteilung* was out in force; a sea of brown. In the last year they had gained new members as never before. People flocked to their local offices to join. But there was no room for complacency. For the good of the movement, they could never stop recruiting, and over the past month he had himself managed to get four unemployed men from the lodging house at

Koppenplatz to come along. This evening it was time to try persuading Marinus, the Dutchman.

The balcony doors on the first floor now opened, and out came the little lame doctor with the clubfoot.

'Comrades!' he shouted in his hoarse, inspiring voice. 'Our time has come. Our Führer has brought us here, to the threshold of a new future, to a new empire, the eternal, holy German Reich. Our opponents have tried all means of stopping us. But we have triumphed. We have triumphed with your help, foot soldiers, people of the streets. You veterans of the hard years, you glorious, ruthless men. You have snatched Germany from democratic misery!'

He dismissed them with a wave, an imitation of the Führer's salute, and was gone. Before long they had formed up, ready to march off. They had just struck up a rousing battle song when Josef Rubashov heard someone hailing him from the hotel balcony. It was Sergeant Wisch from the front at Longwy, now wearing the uniform of an SS general.

The chauffeur stopped the car by the Janowitz Bridge. They proceeded on foot round a building of red granite. In a back courtyard, invisible from the road, stood a palatial house. The front door opened soundlessly. They were standing in an enormous hall, lit by flaming torches. One wall was completely covered in monumental portraits of the Führer. On another hung regimental standards from the war. A marble staircase in the baroque style led them down to the basement.

They were in an empty restaurant. Antique tapestries hung on the walls. Gilded cupids hovered at ceiling level. Music played from invisible loudspeakers. In the alcoves round the walls stood verdigris-coated suits of armour. The ceiling was covered in signs of the zodiac.

Wisch looked at the menu.

'So you've joined the party?' he said. 'I'm glad, Rubashov. You've made the only right choice. I hope you'll learn a thing or two. And commit it to memory. It didn't surprise me in the slightest to see you today, by the way. I've had a feeling for some time that we were going to meet again. When you vanished into the redoubts I knew it wasn't for ever.'

The waiter stood discreetly in the background. Wisch ran his finger down the wine list. He exuded a strong scent of perfume, extract of lavender.

'I own shares in this restaurant,' he whispered. 'The Führer comes here to eat sometimes. Apart from Osteria Italiana in Munich, it's his favourite restaurant. Does that surprise you?'

He took a notebook from his uniform pocket. With some difficulty he inserted a monocle into his right eye.

'And I still keep a notebook. Of things that occur to me. Focusing mainly on the human lot, naturally. Now I'm going to write: *February 27th, 1933. Met Josef Rubashov again. He hasn't aged at all.*'

Wisch smiled as he wrote, while two waiters served the first course: a platter of oysters, gleaming, moist, on a glissando of crushed ice, and a bowl of cellophane noodles.

'*Guten Appetit*,' said Wisch, 'and please do tell me how the oysters taste.' He looked mournfully down into the bowl of noodles. 'I can't eat them any longer. My stomach, I've discovered to my dismay, is a terrible dictator; it rules my life down to the smallest detail . . .'

For the main course Wisch ordered quail in a rosé marinade, after hesitating for some time between stuffed swan and capon in wine sauce.

'And roses,' he added to the waiter. 'Bring a bunch of roses, please. Bourbon roses for preference. Louis Odier, in bud, there's nothing more wonderful.'

'I love nineteenth-century roses,' he continued, addressing Josef Rubashov. 'Ordering roses with the main course is a sign of *savoir vivre*, wouldn't you say? Their shapes, their colours. Unfortunately it's been a long time since I could enjoy their scent. I have some defect in my sense of smell. I've had all the tests. The doctors say they can't account for it. My stomach. My nose. My organs of enjoyment. None of them are what they once were . . .'

133

The quail were brought in, and a simple vegetable soup for Wisch. The waiters discreetly withdrew.

Over the meal they exchanged memories of the war. Wisch gesticulated eagerly, and every time he made a movement, a strong waft of his perfume reached Josef Rubashov. Presumably, he thought, the sergeant was as unconscious of this as of the scent of the roses.

For dessert Wisch ordered cloudberry parfait, but himself took only a cup of weak mint tea. He unbuttoned his uniform jacket. From the inside pocket he produced a tortoiseshell fan and proceeded to fan himself.

'You may be wondering what led me to the party,' he said. 'It was the Führer's geopolitical theories. Very interesting. *Lebensraum* to the east. When the Führer was at the western front, he realised there was no potential there. But in the east! The struggle for space!' Wisch pointed to his party badge. 'I take it you've realised the movement isn't a traditional sort of party? The battle for *Lebensraum* is an end in itself. And the party goes beyond any ordinary political movement. At root, the party is the foundation of a new religion, a natural religion, unlike other parties, and that's what makes the cause so . . . how shall I put it: revolutionary?'

Wisch's eyes rested on the crystal decanter of burgundy standing on the table. His reflected face appeared splintered in its prisms.

'Do you understand what I mean?' he asked earnestly.

'No, sergeant.'

'What I mean, Rubashov, is that the party no longer draws any distinction between nature and human being, and that notion interests me, because it represents a break with a tradition going back many hundreds of years.'

He closed the fan.

'The Jews and Catholics have claimed for centuries that man stands above nature, and therefore has particular rights, but also particular obligations. But the Führer says exactly the opposite. We are one with nature, the Führer maintains, neither more nor less. That makes him the spokesman for a new religion, rather than a political idea. And believe me, this will have consequences.'

134

Wisch sipped his herbal tea and eyed Josef Rubashov's wine glass.

'Superb. At any rate, that's what they say about that wine. *Tête de cuvée*. I can no longer indulge in the juice of the grape myself, because of my stomach. And to tell the truth, it's all the same to me. I wouldn't be able to taste it anyway. There's something wrong with my tongue, as well as my nose and stomach; everything tastes the same. Like this tea: insipid, very slightly salty, a touch burnt. It was the same on the western front. *A votre santé* Rubashov.'

Wisch regarded his teacup with distaste. One of the waiters had dimmed the light in the chandeliers. Great shadows had unrolled across the floor and walls. Wisch appeared to be brooding.

'You must excuse me,' he said after a time. 'Sometimes my thoughts run away with me. I have many memories. Good memories, but unfortunately more of the bad kind. One of those was occupying me just then.'

He summoned one of the waiters and asked for a cigar. He took out his notebook again and jotted something down. He stared at Josef Rubashov through his monocle.

'You see, the innermost principle of nature is battle, at least that's what the Führer says. The will to fight is the will to live, and the will to live equals survival. Look at the animals, he writes in his book. Look at the wolves. The stronger pack drives off the weaker one, and the strongest member of the pack becomes its leader. Any individual who doesn't fight goes under. And a people that isn't permanently fighting is also doomed to perish. Therefore, the Führer says, humans must fight and keep fighting, in fact devote their whole lives to the fight – live and die for the sake of the cause. That's how I understand it, at any rate.'

He shut his notebook.

'Battle was the party's central belief, never forget that, Rubashov, if anybody asks you about it in the future. Fighting is the only way an individual gains any worth. And races must fight each other, just as in nature. The brown rat fought against the black rat, for example, until it had domination of all the sewers of Europe. It took hundreds of years, but in the end the little brown rat was the victor, in every sewer, on every rubbish dump, in the least little privy and earth closet. Learn from the brown rat, the Führer recently said in a speech to a select group of party functionaries at which I, too, was present. Anyone who wants to survive must fight and, at worst, kill – even in an earth closet if necessary. Those were his exact words. Can you imagine: *Even in an earth closet!* And we must show no mercy, he said. On no account must we show mercy. We can't afford to.'

'Why not?'

Wisch stared at him.

'What a question. *Why not?*'

He seemed distracted again.

'Let me just make it clear,' he said, shaking his head, 'that I've no views on the matter myself. I'm more of a mouthpiece for, what shall we say, a theory. Let me ask a rhetorical question of the kind the Führer might use: A gamekeeper who needs to reduce numbers of a particular strain of animals surely feels no pity for the sub-standard individuals he shoots? It's a necessary evil. The weak must go under and leave room for the strong and fit. In battle there can be no pity. Those with the most vitality must seize their right to life. Don't you agree, Rubashov?'

'I'm not sure, sergeant.'

Wisch polished his monocle on his serviette.

'Believe me, Rubashov,' he said quietly, 'I'm only doing my job. In my position, in this uniform, you can't afford to air your own views.'

He picked up the fan to cool himself once more.

'Do you play cards?' he asked with a smile. 'I do like a game of cards after a meal. Skat? Baccarat? Whatever you like.'

'Not any longer . . .'

'Hah! A repentant old sinner . . .'

He had something else on his tongue, but stopped himself.

'And now you're busy recruiting for your local *Sturm*?' he said.

'Four so far this year. And soon one more, tonight I hope, a Dutchman.'

'Interesting. A Dutchman. The 1st Bavarian Infantry Regiment can be proud of you, Rubashov. And time has treated you kindly.

No signs of ageing! Not a day seems to have passed since you and the company cat disappeared without a trace into the redoubts.'

'That's right, sergeant, not a day.'

'Call me Charlot,' said Wisch, wiping his mouth with his serviette.

'Of course, Charlot.'

'Charlot Feder-Wisch.'

'That's a strange name, sergeant.'

'It's the name I perform under,' said Wisch. 'And if you ever have any problems with anything, you must get in touch.'

'I'll do that, Charlot.'

'Well, take good care of yourself, Rubashov. I've got to go. I'm a busy man. A thousand jobs to do. Daily engagements and conferences. Constant meetings, people asking for audiences and appointments. I can hardly find time for it all. I've never been so busy in my life.'

He looked at his watch.

'For example, I've a meeting with Speaker Goering in half an hour. We've important things to prepare for tonight. I wish you luck, Rubashov.'

'The same to you, sergeant. Look after yourself . . .'

They left the restaurant and walked back to the road together. Round the corner, the car was waiting. The door was already open. The chauffeur was hunched behind the wheel wearing a raincoat and peaked cap.

'And good luck with the Dutchman,' said Wisch. 'What did you say his name was?'

'Marinus van der Lubbe.'

'Lubbe, that's right. Best of luck with him tonight. Heil Hitler, Rubashov.'

'Heil Hitler, sergeant . . .'

The battle, the will to live, mistrust of the intellect, he reflected later as he sat on the tram heading for Alexanderplatz. That was what Wisch had talked about. The sergeant's monologue had confirmed his theory that absolutely any opinion could be accommodated within the movement. The main thing was the rapture, ecstasy, the abandonment of self in a greater communion. They all had the right to feel at home there: Wisch and Bauer and he himself and the half-blind Dutchman.

The tram went on up Leipzigerstrasse, across the tangle of traffic at Spittelmarkt and on towards Alex. At the Tietz department store he got off, crossed Prenzlauerstrasse and continued down Hirtenstrasse.

He was on home ground now. He picked his way past junk shops and cartloads of old clothes. At length he reached the cheap lodging house. Lubbe wasn't there, but there was a note on the door: he would be waiting for Rubashov outside the Reichstag.

The streetlights were all extinguished along the Schiffbauerdamm. It looked as though there would be another fall of snow. Not a star was visible in the sky.

He stopped at the Marschall Bridge and looked over in the direction of the Parliament building. The Lycée Français was in darkness, but the lights were on inside the speaker's palace. Behind those windows, he thought, in the light of the chandeliers, the sergeant, the general, Wisch was presumably standing in conversation with Hermann Goering.

He left the palace behind him and skirted along the north side of the Reichstag; and suddenly, in a split second, someone had pulled him against the wall. It was the Dutchman.

'Come with me,' he hissed. And before Josef Rubashov had a chance to work out what was going on, he had forced the door to some kind of storage area from which they made their way into the darkened building.

'I'll enrol in your bloody *Sturm*,' whispered the Dutchman. 'Just give me a minute and you'll have a new member.'

So saying, he handed him a bag and pulled him deeper into the shadows; and Josef Rubashov, far too absorbed in trying to orientate himself and hang on to Lubbe, whose defective sight was causing him to collide with walls and cupboards, didn't get a chance to protest. Finally they stopped in front of one of the tall windows with a view over the speaker's palace and Lubbe hissed in the darkness, 'Correct me if I'm wrong, Rubashov, but isn't that a light in Goering's window?'

But Josef had no time to confirm this, for Lubbe, in the grip of some unaccountable rapture, as if not really master of his own actions, continued his manic shouting: 'Give me that bag, because when I enrol in your bloody Brownshirts, I'm going to do it with a vengeance, with witnesses, in a way nobody's going to forget.'

Lubbe opened the bag and took out half a dozen firelighters, and the next second he had set fire to the six-metre drops of dusty damask that hung draped at the windows of the Reichstag. In an instant they were in flames, but Lubbe seemed less than satisfied with his pyrotechnic exploit, for he was screaming now, screaming and shouting, spewing out his hatred of Germany and the movement as he ran between the drapes and the great wooden benches and set the whole building on fire.

And Josef Rubashov, what was he doing at that moment?

He was standing still, stock still in the burning corridor, his face frozen and his nostrils flared, for he could sense once again that familiar smell, intense, distinct, sour and sharp; and in the vast building he thought he could hear the echoing laughter of the clerk, laughter that was not in the least joyous, but filled instead with a strange, piercing lament . . .

Sensation in the Ring

(1935)

'The Wagner Brothers Pureblood Circus Troupe' says the poster, a poster printed in the colours of the flag: blood red, flint black and plaster white, with little swastikas in the corners, pasted up on a dilapidated fence outside a tent on a plot of wasteland in Berlin-Wilmersdorf this spring of 1935.

Here we have Aryan Guillermo, the juggler known for his clever business with antique Chinese porcelain and his tour de force with flaming torches, performed on a monocycle with a punctured tyre in a costume soaked in petrol. Here we have trapeze artist Greta K, resident clowns Ralph and Alf, *augustes de soirée*, the sensations from France, champions of Charlie Rivel. Here, too, we have knife-throwing virtuoso Ossian and his death-defying assistant; animal tamer Hans Hansen, who smears his cheeks with pig's blood and lets a Bengal tiger lick them clean; here are the magician Adolf Endler, Snake Woman Helga Heinz and the Westphalian fakir Humboldt, with the false teeth. In addition: one bearded lady, one real-life vampire, and a man with only one eye, right in the middle of his forehead, like a cyclops of classical antiquity; plus a host of other artistes and animals and dwarves, horses, trained dogs and an Indian wolfman . . . It's hard to resist this illustrious company, isn't it? Hard to pass up the chance of a visit when you happen to be in the neighbourhood anyway and it's a cold, damp April evening and dusk's dirty hand is casting darkness in great clods over the capital of the empire.

140

The show opens with Aryan Guillermo the juggler, who doesn't look very Aryan; on the contrary, he's as dark as an Arab, with flashing black eyes, wearing a white satin shirt soaked in petrol, his hair stuffed into a yellow turban with a large droplet of glass, intended to look like an emerald, sewn into the cloth. He juggles with a few china jugs and vases. Sends them into the air with his damask-clad foot, balances them on top of each other in a clattering, leaning tower; then he lights the torches and wobbles round on his monocycle to the accompaniment of the circus orchestra in a cloud of smoke. There's a ripple of polite applause and then the ring belongs to the clowns Alf and Ralph, who mostly roll in the sand jabbering hoarse strings of nonsense until they are succeeded by Snake Woman Helga Heinz, with scales tattooed on her skin, a female boa lithe enough to curl herself into a shoebox, hissing. But it's not until the start of the fourth act, Ossian the knife thrower and his death-defying assistant, that Josef Rubashov's interest is aroused.

Out into the middle of the ring steps the smiling knife thrower. He bows and holds his knives aloft in the spotlight, while the percussionist of the circus orchestra announces with a taut drumroll the entry of his death-defying helper. Tied to a wheeled screen bearing the emblem of the movement against a white background, dressed in Wilhelmenian cavalry uniform with multicoloured spangles, glittering and winking like an overloaded Christmas tree, the assistant Herr Bombast is rolled forward into the light. He's a small, frail man with an ancient face and flesh that seems to be made of toughened crocodile skin. This is a man so eroded by age that you could mistake him for a mossy stone if you ran into him in the forest. From his back, beneath the spangled uniform, protrudes an enormous hump.

Ossian the knife thrower and his death-defying helper hold the audience in an iron grip of suspense that evening. Ossian outlines Herr Bombast's body with such precision that you couldn't insert a postage stamp between the knives and the spangled uniform. And to the audience's undisguised delight, the pensioner does not so much as blink with fear as the projectiles whizz past him, slicing the sequins from his gaudy costume and hammering with an ominous thud into the screen, from which he sticks out at an angle because of his deformity. On the contrary; he is even seen to stifle a yawn at one stage, as one of the knives pares the last hairs on his shrivelled head down to root level. He seems altogether bored, sleepy, full of contempt for the hard fact of the shiny steel; and it's this, his lack of respect for the millimetres between life and death, the deep abyss of that tiny space, the complete control of nerves, which makes the act a success, a miracle of cool disregard for deadly risk.

The audience is in uproar. They give the salute and shout 'Heil' for all they're worth. And finally, as the culmination of this orgy of glorification of courage, as Ossian the knife thrower and his assistant are leaving the ring to resounding applause, the crowd bursts spontaneously into the old Horst Wessel Song.

After the performance he finds the Doctor in a caravan dressing room, which the latter shares with Aryan Guillermo.

'Doctor?' he says. 'It's me, Kolya.'

The antique gentleman, surrounded by flowers, party badges, bottles of champagne and billets-doux making more or less respectable propositions, sent in by the ecstatic audience, regards him in the shell-framed make-up mirror.

'Are we acquainted?' he asks at length. 'My memory, you know, sir, is not what it was.'

It's true. In that ancient consciousness there isn't room for an unlimited number of reminiscences, so when it gets too full, it simply overflows, and the memory of whole decades disappears at a stroke. This is a sore disappointment. Because the Doctor, he thinks, his brother in the limbo of eternal life, ought to provide a new lead or at least a key to open the door to the secret room where the answer to his riddle lies hidden.

All evening he sits with him in the dressing room, and as the Doctor wipes the powder from his cheeks with a damp tuft of cotton wool, and whistles whenever Greta K the trapeze artist passes by in her daringly low-cut costume, Josef bombards him with questions about his mysterious disappearance from the churchyard.

He reminds him that he, Josef, had been sitting on a gravestone with his eyes shut while the Doctor hacked at the ground with his sword, and had then opened his eyes to find the Doctor had gone up in smoke. He produces the old contract from his pocket, lights it with a match without doing it any discernible damage, and reminds him of their esoteric experiments. He describes how they found him in the hermit's hovel outside Vitebsk, and his shock when he awoke from the cradle of senility in St Petersburg and realised he had been asleep for fifty years.

He reminds the Doctor of the occult library he claimed to have built up at the court of the autocrat Ramiro Ramiros; of the graphic representations of the seven metals; and of Grigori Rasputin's slow decline, which they had both witnessed at such close quarters that it was impossible to deny it. He recalls, too, their seven-day fast, the amulet hardened in magpie blood, the nails from the coffin of the executed criminal and the collarbone of the double bigamist.

Of all this he reminds Paracelsus, in the hope of stirring his memory. But what good does it do? The Doctor is incurably senile.

Thus the weeks of spring 1935 pass. He cannot escape his fate, he reflects, and in view of that, everything else is irrelevant, meaning-less, fragmentary; for this, the enigma itself, the curse itself, is his centre point. The Doctor, he thinks, is merely a bunch of dis-integrating memories imperfectly held together by a hunched back, but even so he represents the only hope.

By day Josef takes him on canal-boat trips or to restaurants, since the Doctor feels too old for walks in the park. He tries to rouse him as one would a sleeper, with extreme care, so the dream is not lost. But time after time he is obliged to acknowledge that the man's memory is as full of holes as a Swiss cheese. This, however, does not apply to the good old centuries, for he remembers those golden years of humankind clearly and in detail: from the least event of daily politics to what he ate for breakfast and lunch on a stagecoach journey from Paris to Lyons in 1621. It's only over the last century, he says, that the world has started to become blurred to him. But that's the spirit of the age, isn't it? Moral decay, unreliable people, and the substance of things somehow seeming to dissolve before their eyes?

This oldest of old men is not even sure what he was doing in the years before he came to the circus. For a while, he maintains, he was at sea, a sailor on the vast ocean-going liners; and with his hand clasping the handle of the old sword that he still carries with him, in a velvet-covered scabbard hooked onto a belt round his creaking hips, he pours forth an incoherent tirade about the *Titanic*'s maiden voyage, placing it at entirely the wrong date; he tells of the champagne fountains and soirées, and the mud-wrestling between naked women that took place in secret behind a curtain in the engineer's cabin; of the huge iceberg and how he, all alone once the ship had gone down to the strains of Handel's Largo, had swum more than forty nautical miles before being picked up by a whaling boat crossing from Newfoundland to the Azores.

Then he lapses into silence and regards Josef Rubashov, sheepishly scratching his hump. 'Or have I remembered that wrong?' he says gloomily. 'I sometimes get the feeling my memory's feeding me pure fiction.'

One morning they are sitting at an outdoor café in the Tiergarten. It's a warm May day, and from a pavilion close by come the sounds of some festivity. Through the windows they can see it's a fancy-dress party; an ice princess is dancing with a crusader, and a man dressed as the Pope entertains a mandarin. The pavilion door opens and Pinocchio emerges, accompanied by Mr Fox and closely followed by a man with goat's horns and a magician's cloak, a white rat perched on his shoulder. They both stare at the last of these gentlemen, and eventually Paracelsus says:

'Well, he doesn't look like that, at any rate.'

Josef holds his breath.

'Folk have all manner of false preconceptions about that creature, that's for sure.'

He drains his glass of elderflower cordial, having lost his taste for alcoholic beverages two lifetimes ago, then adjusts the cushion at the back of his seat to accommodate his hump more comfortably, his poor hunched back, which has been getting very tender of late and so sensitive to changes in the weather that it can predict thunder or hail several days in advance.

'The question is whether he exists at all, other than as an idea in the imaginations of the uneducated. One hears rumours. Crazy popular legends. Of certificates of debt and elixirs of life. Quite laughable.'

'But you've met him, Doctor, after all,' Josef says. 'You yourself received an elixir of life from him.'

'Me?' Paracelsus stares at him. 'Did I?'

'You told me so yourself, Doctor. In Paris.'

'You must have misunderstood me, my good fellow. I'm a modern man, a forerunner of the age of enlightenment. Would I believe in something like that? My field was anatomy, scientific anatomy, medicine, sir. I wrote groundbreaking papers on intestinal worms, and what thanks did I get? Never-ending disputes with the theologians. I would have nothing to do with superstition, and they couldn't take it.'

He points over to the pavilion, where the devil is now in the company of a butterfly woman with large yellow wings, fastened onto her back by a corset contraption.

'It's laughable, horns and cloven hooves; even in the good old days, in my circles, we distanced ourselves from such humbug. But the priests needed him; without a certain element of threat, it's not easy to lure souls to the faith.'

'But what about your age, Doctor?' says Josef. 'How have you managed to reach such a great age?'

'What do you mean, great age? Dear me. Thirty-six is surely no age at all?'

The image of a senile Tatiana Rubashova comes into his mind, an image of ageing and mental wear and tear.

'But what about the elixir?' he says. 'The night in Paris?'

'What elixir? Are you making fun of me?'

The Doctor raises his eyebrows as if dealing with a lunatic or joker, and then gives a sudden, wheezing laugh that reveals his last, blackened stump of tooth, after which he resumes his storytelling without a hint of embarrassment: this time a completely incredible tale, full of wild paradoxes and painful internal contradictions, about his adventures in the Chinese civil war, his gold-smuggling trips in the Maghreb states, and how he fell asleep in an Algerian desert storm and awoke in a Jesuit monastery in Peru.

This is his existence. The Doctor continues to degenerate before his eyes. The bespectacled clerk does not reveal himself by even the slightest sign. Josef has a feeling that the one he seeks is far away, making the hope that he invests in the Doctor all the more fervent . . .

Early in June, just before the circus moves on, the Doctor's mental state deteriorates still further. He now has no memory at all. He can't even remember his duties as assistant to Ossian the knife thrower, or when the circus is due to leave for Munich and its next engagement. That is why Josef Rubashov finds him alone in his hotel room one evening, without his extravagantly spangled uniform, his boxes of powder and wheeled knife-throwing screen, for the circus has terminated his contract and moved on without him.

He relates some rambling joke he says he heard from Sir Francis Drake, and in the archaic Extremadurian dialect once spoken by the Conquistadors he mournfully describes a game of draughts he claims to have lost to Queen Kristina of Sweden during her exile in Rome after her defection to Catholicism. Then he sighs, falls silent and stares into the distance with the expression of a fish that has just expired.

Despair descends on Josef Rubashov, more heavily than ever before. He cries and curses. He shakes the Doctor's old shoulders and begs him to come back up, somehow, to the surface of consciousness. He threatens him and boxes his ears and tugs at the loose crocodile skin of his hump. But the doctor responds only with a somnambular gurgling sound, nodding to himself as if approving somebody's actions far off in the invisible pantomime of the past, where everything is possible and chronology is dead.

Josef leaves the old man with his sword and his amnesia, takes a tram to the dismal streets of the Mitte district, and there, numbed by his impotence, finds an open restaurant and gets inebriated for the first time in many years.

He is plagued by the thought that Paracelsus somewhere in the depths of his decay holds the key to the puzzle, for he realises it must be lying there, as if on the sea bed, deep down in an ocean trench, virtually impossible to retrieve. He curses the Doctor. He curses himself. He is drunk and close to vomiting. He feels like an insect.

Out in the street, he tears his uniform to shreds, for he has no further use for it. He's tired of their marches, their pugilistic songs and fights in the beer tent. He's tired of their cheap imitation of renewal and strength; he no longer has the energy to go on.

Eventually, he calms down. He goes back to the Doctor's hotel. One last hope drives him on. That the Doctor will have woken up somehow, and will remember again and be able to give him a lead.

But the Doctor isn't there. After calling his name and trying to force the door, which is triple-locked from the inside, Josef has to summon the porter to open it with a master key.

The room is empty. The sword has gone. The clothes and arthritic old trunk have gone, and the window is locked and barred – from the inside.

Once again, as if by a mysterious stroke of magic, the Doctor has vanished.

Philip Bouhler's Butler

(Late 1930s)

'My dear Herr Stillman, for this antique mezuzah I will give you sixteen marks and not a pfennig more . . . What's that? . . . The antiques guide says over four hundred? But you must understand, Herr Stillman, that in these times it's a buyer's market, not a seller's. I'm sorry, I can't go any higher. We're drowning in artefacts here. Look around you! A whole sea of dusty manuscripts and copies of the Mishnah in eighteenth-century gold bindings. Who wants to buy an ivory shofar horn these days? Or silver bathing instruments from a barred-up mikvah? And where's the market? People like you come every night and wake me up in my pyjamas to offload their family heirlooms. But the buying? Is there anybody who wants to do the buying? I'm sorry. I can't go any higher than sixteen.'

Roth the junk-shop owner counted out money from the till.

'Let's say sixteen fifty, Stillman! Take it or go elsewhere. That's assuming you can find any other shopkeeper prepared to do business with you.'

The rabbi took the money and secreted it in a fold in his coat.

'I also have an ark,' he said. 'Italian, sixteenth-century, made by Benveniste for Rabbi Isachar Dow Rokach in Krakow.'

'An ark? What am I supposed to do with one of those?'

'It's not the money in this case, Roth. The congregation is of the opinion that it must be taken to a place of safety. We shall buy it back as soon as times are better.'

'There's no space for Jewish arks here! If you've got silver candlesticks, or golden rolls for the Torah, then I'm interested. I pay fifty pfennigs a gram for silver, seventy-five for gold.'

'Seventy-five pfennigs for gold?'

'It's a buyer's market. Look at my assistant here . . . Rubaslov, he's Russian! Do you know how much he works for? For two meals a day, and three on Fridays, so he can get through the weekend. You're in no position to make demands these days if your papers aren't in order. And the fact that you're leaving on the boat for America can't reasonably be called my problem. I'm sorry. Why are *you* going, incidentally? Plenty are staying. Take the foil-fencing lady . . . what's her name . . . Mayer?'

'We're no longer allowed to work, Roth. We're no longer permitted to teach. We're not allowed to shop in German shops, or own any ourselves. We're not to have valuables or cash amounting to more than a few pathetic marks . . . we're not even allowed to keep pets, not so much as a dog!'

'What can I do about that, Stillman? Open kennels? Am I supposed to deal with this all on my own? It's best to keep your head down in times like these. And let me remind you that I'm breaking the law as well, right now, simply by buying something from you. Or by the small fact of your being in my antiques shop at midnight. I'm taking risks too. If the police were to see us, Stillman, it'd be the house of correction for us. Do you think I can allow myself to be a philanthropist in such circumstances? And give you four hundred marks for something I may not even find a market for? Are you having me on?'

'No, but . . .'

'And anyway, I'm a rag-and-bone man first and foremost. I'm no expert on all this stuff. Jewish sacred objects and arks and prayer bells. It's rags that interest me. It's rags that make money these days . . . and possibly gold.'

The rabbi tried to say something more, but the words wouldn't come and he made for the door. Hunched, almost at a run, he disappeared off into the darkness.

*

149

While he waited for Philip Bouhler to make himself known, Rubashov was scratching a living as an assistant to the junk-shop proprietor. Every day he did his rounds of the back courtyards of Berlin-Mitte. He collected old clothes and scrap metal, the wreckage of people's pasts, and in the evening he emptied out the cart in Roth's storeroom and listened to his shady business transactions.

He was taciturn. He was sombre and introverted, for inside him a battle with amnesia was raging, and not long ago, in the strange house in Tiergarten, he had been on the brink of madness. He'd grown a beard, to look older; he wanted his appearance to be in keeping with his failing memory.

With sorrow he had noted the memories fading; they had been robbed of detail and colour and all the little idiosyncrasies that made them personal. He could no longer remember the details; and weren't the details the foundation of every picture?

Time and again he had cast his net into the pond of the past in the hope of fishing out some details with which to reconstruct the ruined picture. For what else was left, beyond this desperate struggle?

Without memories, he had thought, they were nothing; mere mouthpieces of instincts and needs; dismal trees without roots, a lump of panting human meat driven by the impulses of the moment, living only to seek nourishment and air.

One night after Roth had shut up shop, he went down to the Hamburger Börse. Outside a pub on the Rosenthalerstrasse stood a few young men in uniform. As he passed, they hurled abuse at him. He took no notice of them. They could do what they liked, he thought. They would age like him, and loss of memory would catch up with them, too.

As he continued past Monbijou Park, he realised they were following him. Jew! he heard them shout. Somebody threw a bottle after him. He walked on. Somebody ran up behind him and barged into him. He fell.

They were on him, shouting and cursing at him. He offered no resistance. He registered two policemen standing half a block away, looking in a different direction. The boys pulled his hair. One of them hacked at his beard with a pair of scissors. His clothes were ripped to pieces. He heard himself roar with laughter, loud and unhinged.

The policemen approached them.

'Let him go!' they said.

'Who?'

'Drop him, for Christ's sake.'

'Why? A fucking Jew.'

'Release him! The top brass are here!'

The flock broke apart, scattered and melted away into the Berlin night; and when Rubashov got to his feet he saw the two policemen smiling, smiling shamelessly, and in the background, beside a car, in full dress uniform with glinting medals, the sergeant, the general, Wisch was waving at him to come over.

'Rubashov, you lunatic,' said Wisch as they drove through the deserted streets. 'That could have been the end of you. Walking around with a beard like a Jew at midnight! What's that all about?'

'I don't know, sergeant.'

'Don't know? That's no answer. Good God . . . Meet my friends: Herr Bouhler and Herr Brack.'

There were two men in the back seat. He shook them by the hand.

'Look in the mirror, Rubashov – not a single item of clothing left whole. If you didn't look like a Hebrew before, you do now.'

Wisch, he noted, still had that bad habit of overdoing the perfume. This time it was a different scent: ambergris.

'Not to worry,' he went on. 'When it's a matter of an old comrade-in-arms, that sort of thing can easily be arranged. I've been given new authority over the past year, Rubashov. I hereby appoint you an honorary Aryan.'

One of the men in the back seat leaned forward. It was Bouhler:

'Our friend Eichmann says we should ship the lot of them to Madagascar. So we finally get a bit of peace and quiet in the

Fatherland. And that man knows what he's talking about; he's been down there on official business; he speaks their language.'

'Can anybody explain something to me,' said Brack. 'What are they actually doing here? In our country? And at the same time waging war on us on all fronts. On all fronts and by all available means. Even using children. That Grünspann they were all talking about recently . . . he was no more than seventeen.'

'They even tried to murder our Lord Jesus Christ,' said Bouhler. 'And as if that weren't enough, they claim he's a Jew. A Jew, they say! Jesus was a Jew!'

They were passing through Tiergarten, towards the western area of the city. The chauffeur seemed to know where they were going.

'Wasn't he, then?' asked Brack.

'Not at all. Jesus was Galilean. He came from Galilee. Assyrian blood, racial research shows. One hundred percent Aryan. What's more, there's a theory that his father wasn't Joseph the carpenter from Nazareth at all, but a Teutonic soldier serving in the Roman army. A Teuton named Pantera, who had a relationship with a temple harlot, Maria. They've even found his grave, here in Germany.'

Wisch had got out his notebook. He jotted something down and scrutinised his handwriting through his monocle.

'What you saw in those boys,' Bouhler said, 'was nothing more than the instinct of race. Have you heard about the brown rats, Rubashov? In every single privy, the brown rat defeated the black rat, simply because it was more viable.'

'Is there anything I can do for you?' said Wisch, his voice unaccountably tinged with sadness. 'Do you need money?'

He shook his head.

'A job? A sinecure in some forgotten department? Trust an old acquaintance. Three wishes, Rubashov! Nothing's impossible for a man in my position.'

They stopped outside a villa on a side street in Tiergarten. Wisch opened the front door and they ascended the stairs to a conference room panelled in dark wood.

'You have a particularly interesting shape to your skull,' said Bouhler, seating himself in an armchair. 'You're German, but from

152

the east, isn't that so? From Siebenburg, I'd guess. That would explain the Slavic-sounding name. And phrenology, my good sir, is one of the most interesting occupations imaginable.'

Brack nodded in agreement.

'You're right, Philip, and he has got an undeniably interesting skull shape. Exquisite. Finely sculpted. It's beyond belief that anybody could take him for a Jew. But these things happen in the dark.'

'If you will allow me?' said Bouhler, taking a measuring instrument from his briefcase. 'I always carry my tools with me in case I happen across some interesting example among the great variety of skulls.'

'Note the beautifully straight nose,' he went on as he took measurements with his phrenograph, 'and the exquisitely narrow, well-shaped lips. The attractive curve of the back of the neck up to the head; the elegant ears. Your forefathers were Knights of the Order, perhaps? Congratulate yourself, young man. You are as good as racially pure!'

'We have a project that might interest you, Mr Rubashov,' said Brack. 'The Lebensborn Programme.'

'One has to feel attracted to Aryan women,' smiled Bouhler. 'And one must of course be a prime specimen oneself. That's a basic precondition if we're to maintain the purity of the race. Perhaps you're the man for us, Rubashov? Perfect skull shape. War veteran. Decorated for valour in the field. And you didn't suffer so much as a scrape when the boys had a go at you. You seem to be made of the most durable material. That's just what we need. Brack, go and fetch our lodger.'

Brack disappeared into a back room. Rubashov could hear him talking to someone in there, softly but insistently. After a while he returned, hand-in-hand with a little boy.

'This is Heinz,' said Bouhler. 'Born at one of our centres. A very successful product.'

The boy was in his pyjamas. He blinked uncomfortably in the light and extended his arm in the party salute.

'Take a look at little Heinz. It's extremely interesting. His father is a Sudeten German. His mother is a Romanian German. It's very

153

striking how the purity of the blood has been maintained in exile. Isn't that a sign of how right our theory is?'

The boy yawned. His blond hair was tousled. He put his thumb in his mouth.

'None of that, Heinz,' said Bouhler sternly. 'Would a soldier ever suck his thumb? Only girls do that.'

He gestured to Brack, who led the boy out of the room.

'Would you like to sign up?' he said. 'My instinct tells me you're the man for us. Don't hesitate now, Rubashov. It's a grand life!'

Bouhler stood up and went over to a bookcase. He took a photograph album from a cupboard.

'Look at this,' he said. 'Here are some pictures from one of our centres. The newborn boy in this photo is Heinz. That's his mother breastfeeding him. His father, the Sudeten German, isn't there. He's in the room next door.'

Bouhler turned to the next page, which was entirely taken up with one large photo. It showed naked men sitting on their beds in small cubicles. On the walls were graphs that looked like temperature charts. There were bunches of flowers on the bedside tables. Portraits of Himmler, leader of the nation, hung above the beds.

'Here are our boys,' said Bouhler. 'See what potent men we have. Racially conscious, blond-haired, with all the makings of good soldiers. But they're no bunch of libertines. We're not running a brothel on taxpayers' money here. The breeding takes place in Room 9. We monitor the women's womb temperatures, and when they're at their most fertile, they're sent in here. These boys can get through a dozen a day.'

He turned the page again. A garden shot showed a group of young people sitting under a sun umbrella, eating dinner.

'As soon as a woman becomes pregnant, she's moved to a different block. New ones arrive, like those you can see here. We let them socialise with the boys for a week or so before they're put to use. It's important to get them in the mood, Rubashov. We make sure they have the best of everything. Good food. Fine wines. Fresh air and exercise. That way, we'll never be short of new broods. Heinz's batch, for example, is one of the best yet.'

154

Bouhler closed the album.

'Like we said, Rubashov,' he said, 'just give us the nod. Wisch tells us you're a very special person.'

Bouhler rang a service bell and a man came into the room, dressed as a butler and carrying a tray of glasses filled with champagne. He went round serving them, and finally stood before Josef Rubashov with the last glass on the tray.

The man's face, he saw, was without flesh or skin. It was a cranium he was looking at, a skull that grinned at him encouragingly and said, 'Champagne, sir?'

He blinked, twice. Suddenly it was a completely ordinary man, a servant, a butler, in the process of leaving the room with a bow. He turned to the others. They had seated themselves in the leather armchairs; Brack had taken off his boots and Wisch had lit a cigar. He wanted to ask them: Didn't you see? Do you know him, is he an acquaintance?'

'You go out to the chauffeur, Rubashov,' said Wisch, and his voice was full of sadness once more, 'and tell him to drive you home and write the address down for Bouhler. You want to get away from Berlin, don't you? I'm sure we can manage that, can't we, Philip?'

He took his notebook out of his pocket and wrote something in it. The movement released a strong waft of perfume.

Bouhler nodded. 'Yes, we'll arrange it,' he said with a smile. 'We've another project that I think might interest you, Rubashov. Really. It's most interesting . . .'

He allowed himself to be transported though the night, full of misgivings. His thoughts were slipping and sliding, creeping and crawling, like terrified maggots, until he caught sight of the chauffeur in the rear-view mirror.

'What else could one expect?' he heard him say. 'Scratch the surface of the thin varnish of civilisation and what do we see? The animal within us!'

He could make out no details, only the rounded cap, and the glint of sorrowful eyes somewhere in the darkness.

'Mankind carries the story its own creation with it, in its clenched fists, wouldn't you say? Who knows what this is really all about. Pure instinct?'

Once again he understood this to be the coachman of his guest from the dawn of the century, but maybe he understood nothing at all, for the man's voice was as metallic and distant as if it came from some rusty cranny of his own memory, or from something that was not even a memory, but a crypt of fabricated remembrances, artefacts echoing from the imaginings of some other person.

They were passing through the centre now, the street lights probing through the windows with their antennae of light, but never far enough for him to get a view of the man's face.

'It's not looking good, Mr . . . Rubashov? It was Rubashov, wasn't it?'

'Yes, Rubashov . . . Josef Rubashov.'

'The barometer of history is predicting a storm. No, that's not strong enough. There's a hurricane starting to blow up.'

The chauffeur lit a cigarette, and the glowing tip illuminated his skin: blueish-white skin, an unnatural blueish-white.

'Anyway, it makes no odds. Mankind gets what it deserves, doesn't it? Existence: it all amounts to the same thing.'

He applied the brakes and stopped under the plane trees on Koppenplatz. It was the same man, Josef saw now, the butler who had served them champagne in the conference room.

'Or perhaps I'm going too far? Am I exaggerating?'

Voices could be heard from a group of soldiers walking past; smoke came drifting from somewhere, the pungent smell of burning hung over the neighbourhood, or perhaps not, for he no longer trusted his senses.

'What shall I do to find him?' he asked.

The butler smiled.

'Take a job, Rubashov . . . take the job Messrs Bouhler and Brack offer you.'

The butler opened the car door for him.

'We shall meet again,' he said. 'When the storm has blown itself out, Mr Rubashov. Believe me: we shall meet again.'

156

T4

(1940–41)

'Baroness von Lausitz,' said Bouhler, pointing at the woman, 'was one of the many personas who took hold of her. She is a very interesting case, one of the most interesting I've come across in my professional life. Her real name is Margarete Barsch. She comes from simple farming stock in the Cottbuss area. Sorbian roots on her father's side, but that doesn't explain anything . . .'

The old woman sat quietly on the narrow bed in the hospital ward. Bouhler had removed her straitjacket, but she kept her arms crossed over her breast as if not yet accustomed to the change. Wirth regarded her with interest.

'What's wrong with her at the moment?'

'She isn't suffering from dementia,' said Bouhler. 'No geriatric disorders we've been able to discover. The personality disorders seem to have gone, too. Now it's a speech disorder instead: deep-level confusion of words and their connotations.'

'Brain damage?' suggested Wirth, gesturing to Josef Rubashov to note it all down.

'Conceivably.'

Bouhler looked at the medicine bottles on her table.

'Plenty of research has been done on her over the years,' he said. 'But the question is whether we can learn anything from her. It's a fundamental problem in psychiatry, of course: can we learn anything at all? There must be some use to be made even of this life. What is its purpose otherwise?'

He stroked the woman's hair kindly and handed her a glass of water.

'What's that you've got in your hand, Margaret?' he asked. 'What's it called . . . the thing you're drinking from?'

'Window,' said the woman gravely, looking at the glass.

'Glass, it's called . . . not window.'

'Window,' said the woman again. She bent down and removed one of her shoes. Very carefully, as if it required great concentration, she poured the water into her slipper, raised it and emptied the contents over her head.

'You see,' said Bouhler. 'Who knows what's going on in the depths of Margarete Barsch's mind? And glass-window is actually one of her more comprehensible associations.'

'So before this speech defect started,' said Wirth, 'it was a question of split personalities?'

'It's extremely tragic. At the age of sixteen, Margarete Barsch was afflicted by a psychosis. Very little is known about the causes. The premature death of her mother has been suggested as one. She had to bring up her younger siblings, an onerous responsibility for a young girl. There is some indication that she was seduced by her father as soon as she reached sexual maturity.'

Wirth nodded sympathetically.

'Shortly thereafter we see the appearance of the first of the personalities that subsequently exist in her for over fifty years, one Baroness von Lausitz. The journal kept during her first institutional stay indicates that the personality disorder was powerful enough to alter her whole demeanour. Her face took on a haughty look, just like a noblewoman's. Her gait became that of a woman from a *Junker* family, with a very straight back and dainty steps; her table manners suddenly changed. She even began to lisp like a lady of the aristocracy.'

'Did this von Lausitz have a real-life equivalent?' asked Wirth.

'Yes, strangely enough. And what's more, Margarete Barsch knew her story back to front, which made the whole thing rather

158

uncanny. Baroness Catherina von Lausitz, gentlemen, was the last woman to be burned at the stake as a witch in Upper Silesia. Margarete Barsch knew everything about her. The minutiae of her life. The appearance of the state rooms in the house on her father's estate. The sort of music she preferred. She described in detail the people she had met and mixed with, and the main topics of conversation in aristocratic circles of the time. She described her relationship with a young suitor, a certain Count Pfeifer, and with her Polish wet-nurse, a wise old woman, who later had a part to play in the case presented by the prosecution during the trial. Further investigation revealed that Catherina von Lausitz had, like Margarete Barsch, been sexually abused by her father as a child. The scandal was used against her in the trial: with the help of the devil, it was claimed, she had set a trap to ensnare her parent . . . Margarete Barsch also gave an account of the trial itself, and its climax: von Lausitz's purging by fire. She described it in vivid and horrific detail: the pain, the fat melting under her skin, her body eventually bursting in the extreme heat. She described the stench of burning human flesh. Appalling, isn't it?'

Wirth signalled to Josef Rubashov to stop writing.

'During her first stay in hospital,' Bouhler said, 'she told the doctors that Baroness von Lausitz was a homeless soul for whom she felt very sorry, which was why she let her live in her body. Several more institutional stays followed: Bautzen, Heidelberg, Stettin. Over the years she accumulated more personalities. One year it was the young son of a forester. The next year she added a seamstress. But Catherina von Lausitz lived on in her throughout. The staff at the nursing home eventually began calling her Catherina instead of Margarete. They still do that now, in fact. Here, they simply call her the Baroness.'

The woman laughed and waved to someone over in the corner. There was nothing there but an empty mirror.

'But now she's suffering from other disorders,' said Wirth.

Bouhler nodded.

'She adapted to the language of all her personalities. The language of a forester's son. The language of an eighteenth-century baroness. And when she was a seamstress she spoke as if she had a mouthful of pins. In the end it was as if all those voices began to unravel her own speech. Now nobody can understand what she says.'

'Grave,' said the woman, pointing to Bouhler's stethoscope. 'Grave!' She began to laugh, very mournfully.

'In days gone by they would probably have burned her at the stake, like they did Baroness von Lausitz. But what are we to do with creatures like her today? The possessed? Hot and cold baths? It doesn't help. She's incurable.'

'It's a question of utility,' said Wirth, flicking though the woman's records. 'Can she be of any use to us? And if any more are born like her, can they ever be of any use? Many of these illnesses are hereditary, aren't they?'

'Yes, just like the witches,' said Bouhler. 'Just as the profession of witchcraft was passed on, the second sight, the healing skills, from mother to daughter. But today they're lunatics. Today the witches are in lunatic asylums. So what are we to do with them?'

Bouhler strapped the woman into her straitjacket again. She offered no resistance, merely nodded in the direction of his stethoscope, endlessly repeating the word 'grave'.

'Gentlemen,' he said. 'We haven't much time left. I suggest we move on. There are a few more patients I should like you to meet before we have to leave.'

They walked towards the door. The old woman nodded sadly as she watched them go. She tried to say something, but the words were tumbling around somewhere inside her as if on a merry-go-round, and she would never be able to grasp hold of the right one.

'I agree with you, Philip,' muttered Wirth as they continued down the corridor. 'The truly tragic thing – and we must never forget this – is that these people are suffering, although we can't always see it. And their relatives are suffering too, although they would seldom admit it openly.'

'That's right, Wirth. We must never forget the suffering of these creatures or their relatives. And another matter we should discuss more openly is how expensive they are. Psychiatry annually costs the state millions. For the same amount we could make twenty thousand marriage loans of ten thousand Reichsmark in a single financial year. Or build fifteen hundred working-men's hostels. Or two thousand new flats. Or a hundred and fifty new military hospitals. After all, gentlemen, we mustn't forget: this is war.'

'T4 Institutional Service' it said on Wirth's visiting card, but Josef was still hazy about the aims of the project itself. It had something to do with mental health care, that much he had realised, divided into sections for severe senile dementia and chronic schizophrenia. But there were also other patients in the institutions they visited: mongols and epileptics, patients with paranoia and phobias, and some with psychosis and shell shock from the war. That was what he had managed to work out as he made notes for Wirth, or accompanied him into hospital offices to fill in petrol coupons and mileage charts.

Perhaps they were planning to save money and rationalise care provision? Or link the public sector with the war economy? He wasn't sure. For the project was top secret. A lot of sealed documents and classified memoranda. And Wirth himself wasn't exactly forthcoming.

Fate had been good to him, he would often think. The world had been reduced to the technical operation of driving, some basic secretarial duties and quiet admiration of the German countryside: rivers, lakes, plains and Alps, all this he was able to see, for they travelled over a thousand kilometres a week around the greater German Reich, then back to the Brandenburg house of correction where Wirth had his office and held secret, nocturnal meetings with health-service officials. The project was overseen by an office in Berlin, where Bouhler and Brack were in charge. He met them regularly, out on visits to hospitals and other institutions.

Senior Officer Wirth was a large, muscular man with an innately brutal face that sometimes scared the wits out of the mental patients. He would soothe them with pats on the back as he measured their ears and skulls, just as Bouhler had done with Josef

Rubashov in Berlin. 'It's in the planning stage,' was all he would say about their work. 'You'll know when it's complete.'

So they drove along Germany's new motorways through country-side so verdant and blooming that it was hard for Josef Rubashov to imagine a war going on, somewhere over the horizon.

Early in that second autumn of the war, they went to visit a care institution in Hessen. It was housed in an old monastery on a hill above an attractive, sleepy village, and was about to be renovated. They had already started installing new sanitary facilities, and a local firm had been called in to do the tiling. But the morning Josef Rubashov and Officer Wirth got there, one of the plumbers went down with influenza, and since the job was urgent, Wirth asked him to step in and lend a hand.

He spent two days helping with the restoration of a washroom, while Wirth sat in meetings with Bouhler, who had come to inspect the premises. They laid a new floor of black and white tiles, and the walls were tiled in white. They installed lead piping perforated with small holes, which ran from an adjoining room and had to be fixed to the walls a metre from the floor. Josef Rubashov had nothing against this break from routine; in fact it gave him a pleasant feeling of satisfaction to be working with his hands.

After two days' work, they were finished. Then Bouhler appeared with cakes to thank them all for their efforts, and they sat on the shiny new, tiled floor and chatted quite personally together. What was more, he thought to himself, they all belonged to the same happy band of those excused military service. Bouhler and Wirth because they had responsibilities under the secretariat of T4. And the care-home staff because they had been sent there to help implement the project for reorganisation of the country's mental health provision.

Winter arrived and the snow lay white and glittering on the German plains. The war was at a temporary standstill. In the west, on their island, the English were alone in offering resistance. Wirth discharged his duties conscientiously, and their trips extended so that they were now often on the road for weeks at a time. New orders had come from Berlin: the sick were to be concentrated in larger institutions, and families with mentally handicapped children were now obliged to register them. The point of all this remained unclear.

The weeks passed; the time slipped by like the scenery outside the car windows. And anyone asking Josef Rubashov about his existence that winter would probably have received a smile in reply. Fate, he thought, had been good to him; perhaps his luck was changing . . .

In mid-April they were back at the care home in Hessen to inspect the new complex. Bouhler and Brack were also there, along with a reserved man named Brandt, dressed in full SS uniform, who had been invited along to observe the hospital routines. Bouhler took them along to a waiting room outside the doctor's examination room. It was a beautiful clear day, he would later remember. The hyacinths were in flower in the hospital grounds and the snow was melting from the roofs. The skies of Hessen were streaked with lines of returning migratory birds. Brack and Wirth whispered with the reserved Brandt, and Bouhler offered Josef Rubashov a cigarette. Suddenly they all fell silent. Screams were heard from the front of the building, where two buses had pulled up. Then an external door opened and two nurses entered, followed by about thirty patients.

Josef Rubashov had time to register that there were all sorts: men, women and children, some senile and psychotic. The beautiful old Margarete Barsch was among them. She pointed at a weighing machine standing in the waiting room, and said in her trembling voice: Spoon! In the same way she pointed out several things in the room, giving each of them other names, for somewhere inside her all the objects and connotations of the world were still all jumbled together and recast into new moulds, to make a secret code that only she could decipher.

The patients cried, and some of them clung to each other as if seeking protection. He noticed that they were all dressed alike, in white paper gowns, and tied round their wrists were little labels on which were written their name, plus their date and place of birth. After a while, Bouhler drew aside the curtain to the examination room, and they were sent in one by one to undress and be weighed and measured.

Josef Rubashov could hear it all through the thin walls. He could also hear the sound of the flash as they were photographed from three angles, and Bouhler's calm, kindly voice as he marked them off against a list of birth dates and medical diagnoses.

They came back into the waiting room. They were now naked, and some had a cross marked in blue ink on their backs. A male nurse opened the door to the washroom that Josef Rubashov had helped to complete, and Brack led them down the steps. He left them down there on the gleaming tiled floor, said a few kind and soothing words to them, and shut them in. Rubashov was shaken by a fit of shivering, a sudden wave of terror, the source of which he couldn't pinpoint.

He went into the doctor's room where Bouhler was standing, bent over some papers. He heard Brandt asking about the crosses drawn on their backs, and Bouhler answering calmly, 'To mark out the ones with gold teeth . . . and some of them are of scientific interest, of course.'

It was as if he were going about in a trance; as if he had been chloroformed, or encased in an invisible membrane that cut him off from the rest of the world. Half-numbed by the feeling, he opened the door of a room where two men sat in front of a flag-studded map. Urns stood all around them, and with their gloved hands they were filling them with ash from huge metal vats. He suddenly became aware of Bouhler walking at his side and explaining in a pedagogical tone: 'It's vital we have all the patients' details . . . not long ago we had a query from a relative about one of the urns; in the letter of condolence we'd written that the patient died of a burst appendix, but to our horror it turned out that the patient had had their appendix removed some years before. It must be a mistake, they wrote, they must be somebody else's ashes . . . We also had a case of two patients from the same small place in Bavaria; suspicions were aroused because the cause of death in both cases was pneumonia. But we've learned our lesson. We introduced the flag system precisely to avoid any repetition of such mistakes. We always make sure to have different diagnoses when there are two patients from the same town.'

They came to another room. Some women were sitting at typewriters, typing letters of condolence. He wondered if Bouhler was still talking to him, but when he looked up he saw Brandt was there as well, and Bouhler was showing him some papers.

'In our contact with the next of kin,' Bouhler said, 'we use a three-step system: first, to avoid any unexpected visits, a letter in which we inform them the patient has been moved. A temporary move, we write, building work, unfortunately no visiting for the next month, the practical difficulties make it impossible. Then a sudden telegram with news of the death. We give the cause, usually pneumonia, offer the family our condolences and the ashes. Lastly we send the urn . . . We also, if you would care to follow me, Herr Brandt, have a room for post-mortems: a concrete examination table with drainage channels where we perform autopsies on particularly interesting cases.'

He was only hearing disjointed fragments now, the odd phrase plucked from a language so appalling that its meaning was lost to him: 'We also take an interest in the pathological cases . . . here you can see the rails and the trucks to the crematorium . . . to our dismay we've heard rumours that the children in the village threaten each other with: "Just watch out, or you'll end up in Hadamar's baker's oven" . . . Random euthanasia just wasn't going to work in the long term; the scopolamine injections proved far too expensive . . . we've already promised the staff a little party, beer and sandwiches, when we get to the ten thousandth patient . . .'

But he was no longer listening. He was alone now, walking through long, echoing corridors, and behind the locked doors he could hear the hideous shrieks and prayers of incarcerated human beings. He opened an external door and came out into the hospital grounds. The snow was melting on the lawns; he could hear birdsong. Farmers could be seen in the fields. A gardener was cleaning a spade by a shed.

He walked slowly out to the road and turned down towards the village. He stopped and retched. He fell and got up again. He inhaled, scenting the air; he breathed in the smell of hyacinths and damp earth. But over it, only thinly disguised, another smell, a sickening, acrid smell of burned human flesh that made his insides churn.

He looked about him as if expecting to catch sight of the front among the rolling hills, by the peaceful village, in lovely Hessen, as if expecting to see an artillery battle, a fire trench full of charred soldiers; or a bonfire burning people – witches – at the stake. But all he could see were the chimneys from which the smoke was rising and being dispersed by the wind.

The tears streamed down his cheeks as he walked. He fell again and vomited until there was nothing left in his stomach.

The Darkness

(1942)

He was in a ruined city somewhere, a city of bombed, burned-out buildings, where people sat round open fires. Someone had brought him through a gateway in a wall, and left him in the darkness. Cries in Polish and Yiddish could be heard. He realised he must be in a ghetto.

It was night time. He felt his way down an alleyway. Crying, begging human beings everywhere, children tugging at his clothes, begging for a piece of bread. Mumbling ghosts loomed out of the shadows and vanished again. The people were as emaciated as skeletons.

'Rubashov! What are you doing here?'

It took a while for him to make out the figure in the darkness. It was Wisch.

'Fancy us meeting here. In hell. How did you find your way here, Rubashov?'

He didn't know. He seemed to lose consciousness in one place and regain it somewhere totally different.

'It doesn't matter. There are things I want to show you.'

They went on through the darkness. There were corpses lying along the fronts of the buildings, and children were going through their pockets, hunting for things to eat.

'Half a million people they've crammed in here,' Wisch whispered. 'In an area of a few square kilometres. Expelled from

167

every corner of Europe. It's a Babel. Can't you hear? They're speaking all the known languages of the world, crying and cursing in a thousand different tongues.'

They turned down an alley. Phantoms tore at their clothes. There was a rabbi squatting in the gutter. He held a dead girl in his arms.

In a square there were fires burning by the walls of the houses. People in rags, thin as rakes, crowded round the braziers. This was poverty without parallel.

'You're right, Rubashov,' mumbled Wisch, as if he'd read his thoughts. 'These are medieval times. Darkness filled with sickness and need and mumbling shadows, whose bodies long since gave up on them, shadows cast by the fires onto a wall crowned with barbed wire. Never forget this, Rubashov. Never!'

In a back street, a vendor was selling rats from a cart. The animals had been skinned and hung up by their tails on a wire rack. In front of them crawled a woman on all fours; she crawled like an animal, salivating, moaning.

'They live in cellars,' said Wisch, 'in soot-blackened ruins, in attics, in earth cellars, under flights of outside steps, in churches, synagogues and sewers. In the houses, every room is full to bursting. There's scarcely any food, and the supplies that get smuggled in command astronomical prices. People eat what they find in the gutter, Rubashov. They have their gold teeth extracted to exchange for a hunk of bread.'

He seemed to be speaking to him without moving his lips. It was as if he were hearing his voice from a point deep inside himself.

'The wall is over ten kilometres long. There are six gates leading out, all guarded by soldiers. No one gets out of here alive. We're shut in, Rubashov; we've all walked into the trap.'

He saw that Wisch was crying, soundlessly, but with no effort to hide it. A burst of machine-gun fire rattled nearby. A lorry drove across the square. Drunken soldiers were standing on the back. Laughing, they fired into the crowd, but no one reacted, no one tried to run away.

A mumbling horde pushed past them. Everywhere there was the stench of dirt and death.

168

'There are some who still hope,' Wisch said. 'They're to be sent east, someone says. As forced labour on the building sites of Russia. Or their God will intervene; God will intervene and set them free. Unfortunately they're wrong . . .'

He fell silent. Someone tugged at his trousers so violently that he almost lost his balance. It was a child, a naked little girl, begging.

'The snow will start falling soon, Rubashov. There's no coal, no wood, no fuel, and these already starving people will freeze to death in their tens of thousands. Every morning they'll pile up the corpses on the pavements. It may well be that they cut off the buttocks, or the flesh on the thighs and upper arms. There are shops that deal in human meat.'

Wisch turned towards him. The tears were running down his face. Josef could hear his voice very distinctly now, deep inside him, echoing as if in a cave. Then all of a sudden, he disappeared, dissolving before Josef's eyes as if he had never been there . . .

He must have passed out. When he came round, he was lying in a covered wagon on the edge of the ghetto. A gypsy woman was addressing him, but he couldn't understand a word. The stench of corpses made him throw up. He wondered whether he existed at all. Did he himself exist, did Josef Rubashov exist, or had he borrowed somebody else's demented memory?

He was sweating, and shaking the old contract in front of him. The ancient woman read verses over him. He lost consciousness again, and when he woke up he was sitting in a large hall, at one end of a long table, lit by silver candelabras; the table was spread with a chalk-white linen cloth, he was holding cutlery of pure gold, and on a plate in front of him was a quivering, golden-yellow blancmange. He plunged his fork into it, but it instantly changed into a mass of writhing maggots and the table was now covered with a cloth of blackened human skin; he heard a wildly hysterical laugh and saw in a mirror Wirth and Bouhler, in the bodies of wolves. He passed out.

He awoke again. Before him, in a beautiful meadow with the

scent of wild flowers, Wisch sat playing a lute; he was wearing a shabby suit and old-fashioned spectacles, having resumed the appearance he had had at their meeting at the dawn of the century. When Josef Rubashov leaned forward to strangle him, he changed into a candle flame that fluttered away over the meadow like a burning butterfly.

It was night when he awoke again. He could feel the ebb and flow of fever in his body, and the gypsy woman was still sitting there.

He stood up. Without saying a word, he headed off into the darkness.

He walked the ghetto for weeks without resting. He had a vague sense of this being the work of human beings, of this evil having emanated from themselves, like some monstrous radiation.

Excess flourished on the brink of death. There were underground brothels and luxury restaurants where the smugglers danced to jazz bands. There were gambling dens and saunas, and secret delicatessens where you could buy anything and everything as long as you had money. Prostitutes lined the streets. People of both sexes and all ages sold their bodies for a bit of bread. There were cabarets mocking life in the ghetto; there were hotels for lovers, where those who could afford it could purchase an hour's oblivion for themselves . . . Criminals from other parts of the city hid from the police in the ghetto. They, too, were then obliged to wear the armband with the star: it was a great irony, a cynical joke choreographed by a sick power.

He would never forget: an abandoned boy crying in a doorway; an old rabbi driven mad by his hunger, who wandered from corpse to corpse reading Kaddish. He talked to them all and tried to give them hope. It was the least he could do, he thought: to try to implant some hope into their terrified consciousnesses. But it was useless. There was no way out. Only he, Josef Rubashov, would emerge from this alive, and it filled him with shame.

Even those as yet unborn, he thought, even those who would be born long after this time, even they would be filled with shame, for no survivor, not even he, could understand the terror that reigned here.

One night it became clear to him that he was no longer a believer. God was dead for him, drowned in this sea of suffering. For if a God existed at the same time as this evil, then He wasn't all-powerful, or alternatively His concept of goodness deviated totally from humankind's, and in that case it was meaningless to call Him good. And if God's morality was thus unfathomable, then He was no longer the God they had believed themselves to serve.

Winter eventually relinquished its hold on the ghetto. In the course of a few months, in the freezing temperatures, one-third of the inhabitants had perished. Grass and flowers grew up in the back courtyards, but starving people ate them before they had time to bud.

In the course of the summer, the deformed and the mentally ill came in their thousands from the institutions that had been closed. More Jews arrived, from ever more distant places. They were waiting for something, it hung in the air, the anticipation of something even more dreadful than this; though the idea that anything worse could exist simply defied comprehension. Rumours were circulating, so grisly that they could only be whispered from ear to ear under cover of darkness. Vast factories were said to have been built, vast farms where people were slaughtered like cattle, and boiled up for soap fat. But Josef never heard these rumours, whispered in the dark by mad prophets. For he just kept walking, day and night, without rest.

One evening he was accosted by a mute beggar. She was a young woman, but scurvy had robbed her of her hair and teeth, and terror had taken her voice into pawn and given her madness as a receipt. She took his hands and studied them, as if wanting to tell his fortune. Then she ran away.

With tears in his eyes, he followed her. She dodged between beggars and prostitutes, through doorways and back courtyards, until she vanished into a ruined building in the eastern part of the ghetto. He followed her into the darkness. He found her in the ruined cellar, in a hollow, dug out of the earth floor, trembling like an animal. 'Don't be afraid of me,' he said. 'I'll protect you.'

He stayed with her. He comforted her until she fell asleep and slept the feather-light sleep of an angel. For she was an angel, an angel who had descended from a far-off, forgotten heaven. She was a strange seraph who had come down to bear witness, but then, in the kingdom of terror, in the empire of famine, had lost her reason. She was a deranged stray, and Josef Rubashov loved her. The feeling was unconditional, without memory or future. He loved her because she was lost, because he knew it, and couldn't stop it. And that loss merely intensified his love. His life was predestined to be thus: he would lose all those to whom he was attached, and always be attached to those he lost.

At nights he lay at her side, sleepless, listening to the cold ticking of eternity inside her. She had no past, no awareness of where she had come from or what she was called. She knew nobody. She was alone.

Sometimes he followed her down into the sewers to a place on the other side of the wall, outside the ghetto. They made their way through great tunnels full of excrement and sludge. Sometimes they went on all fours, like animals. They met other people, escaping, or smugglers taking food or weapons to the resistance movement that had started to form in the ghetto. Shadows moved in the stinking darkness; it was a world of phantoms.

In a recess in the base of a fountain on the other side of the wall, a sack of beans or potatoes would be concealed. He wondered with whom she'd once come to this agreement; who was the stranger silently aiding her on the other side? He realised she didn't know herself. He could see she was acting on the orders of some forgotten memory that was part of her former life.

In the middle of the summer, the ghetto began to empty of inhabitants. From a goods yard at its northern end, the people were sent off by train. Once more the rumours were circulating, so ghastly that they shut their ears to them. District after district was

172

emptied out; the police and soldiers herded them at gunpoint to the waiting cattle trucks. Heart-rending scenes were played out: children were torn from their mothers' hands; the old and incapacitated were unceremoniously shot in the back of the neck. A white covering, like snow, descended on the streets of the ghetto. But it wasn't snow, it was feathers and down from the pillows and quilts that the soldiers slit open in their search for hidden objects. Thousands of individuals were sent off every day. When the trains had left, a terrible silence reigned.

One day he left the mute woman alone in the ruined cellar. When he returned she was gone, and he knew they had taken her away.

He went to the goods yard, and what he saw filled him with horror. The people were being driven up into the cattle trucks with whips and dogs, for they were no longer considered human beings, but animals. Like herds of cattle thousands strong, they were forced to the assembly point and up into the trains. Truck after truck was filled; with blows and kicks they were crammed in to bursting point, and when there was no standing room left, the children wedged in on top of them, as if on a shelf. Each wagon was loaded, shut and sealed with barbed wire. In an adjoining siding stood a train that had not yet departed. People died where they stood, held upright among the living even after death. In the heat the people whimpered; they screamed for water and air. Faeces, urine and blood ran through the cracks and down onto the track. It was hideous.

At the assembly point, the weak were kicked to death on the spot. Desperate mothers screamed for their children. A man was bludgeoned to death with rifle butts as his family looked on. Many people went insane.

Josef Rubashov stumbled round in this inferno, calling for the mute woman, running between crying and dying people, and guards who had long since crossed a boundary and were killing as mechanically as they would stifle a yawn. He was carried along in the tide of crying or deathly quiet people; dogs were set on them, whips lashed them onward, like a great herd of cattle to the slaughter, up into the waiting train. For a long time he was lost in grief, and when he came round he was crushed into a truck where the people were shivering with mortal dread, begging for mercy, howling for their loved ones or silently, in mumbling madness, saying their final prayer.

This is the end, he thought. This is the end of humanity, nothing can rise again from this crime; this crime is the end, this is as far as we can sink, this is the deepest circle of hell.

But he was wrong. For the place he then came to, the final destination of this journey, exceeded all his conceptions of evil. It was of such a kind that even Dante could never have envisaged it; no devil could have invented it. There were no adequate words to describe it. It was the work of humankind. It was hell . . .

III

Aberrations

(1946–56)

At the Nuremberg trials of 1946 we see Josef Rubashov again. In a series of photographs taken for the archive of the tribunal he is seated among the journalists in the press gallery. He is wearing earphones and listening intently to the interrogation of the accused. A tangle of wires and cables for the simultaneous interpretation lies before him. We can see that the testimonies are disturbing him.

In another picture he is to be seen outside the palace of justice, in conversation with Gilbert, the prison doctor. He is now wearing a catering uniform and pushing a food trolley. In a third document, also a photograph, he is standing outside the prison rotunda. He is shaking hands with prison governor Andruss. The looks the two men are exchanging express mutual good wishes. We can tell they are saying goodbye.

We don't know what he was doing in Nuremberg during the trial, what role he played, what questions he hoped to get answered. But if we study him more closely we notice a change. He has aged. We're looking at an old man. An aged man with snow-white hair and lined cheeks, with terror's mark of Cain burned into his eyes. We sense that the horrors he has experienced are a force of nature, possessed of a strength that can match the forces of the universe.

Perhaps, he is thinking, his life has no meaning unless there is a reason for what he has lived through.

Perhaps that is why his search must now go on?

In the Copenhagen section of the Danish national daily *Berlingske Tidende* on September 18th, 1948 we find the obituary of Folke Bernadotte, the Swedish diplomat shot dead by an extremist from the Stern Gang while trying to mediate peace between Arabs and Jewish immigrants in the Middle East. In the adjacent column is an analytical piece about English double-dealing during the British Mandate in Palestine, and anyone happening to read to the end of the article will come to a picture that has clearly been put in the wrong place. The photograph actually belongs with the report from the autumn fair at Amager on the following page, a light-hearted piece about tombola stalls and candyfloss, post-war euphoria and the German Ferris wheel from the top of which you can see out over Øresund to the Swedish towns on the other side of the water. And finally: about the two human cannonballs Jing and Jang, the oldest of their kind in the world, by their own account.

We can see them in the wrongly placed picture. They are unmistakable. Dressed in matching zebra-striped body suits with crash helmets on their heads, black with gunpowder from head to toe, they stare into the camera lens. On the left, a man of eighty, white-haired, wrinkled, smiling nervously as if this attention were a necessary evil. And on the right, with a decidedly senile look, an enormous hump on his back, a toothpick casually hanging from the corner of his mouth, scarcely a hand's breadth tall, and lazily propped against the enormous barrel from which they are fired four times a day like stripy meteors in a special aeroballistic double act, acclaimed in market places from Narvik to Navarre . . . yes, it's them: Messrs Rubashov and Theophrast Bombast.

They can also be spotted during the January crisis in Czecho-slovakia earlier that year. In a photograph taken at a meeting at the premises of the craftsmen's union, Gottwald and Masaryk are stiffly shaking hands; and in the audience several rows back, at such an angle that they appear framed by the politicians' bodies . . . yes, it's them again . . . Rubashov staring intently as if looking for a familiar face among the crowd at this fateful moment, and his companion

178

with eyes like empty wells, the crooked posture of something centuries old, like a wizened dwarf oak, shrunk by the rain and salt winds, his face as rough as bark, and gripping a strange, rusty sword in his hand: Paracelsus.

Later, when Jan Masaryk was airbrushed out of the picture in the Communists' attempt to rewrite history, in an attempt to unscrew a crucial screw from the complicated Meccano of history and replace it with a bit of chewing gum, our heroes disappeared too. But the sword remains, a bafflingly anachronistic sword that seems to be tickling Gottwald's armpit, thus making his forced smile and outstretched hand appear an exercise in self-control.

Two things can therefore be ascertained:

1) Josef Rubashov has still not given up. And why should he? With the years extending ahead of him like an everlasting thread, like a dry and dusty desert road stretching away over an endless number of empty horizons.

2) Paracelsus is at his side once more.

They pop up at every flashpoint. We stick our noses into any of the continent's troublespots and fault lines, and who do we find there? Messrs Theophrast and Rubashov.

At the testing of a hundred-megatonne hydrogen bomb in the Urals, we locate them among the crowd of invited scientists, politicians and military men. They are wearing dark glasses and radiation protection suits while in front of them – we can see this very clearly – a cosmic chanterelle of fire and radiation arcs up into the glassy blue sky, where the clouds take on all the colours of the rainbow, and the angels flee with scorched wings, coughing from the smoke. Josef Rubashov, we note, seems hopeful, as if he had bet his last kopek on world destruction and now feels sure of winning, while Theophrast Bombast, that sensualist, calmly stifles a yawn.

Two years earlier, in a film made during Roy Cohn and David Shine's visit to the American legation in Athens: an old man on the caretaking staff (according to Shine's report, his name is Rushabov) is being interviewed using a questionnaire devised by McCarthy:

Cohn: *You're Russian, you say?*
Rushabov: *Russo-Khirghiz, with Swedish-Estonian blood . . .*
Cohn: *What is your role at the legation here in Athens?*
Rushabov: *Nothing specific. I help out when needed. (pause) Sometimes they ask me about translations.*
Cohn: *What sort of translations?*
Rushabov: *Once it was a blackmail letter. I don't remember. (pause) Invitations from other ambassadors . . . the diplomats often socialise privately . . . Documents about this dreadful civil war.*
Cohn: *You speak quite a few languages?*
Rushabov: *(nods)*
Cohn: *A cosmopolitan?*
Rushabov: *I don't know what that implies.*
Cohn: *Jewish?*
Rushabov: *No.*
Cohn: *Are you, or have you ever been, a member or sympathiser of a Communist party? Have you ever subscribed to a Communist magazine? Do you support the Greek Communists? A simple answer: yes or no?*
Rushabov: *I can't remember ever having . . . (is interrupted)*
Cohn: *Have you at any time in the last ten years been in the Soviet Union or in a state friendly to the Soviet Union?*
Rushabov: *Well, the fact is . . .*
Cohn: *So you admit it. (turned to the camera) As you see, a Russian . . . an Asian . . . a Communist employed in a key post at the very heart of one of our most important European embassies.*

Cohn is smiling triumphantly. In the background, beside the table where the two attorneys have gathered a little pile of suspect Communist literature, stands a diminutive, hunchbacked man, almost a dwarf. He has a rusty sword in his hand and is brandishing it in the air as if duelling with some invisible opponent.

*

On April 11th, 1952, *Pravda* runs a series of pictures from a seminar at the Academy of Sciences in Minsk. The platform discussion is led by the physiologist Demikov. The participants describe the latest research in artificial hybridisation of sheep and goats, and Demikov's own experiment, an operation to join dogs and make them share certain vital organs, such as heart and lungs. They even raise the possibility of crossing men with chimpanzees in order to create a pool of cheap labour in the service of the Socialist state. But anyone who scrutinises the pictures carefully, or has access to the negatives and can enlarge them, will find in the audience, to one side of the platform, two familiar faces: one almost asleep, the other with a terrified expression and wildly flared nostrils, staring towards the table where the participants are engaged in heated debate . . . And there . . . Yes, let us briefly take a closer look; let us for a moment observe and consider the figure in the white coat of a doctor, listening attentively as Demikov describes the appearance and capabilities of the new half-man, nodding and making notes, taking his glasses on and off, knitting his brow and occasionally grimacing painfully as if the discussion prompted some unpleasant reminiscence. Yes, it's him. It's undeniably the local government clerk from the beginning of the century.

The text accompanying the pictures includes a full list of the panel members. The man in the doctor's coat is said to be Morgenstern, Detlev Federwisch Morgenstern, East German geneticist from the Humboldt University in Berlin, invited as a particular guest of Demikov's to lead a debate on 'Ethics and genetics in the Socialist state'.

The final column of the piece describes an episode involving Morgenstern. A old man in the audience (Rubashov) gets up and tries to force his way onto the platform, but is stopped by the security staff. As they gently but firmly restrain him and lead him away, he hurls abuse at the East German in 'unprintable Russian'. The latter, much agitated, then leaves the platform and is whisked off in the direction of his hotel in a car driven by a mysterious chauffeur.

Shortly after this, the panel breaks for lunch. When they assemble again an hour later, Morgenstern is still not back. They look for him in his hotel room and all over the conference centre, but to no avail.

The following week, the mystery of the missing East German scientist is highlighted in two articles in the White Russian press. He is now said to have 'Vanished without trace'. An investigation is mounted amid suspicions of scientific espionage, and the security services of the imperialist states are alleged to be involved. There is no record of any research scientist by the name of Federwisch Morgenstern at the Humboldt University in Berlin, and in a cracked calfskin briefcase in the man's hotel room are found four forged passports from different countries. A formal note of protest is delivered to the West German embassy.

In the spring of 1955 the BBC broadcasts a radio documentary series on the lives of gypsies in England. Young reporter Rebecca Highsmith spends several months with a Romany family on their meandering caravan journey along the east coast. It was a programme that lacked nothing, the corporation's yearbook later said, from penetrating portraits to revealing live recordings. You could almost smell the chicken soup and *Bukoli*, the black, peppery bread baked over an open fire, the hard labour of horse slaughter and tanning; and the conclusion of a *Kris*, the gypsy court where judgement is passed according to common law. The band of gypsies includes survivors of Hitler's death camps.

In one recording, made beside a crackling campfire, a man recalls his experience in Buchenwald, and a pipe-smoking old woman, victim of Mengele's experiments, breaks down when the questioning gets too intrusive. We recognise her voice as that of the woman who watched over Josef Rubashov as he lay unconscious in the ghetto.

In the final programme of the series, the old woman dies and Highsmith attends the three-day mourning vigil. At the funeral feast, a 'gypsy comedian' performs, a white-haired old man who speaks with a Russian accent. His name is said to be 'Nikolai the Immortal'. Highsmith describes what she sees:

'He's a comic . . . a sort of clown . . . I don't really know how to explain this. Perhaps it's to do with the gypsies' belief in a transition phase before the dead person reaches the kingdom of the dead; she has to be placated now, so she doesn't come back and haunt them . . . There are people everywhere, crowding round the comedian. They're talking Russian and Romany . . . now let's see . . . no, he's more a sort of fakir . . . he's walking through fire . . . he's walking through the big fire they keep alight in the middle of the camp . . . he's walking on the coals, barefoot on the glowing coals . . . he doesn't seem to feel any pain . . . and now . . . can you hear . . . can you hear the shots . . . they're shooting him . . . they're shooting him with their revolvers . . . and he's responding with a smile . . .'

We don't know what he's doing with the gypsies, or whether he really is related to them in any way; whether his uncanny abilities have somehow made him a cult figure. Nor do we know what has happened to the Doctor; whether they have parted, and if so, why. But one thing is for certain: Rubashov's stay on the British mainland is not a long one.

Later that year he enters a new occult phase, and there is a woman at his side. There is a description of the couple from a coven on the Isle of Man, led by the spiritual heir of Crowley, Gerald Brosseau Gardner. He writes in a letter to Marie Cunningham, the sect's leader in London, of the two disciples' arrival: 'One is the Russian who was once in communication with Lord Boleskin, the woman is presumably his wife.' They rent a room close to the monastery. They participate quietly in the seances. They often sit hand-in-hand, but according to Gardner they want nothing to do with the rituals of a more sexual nature. 'There is a forcefield around them,' he writes. 'The spirit world is uneasy!'

We don't know who she is or where she's from, but Gardner describes her as a lady of young middle age and of central European descent.

183

In March 1956 Gardner writes to Cunningham again. The Russian and his woman are said to have impaired Gardner's 'aura'. To Gardner's vexation, some sect members have broken away and formed a new community in which the mysterious Russian is worshipped as the 'Black Pope'. 'They are utterly wild,' he writes, 'and believe the Russian is in touch with the Evil One.' There are rumours that the man has signed a contract with the devil, and in a postscript Gardner refers to a bet he had with the Russian about the destruction of a strange paper document. 'I lost five pounds and a pint of bitter,' he admits. Soon afterwards, the couple vanish from the Isle of Man.

We know them to be riding the wave of a new spirituality sweeping post-war Europe. Anthroposophy. Theosophy. The teachings of the young Anton la Vey. The Mexican 'Santerían'. White Eagle Lodge. Martinus. The Linbus Society. OTO. The Secret of the Knights Templars.

They appear as guests of honour at a Faust seminar. At a conference on clairvoyance, they sit alongside Hermann Joseph Metzger, Chairman of the Psychosophic Society. They take part in the centenary of the Illuminatio Order and spend several weeks in an alchemical laboratory in Wales. In June 1956 they come more sharply into focus. It is in connection with the possessed boy Lucio in Salerno, in Italy.

This high-profile case of possession by demons occurs around Easter, and a friar from a nearby Capuchin friary, Father Ambrosio, takes on the task of exorcising the evil power. A letter from the friary council to the Vatican describes the boy's torment. Vinegar runs from burst pustules, his fever rises to a temperature of more than fifty degrees Celsius, a cacophony of voices and languages gushes from his mouth. But the written account falls into the wrong hands and is copied by the press. The inevitable hysteria erupts. Amid the afflictions of life in post-war Italy there is a great hunger for sensations. The friary is besieged by journalists, and to give the boy some protection, he is secretly moved to a village in the Umbrian hills.

In mid-July, before any improvement in him is detectable, another letter is dispatched to the Vatican. This refers to a mysterious traveller who arrives one morning on foot from the north, wearing a dusty suit and old-fashioned spectacles, and carrying a leather attaché case under his arm. He is exhausted, and claims he is being pursued, though he declines to say by whom.

The friars let him stay the night. The next morning before going on his way, he asks to see the boy. He falls on his knees at his bedside, at which Lucio writhes in dreadful contortions and utters hoarse curses. The traveller then bursts into tears, and without a word leaves the village, heading south.

Shortly afterwards, the letter continues, two more strangers come walking over the mountains from the north, 'an itinerant faith-healer in the company of a reticent woman'. They ask the way to the house where the boy is being cared for, and there they ask to speak to Father Ambrosio. The letter says that they then question him about the man to whom the friars recently gave shelter, but Ambrosio, pleading his vow of silence, declines to answer their questions.

A third letter again refers to the couple. They have stayed on in the village and are helping the friars to treat the boy. The 'faith-healer' seems obsessed with the case, 'as if his own salvation were at stake', comments Ambrosio. He assists the friars with their rites and undertakes the day-to-day nursing of the boy.

One evening the couple are given permission to go in to the boy unaccompanied. The friars, who are waiting outside, hear screams and voices; unknown tongues fill the house and four crucifixes fall from the walls. As the uproar reaches a crescendo, they rush into the room. The faith-healer and the woman are stretched on the floor, praying in Russian. For the first time in weeks, the boy is sleeping a calm and peaceful sleep.

According to the letter, this event leads to an improvement in the boy's condition. He gradually regains his health, and the couple stay on in the village during his convalescence. In the evenings, the man sits with the farmers in the local bar. He says he has now given up his hunt for the one he is seeking. The friars note his unprecedented good fortune when playing cards and laying bets. Early in September, the couple take their leave; a papal communication has summoned them to the Vatican.

In the notes left by Pope Pius XII, preserved in the Vatican library, one can read about his meeting with the peculiar faith-healer and his woman. The first meeting takes place in a room at Castel Gandolfo.

Pius asks their names and occupation. Rubashov introduces himself as Grigori Ruslov, his woman as Maria Ruslova. They enigmatically ask to be excused giving details of their occupation.

An attendant from the Swiss Guard serves amontillado and fruit in a state room overlooking the Alban hills. The following topics are touched on: demonology, exorcism and sicknesses caused by spirits; the Russian proves surprisingly well informed. The Pope enquires about the state of Lucio's health, and is informed that the boy has entirely recovered.

At a second meeting a few days later the guests sit with Pius in his private library. This time they drink tea rather than amontillado; this time the faith-healer is considerably more forthcoming. With some embarrassment he asks Pius to forgive his secretiveness at the previous meeting. He says he regrets his presumption before God's representative on Earth. He is a sinful man, damned to perdition for all time, and from someone damned to perdition for all time one can expect no better. 'I have seen too much,' he says. 'I have seen more than one human being can bear. The burden of memories is crushing me. How shall I find the strength to have faith?'

Pius cites the early fathers of the Church: 'The battle between consciousness and instinct is what creates the expression of the individual soul. The victory of consciousness is called virtue. The victory of the blind animal is called sin. But without the battle against sin, there would be no virtue, for virtue is no more than the victory won by the principle of good over evil, just as sin has its origin in the inverse relationship. All the evidence, sir, points to your being in the thick of this battle, but you will emerge from it victorious.'

During these meetings the woman is constantly at the Russian's side. Pius describes her as statuesque and serenely calm, wearing a deep-red dress. He dwells at some length on her dress. He notes the way the buttons fasten, the buckle on the belt, the shape of the collar, the mystical signs embroidered round the bottom of the sleeves, and the description is so exhaustive that we suspect it may symbolise something else. The woman nods in agreement with everything the Russian says, and sometimes gives him such a devoted look of sympathy and love that the Pope blushes.

Their stay in Rome is also documented photographically. We see them from a distance, hand-in-hand at a trattoria on Piazza Navona. We see them walking along the banks of the Isola Tiberina and closely entwined beneath a street lamp at the Forum Romanum. All around them, the pictures seem to be trying to say, lie the remains of history, decay, time's erosion of materials, as reminders, pin-pricks on the surface of their love . . . They are embracing on some steps above the Palatine, and on a beach at Anzio, Josef Rubashov is wrapping the woman in a towel. They look happy, wholly embraced by their love. Josef Rubashov appears unaware that he's being watched. The woman, on the other hand, is looking towards the camera lens on more than one occasion.

The final meeting takes place at the start of October, late one evening at the observatory. This time the faith-healer asks to confess to the Holy Father in private. We do not know what is said or what happens during the confession, other than that it leaves the Pope very agitated. Information from assistant secretary D'Annunzio indicates that the Russian asked questions about the Vatican's silence on the question of the genocide of Europe's Jews a decade earlier. Condemnation from the Vatican could have brought about the shutting of the gas chambers. We know that the Council was aware of Kurt Gerstein's project as early as 1942, but until the German collapse there was no papal condemnation. Quick action from the Vatican could also have forced allied bombing raids on the death camps.

Other sources intimate that the faith-healer asked for help on a spiritual matter. We know that Pius the next day sends a personal courier to the imprisoned Cardinal Mindszenty in Hungary, who at this time is the Catholic Church's leading demonologist and critic of Communism. There may possibly be a connection. It is conceivable that Josef Rubashov is the courier in question. For the next time we hear anything of the mysterious couple, it's from Hungary.

In Budapest at the end of October 1956 Colonel Pal Meter, the self-appointed leader of the uprising, is sitting in a military jeep on the way to the Kilian barracks. On the cine film we see his grim, dogged expression and the buildings on fire behind him, with a burned-out Russian tank in the foreground. This is a biotope of death: corpses in the streets, bloody limbs, remnants of faces, fragments of bodies, crying people bending over the dead and kissing their cheeks. We see a young woman in a gunpowder-spattered poplin coat pulling the pin out of a hand grenade, and students aiming volleys of rifle fire into a building where the hated security police are hiding. There's no sound on the film, but it isn't hard to imagine the pandemonium: the screams, the explosions, the wailing, crying voices. And everywhere the reek of cordite and fresh blood, cold sweat, mortal dread and corpses.

The camera rests for a moment on a doorway. A woman in a vibrant red dress swiftly averts her face, and a man enfolds her in his coat. We see him kissing her hair and stroking her back. For two seconds of complete stillness, the cameraman freezes his face. It's the face of someone in love. It's a face from which love flows unalloyed. It's Josef Rubashov.

Something is coming to an end in Budapest. Rumours run round the city. The order of Europe has been rocked. Street fighting in the Hungarian capital. Simultaneously, in London and Paris, in the shadow of the Hungarian tragedy, the attack on Suez is being prepared. It's the usual European sickness: intrigues, double standards, hypocrisy.

Finally, some scenes from the final day of the uprising: the German photographer Vögeli's pictures for *Life* magazine, which create quite a stir. On a pavement, an old man is kneeling in front of what we initially assume to be a woman lying wounded. But on closer inspection – and this is very surprising – we see what it is: a dress, a red dress, spread on the pavement, as if the body lately wearing it had suddenly vanished into thin air.

The man's face is turned to the camera. That unimaginable grief, those eyes in which the pain of the whole world is amassed. He looks as though he is shuddering violently. There seems to be a scream pent up inside him. And behind him, the red fabric is blowing away.

Twenty metres away, another man stands watching. He is not in sharp focus, and is half-obscured by a car, but grief is flooding from him as well, and he, too, is crying. It's the clerk from the start of the century, with a camera in his hand.

Congress at the Watchmaker's

What is this place? Cramped, dark, musty. We're crawling along the floor, with some effort it must be said, over fluff and uneven surfaces and cracks, disguised as . . . well, it doesn't matter . . . a cockroach perhaps, or a spider. And the din: it's deafening. Ticking and striking, ringing and rattling, and a cuckoo calling although it's the middle of winter.

This place is, quite simply, full of something. Time! Time fills every cranny. It saturates the air and drops from weights and clappers and lever escapements; it hangs like bats by its feet from the ceiling.

Up the wall here, camouflaged as . . . let's say a woodlouse, that nice little insect of the dark; definitely one of our favourites. Forget your vertigo. Don't look down. And now we're crawling along a shelf. Good God, it's loaded with the most extraordinary objects. Hourglasses and water clocks, ornamental mantelpiece clocks, big silver pocket watches, equation clocks, astrolabes, timepieces and ingenious conversion tables devised by the astronomer Flamsteed. At last we are beginning to get some kind of overview. He is . . . or was . . . in Holland. At an old watchmaker's in Amsterdam; in a dark watchmaker's workshop, wearing a grubby loden coat, with an earthenware flask of Hollands gin in his pocket.

It was autumn, we can add now that we can see and hear a little better. A scrap of starry sky was winking through a dormer window.

There were shooting stars to be seen: meteorites, a sparkling cipher becoming ever less distinct, blurring together for us, just as the years were blurring together for Josef Rubashov and assuming the consistency of sticky porridge, or a soup that has been boiling for an eternity, so every ingredient and seasoning has lost its savour and been reduced to a mealy, greyish purée. He was old now; and very much worn down.

'Look at this,' said the watchmaker, pointing a bony finger: 'A wall clock from Krakow, made by master craftsman Görtz in the fifteenth century. Two faces. One for measuring the temporal hours, and another for measuring the natural hours. You see, our way of measuring time hasn't always had the monopoly. In Görtz's time, the day was divided into twelve night hours and the same number of day hours. They varied in length, of course, depending on the season. In winter the day hours were shorter and the night hours were longer. Imagine winter in the far north. There, a daylight hour would sometimes be no longer than fifteen minutes. It wasn't something people worried about. An hour was an hour, no matter whether it was short or long.'

The watchmaker moved on, leaning on his stick. And we followed, of course, for what else would we do?

'Eighteenth century,' he said, pointing to a new object. 'The horological revolution. The emergence of the torsion pendulum. Samuel Winston made clocks that only deviated by three seconds a month. The better the clocks became, the more bewitched people were by them. A hundred years earlier, no one minded if a clock gained or lost an hour or two a day. But it's a fact about man and his machines: they challenge him; he wants to improve them, he wants minute hands and second hands and ever more precise measurement. People were as if possessed. The more exact time became, the more dependent people were on it.'

What an old man this watchmaker was. Age had turned in its tracks; his face was so aged that the wrinkles had been smoothed out. He looked like a child; it was as if everything went in circles, the years carrying them back to childhood again.

'This, see, is an American railway timetable. In the nineteenth

191

century there were hundreds of different times. People still set their clocks by the midday sun, so it couldn't possibly be the same time in Boston as in Salt Lake City, could it? In America, there were seventy-six different times running concurrently. There were varying times at different railway stations. And the train had its own time. The clock in the train might show eleven, but the station clock would strike twelve, and in the next town it would be striking one. What confusion. The hours were living parallel lives . . .'

They entered a long, dark corridor. Grandfather clocks stood in rows, like pilasters. Watchcases gleamed. Gilded hands shuffled round clock faces hand-painted with forest scenes. He had to make sure he moved carefully amongst these treasures. His intoxication demanded it. With his reptile brain, staggering, hiccuping; the malfunction of motor skills, the breakdown of thought. At the zenith of a drinking binge that had lasted for four solid years, interrupted only by a few hours' sleep at totally random intervals on the park benches of whatever town he was in, with his belongings in a bag under his head: a shirt, a bottle, an old contract. And his dozing had been almost dreamless; more a kind of illustrated version of being awake.

'This clock belonged to Immanuel Kant,' said the watchmaker. 'In his view, time only exists within us. It's an inborn tool, an ingenious mental tool, that we use to impose order on the chaos of sensual impressions. Time was a phobia for Kant. His whole house was full of clocks and huge star charts and tables, which he could use to work out how the celestial bodies would be aligned on a particular Thursday evening in 2004. His habits were so regular that people set their watches by him. Many great men were slaves to time, did you know that? Sir Isaac Newton. Napoleon Bonaparte. Are you listening, Mr Rubashov? It was Rubashov, wasn't it, Josef Rubashov?'

So he knew his name. How odd. He had no recollection of having introduced himself. But then, he had no recollection of how he had got here. It was those gaps in his memory again. Those sudden power cuts: short circuits, the white spots of amnesia.

'Why do you drink, Rubashov?'

'What concern is it of yours?'

'It's no concern of mine. There's a time for everything. To love. To drink. It's a proverb now, but for our ancestors it was a fact. Every task had its time. Watchmaking time, for example. Or looking after the animals. It couldn't be measured with clocks. Our ancestors would have laughed at us. Every process contained its own time, like a world in itself.'

Processes? Their own time? If there was a time outside time, it was the drinker's. The past became hazy. The future was an unplayed card. You lived in the present. Spontaneity was the watchword. Don't give a damn about tomorrow, the demon within you would whisper, and forget yesterday. Do what you feel like doing . . . Drinking and grieving. That was what he did. Even though she had never really existed. And had he not been immortal, but a member of some animal species, or perhaps a swan, he would probably have pined to death for the want of her. He would have withdrawn into a forest somewhere and lain down under a damp bush, never to wake again. That was the scale of his loss. For his love for her had known no bounds. He had loved her as he once loved his wife, but separately, in a different sphere, since one love could never be like another. But now she was gone. She had been a bluff, a pawn in the game being played for his immortal organism, catapulted out of damned time, dispersed like human ashes, dust, mist blown on the wind. It was truly cruel of us.

'Dear watchmaker. Can you explain something to me?'

'What's that?'

'What am I actually doing here?'

'What are you doing here, Mr Rubashov? What a question. You are expected, of course . . .'

That took him by surprise. The fact that he was expected. Or was the watchmaker a crony from the nearest tavern? It was all the same, he thought. There was nothing left, however you looked at it. Only drinking. *Good health, Mr Watchmaker . . . let's forget everything about time and clocks. Let's drink. On the eighth day, God created aquavit so mankind could forget the disgustingness of Creation.* For thus it was. He used alcohol to try to forget. As he used hate. Because he hated existence, and existence . . . might as well admit it . . . hated Josef Rubashov. It spat on him as he sat with his bottle in the parks. It put him in drunkards' cells. It pointed its finger at him as he staggered around the squares of the towns, hiccuping and drivelling like a village idiot, and sometimes crying as he mourned.

'Look at this.' The watchmaker had stopped in front of a square case. 'Look, Rubashov! One of Taylor's stopwatches. Nineteenth century. Industrialisation. Time becomes money. Piecework rates, the rationalisation of time, machines, conveyor belts, clocking on. Saving time. What an absurd statement! Have you thought about this: an industrial worker produces many times more per unit of time today than fifty years ago. But a poet? Tell me: can a poet save any time? Doesn't a poem have just as long a gestation now as it did then? A poem has its own time. It doesn't take a week or an hour to write, it takes its own time. The poet cannot write quicker. So he's become dearer. So who can afford poets? And who can afford to write poems? The poets are dying out, Rubashov. Is it any wonder the world looks as it does?'

Good Lord, what macabre sort of place is this? A long, dark corridor with no end, dust, spiders' webs, a crazy old watchmaker. And out there, in the depths of space, unbelievably enough, there was a human being. Their rationalisation had got them to that point. Time and progress had brought them that far. Out into space.

'Excuse me, I'm drunk, it's true, but there's been mention of the possibility of visiting other planets. And it struck me that perhaps they'll find a paradise out there. A natural state. A garden of Eden inhabited by other beings. Do you think it possible?'

He suddenly felt lucid. On occasions the alcohol surprised him with insights, rays of concentrated light, unbearably intense . . . But if there was a paradise there, he thought, then mortals would destroy it; they would sow their evil and laugh as they harvested its rotten seed; for that was how they were: impenitents, damned to perdition.

'Did you say something, Mr Rubashov?'

'No. Nothing important.'

'I thought I just . . . How are you feeling? You look pale.'

'You're so shrewd and clever and know everything about clocks and hourglasses, can't you explain to a poor layman what it's really all about?'

'What what is about, Mr Rubashov?'

'Time, what in damnation is time for?'

'What questions you do ask. Who do you think I am? God?'

'It doesn't matter who you are. I just wish somebody could give me an explanation. I've been given an overdose of time.'

The watchmaker opened the case of a grandfather clock. Its belly was exposed, full of metallic intestines: cogwheels, weights, pinions, balance wheels, chains, clappers. He wound up the mechanism with a key.

'Augustan believed time is constantly appearing in us, like cream being piped out of a piping bag. Others maintain that time consists of a number of passing presents, and that the present is the shortest or longest interval of time an individual can perceive as a moment. Others again believe time consists of nerve impulses of some kind. The neurones of our brain, they say, emit signals at a frequency of fifty a second. And these impulses then move through our nervous system. Without interruption, our whole lives, this clock is ticking inside us . . . Perhaps in actual fact there are several times running concurrently. After all, the past is living within us in the form of memories, but people remember differently, and no two people's past is the same. Thus time is also different for every individual. So we live simultaneously in thousands of times, crossing and diverging and leaving different traces in our minds . . .'

He drank. What did he really care about time? As far as he was concerned, it could creep or crawl, slither or hobble or skip rope or sit hidden under a floppy hat somewhere in a Mediterranean trattoria, fast asleep. It could exist in whatever form it wanted, in lengths and breadths, crosswise, this way and that, up and down or drawn off into bottles. It all left him unmoved unless it could serve his purpose. He just wanted to sink; sink like a stone, down into the mild herbal bath of alcohol and forget everything . . . Oh, little Maria Medea, the bluff, the illusion, the great love of his old age.

How could he forget? The meltdown of his emotions, the Sabbath bread of his heart. She had been like a wife, like a sister and a mother and a companion and a father confessor in his dark moments. Time had snatched her away from him, too, undressed and uprooted her and tossed her onto the rubbish dump of history, with the help of . . . well, unfortunately, *us*.

They had stopped in front of a door, a thick oak door with rusty ironwork.

'The clocks have cheated us out of history, too,' said the watchmaker. 'According to the clocks, it's over. When events happen, they are thrown out of time; they are washed ashore on the immovable bank of history, while we sail on down the river – or so the clocks would have us believe. But is it true, Rubashov? Look back over your own history. Isn't it constantly changing, being re-evaluated, being reinterpreted by you? An event today will naturally have consequences for the future; something happens to cast new light on old events, and history suddenly connects with your present in a new way. By that reckoning, the past is just as living and mobile as this moment. It, too, continues down the river of time, though on another course. And artefacts, Rubashov, aren't they still all around us? This door, for example, was made in the fourteenth century.'

The watchmaker touched the handle lightly.

'One last thing, Mr Rubashov, in answer to your question. The best representation of time is perhaps to be found in books. Observe how writers playfully bring it to light. What is a novel, if not an attempt to lay bare the nature of time? There the present is blended with the past and the future. As you read the beginning, you know the end has already been written; it exists concurrently and in parallel, a hundred pages on. Time manifests itself in all its variety. It takes a certain number of minutes to read from A to B, but during that time you make associations both backwards and forwards. In a single line, ten years can pass, and it may take a whole page to describe a single, tiny second. The writer can stop time or accelerate it. He can duck and dive through chronology. So time in all its richness is made manifest in the world of novels.'

The watchmaker stopped speaking, and produced a key from his pocket.

'What are you waiting for?' he asked. 'The meeting has begun, Mr Rubashov. The meeting of time. And you are the guest of honour.'

He put the key in the lock and turned it. There was a click, but the sound was drowned out by a chorus of chimes as all the clocks in the workshop began to strike.

'And think no more of love,' he said, louder this time, to be heard above the din. 'Pull yourself together, Rubashov. You've a lot left to do. Now go on in! The meeting is nothing to do with me. I'm just the host. I offer my premises as landlord of time, so to speak.'

What was the nature of this meeting for which they had assembled in the back room of the old watchmaker's workshop? And who were these people sitting round the table? Antique people, more dead than alive, who had climbed out of the chasm of history with a veneer of mould and old sins on their faces.

Some of them he recognised. Johann Faust, for example, the learned cripple, with a hump on his back just like Bombast's. Others looked familiar as well: one closely resembled the occultist Saint Germain, and another could well be Gilles de Rais. On a stool in one corner sat a cobbler, bearded and barefoot, wearing a chamois-leather apron with ancient tools sticking out of the pockets: sole cutters, pliers, pegs. Who was it – Ahasverus?

One of them had a swinging pendulum in his hand, and another was scraping away quietly on a fiddle. A third was counting gold coins from a bag, and a fourth saying a prayer. Bent over a plate of black grapes was a man in a toga, with such an unimaginably benign face that he suspected . . . yes, why not, it was John, the disciple.

An alchemist was talking to a woman with skin like parchment, and right beside them, sword in hand, stood Paracelsus. There was a buzz of conversation, a chinking of glasses and drinking of toasts. And suddenly someone touched his shoulder, and when he turned round the butler was standing there, Philip Bouhler's butler from the villa in Berlin. 'Well, look who's here,' he whispered. 'Make yourself at home, Kolya. We've been waiting for you.'

He took him under the arm and started to lead him round.

It was a large room, he saw now, an enormous hall, full of books and oak furniture that was black with age, with a layer of dust ten centimetres thick carpeting the floor. There were wax candles burning in brass candelabras.

'You're late,' said the butler. 'We'd expected you to show up before now, but you were busy. Your quest makes you blind to the good things in life.'

'What sort of party is this?' he said. 'And who are you?'

'Me? Who do I look like? Gilles de Rais? I'm the butler, Kolya. The butler! We've met before, you know.'

They walked in a half-circle round the edge of a huge table.

'And love has been plaguing you, we understand, perfidious love. Come come, Kolya, man is in space, and on earth there's a Cold War; progress is undeniably interesting, you ought not to be burying yourself in the futilities of the heart. They're not for us, haven't you learned that lesson yet?'

He indicated the man in the frilled shirt who was swinging the pendulum:

'There's Cagliostro,' he said. 'The cleverest of magicians, but a slave to his brooding. Take him as a dreadful warning. His broodings have become his shackles. He hasn't spoken a word for a century.'

The butler stopped by the man counting gold coins, an ancient figure in medieval attire.

'Raymond Lullus,' he said, 'the maker of gold. A true veteran. The father of the elixir of life.'

The old man stopped arranging his coins in piles and turned to Josef Rubashov.

'You look haggard,' he said. 'Take the advice of an older man and lay off the drink. It's done for stronger men than you.'

Lullus gave him a friendly smile. The sediment of centuries lay in his eyes; a thousand disappointments and wanderings without end.

'Take this,' he said. 'To remember me by.' And he popped a shiny gold coin, a raymondine minted in fourteenth-century London, into Josef Rubashov's coat pocket.

The butler led him on, past long rows of ancient human wrecks, dribbling and senile, rocking in their dry skin, mumbling quietly to themselves.

'What sort of meeting is this?' he asked again.

'Oh, we hold them regularly: same time, same place, you'll find out, Rubashov. And look at you! Your coat in rags, and the smell! How long is it since you took a bath?'

'What business is it of yours?'

'Now, now, it was well meant. You already know Paracelsus, inveterate liar that he is. And here's Ahasverus, the cobbler, our Nestor, the oldest of us all, but severely depressed. A shadow of his former self.'

The cobbler was virtually transparent; his hands were made of dust, he was a relic of a human being, trapped in a never-ending prayer for mercy and compassion, for the chance to rest at last. 'O Lord,' he whispered, 'have mercy, I did not know, O Lord.'

'You seem surprised, Rubashov. Remarkable, that, considering all you've been through. The century has been eventful, has it not? Yet we still have the second half before us. Allow me to introduce Gilles de Rais, the child murderer, and the woman beside him is Countess Elisabeth Bathory-Nadasdy, a jewel, the loveliest of them all. Come come, Kolya, take her hand, the Countess is the famous murderess. She took the blood of six hundred young women to give herself eternal youth.'

More men and women emerged from the shadows, lined, wrinkled, decomposing. At the far end of the table stood an empty chair. In front of it, the table was laid with cutlery, glasses and china for several courses.

'Enjoy yourself, Kolya. You're among friends, among your brothers and sisters in damnation. Who wants to end their days in paradise? Here we help ourselves to the good things of life. And if immortality is really an affliction for you, then get a hobby. It's the only medicine for people like us. In our case it isn't the time that's life-threatening, just the tedium.'

He pulled out the chair for him and motioned to him to sit down.

'Take a seat,' he said. 'The meal's about to start. And heed my advice. Forget love. It's not for our kind.'

The butler was right. Being in love could never be more than fleeting for those condemned to eternity. But he had walked straight into the trap again, eyes wide open.

It had happened in London, one autumn afternoon in 1955 in a bookshop in Oxford Street. How could he forget? The beautiful dark-haired woman standing by the books on chiromancy and healing blue crystals. His memory spared him no details. Her veiled gaze, as if she were permanently just awaking from a pleasant dream. That warm smile. Those nervous hands. And behind her: the window through which he could see the sunshine breaking through for the first time in weeks. Or the shelf of half-bound books on Paracelsus, Donne, Peruchio's work on the Line of Saturn. He remembered it all in dreadful detail, as if it had only just happened, and wished he could remember a little less.

He had been unprepared, but that was what falling in love was like. It attacked you when you were least expecting it. It homed in on the defenceless. It ambushed you from behind in the most treacherous manner. He had capitulated to it in its disguise as an enigmatic smile. It only took an instant. You were coupled up to the invisible generator of love, the forcefield; words were no longer needed because suddenly everything was clear, everything fitted together, the world was transfigured.

Dizzy with falling in love, they had gone to a teashop in Kensington, and then to his room on Chelsea Embankment. There she had read his fate in his palm, for she was a fortune teller, she said, and as his hands told her of his damnation she had cried with sympathy, to the point where he was the one to comfort her.

Oh, he remembered, Maria Medea, the witch, the demon, her sorrow, boundless, like a child's; and he remembered his own sorrow, which came from the thought that this woman – with whom he had fallen in love against all the odds, like a young man, with sweaty hands and throbbing temples – that she would age, that she would one day, very soon from his perspective on time, be taken from him, like the mortal creature he had believed her to be, while he himself would be forced to walk on through the time pockets of the vale of tears, weeping through the millennia, alone and broken by yet another bereavement to add to the long line; and on all these points he was proved right, but in the wrong way, which was more or less what you had to expect, but which you unfortunately never did.

By the light of the table lamp in his shabby room she had told his fortune, reading her way into the filigree of contradictory lines on his hands, but she had overlooked the little break in the line of the heart, the fine pucker that cut the line in two and marked her own disappearance and consequently his own loss; she had forgotten to point that one out to him, and even if she had – would he have listened?

No. Because love rendered him deaf. And the only thing he wanted to hear was the sound of the bells heralding his salvation, and in that she assisted him like no other. She made him promises. She encouraged him. She instilled him with confidence. Obsessed with his salvation, she had sworn to find the one he was seeking.

They had searched day and night. They had journeyed many thousands of miles. They had been guided by her intuition and the visions she had seen in her blue crystals. They had followed scents and trails, hearsay and rumour. And how could he have suspected anything, how could he possibly have had the slightest idea, when they were making love as all other lovers do?

Did spirits of the underworld kneel at your feet and proclaim their love? Did they leave you in a hotel room in Salamanca during a jealous scene, angry and desperate, having smashed the bathroom mirror with the heel of a woman's shoe? Did they send remorseful love letters containing pressed flowers? Did they talk of the evil of the century and the need to look again at the notion of good and evil and redefine the concepts? Did they ingratiate themselves with the great occultists of the age, Brosseau Gardner or the psychosophers, to ask for help in his salvation, only to dissolve into nothingness in Budapest shortly afterwards, leaving merely a red dress behind them?

Yes, they did. They deviated in an unsettling way from traditions. So was it any wonder he was astonished?

But he knew why she had vanished. Or he had his suspicions:

One night during their stay in Rome, he had awoken from a dream in which they had been sitting on a mountain ridge, looking out over a dusky landscape. She had leaned towards him to kiss him, but just as her lips were about to touch him, he suddenly found himself sitting a metre from her. She moved to his side and tried again, but once more, as if by an invisible hand, he was moved a metre further away. So it had gone on until he awoke from the dream in a cold sweat. Then he understood with devastating clarity. He no longer wanted salvation. For if he got it, he realised, he would die, and his loss would be of the same dimensions as if the opposite happened, and she disappeared. The logic was crystal clear. He didn't want to lose her. He no longer wanted his mortality back. He wanted eternity.

That was where his crime lay. He wanted eternal love, for he had come to love this woman so much that he could not bear the thought of ever losing her. The logical consequence of this was that they would continue the search, not to ask for mercy, but rather to ask a profane favour: that the woman be allowed to join the ranks of the immortal, uniting them until the end of time.

But in that decision, he surmised, lay his tragedy. For that loophole was not part of his punishment. On the contrary, it would undermine the whole point of it. Because the loneliness, the bereavements, were its sine qua non. In this way, too, the essential nature of being in love was revealed to him: it only exposed what you wanted to know, it only inspired you to dream, while everything else, all the unpleasantness, it kept hidden behind its back, smiling on its victim with white teeth that were merely sham.

He told her all this. He proposed continuing the search, but with the aim of having her, too, accepted into the company of the immortal. And that was when she disappeared. Shortly afterwards. That was when she had dissolved, in the city of Budapest. That was when she no longer fulfilled a function; or it was when she accomplished her real task. To leave him in the lurch as he stood at the height of his love, to leave him crushed, broken and unhappier than ever.

It was cruel of us, we admit; really artful.

The meal at the watchmaker's was still in progress, but he got up and made for the door. Paracelsus was observing him, without recognising who he was. He put the bottle aside. It wasn't helping, he thought; he couldn't forget her, it wasn't getting him anywhere.

The butler was waiting at the door.

'Are you leaving already?' he asked. 'Come come, why don't you help yourself to all this time? Is it boring you, Rubashov?'

A spider crawled across his cheek, down his neck and onto his shirt collar.

'Yes,' he said. 'I'm leaving.'

'Perhaps solitude would suit you better. Living far away from other people.'

'Perhaps. Maybe I should try to avoid them.'

'Take my advice,' said the butler. 'Seek out a desolate place. That's what it says in our tract: Seek solitude.'

'Perhaps. All I want to do is forget.'

The spider crept across the butler's shirt collar, onto the headrest of the armchair . . . onto that leather-smelling, dusty surface, where it was difficult to make progress over the many obstacles, cracks and slits.

The butler smiled.

'It's ennui,' he said. 'Our arch-enemy, ennui.'

And as the buzz rose from the lugubrious chamber where the living dead were holding their meeting, and amnesia and eternity reigned, Josef Rubashov raised his eyes to the dormer window. Out in space, he thought, there was a human being, a cosmonaut, utterly alone. And he wished it could have been him.

An Attempt at Hermit Life

(1961–3)

Confidential
Captain Littbarski
MSS Patrol Area Chausseestrasse
Berlin

Comrade Littbarski,

As indicated in the previous memorandum, the Ministry leadership is extremely anxious to clear up the mystery of the fugitive from the Republic in the Boyen-Gartenstrasse sector. At the last meeting with Comrade Mielke at MSS Ruschestrasse, the following questions were raised:

How did the man get into the restricted area?

How long has he been in the area (approx. date of sighting?)

Can his movements be tracked – is there a system to his changes of location?

How does he avoid our alarm systems? (Comrade Erb, responsible for the Acker-Brunnenstrasse sector, has opted to carry out a technical check of the automatic firing devices – who in your area could undertake a similar check? Lieutenant Meyer?)

How does the man escape the dogs? Could he have established a 'relationship' with the animals? Has the matter been raised with the dog handlers?

Finally:

What does the man live on? How does he obtain supplies? Should help from collaborators on our side be suspected? Have any break-ins in our storage compounds been reported?

In accordance with the resolution (see attached minutes) the matter has been placed on the desk of Comrade W.U. for the special attention of Politburo member Mielke.

Your speedy response is imperative. Answers to be sent to Reinecke, MSS Appraisal Unit C4.

Courier's Bag
Confidential
Reinecke
Appraisal Unit
Ministry for State Security
Ruschestrasse, Berlin

Comrade!

In accordance with instructions from Becker, Lieutenant Meyer is setting a new mantrap in the area of Boyen-Gartenstrasse, St Hedwig's churchyard and the Spandau Canal (see attchd diagram). Meyer thinks this likely to produce a satisfactory result in the matter of the fugitive from the German Democratic Republic before the weekend.

As regards the breaching of the defensive barrier, Meyer has put forward the hypothesis of a break-out from the property Brunnenstrasse 138, where the cellar has not yet been adequately sealed. The man could possibly have gained access to the patrolled area through one of the coal holes (20 x 30 cm), which the technicians had ruled out despite the protests of the patrol commanders (see my submission 'Strengthening of the anti-fascist defences in patrol area 4'). Another potential route, according to Sergeant Köhler who has served longest in this sector, is St Hedwig's churchyard, which has still not been closed to mourners. Köhler thinks it would be feasible to dig a tunnel from one of the larger family graves – but in that case we should have found where it emerged into the prohibited zone.

Our first sighting of the man dates from June 17th, i.e., six months ago. (Report from former guard Janssen of having sighted the fugitive as early as November the previous year is not considered credible by Meyer or myself.) According to evidence from privates Kerbach and Müller, the man was discovered asleep under a tank-trap. They state that they opened fire, whereupon the man (uninjured!) fled under cover of darkness in the direction of the Spree. (Kerbach maintains he emptied a whole magazine into the suspect from a distance of no more than ten metres – the event led, as you are aware, to a preliminary inquiry, after which K. remains suspected of aiding and abetting escape from the Republic. Re Janssen's evidence: this can perhaps be explained by his excessive alcohol consumption following his wife's death.)

In reply to your question about the pattern of the man's movements: these are unpredictable – no system is discernible. Herzl, guard commander at Johannistal/Teltow Canal, reported the same irregularity of movement during August, when the man was in the south-eastern sector of the wall; all reports indicate that he covered many tens of kilometres within the restricted area during the period August/September (see reports of sightings from the other districts, including Potsdam).

His tactics for evading our alarm systems, particularly the new mines, are as much a mystery to us as to you. With regard to the dogs, there is nothing to indicate that the man has built up any 'relationship' with them. (Ingrid's bitch puppies, Ingridchen I, II and III, were put down in May after the unfortunate incident with the two alleged Russian officers; the new animals, may I say, are of another calibre entirely.) On the contrary, we have found pieces of cloth from the man's clothes, which appear to have been torn off him by the dogs.

As regards the provision of supplies, Meyer has put forward the theory that the man is eating the carcasses of the common hares that occasionally get caught in the traps, especially on the carpets of spikes at Kielerstrasse; or that he somehow manages to steal food from the dogs.

Another question raised during discussions among the guards is where the man spends his days. Since almost all sightings of him are in the evening or at night, one wonders if he has some kind of hiding place – an as-yet-undiscovered bunker or similar – or whether he goes back through the inner sealed line to Berlin-Mitte.

The new guard-duty roster permits me to remain in the Chausseestrasse area over the weekend. With luck we may have the man in MSS protective custody by Monday.

Littbarski

A soundless screen: the snow whirling and falling in the illuminated circles of the searchlights; a diffuse red light, like diluted fire . . . and there . . . the flakes, the crystals . . . the ground covered in a white pelt . . . the tracks of a hare, almost covered over by the snow, and the tracks of a human being . . . heading east. Then they head back, the tracks, turning off to the outer protective wall, in the direction of the anti-tank obstacles. The footsteps through the snow, plodding, the snowflakes falling, the searchlights blinking, it's hard to see; a sudden wind hurries along the concrete wall, like a messenger, howling, whistling, in a black cloak decorated with cold. The tracks in the snow; now they stop . . . one last step . . . and there, in the lee of an anti-tank obstacle, he sits. He brushes down his coat . . . he stares out into the darkness, scanning the length of the wall as it stretches away to the distant watchtower, to the Spree, to the western sectors where the neon lights are winking and people are hurrying about their business, hunched up, keeping close to the buildings, this windy December evening as the snow keeps falling.

Faithless is the city to which he had returned. Gone were the splendour and the monuments, the Art Nouveau façades, the luxury hotels, Haus Vaterland, the imperial palace, Kempinsky's Bar and half a million people. Tiergarten had been laid waste and nothing was left of the Prinz Albrecht district but a heap of gravel.

They'd built new things instead. A wall, for example. Or two, to be precise, running parallel with each other for scores of kilometres, round half the city in a vast circle. It was a wonder, the eighth wonder of the world. What labour lay behind this monstrous architectural marvel, what technical refinement, what mustering of resources and what political self-sacrifice. It was in the same class as the Pyramids. Or the Hanging Gardens of Babylon. Or the Pillars of Hercules. Even just the building materials it took: all those thousands of tonnes of mortar they had to mix. And the barbed-wire ornamentation, the barbed-wire arabesques, the rolls of barbed wire which, if uncoiled, would go three times round the world – that alone was record-breaking. Or the armies of workers they mobilised: thousands upon thousands of bricklayers, carpenters, concreters, hod-carriers, surveyors, errand boys, engineers, entrepreneurs, and all manner of pompous asses from the Party. It really was a monumental piece of work, a historic feat, a world record for the technical skills of construction.

In the shade of this wonder he had been happy; he and the hares, the sweet little common hares who spent their days copulating and whose tribe therefore increased explosively, along an exponential curve, so they now numbered tens of thousands, or even hundreds of thousands, here in hare paradise. Yes, he had loved it. The peace, the solitude, the changing seasons. Here, he had thought, I could stay for several eternities; this is my no-man's-land, this is my neutral zone, my sanctuary on Earth.

It certainly was a paradise. Man and hare in happy combination, and the animals were so trusting he could pat them, and feed them dandelion leaves in summer. Not a red fox in sight. Plenty of food; clover and crisp, low-growing scrub, tender shoots, and flowers in all the colours of the rainbow. Perhaps very occasionally a military jeep or a guard patrol to break the silence, or an Alsatian that had managed to slip its leash and then ran round barking randomly, gnawing on old footballs kicked over by mistake. But other than that: silence . . . peace . . . a land of milk and honey.

Admittedly he had seen a number of escapees in the early days. People jumping from third-floor windows of the houses still standing along the border, or driving their cars through the barbed wire in places where the wall still wasn't complete; but then it got harder, or at any rate took greater cunning. The Volkspolizei had the buildings along the border demolished or sealed. They strengthened the protective wall and built a new inner fortification. They offered bounties: the guards could earn 250 Ostmark for each human kill, plus a bottle of quality Russian vodka and two days' leave in a Polish brothel. Then came the mines and the automatic firing devices, the electric fences, the beds of spikes, the noise, the fear, the cameras, the splinter bombs, the broken-glass obstacles, the despondency, the dogs and the underwater barriers in the canals. That severely stemmed the flow of escapees, but didn't cut it off entirely.

Human will is so hard to break down. It's like the worst kind of ivy; no herbicide is strong enough. People started planning instead. They got more crafty. Both sides climbed the league table and won promotion to a higher division; the more the Volkspolizei strengthened their defences, the slyer the escapees became. These days, on the rare occasions they happened, the escapes were mounted with far greater refinement. On winches along the power lines, for example. Or in diving gear across the canals. People crept through the sewers or dug tunnels. He had heard them digging away, fifteen metres below the ground. One tunnel was one hundred and forty metres long, and fifty-seven people managed to make use of it before the Volkspolizei flooded it. Another was dug by a dozen energetic pensioners, the eldest of whom had just turned eighty-one. A third was exposed when the entire street above it collapsed like a disastrous soufflé.

The imagination of a human being knows no bounds when it comes to catching and killing, nor when it comes to escaping and getting away; for those are the conditions governing human life, those are the rules by which people have been playing the game for hundreds of thousands of years, and so they went on, never stopping. There were firms of people-smugglers who advertised their services on flyers and in the western newspapers. There were folk who swam across the Spree in rubber rings, and one lot drank the captain of a sightseeing boat under the table, then hijacked the boat and steered it across to the American sector. There were people who forged diplomatic passes or hollowed out the back seats of their cars, like loaves of bread, and smuggled others over the border; and the most supple squeezed into a dance band's amplifier or an ordinary suitcase of laminated plastic.

Some brought ladders and jumped wildly across no-man's-land, but they seldom made it. They died . . . And there was nothing to be done about it, for that was the way they were made, to kill and to die.

One night Rubashov had been woken by shouts of joy as he lay asleep in his undetected bunker in the prohibited zone, and when he climbed out he saw a man floating across no-man's-land in a hot-air balloon, hooting ecstatically. And then there was the most extreme case of all: the lads who went to the cinema on the Kurfurstendamm every Monday night. He knew them well. They got out through a ventilation shaft in one of the sealed houses, bringing with them a rope ladder that somebody attached to a tree for them on the other side of the wall, in a blind spot invisible from the watchtowers. He had spoken to them many times. What are you doing here, they would ask, and of course he couldn't give them an answer. Maybe they didn't expect an answer, either. They just smiled, threw the rope ladder over the wall and waited for their accomplice – some film buff, no doubt, who thought it fantastic that two lads were prepared to risk life and limb to see *Lawrence of Arabia* with Omar Sharif at the Ufa Palace by the Zoo – to fix it into a tree on the other side of the Iron Curtain, and sometimes on their way back they would give him cigarettes.

It was one of those cigarettes, incidentally, that he was smoking as he made his way in the darkness along the death strip, cautiously so as not to trigger any of the automatic firing devices. He was smoking and enjoying the tranquillity produced by absence of other people. Tonight, for example, there was no sign of anybody trying to escape. It was peaceful, deserted, an empty, snow-covered paradise.

Yes, here it was peaceful, but how was it out in the world? There

210

was no paradise there, and nor did anybody expect it. Everyone was waiting for the nuclear winter. One morning near Spandau, Rubashov had looked out over some allotments on the western side. There, a man in a boiler-suit was in the process of building a shelter for himself and his family. He had watched the man work for several hours. It interested him. This desire for survival that was the direct opposite of his own craving. The man excavated a hole the size of a prison cell, and over it, like a thick, protective roof, he parked his car. He filled the car with soil, covered it with tarpaulins, and shovelled a few more cubic metres of earth over the top. He dug trenches for a new water pipe and a sand filter for the dreadful rain that would fall from the doomsday sky; he installed an ingenious ventilation system, an earth closet, and an underground lobby where he presumably planned to hang his contaminated protective suit after he'd been out looking for food or for other survivors in the atomic desert. Finally, he took in large stocks of dried and tinned food: beans, peas, lentils and canned meat, plus a crate of iodine tablets.

'If you are caught in the open,' said the disaster-information manuals that the city authorities were now posting out to the population:

'do not look at the light. A split-second is enough to make you temporarily blind. This is especially important at night, as your pupils are dilated. Within a few seconds of the detonation, blast waves of heat will spread over an area of several dozen square kilometres around the point of impact. Remember that the waves need to hit you in order to harm you. Your only thought must be to take cover. Find a wall or some other fireproof obstacle standing between yourself and the detonation site. Heat, like light, travels in straight lines. Even the smallest obstacle can offer protection: a ditch, a hole in the ground, ground that slopes down in relation to the detonation site. If you are in a car: open a window so the pressure wave does not shatter all the glass. Lie down immediately on the floor or seat. Cover all naked skin as well as you can. Within one minute of the explosion, the first crisis

211

*will be over. Seek out a proper shelter to escape the radioactive
fallout.'*

Rubashov didn't understand them. Why this will to survive? He
was hoping for the opposite. He dreamed of the missiles, the
blinding light, the initial radiation, the residual radiation, the blast
wave and the manna of radioactive rain. He put his hope in the vast
mushroom cloud, the extreme heat that within seconds would
vaporise everything living and dead within twenty kilometres with
a flaming sword whose temperature could match that at the core of
the sun. The prospect of the huge funnel of the bomb filled him
with ecstasy, the mushroom cloud that would form as the heat rose,
leaving a vast vacuum beneath it into which sand and gravel and
pulverised stone – what was left of Berlin – would be sucked up as
if in the draught from a cosmic tiled stove. Or the radiation, the
invisible radiation, that would sever the electrical contacts between
the molecules of the body and send the cells into a micro-level
meltdown. Or the mighty shockwave that could deceive them by
taking another course, shooting up into the outer atmosphere
under cover of their blind terror and travelling five hundred
kilometres before striking again on some part of the Earth where
they were least suspecting it. Or the fallout of radioactive particles!
Just breathing in one tiny, contaminated fragment of dust would do
it; just happening to swallow a single poisoned grain of sand, if you
impolitely happened to yawn in the darkened shelter without
putting your hand over your mouth, because you thought nobody
could see; or getting a microscopic flake of soot in an open wound
. . . then that was basically the end of you; the beta and alpha
particles would wage a ruthless civil war in your body, 'Take no
hostages, no sparing of women and children!' and the gamma
radiation would corrode them down into a foul juice of blood and
human flesh.

Radiation sickness would blight their last days; wasted by attacks
of diarrhoea and stinking vomit, their bodies covered in mauve
patches, gushing fountains of internal bleeding, hair loss, the
unconditional capitulation of the lymphocytes, the desertion of the

white blood corpuscles, the profound resignation and lethargy.

Or the collapse of the central nervous system. The ghastly twitching, the wasting of the muscles, the idling hiccoughs of the heart, the last sigh of the breathing organs, coma and death. Perhaps a couple of them would survive the initial slaughter, but at what price? Cataleptic seizures, brutal leukaemia, kindly lung cancer, and skeletal cancer that made them rot from the centre outwards.

Was that a life?

Perhaps not for a mortal, no, but conceivably for Josef Rubashov.

That was maybe another reason for his being precisely here, in Berlin, because there was international consensus about where the first missile was likely to land. And if his curse proved able to defy even the heat of the sun, at least afterwards he would be able to enjoy great solitude, greater even than that he had found between the walls, once the last of his race had been annihilated in the pyrotechnics of Armageddon . . .

He continued on his way, parallel with Gartenstrasse. The wind, he noticed, had dropped. It was so quiet now he could hear the snowflakes falling and the barbed wire rattling in the breeze.

It was strange, he thought, but almost two years' peace in this depopulated area had calmed his nerves. Months could pass without his seeing a living soul, especially in the southern stretches where security operations had been automated. He might sometimes stop in one place, like here, stay a few weeks, because his existence only offered those two options: walking or resting. He didn't eat any more. He had completely stopped taking nourishment, and it had been over a year since he had last relieved himself.

In his hiding places – an undiscovered potato cellar that had happened to end up in the restricted zone; an old bunker from the war, with one exit accidentally left unsealed – he could lie for days watching the ants or a spider working on its web. He thought: *I am no longer governed by my needs; all my wishes are gone. What purpose do they serve? They simply give rise to others, which must be satisfied at any cost – an eternal sucking on the empty dugs of desire.*

The snow whipped him in the face as he walked on along the

213

guards' path. He wasn't thinking; not a single emotion was active within him, not a single temptation or urge. He had succeeded in attaining the ideal state, a status quo between body and soul, between desire and consideration, instincts and self-extinction; he was quite empty, apart from that vague, gnawing hope that they would give in to their thirst for blood after all, fire off the first missiles and let the winter come – a winter that would make this December look positively tropical.

He walked on, ploughed forward, with snow up to his knees, snow encasing his bare feet, which had long since stopped feeling the cold or the heat . . . he walked . . . and suddenly wasn't walking any more . . . for there was no longer ground beneath his feet . . . it disappeared . . . was pulled from under him . . . and, filled with astonishment, he plunged into a deep pit.

Transcript of Interrogation 1
Nicholaus J. Ruschahof
MSS, Lichtenberg
Present: Comrade Reinecke
          Comrade Wolf
Stenographer: Heimann
MSS archive 11 009

Reinecke: *We asked this before, your name, Ruschahof? Is that really right? It doesn't sound particularly German . . . Are you a member of one of the expelled populations? East Prussian? . . . from Königsberg? . . . are you one of those Katschubs?*
Ruschahof: *No*
Wolf: *There is no citizen of the German Democratic Republic with your name. Why don't you admit it, they sent you from Bonn, didn't they?*
Ruschahof: *Not at all. I'm here voluntarily.*
Reinecke: *Let's put the question another way: is any foreign state involved?*
Ruschahof: *I'm not employed by anybody.*
Wolf: *At your age! What sort of people do they think they're*

dealing with here?

Reinecke: *How long have you been in the area, Ruschahof?*

Ruschahof: *Roughly a year and a half.*

Reinecke: *You're lying. That's impossible. How could you survive? Don't you ever eat?*

Ruschahof: *No.*

Wolf: *Well, what do you do, then? Coprophagate maybe . . . like the hares? My God, what shall we do with this fellow, Reinecke?*

Reinecke: *Our first observation of your movements is dated June 17th. How many times in the period since then have you entered the restricted area?*

Ruschahof: *I've been here all the time . . . I didn't want to get out.*

Reinecke: *And from which direction did you enter in the first place . . . from the western side?*

Wolf: *Or have you got accomplices on our side?*

Ruschahof: *I don't know a single person here.*

Reinecke: *From which side? West or east?*

Ruschahof: *I can't remember . . .*

Wolf: *We want names, Ruschahof! The names of your colleagues. Start with the bosses!*

Ruschahof: *There are no bosses.*

Wolf: *You're lying . . . and you've bought people on our side . . . war agitator! Infiltrator!*

Ruschahof: *I haven't . . .*

Wolf: *Look at me when I'm talking to you, man! This is serious. We can get tough if we need to!*

Reinecke: *Let's take it from the beginning, Ruschahof. How did you get into the restricted zone: parachute?*

Ruschahof: *It was easy back then. You hadn't finished all the building work. I can't remember, I suppose there was some chink to creep through.*

Reinecke: *Would you be kind enough to explain to us where your depots are?*

Ruschahof: *Depots?*

Reinecke: *Provisions and . . . explosives . . . Where are they buried?*

215

Ruschahof: *I haven't buried anything.*

Wolf: *The Trojan horse! They sent you in to blow holes in the wall, that's obvious, the way I see it. Do you know what we used to do with people like you in the old days? Fascists? We chopped you into little bits if we caught you.*

Reinecke: *Can you explain how you during this time . . . and let's not exaggerate now, Ruschahof . . . you can hardly expect us to believe you've been living in no-man's-land without food for almost two years, but the dozen or so times, say, you've been over to reconnoitre and set up your depots.*

Wolf: *And listen, don't think you can convince us you're a fugitive from the Republic. Ruschahof! The hell you are! That name doesn't exist!*

Reinecke: *To get back to what I was saying . . . How have you been able to avoid triggering our alarm systems?*

Ruschahof: *You learn as time goes on where you can walk and where you can't.*

Wolf: *Balls! There must be maps over on your side somewhere. What Judas provided you with the plans? Or is that why you're here: to draw up new ones?*

Ruschahof: *I haven't got any maps.*

Reinecke: *How did you avoid the traps?*

Ruschahof: *I made a few mistakes in the beginning . . . then things improved . . . I even got to know the dogs.*

Wolf: *The bloke's mad. Stark staring mad. What shall we do with him? Shall we exchange him for someone on their side?*

Reinecke: *Come on, Ruschahof . . . a bit of cooperation would be nice.*

Wolf: *Or he can quietly disappear. Which state are you working for? Answer me!*

Reinecke: *Listen, Ruschahof. All we're asking is some willingness to cooperate. We'll take a short break. Then we'll carry on. We won't give up, you know, no matter how much you squirm. We'll never give up . . . Heimann? Did you get all that?*

Transcript of Interrogation 1V
Nicholaus Ruschahof
MSS Lichtenberg
Present: Reinecke
          Philby
Stenographer: Heimann
MSS archive 11 009 d

Reinecke: *Good morning, Ruschahof. This is our special guest . . . Mr Philby . . .*

Ruschahof: *Good morning . . . Are you going to let me go?*

Reinecke: *All in good time . . . You'll be free to leave the country very shortly. Before that, we just want to assure ourselves of your . . . well, cooperation and silence. We hope to remain in contact with you even in the future, contacts that would then be in the hands of Philby here.*

Philby: *Good morning, Nicholaus.*

Ruschahof: *Good morning, Fullbee . . .*

Philby: *Philby!*

Reinecke: *Our investigations have shown that you may well have given correct information, that you really have been out there as long as you claim.*

Ruschahof: *You can think what you like.*

Reinecke: *If true, it must be unprecedented.*

Ruschahof: —

Philby: *You're a remarkable person, Nicholaus. Everything points to it.*

Reinecke: *Truly remarkable.*

Philby: *You have certain unique characteristics . . . never eating, for example. And this sheet of paper you carry about with you?*

Ruschahof: *I'm rarely hungry.*

Philby: *But you haven't eaten a thing since you got here. Four weeks, Nicholaus. Without so much as a crust of bread. How do they train them like you?*

Reinecke: *Are you like a camel, Ruschahof? A blow-out and huge*

217

amounts to drink . . . then you don't need anything for a month . . . until you reach the next oasis.

Philby: *And we have certain perks to offer you at our oasis . . .*

Ruschahof: *Such as?*

Reinecke: *You'll find out, all in good time.*

Ruschahof: *When will you let me go?*

Reinecke: *Soon. If you're willing to cooperate. Comrade Philby will contact you, if so. You're undeniably capable . . . You like the job, I take it?*

Philby: *Don't worry, Ruschahof . . . you can carry on working for your side . . . We can even help you lay your hands on a few normally unobtainable documents. But we need favours in return.*

Reinecke: *It's nothing to be ashamed of, Nicholaus. Philby's been doing it with no trouble . . . You just carry on as usual, but with dual loyalties.*

Philby: *And with double the income!*

Reinecke: *With triple the income . . .*

Philby: *Quadruple, sometimes.*

Ruschahof: *What is it you actually want?*

Reinecke: *It's impossible to be precise at the moment. One never knows when circumstances will require us to call on extra forces . . . You can consider yourself held in reserve, Ruschahof. You'll only be mobilised in case of need . . . and you'll always be approached in person by Comrade Kim.*

Ruschahof: *And when will you let me go?*

Reinecke: *Whenever you like . . . after certain promises.*

Ruschahof: *What difference does it make to me. You can keep me locked up. Throw the keys away: I'm perfectly happy in your solitary confinement cells.*

Philby: *You're a remarkable person, Nicholaus.*

Ruschahof: *Is there anything wrong with wanting to be alone?*

Philby: *We can always put you somewhere else, if the silence gets too much . . . We've got places where a score of people are crammed into five square metres . . . for years on end . . . Would you like to go there, Ruschahof? To Moscow, or further away? We can arrange it. I know lots of places in Moscow. I live there.*

Ruschahof: *For God's sake . . .*

Philby: *So . . . we're finally getting somewhere. Comrade Reinecke, would you mind leaving me and Nicholaus alone for a moment; we have some details to discuss.. You too, Heimann . . .*

Memorandum, Evaluation Unit
(for circulation)
Inofizielle Mitarbeiter 'Ruschahof'
Source: Philby, KGB Moscow, MSS Leipzig

Ruschahof was captured in the restricted zone between the anti-fascist defences on the night of December 12th and immediately taken into protective custody for interrogation at MSS Hauptabteilung Berlin (East). Transfer to Leipzig was arranged by Reinecke on the 18th. The undersigned, having flown in from Moscow, took part in the interrogations.

The man is unknown; it has proved impossible to confirm his identity. Investigations by IM 'Holz' in Berlin (West) have yielded nothing. He is not on counter-espionage lists, nor among those reported missing. Enquiries through Interpol by IM 'Foxhunter' have produced no results. The name Ruschahof is presumably false. He may belong to an older cadre that has been activated after a period of isolation, perhaps in England.

When captured, the man had nothing but the clothes he stood up in. The inside pocket of his coat contained a lead pencil, a cigarette packet of the Cabinet brand, and an illegible paper document. He was barefoot (!).

A medical examination was undertaken by Dr Hirsch, Leipzig:

The man has extremely reduced requirements for liquid and solid nourishment (no traces of narcotics in the urine sample). Resting and working pulse: normal. ECG: normal. Blood pressure: high.

Oxygen absorption: low.

At Reinecke's request, the man underwent psychiatric

examination and was found to be in good mental health. No symptoms of geriatric disorders: memory loss, etc.

The man's age is estimated by Hirsch to be between sixty-five and ninety.

Distinctive features: Wrinkled skin. White-haired. Speaks fluent Russian and German, but with an accent, possibly Czech.

Generally the man appears stable. During his imprisonment he displayed no sign of nerves whatsoever.

After four weeks in protective custody, Ruschahof accepted the offer of an assignment within MSS Foreign Operations. Contact: the undersigned. Outward transit will be via 'Exit Eisenach'. Base: MSS apartment Freiburg, and KGB Hannover, various addresses. Can be reached by telegram or telephone (use scheduled code).

Low state of alert until further notice. Comrade Reinecke has proposed gradual infiltration of the Irish target groups (Belfast, Derry). The man is not required to make reports: all contacts will be made via Berlin (West) and Frankfurt.

One proposed option is to use hitherto inactivated cells to monitor the man for a two-year period; in the meantime no assignments should be delegated to him.

Pay as per standard agreement, with which he seemed satisfied.

See also Appendices: personal case study, interrogation transcripts, medical report, etc.

Comrade P.

Meltdown

(1969)

We are in a street. An empty playground in front of a nursery school. A smashed-up shop. Burning car tyres in dense smoke. Overturned vehicles used as barricades. Piles of broken paving stones. Flags in green, orange and white. We can see people bleeding to death on the footpaths, screaming, howling people, blinded by tear-gas; crowds surging to and fro, black balaclavas on one side, and on the other British forces, also masked, in dark, tinted visors, armed with batons and rifles loaded with rubber bullets, and gleaming water cannon; and behind them: the Ulster Unionists, boys the same age as Liam O'Daherty, the gentle boy whose eyes and binoculars we are currently borrowing, or Stiofain Morrin, who's standing guard outside the room where the prisoner is held.

Rubashov was in West Belfast, the Catholic area of the city. In a dark room with the lights out, together with two men from the Provisional IRA, plus another man, a prisoner from the other side, a poor man from the UDA, Ulster's freedom fighters, who had been shut up with his toys, his bumble bee, his box of matches, in a cleaning cupboard.

But there was also a woman with them. She stood engrossed in an expressionistic drawing on a sheet of paper unrolled on a table. Her name was Fanuela, just like . . . no, let's leave that for a while . . . a beautiful woman of southern Irish origin, from Cork maybe, or Tipperary, who had been smuggled across the border, into the city,

221

by the Dominican friars on Bombay Street – God bless the holy – in a brown cowl, disguised as a monk.

'Look at this, Rubashov,' she said, at the same instant as another gas grenade exploded half a block away. 'Take a close look, because you need to learn this plan off by heart.'

She pointed with one of her long fingers to a cross in one top corner of the map. Her hand was beautiful, he noted; everything about her was lovely: the gentle features under the white veil she now wore, the shapely body in its tunic; she made him think of an angel.

'This is the entrance. Nothing to worry about there. Your pass is genuine, we've just fiddled with the name a bit. And the photograph.'

He looked at the plan, a detailed diagram of an interior with several transparent overlays. *Lancashire*, it said; *English power station. Boiling water reactor. Electrical output: 700 MW.*

'The second checkpoint won't detain you, either. We've managed to get one of our men employed on the security staff, a Finnbar Donnes, whose father was involved in the border campaign. It's after that your problems start.'

She pointed to a second cross. *Reactor vessel*, it said.

'From then on, you're on your own. You'll have to get yourself into the passage under the reactor hall, over this way, to the main circulation pumps. No one must see you. It all hangs on how cool you are.'

She looked up from the plans.

'Why are we doing this, Rubashov?' she asked dully. 'What's our motivation?'

'The slaughter on the Bogside,' he replied. 'The Loyalists want us out of Ulster.'

'They want to wipe us out, Rubashov. They want to wipe us out as a people, and crush our religion. Thirty-six thousand Catholics live in Derry, and only seventeen thousand Protestants. But even so, it's the Protestants that wield the power. Whose fault is that?'

'The English.'

'Not just them. The Protestants are clever, you see. They changed

222

the constituency boundaries to include the country areas, and it's nothing but loyalists there.'

He was aware of her perfume, a scent of grapes and flowers and . . . was it incense, holy incense?

'Last week six men knocked at the door of a house in Cawnpore Road and asked for Mr Behan. Behan's the father of four sons, two of them altar boys, and he's been loosely associated with Sinn Fein since the leafleting campaign in May. He's not in, his wife said, he's gone to sign on the dole at Social Security Office 3. We'll wait for him, they said, we've all arranged to go to the trotting track together. So they sat there in the living room, and some of them had gold crucifixes on chains round their necks, so the wife thought they were Catholics, and they all spoke in West Belfast dialect and sounded as if they worked at the docks. Just sat there, were served tea in the best china cups, and patted the kids on the head; waited for him to come home, with his cheque for twenty pounds. Then they executed him. They killed him, Rubashov, as he stood there in the hall worrying about how he was going to pay the rent. Slaughtered him like a lamb at Easter. Shot him in the back of the neck with a British military pistol. And his wife? Do you know what they did to his wife? They knee-capped her. With a Black & Decker drill.'

Fanuela directed a fierce glance at the prisoner's cupboard.

'We could probably have lived with the discrimination for another year or two. Being excluded from all political influence. Seeing all the state-sponsored building programmes going to Protestant districts. The set-up grants only going to Protestant businesses. Protestants getting gun licences without any checks. We could probably have endured the torture in the British prisons, and the fact that they stick force-feeding tubes down into the guts of the detainees on hunger strike for the right to be treated as political prisoners. But we can't tolerate what's going on now! It's not possible, Rubashov. Not with Protestant snipers on the roofs of West Belfast shooting people outside churches after mass. Or British paratroopers breaking up peaceful Catholic demonstrations, but turning a blind eye when gangs of loyalist murderers can stroll down the street in Clonard slaughtering everything that moves. We can't take any more of this. So we're fighting back. And we're going to win, Rubashov. Because we've got the people behind us. We've got the future ahead of us. More than half of all children born in Ulster today are Catholics. We can thank our faith for that. The only faith. The true faith. Believe me, Rubashov, good will eventually triumph.'

She was right, he thought, as he studied the detail of the plans. They had sympathisers everywhere. There was always a spare bed for a brigadesman on the run. The doctors operated on gunshot wounds without asking any questions. The monks provided hiding places. The Gardai looked the other way as they smuggled weapons across the border.

'So you'll have fifteen minutes to prime the charge,' Fanuela went on. 'For the sake of Ireland and the true faith. The reactor cover will be in position for change of fuel between 15.00 and 16.00. Now look at this. It's the containment cupola. That'll be open too, as will the equipment lock. You'll be directly underneath. The bomb's got a timer. It'll go off at 16.05. At exactly 15.55, Donnes will turn off the emergency cooling system. So you'll have ten minutes to get out.'

'I don't want to get out.'

'You'll die if you stay in there, Rubashov.'

'I hope so.'

'I can't make you out. Why the sacrifice? What we need are cold men, ice-cold men who keep themselves alive as long as possible. There are so many other missions still waiting. We can't lie down and die until we've won.'

'This is a suicide mission. How many of your people are prepared to go in and do this?'

Fanuela smiled.

'Not many,' she said. 'Only you, Rubashov. You're the only one who volunteered for this mission.'

She indicated the plan.

'You won't have time to feel a thing. It'll be an explosion like no other. With the cooling system knocked out, the fuel rods will melt.

And when the molten fuel comes into contact with the water in the reactor, there'll be a steam explosion. What a firework display! They'll hear it as far away as London. Everything'll go sky high: the control room, the waste-storage areas, the transformer, eventually the whole power station. And the meltdown, Rubashov, all that molten material heated to thousands of degrees will sink through the earth, just where you're standing, and turn the whole area to fire and gas.'

Was it true? Might his hour have come? There had to be a limit to what his organism could withstand. There had to be a limit to the scope of the curse. Here, somewhere in the confusion of lines on the plan, his salvation might lie.

Fanuela's walkie-talkie crackled into life. 'Foot patrol making its way up the Kashmir Road,' said a man's voice.

'That's okay. *Morgan?* Can you hear me? Open up a new front on Donville Street.'

'Got you.'

Flakes of soot were dancing in the wind on the other side of the window. The roars were rising from the barricades. Shots were heard a few streets away, where *Morgan* was opening up the new front.

'There's just one other favour we need you to do for us before we send you over to England,' she said. 'You've got to exchange that loyalist pig for one of ours. There's a prisoner swap tomorrow.'

She rolled up the plans and went over to the tiny room where the prisoner was being held.

'Him, I mean. He's the one we're exchanging.'

Stiofain Morrin put the key in the lock. The saint, as he usually thought of him: with those bright-blue eyes that seemed to light up his forehead with a soft, white light, in a circle, almost like a halo.

The room was hardly any bigger than a prison cell. The prisoner was lying on a couple of blankets on the floor. He was holding a matchbox in his hand. With a stub of pencil he had decorated it to look like an electric razor. These were the sorts of little toys he came up with to console himself in his isolation. There was a bumble bee in the matchbox. He'd caught it when it accidentally blundered in

225

through an air vent. When he shook the box, the bee began to buzz, making it sound like an electric razor. He ran it gently over his bearded cheeks.

'We're letting you go tomorrow,' said Fanuela. 'If it was up to me, we'd be executing you. But there's going to be a swap.'

The man nodded and went on rubbing the matchbox round his face. There was something peculiar about him, too. Everyone was so strange in this flat.

'We took him on Bombay Street four weeks ago,' Stiofain Morrin said hoarsely. 'He was leading a group of UDA supporters. They smashed the crucifix in the church. A devil.'

Good and evil, he thought. Catholic – Protestant. He didn't care. All he could think about was the reactor. Ultimately it was technology that was going to save him; technology, which had got them to the moon and the bottom of the sea, which had made them masters of the very core of matter, to the point where they had learned to split its atoms. Technology that could cure all curses, known and unknown. Technology that had given them heart transplants and the organ trade, and pigs' kidneys, which had initially scared him out of his wits, but had then given him such a vitamin boost of hope when it dawned on him: if humankind can make itself immortal, then it ought to be able to make me mortal.

'Rubashov, are you listening?' said Fanuela. 'Tomorrow you're to take him to a pre-arranged point on the Falls Road. One of their top people will meet you there, a woman, someone called Lilith. You stay there with your revolver stuck into this pig's neck until we know our man is safely back. Then you're free to go to England for the last stage of your mission.'

That summer as the nineteen-sixties were about to give way to the seventies, he would dream at nights of the power station. He dreamed he was walking through dark and winding passages with electric cables running like long, brightly coloured snakes along the roof, through a labyrinth of surprises. It was like a ghost train at a fair. Whenever he turned a corner sharply, something unexpected was waiting for him. Once it was a luminous face, a demon's face, looming up at him before vanishing again. Another time it was a black cat falling from a trapdoor in the ceiling. Once, the floor had gaped open in front of him and he had been staring down into an interminable tunnel stretching to the centre of the Earth; and in its depths he could see the meltdown, glowing white-hot. The corridors took him further and further into the building, through huge rooms and brightly lit halls. In one of them hung a mirror, and when he stood and looked into it, his image did not appear on its silvered surface. In another, a picture of the Madonna stood on an altar, and when he touched it, it began to shed tears of blood and address him in Fanuela's voice:

'Destroy me,' she said, 'melt me down . . . into magma.'

A third hall was a kind of glasshouse. Out of the floor grew petrified trees, their branches weighed down with shrivelled black fruits, and there was also a door. He opened it and found himself in a control room; and in an armchair, a burning armchair in front of a vast instrument panel, sat their prisoner with an enigmatic smile, rubbing the buzzing matchbox around his cheeks.

He crept past without a sound. He went through an open airlock and then down a spiral staircase. He was under the reactor vessel now, the vast, cylindrical tank, in a dark canyon of graphite and steel, and from a point somewhere above came a clatter as the cover opened and men in protective suits exchanged the fuel rods.

He opened his bag and took out the primer. He got the nitroglycerine ready, four charges connected in series, and taped them in position in four different places. He noticed a clock hanging on the wall. The clock face was made of a skull, and the hands were the ribs of a child. Everything was ready. He shut his eyes. Soon, he thought, very soon, it would all be over.

By the next morning, life in the Falls Road was getting back to some semblance of normality. Street cleaners were clearing the broken glass from the pavements. The barricades were being dismantled with the aid of a tractor. A grocer's had reopened, as had the nursery

227

school. A woman was standing outside the building, by the fence; an old woman in a black shawl and skirt.

'That's Lilith,' said Fanuela. 'The leader of their cell. You're to go over to her with the prisoner. You handcuff him to the railings and tell her the keys will be thrown out of the window as soon as our man's safe. And you chain this case to the same railings. It's the money. They insisted on being paid, as well.'

O'Daherty placed a case on the floor, a brown leather suitcase, bound up with insulating tape.

'As soon as this is done, you'll get your tickets for England. False papers and a primed charge. Then you can die inside the power station, Rubashov, if you insist. Die for the true faith.'

He had had hope before and seen it obliterated, but this time, he thought as he made his way to the prisoner's room, very soon, salvation might be at hand. Perhaps he would dissolve, melt away, turn to fire and gas. Perhaps all the dammed-up time he carried in his body would finally explode from his organism as the wall of his dam collapsed. For he had been living on credit, the credit of his curse; he had been living on a loan for which he had never asked, way over his originally allotted time, in a castle in the air, con-structed of years, beyond his temporal resources, without making any of his repayments. After what he had lived through, he should have been compost and worms long since, and now – the thought was suddenly overwhelming – he would be restored to the earth, to the natural cycle, to mother nature in a single ecstatic moment. He would die in peace, would reclaim his human right to a grave, deep in the earth, like a spark from a gigantic explosion, burning, molten, a puff of flaming gas that sank and sank and was gone for ever.

'Everything ready, Rubashov?' Fanuela asked. 'You know what you've got to do?'

He nodded.

They opened the door to the tiny room and brought the prisoner out. He saw him in daylight for the first time. He was a short man, shorter than he'd imagined. He gave them a mysterious smile and shook the matchbox, making the bumble bee buzz.

228

'You'll be able to shave yourself properly soon, you pig,' said Fanuela. 'Your friends are waiting . . .'

They went down the stairs. The prisoner's left hand was handcuffed. He was bare from the waist up; the dark hair on his chest grew as thickly as animal fur. He was dirty after his weeks in solitary confinement. He stank of sweat. He ran the matchbox over his cheeks; and his eyes, like the smell, Rubashov now realised, were in some way familiar.

'Do we know each other?' the prisoner asked. 'You seem somehow familiar. Have we met? In happier circumstances?'

But Josef Rubashov was so taken up with the thought of his own salvation that he wasn't even listening.

They came out onto the Falls Road. Children were running around the playground, shouting. He secured the prisoner and the case to the fence. From a toolshed by the pre-school, four men came walking towards them, four short men, as hairy and dark as the curious fellow with the matchbox, and between them a blond brigadesman, also in handcuffs, was walking, or in fact being dragged. The men in Fanuela's flat were all blond, thought Josef Rubashov; tall and blond, whereas the men in the loyalist group were short and dark.

Lilith was a very old woman, he saw. Ancient, lined and wrinkled to such a degree that her face had completely lost its shape. The prisoner smiled at him, and the bumble bee in the box accompanied his smile with its hum.

Now, he thought, very soon, he would take his leave of the human race, and it made him feel tenderly disposed to them. He felt tenderness for this old woman, Lilith, and for the prisoner with his matchbox. He felt tenderness for Stiofain Morrin and Liam O'Daherty and for the children running around their playground. Stick it out, he thought, one day the barricades will be gone, one day everyone will come to their senses and bring it all to a happy end, for there was no point to this battle, there was no point in differentiating between people; there were only the mortal and the immortal. And when he saw Fanuela giving him the signal from the window, he went back to the flat, waving to the children in the playground, and to the old woman Lilith, and everybody smiled and waved back.

Then he returned to the conspirators' apartment on the Falls Road, where the lovely Irishwoman was waiting in the dark, where the plans of the power station were, and the parcel with the charges, for with the help of these treasures he would at last, very soon, be able to rest.

It was most odd: Fanuela wasn't there, and nor were O'Daherty or Morrin, and the plans had gone from the table. And in the window bay, enveloped in a sort of shawl of light, stood a figure that looked vaguely familiar, yet utterly unfamiliar, an archangel, said a voice inside him, *an archangel, Fanuel,* or some other celestial being that had stationed itself in the flat.

'The plans,' he said. 'What's happened to the reactor plans?'

The being laughed at him.

'What plans, Rubashov? Are you sick?'

'O'Daherty and Morrin . . . and where's Stiofain?'

'Are you having some kind of joke? Who is Stiofain?'

He felt dizzy. For a brief moment, the universe trembled with such force that a crack opened, cutting through existence. He could see it clearly: a crack dividing his field of vision in two, dividing matter. And there behind it: a white light, as if there were a room, a room illuminated by a heavenly meltdown, which he was now watching from another room: the darkened room of his reason.

'They were here this morning,' he said. 'And the plans, they were on the table.'

The being laughed derisively.

'You're mad, Rubashov. There's never been anyone here but you and me. And him, out there, your guest of long ago, our prisoner.'

'The power station,' he tried again. 'I was to blow it up.'

'Blow what up? With what? The battle's here and now. The battle's always here and now; never tomorrow or the day after.'

It was an archangel, he could see now, as clearly as anything; the pair of wings under the back of the tunic, the white light radiating from him, a flashing halo, flashing as if there was some holy loose contact – an archangel, Fanuel, giving that loud and deranged laugh. And he could also see what the angel had in his hand: a transmitter; a remote control with an aerial that he was pointing towards the street where their man, the blond giant, was being released and walking towards the flat, while the hirsute prisoner still stood there, chained fast to the railings, with the suitcase, surrounded by the nursery-school children.

'Long live good!' said the archangel Fanuel. 'Long live the true faith! Death to the traitors!'

In the darkened room, it began to dawn on Josef Rubashov what was about to happen. He saw the children down below, and the rain that had started falling on the broken paving stones; and the prisoner, and Lilith, looking like a little female devil, now with her umbrella up, and the two of them smiling at each other as if they hadn't met for a very long time.

'Death to the traitors!' repeated the archangel expressionlessly. 'Death to everyone. Death to the Zionists. Death to the Arabs. Death to the Communists and capitalists and death to the Protestants . . . long live the Catholics!'

'There are Catholic children out there,' he said.

'And Protestants. It's a bloody integrated school, Rubashov. You have to allow for a few losses.'

He watched the angel fingering the remote-control button, distracted, mumbling rapturously, great wings hanging slack, sweaty under its halo; and he understood and didn't understand; and he recalled Fanuela's accomplices, Stiofain – Stephen – Francis, Philip, Basil, Theobald – what strange names! – the fanatical host of saints and martyrs who had come and gone in the conspirators' flat, and he thought he finally saw something of the battle between good and evil: that it could be waged in absolutely any name, in absolutely any guise, and the positions were interchangeable, because it was the battle itself that mattered and the ends didn't justify the means, for the means were in fact everything, they were inviolable, infallible, holy, and the eternal battle was an end in itself, fuelling the conflict that drove the machine of the universe. And tottering, hobbling, with his whole, centenarian being in revolt, he left the flat, went down the stairs where the tall saint who had just been released met him on the second landing with a grimace, and out onto the street where the children were flocking round the chained prisoner, the drab clerk, Feder-Wisch, now wearing his glasses from the start of the century, who was showing them his matchbox with the live bumble bee and smiling gently.

'The case!' he screamed, but his voice was drowned in the storm . . . in the bloodstorm . . . a meltdown of blood and flesh . . . splashing and hailing down on him, and bodies lay broken on the tarmac and on top of the parked cars, amputated arms and legs from which a red, viscous mess was quietly pumping; and an old woman who had happened to be passing was now a torso, her head attached by a few strings of tendon, facing down onto the pavement, where one of her eyes was floating in a puddle of water; and the prisoner, or to be strictly accurate his head, came rolling towards him, bobbing like a football over the bumps in the tarmac, laughing and crying by turns until it changed into a whirlwind that swept away down the street in a haze of red; and at the window stood the archangel Fanuel, laughing hysterically; and Rubashov could feel something warm and sticky on his cheek, and when he peeled it off he saw what it was: the pink tongue of a child, in which a tooth was embedded, like a sliver of almond in a sponge cake.

A foot was lying on the paving slab in front of him, severed along the top of the sock; a child's head had wedged itself between the railings. And after a moment – or was it maybe much earlier, or possibly some time later – he was aware of the smell of rotten eggs and vinegar, and holy oil and incense, and then the terrible blast wave, and then: a screen going blank, and the world . . . the world went black.

Guest Appearance in the Ether

(Late 1970s)

The nineteen-seventies are drawing to a close in stereo. Ownership of colour television has been commonplace for some time. Now this medium, too, offers us glimpses of Josef Rubashov's life. We can see him in colour and hear him in stereo, but what we see and hear is not encouraging. This is a man in decline.

Is it any wonder, we ask ourselves. Planting Maria Medea in his life at a stage when love appeared his only route to salvation, that was cruel. Not to mention events in Belfast; that was refined and artful.

Extending the lighted candle of hope to him over and over again, only to snuff it back out the second his concentration lapses, is inhuman. It shows a complete lack of love and brotherly concern. But then, we've never claimed to be in possession of such qualities.

We have him under surveillance, sometimes from the corner of our eye, sometimes in full focus. He's a white flashing dot on our moderately comprehensive radar screen. Sometimes we zoom in on that dot, and then we may happen to find ourselves looking at the hilly Catalan landscape and the city of Barcelona dozing beneath a blanket of smog and moisture, between the sea and the heights. We follow the dot from the Columbus statue along las Ramblas to the Sagrada Familia and up to the television centre, the studio complex, Studio 4, where once a week, in front of an audience and transmitted live to the region, they present the wildly popular series *On the Frontiers of Science*, hosted by that well-known former weather forecaster of Channel 2, Enrique Xuspo Torres.

A television studio makes a fascinating laboratory for the study of late twentieth-century man's exhibitionism; trapped in an ultra-technological collective, slave to time and machines, watched over by cameras, reliant on technocratic assistance because he's out of his depth with the technology and only a host of experts in more or less voluntary collaboration can prevent the entropy of the entire thing.

Is it a madhouse, we ask ourselves as we stand there in the human anthill of the studio. With all those ominously flashing lights and flustered people running this way and that, shouting over each other. Is it a theatre, we wonder, peering into the dressing room where Enrique Xuspo Torres is having his cheeks embellished with rouge and his eyes with mascara, while he fantasises about the busty blonde to whom he has just managed to direct a ruthless look of sexual hunger as he popped his head into the auditorium to inhale the perfume of his largely female studio audience. Is it a spaceship, we exclaim in amazement as we stare at the production control room.

Now four remote-control cameras are wheeled forward on the studio floor, all of them the latest design that can be operated directly by the monitor technician and don't require film camera-men, who are so often union activists and prone to strike. The floodlights and spots are turned on from the lighting control area. Scanners begin to hum. Outside the control room, the producer stubs out his cigarette. A script girl, Antonia Àlvarez, until very recently one of the five lovers whom Enrique Xuspo Torres likes to maintain in a complicated shift pattern whenever his neurotic wife Ursula is admitted to the clinic, makes final notes on camera selection. The audience is being instructed in the difficult art of applause by a floor-manager. Then Enrique Xuspo Torres leaves the make-up room, passes the little waiting room where the evening's guests are awaiting their turn to bask in his radiance. Equipped with his famous ivory smile, which will soon have the women sighing in their sitting rooms all over Catalonia and the men in the bars theatrically raising their eyebrows before turning over to the sport, he takes his place on the studio sofa. He pours a glass of mineral water. He fiddles surreptitiously with the nicotine gum he likes to chew on the sly. He sighs with the sense of well-being that unfailingly comes over him at the thought that he will soon once again, for an hour, be playing the leading role in millions of women's lives. The spirit has moved him and he nods to the control room. The producer looks at his watch. The countdown has started. The theme tune is already blaring out of every television set in the region. We're out in the ether . . .

'Several thousand years ago,' says the presenter, smiling into the on-air camera, 'the human race was probably colour-blind. Early Indo-European languages, for example, have no words for colour. We may ask why our forefathers had no knowledge of them. Did they perhaps live in a black-and-white world? Xenophanes only knows three colours of the rainbow: lilac, red and yellow. He shares that defect in his powers of perception with Aristotle, who also speaks of "the three colours of the rainbow". Democritus, who appears somewhat later, adds black and white. What does all this really signify, dear viewers? (Dear female viewers, he felt like saying; *tigresses!*) When we look up into the sky today and observe the optical phenomenon known as a rainbow, we see all the colours of the spectrum. From red, orange and yellow via green and blue to indigo and violet. Why then, we may ask, doesn't Xenophanes refer to, say, green or blue? Couldn't he see them? Didn't these colours exist in ancient Hellas? Can it be the case that new colours have been added over the centuries? Or have they always been there, and gradually been revealed to us over the generations? This evening, dear viewers, that will be the starting point of our discussion. May the same thing in fact apply to the whole universe and its secrets: that we only discover them by degrees?'

Enrique Xuspo Torres paused for effect, letting his gaze water the studio audience's flower border of ample cleavages. The blonde in the front row, he noted, had that slightly dreamy look in her eyes.

'Not that long ago,' he continued in honeyed tones, 'they believed the Earth was flat and the centre of the universe. Now we know it to be otherwise. Not so very long ago, they thought gravity an inexplicable phenomenon. Today we can describe it mathematically. Are there still, dear audience, in the second half of the twentieth century, things that can't be explained? That's what we'll be looking at this evening. Phenomena that still lie outside the field of science, but which our grandchildren may take as self-evident and explain quite simply by an equation.'

The presenter rounded off his last sentence, as was his wont, by staring deeply into the camera and running the tip of his tongue along his top lip in an intimate and obscene manner, then left it to the producer to interrupt transmission for a commercial break. And during the break, which fittingly enough featured a full-colour encyclopaedia on the evolution of humankind from the primitive nomad of the steppe, *Australopithecus africanus*, to an advanced monster in a spacesuit that would soon be hoisting a flag on Mars, he casually chewed his nicotine gum, gave the blonde a greedy wink and had the floor-manager invite the first guest to take a seat on the sofa: Dutch professor of parapsychology, Wim van der Weiden.

'Wim, welcome to the studio this evening,' said Xuspo Torres once the audience applause had died down. 'We've invited Professor van der Weiden here as a representative of the parapsychological research institute ISO: International Studies in the Occult, based in The Hague. But also in his capacity as discoverer, recorder – one might even say collector – of parapsychological phenomena, or *miracles*, as some may still prefer to call them. But you began as a mathematician, isn't that so, Professor van der Weiden?'

The professor nodded earnestly and looked deep into the camera.

'Senior lecturer,' he said. 'In cybernetics.'

'Let's start there. Can you tell us very briefly what characterises a cybernetic view of life?'

'You might say,' the professor replied, 'that cybernetics sees the universe as a gigantic computer in which programs large and small are being run alongside each other. The program for time is vast and hugely complicated. The acorn, on the other hand, is a much simpler program. The acorn, a cyberneticist would say, is the program for an oak tree. Even a simple atom can be seen as a mini-computer, or a little computer punch-card, a chip . . .'

236

'We're not talking *tapas* here, viewers,' said the presenter in an attempt to score points off his guest.

'No, certainly not. We're talking computer chips. The atom is, so to speak, a mini punch-card. The first hole tells us the number of particles in the nucleus. The second tells us the number of electrons in the shell. The third tells us the energy value of the electrons, expressed in this case by means of Planck's constant. Another example is DNA. DNA structures, too, can be seen as computer programs, and quite complicated ones, at that.'

'You mean there was a program for each and every one of us even before we were born?'

'Exactly so.'

The presenter made a scarcely perceptible gesture to the control room, which could only be construed as a hint that the camera had remained on the Dutchman's face for too long and should now focus on himself again. The monitor technician made sure the star got his way.

'And from this rather mathematical way of looking at the world you expanded your investigations, as I understand it, but still using mathematics.'

'Through science – which came into my life quite late – I was forced to ask myself a question that revived metaphysics. Why did nature opt for a mathematical pattern? And, moreover, a pattern that we can comprehend? Natural science, you could say, is one program within the larger program, a knowledge program that's growing and growing, and will ultimately, I'm convinced, be able to explain the structure of all the other programs of the universe.'

'You mean, some being has given us the mathematics to be able to discover precisely who that being is?'

'That's my personal conviction.'

'And it goes without saying that such a great intelligence therefore has mastery of patterns we don't yet understand, but may be able to decipher in the future?'

'Yes, that's more or less it.'

The on-air camera had again turned to the Dutchman, and the presenter made the most of the opportunity to get rid of his nicotine gum and send another of his looks to the blonde in the front row.

'Then you went a stage further,' he continued, signalling again that the camera had dwelt too long on the Dutchman, 'by taking an interest in mathematical mediums, which would later lead you on to certain other varieties of medium.'

The Dutchman smiled and nodded.

'The first one I heard of,' he said, 'was an Indian, dead by then, called Srinivasa Ramanujan. A very strange character. I think you have a picture of him somewhere.'

In the control room, the producer gave the order for file scanning. A scratched monochrome photograph appeared on the output monitor, showing a young Tamil crouched in the rain on some steps in Oxford, wearing galoshes and a poorly fitting, dogtooth-check suit.

'Ramanujan,' said van der Weiden, 'was born in the city of Madras at the end of the nineteenth century, the only son of a poor elementary-school teacher and a low-caste seamstress. He had a far-from-adequate education, and therefore approached mathematics from an extremely unconventional angle. As an artist, you might say, through intuition and an almost fanatical trust in his own subconscious. At the age of eighteen he was already writing down numerous theorems, without spending time trying to prove them. And many of them – for example, the one for differential calculus in the seventh dimension – have proved years later to be correct.'

'So Ramanujan was a mathematical medium?'

'Like so many other great scientists: Newton, Paracelsus, Schrödinger: it's always a question of being in close contact with dark forces. But unlike them, he lacked education. He was said to have gained insight into the nature of mathematics as a thirteen-year-old by sitting staring at the equations in Carr's famous 'Synopsis of Pure Mathematics'. So his genius allegedly began with a kind of graphic understanding of mathematics. He himself maintained that the theorems came to him through revelations from the goddess Namagiri, a sort of female devil whom his mother had worshipped at the time of his birth.'

Xuspo Torres signalled to the control room to stop scanning and go back to the studio camera. The script girl Antonia Àlvarez was regarding him hungrily through the glass with her cow-eyes. He avoided her gaze with practised ease.

'Some kind of demonic muse, you mean?'

The Dutchman smiled.

'From an early stage there were many legends attached to him. The renowned Oxford mathematician Hardy . . . an acquaintance of mine, I was about to say. You see, I've lived for these people for so long – for all sorts of unusual people! – for so long that I almost feel I know them all personally . . . Anyway, Professor Hardy heard about Ramanujan and arranged for him to come and work under him in England. In 1914, such a fateful year as you'll recall, he came to Europe by boat. Unfortunately it was a real culture clash, and his stay didn't last very long. He began to suffer nervous symptoms and returned to India as soon as the war was over. He died prematurely from TB, at the age of only thirty-five.'

'Various other legends have grown up around him,' said the presenter. 'In India there's a small sect, an offshoot of the Blavatsky movement, that worships him as one of the "wise men of Tibet".'

'So it's said, yes. He's supposed to have attained immortality and is living today in a hidden valley in Tibet.'

Another picture, of a dark-skinned woman, appears on the screen.

'And this is another Indian you discovered personally,' said the presenter.

'This is Miss Shakuntala Devi. For the last ten years she's been travelling round the world, astonishing scientific gatherings with her mental arithmetic. In this picture, taken in Texas, she's just correctly found the twenty-third root of a number with two hundred digits. Can you imagine the length of such a number? And all in less than fifty seconds.'

The programme presenter decided it was time to hold up the book, fat as a Bible, its cover adorned with mysterious symbols, that had been lying on the low table in front of them since the start of the programme.

'You claim in a recent book that she's a stock example of a mathematical medium. *She is linked up to the larger computer*, you write.'

'That is correct, and the same can be said of these two lads.'

A photograph of two brothers came up on the screen.

'These are John and Jim Bull, mentally handicapped twins. They can beat any computer at finding prime numbers.'

'You also write in your book that we accept these gifts, strangely enough. We attribute them to human intelligence and thereby flatter ourselves.'

'It's impossible to beat a computer at finding prime numbers. Yet they do it.'

The presenter sent a look of irritation in the direction of the control room. The camera had again dwelt on the professor for far too long.

'It's a different matter for gifts outside mathematics,' he said. 'Those we don't accept. We have names for other paranormal gifts, like mumbo-jumbo and hocus-pocus.'

'There is perhaps a grey area, namely what people can do when in the grip of religious hysteria,' said van der Weiden. 'Sometimes, although it conflicts with all known physical laws, we may accept that people can walk barefoot over red-hot coals during primitive initiation rites, or that Eskimo shamans can lie in freezing water for four days. We accept it reluctantly, as a fact that goes against scientific laws. By contrast, strangely enough, we no longer accept the devil. The concept of a devil is obsolete, we say, an invention of our superstitious forebears. Although the devil is just as possible or impossible, by the same standards, as it is to walk barefoot over a bed of coals at two thousand degrees without burning your feet.'

The presenter turned to the camera.

'After the break we shall be meeting some more extraordinary people. All discovered by Professor van der Weiden. Their gifts, which you will see put to the test, are however not as easy for us to accept as John and Jim Bull's. So stay tuned, dear viewers. We'll be back very shortly with more exciting guests, here on the frontiers of science . . .'

The camera didn't catch the pained grimace that contorted Enrique Xuspo Torres' face into a caricature of the Spanish heart-throb image, half-Jesuit, half-bullfighter, that he always took such pains to convey to the sitting rooms of the region. For the camera was the root of the sense of wounded pride now running through him. He got to his feet to go and take the producer to task. Again the technicians had let the lens dally far too long on Professor van der Weiden, although it was actually stipulated in the contract he had signed with Catalan Television after hard nights of negotiation that he, Enrique Xuspo Torres, should be in shot on his own for at least 60 per cent of the transmission.

The commercial break, which featured shampoo, dog food, slimmers' olive oil and the San Fermín fiesta in Madrid, for which a number of tickets were still available for Catalonia's bullfight lovers, lasted exactly three and a half minutes. Afterwards it would have been impossible for the viewers to detect any trace of the argument that had raged between the presenter and the studio staff in the meantime; not to judge by Enrique Xuspo Torres' face, anyway, which had its usual promisingly suave, stoically far-away look when it came back into shot, the only deviation from his normal self possibly being the flush of anger tinting his earlobes red. He had let his wrath descend particularly on the script girl Antonia Àlvarez, that cow, since he had considered it her duty, not least in her capacity as his former lover, to present him in the best possible light and make sure he was on screen as often as possible. After his accusing outburst she had left the control room in tears, as the technician and the producer assured him that the unfortunate incident would not be repeated. There was something about the new technology, they said, something about the automated studio cameras. Reassured, he returned to the studio sofa the second before the commercial break ended, and even had time to beam out a horny look to his blonde prey in the first row before they were on air again.

'Welcome back to *On the Frontiers of Science*,' he smiled. 'As you see, Professor van der Weiden is still with me on the sofa. Other guests will soon be joining us, because the professor has arranged for some of his protégés to be with us tonight. All of them people with unusual gifts. So without further ado, let's welcome our second guest of the evening: Mr Alex Sanders!'

A man was now being guided past cameras and control desks by the studio controller; a short man with slicked-back hair, dressed completely in black: black cord trousers, black silk shirt, black bow tie and black socks and shoes. Only one flash of colour provided a contrast to this solid darkness: an emerald-green crystal flask sticking out of the pocket of his black jacket.

'Mr Sanders,' said the presenter after inviting him to take a seat, 'you have been called the Cagliostro and Saint Germain, the Rasputin and Aleister Crowley of our time. Impressive epithets for a man who has only stepped into the limelight over the last year. What do you think of these comparisons yourself?'

'I'm flattered,' said Sanders, revealing that his eyelids, too, were black; covered in a black powder. 'But my innate modesty forbids me comparing myself with those great names.'

'Let me briefly explain to the viewers that Mr Sanders is the leader of a community of witches, a coven, in London's Notting Hill. Later this evening we will pay them a visit and see what lies concealed behind the doors of a modern-day black temple. Maybe Mr Sanders will also look into the future for us, something at which he's said to be very skilled. Or, like Uri Geller, he may attempt to influence objects and people from a distance by the power of thought. But first, Mr Sanders, in your system of beliefs, one of the central tenets is worship of the power we get from the so-called third eye, isn't that so?'

Sanders nodded, clasping his hands together on the table in front of him.

'That's right, Enrique. We think all human beings possess latent occult ability, and that this can be coaxed forth by activation of the so-called third eye, or the eborial gland, as it is known. The cyclops eye, the people of antiquity called it. Once, way back in our evolution, there was an open eye here. One can still find evidence of it by carrying out an autopsy.'

'But that eye has now become a gland. And not just any old gland. Because, if I've grasped this correctly, mighty forces can be unleashed by the activation of this gland?'

Mr Alex Sanders smiled into the camera and then turned to

Professor van der Weiden. The latter, who until then had been sitting quietly, staring dreamily out over the audience, nodded almost imperceptibly, as if in agreement. Sanders turned to Xuspo Torres again:

'I could give you an example of that force.'

'Please do,' said Xuspo Torres. 'Our viewers are no doubt eager for a demonstration.'

Mr Sanders fixed his eyes on the presenter. It all went quiet. Not a sound from the studio audience. Even the hum of the monitors seemed to fade. The camera rested on Xuspo Torres, but what it registered was not to his advantage. He was breaking into a sweat around the temples. Inexplicable terror darkened his gaze. He was trembling violently and swallowing repeatedly. Finally, with a great effort, he managed to get to his feet.

'That will do for now, Mr Sanders,' he said hoarsely. 'We'll move on to this evening's next guest. Another of Professor van der Weiden's protégés, a Russian this time: Josef Nikolai Rubashov.'

As Enrique Xuspo Torres was draining his glass of mineral water, trying desperately to distract himself with a flight of fancy in which he undressed the buxom blonde, now observing him from the front row with a slightly sceptical air, the Russian made his entrance. Xuspo Torres shook his hand mechanically, since what had just occurred had caused his legendary powers of concentration to malfunction, and what he had experienced had been sheer horror.

The look Mr Alex Sanders had given him had not been an agreed part of the proceedings. When they had run through the details of the programme that morning, his look had only caused an inexplicable itching of Torres' neck, but very faint, so faint that it was really more like the sort of urge to scratch that one might feel on seeing an ants' nest – i.e., a case of auto-suggestion. But just now, that look had as good as paralysed him, squeezing his heart into a hard, black kernel of terror and temporarily cutting him off from the outside world. And very distinctly, from a point somewhere inside his own skull, he had heard Professor van der Weiden's voice saying with a laugh: 'Enrique, you conceited old boar! You didn't expect this.'

He played for time by trying to assess his new guest: an ancient

243

fellow with white hair, a matted beard and a face that was a spider's web of lines.

'Welcome to the programme, Mr Rubashov,' he said, collecting himself. 'You, too, were discovered by Professor van der Weiden, if I'm not mistaken?'

The Russian nodded and looked vaguely about him. He was scratching his ear with a scrawny, trembling hand. This made the presenter feel a little calmer.

'This was how it happened,' van der Weiden said. 'If you don't object, I'll do the talking, Enrique. Josef Nikolai is a man of few words. As we can all see, he's a very old man, almost older than one can imagine.'

Enrique Xuspo Torres nodded. The attack had passed. Let the Dutchman talk, he thought. He would pull this programme off as he had all the rest and then, once these crackpots were out of the studio, the sooner the better, he would ring his wife Ursula and explain in exasperated tones that he unfortunately had to stay all night and work overtime on the next feature, about the eels in the Sargasso Sea; then he would take his blonde female admirer to the nearest hotel and give her ample proof of his manhood.

'I found myself on Josef Nikolai's trail by sheer chance,' said van der Weiden. 'Thanks to this article, in fact.'

The Dutchman took a press cutting from a briefcase. At the top was a picture of a crash site.

'It's on Tenerife,' he said. 'In March last year two Boeing 747 jumbo jets collided at Tenerife international airport. As we all remember, the death toll was five hundred and ninety-seven, making it then the greatest disaster in the history of commercial aviation. There was only one survivor: an old Russian man.'

Van der Weiden held the article up to the camera.

'We can also see him being kept under observation in hospital at Las Palmas. Strangely enough, he escaped without a single scratch.'

The professor looked enigmatically into the camera as he produced another newspaper article.

'Four months later: the terrible bus crash in Macedonia. Fourteen people were killed when a minibus ran out of control on a mountain road and plunged down a ravine. There was only one survivor: the same Russian . . . To get to the point, I started investigating this remarkable individual, who has this strange capacity for surviving catastrophes. And he who knows exactly what he seeks, like a skilled hunter, seldom has to wait long for results. I found that over the last thirty years or more, Josef Nikolai has escaped half a dozen similar disasters, all documented by AP, UPI, Reuters and a host of newspapers, radio stations and news agencies . . .'

'The professor's first thought,' Mr Sanders interjected, 'was somewhat speculative: he conjectured that Josef Nikolai cannot die. A sort of modern Uta Napishtim, the immortal figure of the Gilgamesh epic. He who was warned of the catastrophe, the great flood, by the god Ea and therefore built an ark: the biblical Noah.'

Enrique Xuspo Torres was beginning to pluck up his courage again:

'But no one is immortal, of course,' he said. 'Neither God, nor the devil, nor science can get us that far, even with the help of cybernetics, isn't that so, gentlemen?'

'Agreed. But Josef Nikolai is very old. As a result of various enquiries behind the Iron Curtain, the professor located his baptism certificate. Mr Rubashov was born in St Petersburg in the year 1869.'

Xuspo Torres shook his head. Fools, he thought: 1869! These were the worst nutcases he had ever managed to assemble beneath a studio roof.

'To cut a long story short,' Xuspo Torres orated, 'you, professor, managed to find not only the baptism certificate, but also the man it referred to, take him under your wing, and even find him work . . .' A picture came up on the scanner of a casino in Malaga. 'Because Rubashov turned out – and I'm no longer referring to his alleged age, which seems utterly absurd, or to his preposterously good luck in disasters – Rubashov turned out to possess . . . well, what shall we call it? A strange sheet of paper, which the professor here, at any rate, claims is indestructible.'

The scanner switched to a picture of Josef Nikolai Rubashov standing on the casino stage with his contract in his hand, surrounded by an audience of astonished gamblers.

'And with this extraordinary paper he has, they say, made appearances at gaming clubs up and down the sunshine coast, inviting the public to try to destroy it in exchange for money.'

The camera was back in the studio, though it was not on the presenter, but on his three guests. Xuspo Torres tried to manoeuvre himself into the shot.

'Would you like to show us this remarkable piece of paper, Mr Rubashov?' he said, unable to conceal his irritation with the technical hitch. 'It would be very interesting for us to try our hand at what is said to have defeated so many before us.'

The Russian nodded vacantly and produced from his trouser pocket a yellowed document, folded in two. Without a word, he passed it to Enrique Xuspo Torres.

'We're back where we started, dear viewers,' said the presenter. 'Are there phenomena today that science can't explain? Are there colours in the rainbow that we still haven't discovered? Or is all this, as I personally suspect, nothing but bluff and trickery. This document, for example, with its illegible writing, is it really indestructible? Dear television audience, we are having some technical problems with our cameras here in the studio tonight, so we'll take the next break now. Those eagerly anticipated answers will have to wait until we're back . . .'

But there were no more commercial breaks that night. Something quite different was sent out into the ether from the control room: a film recording made in Mr Alex Sanders' black temple in Notting Hill, and not by any means the rather tame recording that Enrique Xuspo Torres had himself supervised in London a month before, in which Sanders had burned a little incense and worshipped a demon. So while the presenter was once more in the control room giving the script girl and the producer a good telling off because the cameras were playing up, and because they were the two who at an editorial meeting had forced through the decision to automate the video output . . . while the studio staff were then distracted as they tried to calm the agitated TV star, the unannounced item was being broadcast into everyone's sitting rooms without any of those on duty noticing what was happening. It was a most peculiar interior that the viewers saw on their screens that night. In the middle of a vast, black-painted hall, at a chequerboard table, sat Mr Alex Sanders and Professor Wim van der Weiden, drinking mint tea from a Victorian china tea service. Around them in mid-air, as if weightless, the furniture was performing a dance. A grand piano came floating by, light as a cloud, its keys playing a merry quadrille. A chesterfield sofa was going up and down the wall like a lift. Dusty bottles flew about, full of what looked like mist, and round the professor's head circled four alarm clocks, like planets round a sun. Cuckoo clocks with legs went bobbing across the table. China dolls danced and sang. Fabulous beasts materialised and disappeared, and around the floor scurried thousands of rats, all dressed in tail-coats.

The studio audience, who could see all this on a monitor, watched with rapt attention until the film was almost over. With only seconds of it remaining, they broke into a spontaneous round of applause. Only then did the people in the control room wake up. 'That's not the film we made in London,' said the producer, pointing at the monitor. But it was too late. The lights were blinking for another take and Enrique Xuspo Torres rushed back to the studio sofa.

'Welcome back, loyal viewers,' he panted. 'You're back in the studio. As you have no doubt realised, we are still experiencing some technical problems, with the cameras and with the pre-recorded items from Mr Sanders' black temple. We hope this can be put right and that, with everyone's cooperation, we'll be able to follow our well-rehearsed schedule for the rest of the programme . . .'

With these last words he turned to Professor van der Weiden, and no one could fail to notice the glare of hatred he gave the Dutchman.

'As I say, we're still here,' he went on. 'We've got everything under control and, if I remember correctly, we promised you an experiment on Mr Rubashov's document. That we would try to destroy it, in fact. Could I trouble you for a match, professor?'

'No need,' said Mr Sanders. 'What you want, Enrique, is a fire.'

And at that very instant, the piece of paper the presenter was holding in his hand burst into flames. He threw it down onto the table, and another look from Mr Sanders extinguished it.

Enrique Xuspo Torres was sweating now. He could feel his

forehead glowing and his heart running amok, and not even the blonde's cleavage could offer him any respite.

'You can see for yourselves, dear viewers,' he said 'The paper has not been harmed. What we have just witnessed, when Mr Sanders set fire to it, is another example of a hitherto unexplained phenomenon. So-called telekinesis. One of Professor van der Weiden's other protégés, by the way, is the Israeli telekineticist Uri Geller . . .'

'That's totally incorrect,' interrupted the professor. 'And irrelevant!'

The programme presenter was sweating profusely now. He noticed that the cameras had taken on a life of their own. Like great praying mantises on wheels, they were moving around the studio filming corners, patches of carpet and trails of coloured wiring.

'You viewers,' he said with a slight stammer, 'have doubtless all heard of Uri Geller, the man who can bend spoons using the power of his mind. Or make broken clocks start to go again . . .'

'Any idiot can do that,' said Mr Sanders. 'That means even you, Mr Torres. Let's test that experimentally with this Polaroid camera.'

A Polaroid camera suddenly materialised in Mr Sanders' hand. He pointed it at the presenter.

'What are you thinking about, Torres?' he said. 'Concentrate on whatever thought you have in your head this very moment! Influence the camera!' And without waiting for an answer, he pressed the shutter and then ejected the negative from the inside of the camera.

'What we are about to witness, dear viewers,' said Professor van der Weiden with a smile, as the cameras regrouped around the studio sofa, 'is Mr Torres' somewhat primitive imagination, transmitted by telekinesis.'

And at home in their sitting rooms, the television audience could now see the Polaroid picture Sanders had placed on the table. Gradually the image developed. It showed Enrique Xuspo Torres himself, naked, but with the snout of a pig, lying between the legs of script girl Antonia Àlvarez, his hairy buttocks stuck in the air, his anal cleft generously exposed to display his walnut-sized haemorrhoid.

248

'It's not true,' protested Xuspo Torres as Mr Sanders pointed the camera at him again and took another snap. 'I wasn't thinking about that at all. What's happening, Sanders? Get rid of that thing!'

'You have a very rich imagination, and an equally rich gift for telekinetics,' said Alex Sanders, holding up the second photograph. 'This really does beat most things we've seen.'

This time Xuspo Torres was to be seen with waggling dog ears and the tail of a monkey, sucking on the left nipple of the busty blonde in the front row.

'It's a lie!' he shrieked. 'I would never . . . Control room, can you hear me? Stop transmission. Stop, I said! Play the ads!'

But the recording didn't stop, because the cameras and equipment were living lives of their own on a higher plane, like devils or angels, and the most remarkable scenes were now being beamed out to the sitting rooms of Catalonia from the studio floor of the television centre in Barcelona. Visible in close-up on every screen was Enrique Xuspo Torres' half-crazed face. Sweat and mascara were running in rivulets down his cheeks, taking clumps of powder with them, and the secret he had kept so well since his time as a weatherman, the toupee, suddenly sprouted bat-wings and to his utter horror took off across the studio, leaving him disfigured and exposed. Mr Sanders and Professor van der Weiden, by contrast, remained calmly seated on the sofa with their feet up on the table; then with the hypnotic movements of a magician, Mr Sanders produced the green crystal flask from his jacket pocket and released something, which to judge by appearances was nothing other than a genie in a bottle, semi-transparent and dancing happily to an old ragtime tune, its tail stuck in the neck of the flask. Black tulips rained down from the ceiling. The cameras rose into the air and hovered there. The slide scanner leaped through a succession of private moments from Enrique Xuspo Torres' life: that time he took script girl Antonia Àlvarez on a clandestine romantic trip to Switzerland and seduced her violently in the pool, with his hat on. Or that dawn in the dark night club in Córdoba when a shady member of the government stuffed bundles of hundred-dollar bills into his pocket so that he would sing his praises in the press in the days leading up to the election. Or naked and drunk at the transvestite club in Barrio Chino; or that time he lost his head and strangled a cat after failing to get selected for the FC Barcelona junior team. As smoke and flames spewed from the control room, a miniature rainbow formed in the spray from the sprinkler system and the studio personnel ran for their lives, his wife Ursula's voice could suddenly be heard in a direct link to their home telephone, calling him a swine and a lecher and informing him of her intention to file for divorce. Fountains of champagne gushed from the floodlights, and goldfish flapped around the floor in their thousands. The audience, frightened out of its wits, rushed for the emergency exits, led by the blonde whom Xuspo Torres had already bedded in his imagination. Demonic laughter filled the air, wall sockets coughed flames and sparks. And in the midst of all this live transmission chaos, right beside programme presenter Xuspo Torres, who like a captain loath to leave his sinking ship had clambered up a floodlight and was vainly appealing from his mast at the top of his voice for a commercial break . . . yes, beside him, on the studio sofa, sat Josef Nikolai Rubashov, distant and introverted. He was holding his old contract and radiating utter dejection and decay. We felt really sorry for him. We suffered with him. We truly wished him a better fate. He was so old, his reactions so sluggish, his sense of smell so reduced, that it was only now, with the chaos already at its peak and us calling him in our voice from the start of the century, that he realised who we were. Then he got up. And with a crazed look, his hands outstretched to seize us by the throat, he tottered towards us with his old man's steps.

Not that we were afraid anything would happen to us, that would have been ridiculous for beings in our position; but we took it as a signal that the evening was over. And so we vanished, we dissolved, while the television sets of Catalonia were still being shaken and rattled by inexplicable poltergeists, and a box with the message *Temporary break in transmission* came up on the screen.

Odysseus

Invisible, concealed in a rat hole or a bit of green glass on the floor (it's quite true!), we are observing him in a cellar in Copenhagen's Nørrebro district. A watery winter light falls through the small, high windows. The light forms pillars, columns and proud, straight-backed capitals, in which the dust dances and whirls like microscopic acrobats whipped by an invisible animal tamer.

In one corner, on a battered mattress, sits our man Rubashov. He's wearing his threadbare jacket from the First World War. His trousers are tattered and his shoes have no soles. His face is coated in a layer of dirt. His chin is resting on his knees and his eyelids are half-closed over pupils no larger than a pinprick. It's very quiet. Not a movement. His body is at rest, turned in upon its own ecstasy. Every nerve and cell, lymph and capillary is closed around timeless delight. On the walls: yellowing advertising posters from one of the city's breweries, but the colour has come loose from the damp plaster and is lying in flakes on what was once a beautiful oriental carpet. A rat (it's not us!) scampers without concern across the floor to the pile of rags at one end of the room in which it has made its nest. Tiny baby rats are moving inside; blind, pink, hairless, their blood vessels on the surface. They are squirming and whimpering for poison, their little noses wrinkling and sniffing in the darkness.

But he is not alone. By the door with its missing panel, its worn wood tattooed with graffiti . . . there . . . yes, just there . . . another

251

figure is lying. Is it a man or a woman? Hard to tell, even from this close range. It's some kind of human being, at any rate, though the body weighs no more than thirty kilos. The sharp contours of vertebrae and other bones can be seen under the scraps of clothes. Its scalp, which was once, until very recently, covered in thick, luxuriant hair, now has gaping patches of white. Its nails are bitten down to the quick . . . Or was it the rat, the hungry mother rat, trying to gather some food from the nourishing human protuberances known as fingers?

A tourniquet is hanging loosely round its upper arm. The skin on the inside of the elbow is perforated with holes and scars, so many that they have formed a rough crust, almost a carapace, overlapping scales like some tropical lizard. Its legs, too, are perforated. Its stomach, calves and neck have been pierced all over . . . needles have even been jabbed into the whites of its eyes . . . jabbed in and out . . . out and in, as if this person had wanted to release something shut inside, drive out an evil force with the help of a needle tip, a poisonous solution; or puncture the bubble of its life, puncture the thin varnish, the skin, this fortress of body and soul, two square metres of it, one-fifth of man's body weight, which encloses and defines him with all its little characteristics and colours, epithelium, melanins, melanocytes, making him into . . . well, what?

A bloody syringe is still dangling there, its tip stuck into the flesh. And on the floor: a blackened spoon, a burned-down candle, a bottle of mineral water. But it's by no means certain that these utensils are responsible for transforming this human being into a horizontally outstretched skeleton, for nature has begun to fear her children and is therefore sending them incurable viruses, microscopic avengers, in pure self-defence, and it may be these that have turned this person into a lifeless wreck.

The dust acrobats twirl, performing their ballet of the birth of the universe, dancing and dancing and rousing our man from his trance.

'Poul,' he mumbles, his voice dry as bark, 'Poul?'

And when no answer comes, he pulls himself up and with a tremendous effort, borne down with memories of more than a century, totters along the side of the room, in the cocktail of light and dust, to the prone body on which the bluey-red patches are spreading, like liquid, like juice spilt on a cloth, like blood on a cotton-wool compress.

'Poul . . . answer me,' he whispers, turning him, rolling the body over, this virtually weightless creature who perhaps in actual fact has always striven for . . . lightness, lightness, a gravitational rebel, a weight revolutionary, striving to float, to perform the pantomime of the freed soul . . . turns him over and realises that sickness, nature's avenger, or perhaps the toxic substance they have fraternally shared from the same syringe, has proved too concentrated for that mortal heart . . . No pulse, he notes, and no breathing either, and the outer membrane of the eyeballs had dried and wrinkled like the skin of a raisin. The she-rat who eats their waste – their vomit and excrement . . . and who is therefore also addicted to the same toxic substances – the little she-rat hisses from the floor and tries to nip his ankles. Then he closes the boy's eyelids with his fingers, that ancient human ritual, so the soul doesn't try in vain once more to enter through those windows and take possession of its worn-out body. Shuts the eyes with his hardened fingers and leaves.

Rubashov lived for several years on one long, unbroken, drug-induced high. He was insatiable. He was a bottomless, living dustbin. He took in their toxins through every orifice of his body. He tried anything he was given. For months he was in a hallucinatory state, in which the external world disappeared and an inner universe with its own natural laws took over. Visions danced before his eyes, ghostly figures stepped forward and spoke to him through faces in their bellies. He was turned into whatever the visions offered him: the secret inside a locked casket, a candle burning in a damp cave, a figure in an insoluble equation, a murderer's dagger, the longing of a convict, a carafe of dew in a dream of a desert.

In Milan they gave him a substance so toxic he lost consciousness for two months. In Scotland he lay motionless on a bunk for a whole autumn, listening to the voices created by rainwater dripping through a hole in the roof. He took larger and larger doses. But the effect slowly lessened. His body habituated itself. In the end he no longer felt anything. Then he gave up and began his walking.

Night and day he walked. There was no objective, he thought, no secret openings in time through which he could make an exit. There was just the endless succession of horizons, lunar months, cycles, the changing of the seasons . . .

In northern Scandinavia, the deep-frozen ground mirrored his inner cold; the tundra was an image of the map of his soul. His eyes were like the spectral expanses of high moorland. His heart was as hard as the ancient granite mountains. He didn't see another human being. He talked out loud to himself in order not to go out of his mind.

Winter came. He plunged on through snow a metre deep. Huge shadows were cast by great, white accretions; they assumed the form of forgotten, primeval beasts. He saw them rear up on their shaggy hind legs, he heard them cough and roar with the voice of the wind, heard their jaws as they salivated and struck to devour him. But when they realised who he was, when they saw his boundless sorrow, his curse, they lay down again and went back to sleep in the snowy night.

Far up in the north where the coast meets the sea of ice, he stopped. That was how he was doomed to live, he thought: deep-frozen.

He walked for weeks over the pack ice; he stumbled on, slipping, plodding and howling out his dread. The pole star was his guiding light. The wind his only companion.

A storm broke up the ice sheet. He lay on his back on a floe the size of a raft and let himself be carried south by the current. Snow fell on him, a layer of ice formed over his body. He didn't care, why should he? Why should he ever move at all?

At one point he was joined by a starving seal. It lay on the edge of the ice floe, trying to catch fish. It grew weaker and weaker, stiffer and stiffer, until one morning it rolled over on its side and gave a final sigh. Another time, a great sea bird alighted on his chest and rested there. He was lying so still inside his crust of ice that it didn't notice him.

The current washed him ashore in Narvik. Spring had arrived. Flowers were coming into bloom on the mountain slopes, the meltwater was rushing in the streams. He hitched a lift south.

At the harbour in Trondheim he made his way on board a cargo ship. He fell asleep among the crates of fish in a cold store.

He awoke in a town on the Spanish coast. It was early autumn and he realised months had passed since he had last been conscious. He stared at his face in a shop window for a long time. He had aged again. He was ancient, a parody of a human being. A delta of lines ran across his cheeks, his pate was bald, worn as smooth as driftwood, his beard had softened into fine, white silk. Of his teeth, only four remained.

He smiled to a woman passing by. He could see she found him disgusting. He was glad. If they were disgusted, they would keep away. He found a stick in a rubbish bin. He could see it was just what he needed. His joints were stiff, his back had twisted like an old tree. Leaning on his crutch, he limped out of town.

On a remote Asturian beach, the beauty of the scenery induced him to make camp for the night. When he woke up, he saw no point in going on.

He fed himself on sand. There was nothing he needed: no people, no life, no laughter to remind him of their false joy.

His vision had also deteriorated. He was glad of it. His hearing, too, seemed dulled, and when he drank the sea water he couldn't taste its saltiness. That gave him a sense of satisfaction. When the senses had gone, he thought, nothing remained; only darkness, a rushing sound and gasping breaths.

The screech of the seagulls woke him. He tried to get up, but it was impossible. For a moment he thought paralysis must have struck, and the thought filled him with pleasure. Then he saw: it was oil, a coating of solidified oil ten centimetres thick, a pitch-black giant's tongue poking out of the jaws of the sea to lay its tomb lid over the beaches.

He followed the coast eastwards. Dying birds everywhere, black, sticky, their eyes glued shut by the sludge. Porpoises, their bellies distended, gave off a fearful stench. Millions of dead fish washed against the shore with the waves. It was as if he had been given a new way of seeing, and what he saw filled him with grief. The earth was dying, the earth was bleeding to death before his eyes; they had poisoned it, given a lethal dose of poison to the earth that had sustained them for century after century.

He walked through woods where the trees were rotting from inside. He looked out across lakes in which all life had been snuffed out, with shores where only poisonous hogweed could grow. Desert landscapes stretched away where luxuriant meadows had been not long before. Immense wounds gaped in the earth, bleeding craters where metals had been mined; seams and veins they had sucked dry and then abandoned. The seas were dying, the fields poisoned; there were places where a mouthful of soil was enough to kill a person. Vast areas of clear felling extended where primeval forests once grew. The soil was eroded by landslips. Soot and emissions darkened the sky and its leaden clouds watered the ground with its acid rain. From concealed caverns in the mountains he sensed the hideous radiation of their nuclear waste. High in the atmosphere, holes were forming, corroded by their toxins, through which the sun's lethal red light beamed down. Whole species were heading for extinction, and humankind would soon be sharing their fate.

They deserved it, he thought; they deserved to be crushed under the landslide they themselves had set in motion. The human race was interested only in its own consumption; that was why its factories worked day and night to create new vices to satisfy . . . Soon he would be walking alone across these barren wastes. Beneath a pitch-black sky. Alone through deserted cities and dead forests. Through a world life had evacuated in panic. A waste collection site. The refuse tip of their civilisation.

In the cities, he slept under bridges. He witnessed tramps fighting over bits of bread and pulling knives on each other for a bottle of wine. In the soughing of the night, he would sometimes awake to the sound of people crying: women who had been raped by their husbands; daughters abused by their fathers; men crying with guilt. They'd lost control, he thought; they were in freefall. But only then, under cover of darkness, behind locked doors, could they give themselves up to their nameless terror.

He saw people cowering in their houses, held together by the mortar of horror, at windows scratched with self-contempt. They trembled like beasts to the slaughter in their vehicles, and he saw them driving aimlessly along streets of loathing, their eyes already those of dead souls. Perhaps they were already dead, he thought. Perhaps, after what the century had done to them, they had all died long ago?

One night in Yorkshire, England, he was the witness to a murder. In a woodland clearing by a remote country road, a lorry driver raised a hammer and smashed the skull of a young prostitute. It made a quiet crunch, like cracking open an egg. The man laughed as he raped the corpse, laughed and stared up at the sky with orgiastic gaze. A terrible chill descended on Josef Rubashov, but it had nothing to do with what he was seeing. It was the chill of indifference. He could have helped the girl, he thought; he could have prevented the deed. But he didn't. He was indifferent; indifferent to everything, to murder, terror and a woman's scream for help.

He went on, shivering with cold. It was this indifference that was freezing him, an internal arctic low-pressure area, an inland ice of the soul. He dreamed of warmth, of being heated up, of being burned. But he knew it was pointless. He was indestructible, he stood above hot and cold, he was as indestructible as their evil, and he would outlive their atomic-power stations by millions of years.

'Josef Rubashov? Is that you?'

The voice belonged to an ancient man in a dark cellar bar in Sofia. It was the start of the nineteen-eighties. The man was sitting alone at a table with a full glass of Calvados before him. He was a startling apparition. He was wearing dress trousers, a dirty shirt with a starched front, a dusty bow tie and a striped waistcoat. It was Philip

Bouhler's butler. The butler was an old man now, bald and crippled with arthritis. His voice was so weak it could hardly be heard.

'I scarcely recognised you, Rubashov,' he whispered. 'It's time . . . it passes too quickly.'

He wheezed and raised the glass to his lips with shaking hands.

'Wait,' he said. 'I'm not alone.'

He disappeared into a back room. When he returned, he was pushing a pram.

'Look,' he said. 'We're all getting hard to recognise . . .'

In the pram lay Paracelsus – that is to say, what little was left of him. He was now no bigger than a child of three, a miniature human being. He had been transported back to a childhood four hundred centuries distant. He could no longer speak. He was oblivious to the world around him. In his hand he held a baby's rattle, raising his chubby child's arm now and then to shake it above his chest. His executioner's sword had vanished. He gurgled quietly when Josef Rubashov whispered his name.

They joined forces. People often turned to watch them go, whispering and pointing among themselves. Women would occasionally come up to see what was in the pram. But when they caught sight of Paracelsus, that living corpse the size of a child, they crossed themselves and ran away . . .

One night in Rotterdam, at the port, they found Gilles de Rais. He was sitting by a fire, stirring the embers with his fingers while his eyes followed the dark outline of a lighter bobbing in the swell. He was dressed in sackcloth and rags, and his feet were bound in newspaper. Like Paracelsus, he had ceased to speak. Time had come to their aid, said the butler. Time would presumably break them down. Wasn't that a clear sign? That time had taken pity on them. That time had discovered the injustice of their curse and rebelled against it. But there was nothing to indicate they would die; they simply went on ageing.

They encountered some of the other immortals, too. Or maybe they'd always been there. Maybe they'd always been close to them, constantly crossing their path. Maybe it was only now that Josef Rubashov's eyes had been opened to them.

Raymond Lullus was living in a disused mine shaft in the Ruhr. In a mental asylum in Hamburg, strapped into a straitjacket in a padded cell, sat Countess Bathory-Nasdy. One evening in the Paris metro, Rubashov and the butler spotted Cagliostro and Saint Germain getting off a train. They called to them, but they were swallowed up in the human throng on the platform.

Paracelsus went on shrinking until he was no bigger than a newborn. The toothless mouth, the bare head, the skin growing ever smoother, so the old tracery of lines totally disappeared – he could no longer be distinguished from a tiny baby. The butler was getting older, too. Like Josef Rubashov, he needed a stick for support. He spoke increasingly rarely. Eventually he was as mute as Paracelsus.

Late one autumn, Rubashov lost them. It was by a motorway in France. There was only one vehicle in sight, a black car disappearing over the horizon. The sun was slowly rising over the hills. Crows were cawing from a dead tree. Far away, from another time, he thought he could hear the guest's melancholy laughter.

Then the days and years vanished in a meaningless rushing and roaring. Time had played a trick on him, he realised. Time was using him as a pawn in an incomprehensible game. When he looked up Rasputin in books, there was no mention of his taster. When he saw portraits of van der Lubbe, Philip Bouhler or Christian Wirth, he didn't recognise them.

Time was a waking dream, and he had been forced to participate in that dream. Time destroyed events and invented new ones. Time was as perfidious as memory. Time was as forgetful as Paracelsus. Whenever She made a change in the present, the past was also affected. She gave and took without any justice. She would never come to his aid.

At the epicentre of an Italian earthquake we can see him limping onward. The ground quakes and cracks, he falls and lies still. Behind him: what is left of a village, a vast heap of stones and broken tiles. Dull screams can be heard from those buried alive.

Mad dogs run round the ruins, barking. He gets to his feet and staggers on. A new tremor. The world flickers, the field of vision jumps, like a film on a shaky projector. A whole rock face comes loose from its ancient moorings and rolls down the mountainside towards the valley. He dances for joy as the enormous landslide looms towards him in a cloud of dust, making the sky darken and turning day into night.

He comes to his senses in total darkness, buried under thousands of tonnes of stone. He is lying in some kind of air pocket; in a subterranean cave. He feels around him with his hands, measuring his prison. The space, he discovers, has the dimensions of a coffin. He shuts his eyes and luxuriates. In the absence of death, this is the best he could have hoped for. Darkness. Silence. Alone, at last.

The weeks go by and he is still happy. The space is exactly the right size to allow him to change position when the ground beneath him gets too uncomfortable. He dreams of darkness and wakes in darkness, and soon he can no longer distinguish between his sleeping and waking states. The dormouse he catches in the second week, trapped in the same grave as himself, is it a dream? He tames it and trains it to perform tricks.

He eats spiders and sucks on desiccated beetle casings. He invents a game based on the random rate at which little stones break loose from the tomb roof and land on his face. It's hot in the underworld. If he strains his ears he can hear the fading sounds of other buried people.

A thin trickle of water runs down between the rocks. He licks it up when he is thirsty, and urinates where he lies. A slowworm strays into his grave. He plays with it, lets it coil between his fingers, down the front of his shirt, through the holes in his trouser pockets. When they have both tired of the game, he lifts it by its tail and holds it above his face, opens his mouth wide and swallows it whole. For several days afterwards, he can feel it moving about his stomach, writhing and hissing until the acids slowly get to work on it and the movements cease.

In the fourth or possibly fifth week he hears noises a few metres above the grave. A rhythmic knocking, metal against stone, and

260

then a dog's bark. He rationalises the occurrence as a hallucination, for he has been communing only with the dead these last days, and they have been addressing him with a clarity you seldom hear from the living. But the noises continue, regular and unnerving. He lies on his back and puts his hands over his ears, but the grave is filled with a blinding, ice-cold light that hurts so much he screams. Agitated voices fill the underworld, and believing he has gone out of his mind for good, he throws out his arms in a gesture of resignation. Then he feels the shaggy coat and the tongue wetting his face. He weeps in disappointment as they slowly hoist him out with a winch. He howls and thrashes his arms, having never asked for their rescue.

Walls fell and empires crumbled. New wars broke out, fuelled by hatred left over from the old ones. He walked constantly.

In Bosnia he made his way through forests and across huge bogs where corpses floated like stinking pontoons. He saw devastation everywhere, villages burned to the ground, ruined churches and mosques. Great streams of refugees passed him, going the other way. They were lugging bundles and leading reluctant, emaciated animals. Their faces were white with terror and streaked with tears. On the horizon, their homes were in flames.

It was a lunar landscape, cratered by grenades and artillery fire, a wrecked world where deserts of soot spread in all directions and the woods had been incinerated into fields of stubble, as soft and black as velvet. In the dusky, ghostly villages the embers were still red in the stoves, doors were slamming in the wind and abandoned chickens cackled as they ran through the streets. Corpses lay scattered about the fields, castrated, tortured.

Vultures hovered like black clouds in the sky. Stars twinkled sadly. Snow and rain fell. Far away, like thunder, the rumble of artillery could be heard.

He stood on the shorelines of seas of decaying bodies, of flesh and bone and twisted limbs, of craniums with blackened scraps of flesh still clinging to them and their hair still growing. Crows pecked out the eyes of the dead. Rats tore at rotting flesh. Fermentation processes made the corpses rock and move, as if life hadn't yet totally departed them. He closed his eyes and tried to pray to God, but confronted with this atrocity, his mind refused to form his words.

Round burned-down farms, the bodies lay in piles. Nothing was left of the sexual organs of the rape victims but bloody pulp. Men had been mutilated and children clubbed to death like calves. A woman had been slit open like a slaughtered animal and a foetus lay by a mess of placenta and intestines. Ants were swarming in the brain of the unborn child. There were bites from a cat in the woman's belly. He saw everything in black and white, for no colour existed to do justice to this pain.

Huge explosions made the ground judder. In the night sky shone stars he had never seen before. He wondered if Judgement Day had come. Was this the end of the world? Had the rulers gathered from the four corners of the Earth, from Gog and Magog, for the final decisive battle?

In one Serbian village, smoke was still rising from the ruins. He reeled about in the devastation, now almost blinded by the sights he saw. Soot fell in flakes like dry, black snow. A sudden cry made him stop. In the village street, wrapped in a blanket, lay a newborn baby. He couldn't believe his eyes. It seemed to go against the order of nature for a human being to be alive here. He picked it up and held it close to his chest; calmed by the warmth of his body, it stopped crying.

Sitting on a hearthstone in a burned-out house, he stared out into the night. The moon regarded him with the neutral expression of a gambler. But held tightly against his chest, like a doll inside his coat, the baby slept.

He could hear the light breathing, and the sound made him remember his own son from the beginning of the century. He remembered Leopold's fair hair and sea-coloured eyes. He remembered the prattle and the smell of innocence and talcum powder that rose from his pores. He remembered the little creases between the toes, and the reflex that made the fingers close round an object and grip it. He remembered it all with uncanny clarity . . .

He carried the boy on his back, in a sling he made out of leather straps and a torn-up tunic he took from the body of a slain Muslim. He cared for him with a feeling that was love and guilt in equal measure. It was as if he was repaying the debt for the death he had provoked, as if he was redeeming himself from having brought such misfortune on others by his offence on the last night of the previous century. He kept well away from the front lines. He didn't see a soul, and that made him feel safe. Where there were people there was also evil, and he shunned them for the sake of his precious charge.

He spent his time in remote forests, and in areas so devastated that no living being went there. The thought that the boy might survive kept his spirit alive. Under cover of darkness he crept up on farms and ruins to steal food – but if he found none, he cut his own hand and let the boy drink his blood. He realised it couldn't go on for ever. He knew he wouldn't always be able to carry him with him. Sooner or later he would have to leave him. But he tried not to think about that moment.

Summer came. He walked over dusty mountain passes and through acoustic valleys where the bellows of fighting soldiers had gone on echoing for months after their deaths. But the climbs took their toll on his strength and he decided to rest.

In one valley he found an abandoned farmhouse and, overcome by his own exhaustion, made preparations for the night.

He was awoken by the boy's cries and sat up. Four Serbian soldiers stood in the room. They were holding the boy by his legs, upside down. He screamed at them to stop, but before his voice had died away, they dropped the child on the ground. A soldier stabbed a bayonet into his stomach and held the boy up in front of him, like a speared animal, while his intestines came spewing out and the light of life went from his eyes.

The shock was so intense that he fainted, but when he came round he was lying naked on the floor, his hands tied behind his back.

They raped him, but he felt nothing. It was as if he had been wrapped in thick cloths and everything happening to him was really happening to someone else. He could hear their groans and taste the salt when they urinated on his face, but it seemed to happen at a great distance, perhaps in another life, or to a stranger who had lent him his consciousness for a brief while. He heard them buttoning their trousers and getting ready to go. They were laughing and joking, and before they left they doused the floor in paraffin and set it alight.

The house was a kiln where everything became charcoal. Lying on the floor, he watched the child turn to ashes. But once the ropes that bound him charred and fell off, he got to his feet and staggered round in the sea of fire.

The heat scorched every hair from his body. He took the old contract out of his pocket. He brandished it frantically in front of him. He jumped and hollered until he felt his vocal cords start to tear away from his throat.

Autumn came, and the winds drove him west. He had no idea how his legs could still carry him. He had no idea how he managed to see or hear or fill his lungs with air. He had no idea how his body could defy the immense weight of his soul.

One night in the Bosnian village of Omarska he witnessed the Serbs burning people alive. Soldiers stood around a bonfire of burning car tyres. They forced the prisoners of war onto the pyre in groups of four or five; those who hesitated were shot on the spot. It went on all night. All night they burned people. All night they murdered.

To avoid the living, he walked through the forests, but there was nowhere to hide from the dead. As he sat by his fire at nights, he saw their faces materialise in the darkness. They stood in a circle around him, misty and mute, exuding the smell of humus and the grave. They were the war's victims, victims of a century of war. They sighed and displayed their wounds, and some sat down beside him and put their transparent hands into the fire. He left them undisturbed until they tired of it and went away of their own accord.

One evening in Sarajevo, we showed ourselves to him. It was a winter in the mid-1990s. We appeared without disguise and made sure he could see who we were. The moon was shedding light onto the narrow, ruined street where we were standing. We held our hands out to him, to show we meant no harm. We explained wordlessly that we, like him, had to be there, were condemned to bear witness. And that the evil ascribed to us is humankind's own.

But he didn't care about us any more. He was indifferent. Nothing moved him any longer. He simply shook his ancient head. He turned his back on us. Just turned and went.

Short Biography on the Threshold of the End
(New Year's Eve 1999)

In Iroquois cosmology, Earth's daughter gives birth to twin sons. The youngest is called Flint, a failure of a boy who inflicts all sorts of misfortunes on the peoples and tribes of the world. He is not to be compared with the Canaanites' Baal, or with Ahriman, Ischtar, Dionysus, Loke or the biblical judge who makes a wager with God and puts Job to the test. But on this Earth with all its time, its multiplicity of languages and its jungle of migrating legends, it seems to be the case that mistakes happen – that one person is confused with the other. We know this all too well, for we have been around a long time.

We? Let's pause for a moment to consider this grammatical pitfall. We could also say 'I', but we don't. We assume so many forms that it's difficult to refer to ourselves as 'I'.

How can you maintain the sense of possessing a solid personality when you have to appear disguised as a whirlwind or a candle flame? Or an indivisible I when you are manifesting yourself as a herd of pigs? Appearing as a bit of glass or a dice also tests your sense of self to the limit, and thus we obviously feel we have a lot more in common with, for example, Margarete Barsch than with, let's say . . . Well, it doesn't matter; it's like we often say when the confusion is at its height: it amounts to nothing more than pointless polemics between pronouns.

Form, or lack of it, is both our greatest problem and our greatest asset. It creates quite exceptional mobility. People are surprised, to say the least, when we step straight out of a mirror. Or when we materialise out of thin air in a darkened room.

Not so long ago we were in a restaurant and decided to pay a visit to the gentlemen's toilet where a muddled person of the male sex was celebrating black mass, locked inside one of the cubicles. On the way in, we created quite a stir. We simply couldn't resist the temptation, as we passed the urinals and spotted the mirror covering the wall above the porcelain channel . . . we couldn't resist the impulse to squeeze in between two tipsy gents in suits who were emptying their bladders while smoking their cigars. Good evening, we ventured, quite matily, as men do when collectively relieving themselves. That did it. The fact that we were standing there emptying our bladders between them – without being visible in the mirror.

So in our case, form is a decided advantage, but also a short-coming, so we do our best to adapt. Some clients demand a certain level of propriety before they'll make their mark on the document. Strict men who would prefer to meet in a hotel lobby or at the restaurant of the masonic lodge or, for the atmosphere, in a gallery in a Gothic cathedral. Businessmen are worst, closely followed by military types. With them, all the papers have to be read thoroughly, not once but twice, and at the last minute there's always some sort of quibbling or haggling and a paragraph that needs changing for the sake of appearances. They want to be making the decisions, that's all, and to simplify matters we let them do it. On those occasions we appear discreetly dressed, in a suit appropriate to the season, and sometimes escorted by our chauffeur. Like now, for example, in this air-conditioned space the size of a ballroom on the thirty-fourth floor of a high-rise office block with tinted picture windows. Here, we are even expected to wait our turn. ('I know you've got an appointment, sir, but the director is in an important meeting at the moment. Please take a seat; there's a coffee machine in the corner.')

That causes us to ask certain questions about the way things are going. You have to admit that people at the end of this century have grown more sceptical. Maybe that's healthy? Some refuse to believe in us despite having issued the invitation themselves. Then it doesn't matter how many quick-change transformations we try. 'Prove you're really you,' they say. Or: 'I don't believe this, it's all just superstition; you simply can't be proved empirically!'

This modern attitude to metaphysics can be quite a strain. They flirt with it, but when it comes to the crunch, they start talking science. Maybe it was easier at the start of the century. At least in those days there were still plenty of backwaters where folk clung to the notion that the Earth was flat, and were always keen to voice their belief in God and the devil, who – if you studied the form they took in people's minds – were bewilderingly alike. God and the devil were in principle both as bad as each other, with the distinction that massacres and famines were called afflictions if they were viewed as having been sent by the Almighty. As regards us, we got the blame for most things that weren't tipped to be legitimate afflictions.

Beyond that, and we say this without the least sense of superiority, it seems unnecessary to attach too much significance to this particular century. Basically it's just one among thousands, a drop in an ocean of time. And when you've been around this long, you easily get them confused.

As well as form, we also have problems with time. To us, time in essence means mainly disorder, many thousands of years in a calendar of loose sheets that are shuffled and cut until there's no coherence any longer. Causality, as Rasputin so aptly put it at the dawn of the century, is only for those who need a God. For beings with our sort of overview, cause and effect are pure illusion. Because if what happens on a particular Saturday is really only the technical result of something else that happens, or has already happened, the following Saturday (i.e., is caused by a fact further on in time), well, then it becomes utterly meaningless to think in terms of cause and effect. These are matters you can ponder on as you wait for your next meeting. Like here, for example. On the thirty-fourth floor.

And while this chaos of causality is unfolding in every conceivable temporal direction, we simply try to keep the dreariness at bay. It's a real torment to us at times, the dreariness. For a while, the theatre brought us some consolation (Tertullian was quite right there). But if you've seen the Greek dramas, you've basically seen it all; the rest are just variations. We've completely given up going to the bathhouse because the hygiene standards have got so bad. The taverns are still tolerable. But actually we spend most of our time sitting by streams, trying not to think about anything in particular. That's where you're most likely to see us. On a park bench by a placid river. With a muff, if it's winter.

Our smell is another problem. It's been with us for as long as we can recall. It's presumably secreted by some gland or other, and it sometimes results in our exaggerated use of perfumes, which defeats the object because we then run the risk of arousing just as much olfactory attention, though for opposite reasons. But with age, thank God, you learn to live with your defects, sometimes even to value them.

But we can't escape the dreariness, and it get worse as the years pass. We've developed a few strategies for banishing it. Meditation's one. Writing Lucifer letters, always a popular purchase in medieval markets, is another (like this one perhaps, a Lucifer letter, from us, to you human beings, to draw attention to some of your problems). Comprehensive historical and mathematical studies are a third. But astonishingly enough, a surprise even to us, gambling is still high on our list. The astonishment naturally arises from the fact that the element of suspense is totally lacking in our case. That's the crucial difference between us and, say, the young Josef Rubashov. It simply isn't exciting when you always win. And yet, that is what we experience: suspense.

After all these years, we still can't get enough of skat, baccarat or laying bets. Or even an ordinary tombola. That ticking, rotating wheel arouses irrational feelings of happiness in us; it makes us want to cry. Or in the casino, surrounded by beautiful human women, because if there's one thing for sure, it's that girls find those who have luck, success and self-assurance totally irresistible, a fact for which history never ceases to provide examples, starting with the serpent.

269

To digress briefly on the subject of this reptile, we have a real weakness for the Ophites' theories concerning the serpent in paradise. The Ophites thought the serpent was really a secret agent sent out by God with the mission of making sure humankind got the forbidden knowledge. Forbidden from the viewpoint of the Demiurge, because he was the one in charge of paradise, and he had managed to deceive the simple human beings by means of sorcery and pompous rhetoric into believing he was the Supreme God, though in fact he was merely the creator of the material world. The true God, on the other hand, was – according to the Ophites – pure spirit, as was his kingdom. And the serpent was his messenger to the humans, with the task of imparting the knowledge of the Demiurge's evil empire of bodies and materialism, so they could begin their long trek to salvation. It isn't like that at all, of course, but we still like the story because it's edifying and also restores to the serpent, that undervalued little reptile, a modicum of its lost reputation, which like love, as every young child knows, takes a long time to build up, but only a moment to destroy.

Besides, we also have quite a few interesting memories to think back on. Take this garden, for instance (it's true!), this park with its vineyards and beautiful springs. It's night time. The sky is clear and starry. The air is full of scents: aromatic oils, grilled lamb, dates, magnolia. We walk up the hill; it's a very ordinary night, apart from the fact that it's a holiday and there are festivities in the city; we just want a bit of fresh air, and suddenly in the darkness we come across three men lying there, sleeping off the drink, we assume. We'll have to step over them carefully, because it's impertinent to awake a sleeping stranger, especially if he's intoxicated. We go on up the path lined with date palms and find ourselves standing by a wall. Behind the wall kneels a man with tangled hair looking completely crazed, on account of some lovers' quarrel, we guess. He's kneeling and pressing his face to the dry grass and whispering in a rather rustic accent from the north: Father, Abba . . . I cannot go on . . . let it pass from me . . . remove this cup from me . . . I cannot go on! A drunkard, we think, that explains things, especially at this time of night. But then we see him get up, trembling badly (with such mortal dread), weeping, stumbling, not noticing us, he goes over to the three men on the hillside and, when he finds them asleep, he's beside himself with rage and gives them a proper telling off. We think no more of it, since we're only here for a breath of fresh air, much needed after a hard day's negotiation with a Roman overseer, so we take a bit of a detour via the southern side of the hill, but no sooner are we over the crest than we run into a column of soldiers from the temple guard, tramping noisily through the grapevines, and for want of something better to do, giving up on the idea of being left in peace, we fall in with them, gripped by the general air of suspense. We march on for another few hundred metres, now with the help of the torches that the soldiers have lit to orientate themselves in the darkness, then we come to a halt by a little grove of tall pine trees. There, in the flickering light of the torches, we now see the three men who were previously asleep up on the hillside, plus various other people, men and women (which is unusual in this city, seeing them together, especially at this hour), and at their head: the kneeler himself. He seems considerably more sober now, but just as terrified as before, if not more so, and has plainly committed some crime and is about to be thrown into prison by the temple guard. Prompted by pure curiosity, we position ourselves near the front of the column, where pandemonium has just broken out, and one of the men who was asleep on the Mount of Olives, to the kneeler's annoyance, is dozily brandishing a sword. 'Who are you?' one of the temple guards asks us. 'Er . . . Malkus,' we answer. We have to say something. We could equally well have said Antonius, but that would probably sound a bit too Roman, and we're dealing here with a local populace not tremendously enamoured of the Romans, to put it mildly, and fond of arranging little assassinations.

All this in parenthesis, and with apologies for our tendency to tease: that's the language we speak, that's all, the way we sound, and what we are really trying to show is the equivocal role of chance in history. This episode, you see, gives rise to the Malkus legend. For a long time Malkus was also seen (rightly) as the witness who

271

listened to the Master's litany on the Mount of Olives, since it clearly couldn't be the disciples, because they were asleep, poor saints, according to the canon of the New Testament.

Our memories are a history in themselves; they could fill a few thousand volumes of memoirs. Alexander the Great, for example – was – if the truth be told – a real weakling. Caesar was dyslexic, and anyone who tells you otherwise is lying. Machiavelli was a bed-wetter and Goebbels had a clubfoot. It's amazing what infirmities are lurking behind the façades of the famous figures of history, which has led us to cultivate a theory that it may be the ailments, clubfeet and bedwetting that determine their success and , especially the latter. No driving force outdoes that of a complex, we've realised, not even the sexual urge.

But memory is one thing and documents are another. We have been conscientiously amassing the documentation for as long as we can remember, and there we permit no speculation, only facts. The contents of Josef Rubashov's filing cabinet, for example, are a mere drop in the ocean, and certainly not particularly comprehensive when compared to others in our collection, but it's extremely well maintained and therefore serves superbly as an example of what we do. And this is what we do: collect facts, wage war against oblivion.

Really, we hear you ask. But what about hell, then?

We shake our head at that. There is no hell as far as we know, apart from the one on Earth. And perhaps there's no God or devil either. To make life easy, we say we're the one they think we are, anything to make operations run more smoothly; and it's true that we do share some of the attributes of that mythological figure. Just as it's true that the image of him has its roots partly in us, particularly our administrative ingenuity, our feeling for correct judicial procedures and legal hair-splitting; in short, the writing of contracts. But that image also has its roots elsewhere: in Ahriman. And in Dionysus. And in Job's judge. And maybe also in the Iroquois' Flint.

God and devil are names that stand for quite shifting concepts. Yet it must all have started somewhere, clearly. Humans must have got their free will from somewhere. But we seldom permit ourselves any theological reflections. We have always existed, that's enough for us; likewise the compulsion to document.

To digress again, it's quite easy to pass ourselves off as a mathematician, and in fact our extensive studies in the subject do seem to point to mathematics as the programme of knowledge most likely to explain the master programme of the universe one day. The question is, to what end?

Oh yes, we have found mathematics fascinating on occasions: people like Pythagoras, Newton and Ramanujan with whom we, in some disguise, have had inspired and learned discussions lasting into the small hours. Even if we were mostly out to create a bit of scandal that time in Barcelona, which we sometimes find terrific fun, we did actually mean what we said to some extent.

We like mathematics, and we like scandal just as much, but our main task always remains humankind. Perhaps they are right to view us as the devil. Perhaps we, in contradiction of our own argument, really are the one they claim? But with our wider perspective, we still say it's just a word. And the only thing we can cling to is our task.

Dust has settled on Josef Rubashov's files now the century is nearing its close; the photographs have yellowed, damp has darkened the papers. Time is inexorable in its wearing down of the material world, and not even Josef Nikolai wil be spared in the long run, whatever he may imagine. At times we feel we might have chosen to present material from the case histories of more famous people. But the choices we make are often without foundation, prompted by the whim of the moment rather than logic and considered decisions. And once a choice is made, all others are ruled out for that occasion.

We sometimes find ourselves musing on this as we leaf through his documents to assemble this compilation, since even if we wished to, we haven't the time or space to present everything here. Some of the items chosen for inclusion are ones generated by ourselves. Others we have naturally tracked down among contemporary sources.

Here on the thirty-fourth floor, for example, we have with us a

273

portrait of him, a photograph severely ravaged by calendar time, retrieved from our secret archives. It shows Josef Rubashov on a solitary walk along the shores of Krestovsky Island in St Petersburg in 1911, when he was on the highest rung of his happiness, still unaware of his impending fall. We took the shot ourselves and, even then, you can see it in the melancholy shadows and cold sky we unconsciously chose as a backdrop . . . even then we knew that his life would take the form of a tragedy.

Loss is perhaps the only constant in humankind's existence, corruption its godmother, and Rubashov had to experience this as few others. He has been forced to trudge through a century which was in form unlike those that went before, but in content merely a repetition, played out within a framework of rules devised at the dawn of history. He, like every other member of his race, is a victim of humankind.

As we say in our Appendix to his file: *Josef Rubashov symbolises all the widows, widowers, orphans, the abandoned, deceived, mourning, terrified, all those tormented, bullied, expelled, enslaved, persecuted, tortured;* but he has a uniquely dual role, as he also represents: *all the survivors, those whose fate has often been many times worse than those they survived. He is a case study in the mechanisms of suicide, he symbolises the wretchedest of the wretched: those who want to die, but cannot.*

It sounds like some cold eulogy from the pen of a bureaucrat, but it is a tribute to those who have been forced to remember, or rather, to those who have never been allowed to forget. It is a dreadful fate, but also a task of the utmost importance. Among this group of people, we also number ourselves.

Soon, the filing cabinet will be full. The material is growing bulky, documents by the thousand. We swoop down on him periodically and observe him through a long human life. Through a long life of seeking and battling for his right to die, he moves us, we have to admit. He touches our hearts very deeply, because he has managed to retain his sympathy against all the odds.

But we are awoken from our reverie. The secretary is telling us that the director will see us now. We've never done business on the thirty-fourth floor before, at least not in St Petersburg, but we're always glad of any opportunity for variety.

From up here we have a matchless view over this tortured city. And somewhere down there, we know – in the milling throng of people, good and bad, rogues and human angels – somewhere there, on this New Year's Eve at the end of the century, is Josef Rubashov.

The Spirits Take Their Leave

On the fourth floor of an apartment block on Sadovaya Street in central St Petersburg, in an old, patrician apartment where the high-ceilinged rooms were embellished with elegant stucco work, and where a multitude of times were constantly slipping into and out of each other through the secret passages of existence, the ghosts were jolted from their sleep. They had been roused by the gong of history, the excited ticking of chronology and the noise from the people in this city of many million inhabitants, who now, this evening, were reverently approaching a new epoch. Among those finding themselves restored to consciousness by the unusual gravity of the moment, by the military formation of calendar time into not only a change of century but also a change of millennium – in short, by the degree of symmetry that can even awaken the dead – was an old batman of Polish birth called Waida, whose life had been ended by a broken heart as he sat by the open window of the room overlooking the inner courtyard, one winter's night in 1908.

Waida the ghost opened his eyes with an oath in the very room where he had departed from life, surprised to see the framed portrait of old Mrs Orlova, the major's widow, hanging on the wall beside a full-colour poster of an Azerbaijani tennis star, who nine decades later had become the darling of the girls of St Petersburg. Startled from sleep, he looked down at his translucent feet, where scenes from his life were being replayed on the film screen of his toenails, and found that he was floating five centimetres from the floor, which was still covered by the old widow's heirlooms, the costly but threadbare carpets from Samarkand. *I'm dead,* he thought, *yet I'm alive. How peculiar!*

He marvelled at the array of objects whose uses he did not know. A computer screen on a desk he took for a silted-up aquarium, and a pair of earphones for modern earmuffs against the Russian winter cold. An impulse to look out of the window at the view that had been his for thirty-four years was a fact almost before it was born. He realised that in his new incarnation, movement consisted of thought, so he no longer needed to make any effort to change his position.

It was a city of light he saw spread before him; strangely flashing signs in all the colours of the rainbow; sparkling electric streetlights; two droning stars were moving across the sky, and the batman understood wordlessly that they were flying machines, invented by humankind after his death. Along the streets ran thousands of streamlined automobiles; horses, he could see, were now an extinct species.

Propelled by thought, he passed straight though the wall and found himself standing in his neighbour's room. There, as blurred as mist, lying on his stomach under the bed, a dead Zweig was grovelling for his chamber pot without any noticeable success. *Somebody's stolen my pot,* he heard the lawyer's clerk mutter. *That's out-and-out cruel. Just as I was waking up and needing to relieve myself.* The voice couldn't be heard in the room, only in the batman's own ghostly consciousness, which seemed to be rather like the receiver of a telegraph station with some sort of built-in dictionary or simultaneous interpretation system, because Zweig was cursing about his lost pot in the incomprehensible dialect of the Volga Germans, but the batman nonetheless understood every word.

He was surprised that the lawyer's clerk had found his way back to the widow Orlova's apartment, for the German had died two years before him, in the city of Viborg where he had gone with an uncle for a winter holiday; late one night, after a serious drinking session, he had fallen asleep in a snowdrift outside a place of entertainment, never to wake again. *You were like me, Zweig,* thought Waida, *unhappy in life. We never got the women we wanted, and never earned a kopek more than it took just to keep ourselves afloat. Life's unfair. Only the scoundrels are rewarded with riches. The little people, like us, who tried to live respectable lives, what reward did we get? We died as we lived, in poverty, in obscurity.*

Waida the batman transformed his thought into electrical impulses that whizzed through the circuits in the walls, round and round at the speed of light. When he got dizzy he climbed out through a ceiling light, and with a parachute made of a delicately stitched patchwork of rose petals from a two-thousand-year-old garden from the dream of one of his ancestors, he floated to the floor in the room that had once been occupied by Rubashov the gambler. He gave a sob at the memory of the tricks played by chance and coincidence. For the fact was that when Rubashov had been thrown out after a dispute about the rent on New Year's Day a century before, the door had been opened to the batman's personal Waterloo: haberdasher's assistant and young woman of easy virtue Andrea Nekrasova, an apparition to whom he had for ever lost his heart.

Waida recalled the love that had radiated from him that day she moved in, for at first sight she had lit a fire in him that even death had failed to extinguish. He was amazed. By the light of a centennial moon he saw her sitting on the stool by the window that Easter evening in 1901 when he had plucked up his courage to propose, only to be instantly turned down. She looked just the same as ever, sighing as she pulled apart an obscenely painted *matroushka* and marked on her calendar a lovemaking assignation with a deputy director long since deceased. *Andrea!* he whispered. *Nobody loved you as I did, and in death my love is stronger than ever. And yet you never cared about me. How many times did you humiliate me by throwing my bunches of flowers out of the window and dismissing my love poems with a prosaic yawn? Or when we saw each other in a restaurant on Sredny Prospekt and you pretended not to know me.*

278

Get lost, Waida! he heard her reply in her affected Muscovite dialect, which barely concealed her true roots: a peasant village on the far side of the Urals, where she had been a farm maid until famine had driven her to St Petersburg.

The moon vanished and was replaced by the dazzle of the New Year rockets, and with the aid of thought the batman undressed her, so he could see her naked for the first time. *Stop that,* she said, but without trying to conceal either her sandy pubic hair or her pale, perfect breasts with the nipples painted ochre. *Or pay ten roubles for a look, Waida. And if you want sex, it'll cost fifty more, or a three-course dinner with champagne at Myslinska's; I know what I'm worth, Mr Batman, I'm not just any old whore.*

Waida laughed and felt the hundred-year-old wound to his heart being healed by the plantain leaves of death and the cobwebs of invisible angels; and he knew that sometime, sooner or later, he would win her love, for he now had infinity at his feet, and that encompassed all the possibilities of the universe. In infinity, he thought ecstatically, everything that had ever been created, or could or should have been created, was latent. There lay everything that had not yet been put into effect, every pair of opposites in harmonious union, and now he could calmly bide his time. With a smile he attired her in the expensive dress he had seen in a shop window on Nevsky in 1902, but never been able to afford to buy; and he prevented her climbing into the cab that one morning the following year would carry her to the end of her earthly life, strangled with rusty wire on the floor of a hunting lodge of a landowner in Novgorod, who later bribed himself free and emigrated to Siberia.

How did it feel, my love, he said, *to die by a murderer's hand? You poor child!*

There are no words to describe that fear, replied Andrea Nekrasova. *The certainty that life is going to end, and not through illness or accident or choice; now evil itself has assumed the form of a rich gentleman and I am going to die like a slaughtered animal on the floor.*

Big tears rolled down her diaphanous cheeks where a beauty spot was still visible as an emblem of her dubious profession, and her

279

hands twisted like two frightened animals round the birchwood doll. *I was looking out of the window when it happened, Waida, and the wire round my neck was like fire and ice at the same time; and my thoughts ran riot: this isn't happening to me, it's happening to one of my poor sisters who receives her clients in hovels hired out by the hour. I hate men, Waida, yes, the whole lot of them, you included.*

In the certain knowledge that losses were no longer possible, the batman let the image of her dissolve. His ghostly form flowed through a telephone cable and emerged from an electric wall socket, and he found he was still in Andrea Nekrasova's room, to which the carnival music of modern car horns and cries of the celebrating crowd were now carrying. A blurred figure was sitting at a table in one corner, drinking from something he took to be a teacup. The creature grew more distinct, and eventually the batman could see it was an ancient man with a white beard; being dead himself, he instinctively knew he was dealing here with one of the living. He sat down on the table, cross-legged like a tailor, and observed the old man shamelessly through the curtain of invisibility. *Mr Rubashov,* he whispered, still unsure whether the living could hear him. *Is it really you?*

Clearly life, too, was full of miracles, for the old gambler should have been dead and buried long since; he was as old as Noah. The batman wondered what could have brought him back to the lodgings of his youth. Common sense told him it couldn't be to pay the rent arrears from 1899; any legal liability for those would have expired long ago. *Repetition has brought him here,* he thought, *for if you have reached such a great age in life, simple statistics show that you are bound to start treading in your own footsteps, because everything has already been done.*

While the batman was inhaling the scents of the man's old age and looking round the room, where the light was all electric and the furniture looked uncomfortable and modern, although in fact the old samovar was still there, along with the steel engraving of a three-masted schooner on the wall, he recalled the young man who had lived in the room an eternity ago. He remembered a well-dressed youth from a merchant family, who had got into debt with pawnbrokers because of his compulsive gambling, but had managed to retain a certain dignity even so. He remembered the young man's morning walks and the way he always politely raised his hat to the other lodgers if he happened to meet them in the street. He remembered he had had a weakness for cats, had grieved over widow Orlova's ban on pets in rooms, and had been courting a beautiful actress at the Théâtre Française. And he remembered that young Mr Rubashov once, when he, Waida, had been completely without funds after a short illness, had given him ten roubles, for which he still felt gratitude. There wasn't much resemblance, he thought, between that youth and the ancient man who now sat in the room, drinking tea and staring into space – how could he know it was the same person, even?

Waida the batman lost interest and floated away, still in his tailor pose, through the dark apartment where epochs and times flowed into each other to make a seething brew of eternity.

In widow Orlova's kitchen he came across a very young woman. Some relation of the major's wife, he guessed, because she looked very like the woman in the old photograph. She was surrounded by suitcases and neatly folded clothes; presumably she was about to go on a journey, because she had that peculiar leave-taking gleam of sadness mixed with relief in her eyes. He bent his ear to her brow and listened to the crackle of her thoughts: *New Year's Eve and everybody I know's out celebrating; why aren't I? Because I'm getting out, leaving this bloody city and all the ominous signs, and not least, my sadness about Sasha, not least that . . .*

Who are you, young lady, whispered the batman. *And where are you going?*

Her? It was a different voice that answered, from some invisible part of the kitchen. *That, Waida, is young Miss Yelena, great-granddaughter of the major's widow Anna Orlova, née Klemov, deceased 1918, from whom you rented a musty room for no fewer than thirty-four years. The girl herself is named after the title of a couplet by the songwriter Vysotski, unknown to you, batman, popular long after your death, and what do you care about the living, anyway, go and lie down, go back to your eternal rest, you're a hundred years after your time!*

281

Astonished, and floating with his back to the ceiling, Waida the ghost heard other voices from invisible mouths: the girl was born in '79, they said, *and we're not talking about the 1800s, Waida, and she's not remotely familiar with the Holy Mother Russia you call yours. Try to get that into your head; what does she know of your love for the haberdasher's assistant; what does she know of your secret dream of going to a ball at the Winter Palace; what does she know of long-bearded metropolitans, mysterious Skoptsist orders, convents and monks, holy fools, the Russo-Japanese War and the battleship* Potemkin, *where they mutinied for a few bits of rancid pork? Father Gapon and the black hundreds? They mean nothing to her. Rasputin? An article in the Sunday supplements when there's no news. You have nothing in common but this apartment, where the living and the dead have apparently got to get along for one evening, and the fact that you coincidentally both happen to be Scorpios and are both still suffering the after-effects of a defeat on the battlefield of love. Pull yourself together, Waida. Go and lie down in the nearest grave!*

Waida the ghost looked about in the hope of seeing the person or people speaking, but only he and Yelena were present. He noticed he had moved from his elevated position by the ceiling, and found he had turned into condensation between the two layers of the double glazing in the kitchen window looking out over the street. *Very odd,* he thought, *these constant changes of form; and what will happen, I wonder, if the temperature goes down; will I turn to ice, and become solid material?*

Outside, neon signs were winking their advertisements for foreign fizzy drinks and a column of taxis was transformed into a string of shining pearls, trickling through the night's hand. The crowds on the footpaths were converging on Nevsky. Cries went up: Long live the President! Long live the Republic!

In his condensed form, Waida the ghost shed tears for the empire he now understood to be gone for good, and the moisture clouded his gaze, making the view over the Neva, the quayside, Liteyny Avenue and its rows of brightly lit fast-food restaurants and brothels with red lights run together like the colours on an artist's palette. Rockets exploded in the sky, and with the all-seeing eye of death he discovered the great hole in the ozone level, high up in the atmosphere.

He went back to the kitchen.

Waida, said a new, demanding voice. *Can you hear me?*

He listened as he stroked Yelena's hair, because she looked as though she needed comforting.

I'm here, he answered. *You just carry on with your invisible talking, and teach me everything about life after death.*

All right then, batman. Like the girl, you're utterly ignorant of Russia's role as an ideological laboratory over more than half a century: Trotsky fleeing on the sledge, Lenin playing skat in a sealed train on the way to Stockholm, the fall of the Tsars, the revolution, the civil war, Stalin, the murder of the kulaks, the Great Patriotic War, the turning point at Stalingrad, the Gulags, Khrushchev with the shoe, Brezhnev with the hat, Andropov with the hat, Gorbachev with the bald head. Well, with a little effort she might recall the last of those, because of the birthmark on the crown of his head that stirred every child's imagination; and the Communists are still there in the Duma, and becoming increasingly active, although the available information indicates that young Yelena voted Liberal in the first election of her life a year or two back . . . but, and listen to this, Waida, you might learn something you never grasped while you were alive: in spite of this, you do have many experiences in common with this young girl. Her Russia is in actual fact, whatever we said previously, a repetition of yours, for it is to some degree true that history goes in circles, or rather that it's lacking in imagination and can't think of anything better than repeating its old faux pas; then as now, injustice and unparalleled poverty prevail; then as now, starving small boys sell their bodies to paedophiles at Moscow railway stations; humankind is evil, Waida, and has grown no better, that's for sure; St Petersburg is still the home of the homeless: only last night they found no fewer than fourteen corpses, frozen to death under St Petersburg's beautiful bridges; every last civil servant is corrupt, every last office girl is a prostitute, the mafia does its business openly, bribes are a bigger item of expenditure than taxes and wages, people are starving and freezing and boozing just as in your time, nothing has seriously changed for the better; your

Russia, Waida, and the girl's, is a catastrophe.

Widow Orlova's great-granddaughter, the batman noted, gave a start when the disembodied voice mentioned organised crime, so he floated over to hang from her left earring, legs dangling, and listen again to the crackle of her thoughts:

The mafia is responsible for me standing here packing my bags instead of celebrating out there, seeing in the new millennium. First there's the protection money I have to pay as landlady here. My great-grandmother once owned this apartment, but the communists took it from her and turned it into a liaison centre for the Cheka in the war against the Whites, and seventy years later under the new property legislation I got it back. Fate and heating costs forced me to rent out rooms by the month, just like old Anna Orlova, though now only old Rubashov is left, and I hope it's sunk in that he's got to vacate the room by tomorrow at the latest . . .

Rubashov, repeated the batman. *I was right, then. It was Rubashov! Just so: Rubashov!* He heard a voice right beside him again. *A peculiar old man, talks to himself as if he's senile, and he'll often stand for ages in front of the portrait of Anna Orlova, watching her with the sort of look you might give an old acquaintance, which is impossible of course, isn't it, Waida, because that would make him way over a hundred years old. Though the question is: would more lodgers have helped to pay what the mafia are demanding from young Miss Yelena: four hundred dollars a month to protect her property, which they deferred collecting for nearly six months, but now their patience has run out. How else could she interpret the noose hanging on the door handle the other week, or the late-night telephone calls? She's scared to death, poor girl, and that's why she's had to turn to the same organisation, though another department of it, one that deals in forged papers in a modern office block on Krestovsky Island, where she's been lucky enough to get for exactly four hundred dollars a baptism certificate giving her new family name as Mandelstam, all its official stamps 100 per cent kosher, and with that document attesting parentage not her own, tomorrow she'll be . . .*

But Waida the ghost didn't wait for the end of the account, the part explaining why young Yelena wasn't out with the New Year partygoers, including the tragic story of Sasha, Alexander, the boy who disappeared in the Chechen War, and the part with the exact departure time of the Lufthansa flight to Berlin, the German capital, where a new future awaited her as an immigrant of Russian Jewish birth, who would make a first attempt to forget the state of anguish in which love had left her. No, Waida the batman didn't wait for the disembodied voice's explanations, because something outside in the street had caught his attention.

Assuming the form of some light reflected on the window pane, he watched a black limousine park outside the boarded-up bread shop on the other side of the street, and something told him that the man in widow Orlova's old flat was expecting an important visitor that very evening.

Things are brewing up, said the ghostly voice beside him in a tone that might as well be referring to the weather as to the car. *It's going to be an unforgettable New Year's Eve, batman, depend on us.*

Outside, the snow had begun to fall in fine crystals, coloured by the neon lights of the city and the rockets that were exploding with ever-increasing frequency and cascading over the sky like beautiful, flowing hair. Waida saw, half a block away, policemen brutally dragging off a drunken beggar; time was approaching the stroke of twelve and a surge of sound rose from Nevsky, where the nation's President would at any moment be making his speech via the huge video screens. The snow fell more and more thickly. A chauffeur got out of the car and opened the door for his passenger. A woman who was passing crossed herself and hobbled hastily away towards Nevsky as if she had just seen death. If so, it was death dressed as a butler, thought the batman, because the chauffeur was wearing servant's livery of the last century, and beneath a bowler hat the empty eye sockets of a skull gleamed gently.

For understandable reasons, the young landlady Yelena hesitated before answering the door this New Year's Eve. Admittedly the knocks were discreet, but rumours and newspaper headlines were running through her mind. She remembered the story of the dozen pensioners who in their poverty had sold the deeds of their council flats to a gang on Vasilievsky Island and, after making their marks on the contracts, had vanished without trace. She recollected a street vendor by the Kirov Bridge who had refused to pay protection money and was found two days later in the Griboyedov Canal, all his fingers cut off with a pair of secateurs. Another, she recalled, had been found with a message stuck down his throat, warning the business community of the consequences of paying their insurance premiums late. She thought of all this as the knocking at the door began again, and a voice told her to stop hesitating, because ultimately no one can escape their fate. So she opened the door, and a glimpse of the late-night visitor calmed her.

He was a foreigner, she assumed, as there was something about his strange taste in clothes that she couldn't account for. He was wearing moth-eaten tails, and across his shoulders hung a black cape with a fur collar. He appeared to be in his forties, and the long face with the gentle eyes was crowned with a dusty green top hat, with a hole in the middle that looked like a cigar burn.

'I am looking for Mr Josef Rubashov,' he said politely, 'your only lodger in these hard times, if my information is correct, young lady.'

Yelena realised she'd been wrong about the man's background, for his Russian was impeccable, if a little old-fashioned. She looked at Anna Orlova's old wall clock, which still hung in its place next to the row of undusted ikons in the hall.

'It's late,' she said, 'nearly midnight. Is he expecting you?'

The man standing in front of her lowered his voice:

'Absolutely not. That would defeat the whole point of my visit. We are old acquaintances, Mr Rubashov and I. Though a long time has passed since last we met, and I wanted to surprise him.'

An antiquated fountain pen was sticking out from under the visitor's top hat. He was pink from the evening cold, and on his cheek there was a fresh shaving cut. He was wearing white gloves and carrying a leather briefcase.

'Miss Yelena,' he said tentatively, looking at the nameplate on the door. 'I can assure you that if you let me in so I may surprise my friend . . . then you, Miss Yelena, will henceforward permanently be spared the blackmailers of St Petersburg's stinking underworld, who I understand have been persecuting you since this somewhat lugubrious apartment was restored to you. No, do not misunderstand me! I am not a member of that group as you momentarily feared, but even so, believe me, I am in possession of particular means, which, so to speak, can give you a certain immunity . . .'

The young landlady regarded the strangely dressed figure with amazement, and some instinct told her that this man, who seemed so young and yet so old, considering his taste in clothes and turns of phrase, was a gentleman who kept his promises, and whose help could be counted on if needed.

'I am even prepared to stake my good name,' he said gravely, 'my *honneur* as a *monsieur décoré*, with God knows how many titles and orders since time immemorial, that you will never again be pestered by these loathsome hooligans. Believe me. I am fully empowered to have them punished. At this very second, in fact. Yes, at this precise instant, if necessary!'

And unaware that the visitor's words were at that moment being put into action, and that the St Petersburg police would be reporting at a confused morning conference the very next day that no fewer than twenty-four of the city's underworld villains, protection and blackmail specialists in the Sadovaya/Kirov Prospekt area had in the strangest of circumstances, been found incarcerated and, frightened out of their wits in a prison cell in the Peter and Paul Fortress, together with a suitcase full of compromising material that would stand up in any court, plus a letter of greeting from a certain Monsieur Charlot Feder-Wisch, who said he preferred not to be there in person . . . for ever unaware of this, she opened the door wide to the late-night visitor and let him in.

'Do come in,' she said, 'but please don't stay too long. Mr Rubashov has got to get up early. We're both moving out tomorrow . . .'

Miss Yelena would never forget the man who stepped over her threshold that night. In the light of the hall lamp she could see him more clearly: he was boyish in appearance, his growth of beard was sparse, his eyes dark and his face freckled. When he took off his gloves, she saw that his nails were painted blue. And to this man's peculiarities she was soon able to add another: his smell. Behind an initial defensive wall of scent, which incidentally she was able to identify as a modern brand of perfume for men, Hugo Boss, with which he had generously splashed himself, lurked another, less-than-wholesome smell. She wrinkled her nose unconsciously. Her thoughts went to the sulphate factories by Lake Ladoga and days of low pressure on Petrovsky Island, where many households relied on low-grade coal for heating, but before she could conclude her associations, the visitor interrupted her.

'Nothing to trouble one's nose with,' he said apologetically. 'It is presumably some side-effect of digestion. Probably, when all is said and done, it is the result of an undesirable lifestyle: late nights, a great deal of stress, in my capacity as *maître des plaisirs* among all manner of sinners and hedonists. The good life, in short, takes its toll.'

The visitor took off his coat and surveyed the hall. From the trouser pocket of his dress-suit he produced a cigarillo that, strangely enough, was already alight, or perhaps lit itself instantaneously.

'If you have no objection, Miss Yelena,' he said, blowing a coquettish smoke ring, 'I would prefer to present myself unannounced. Just show me the door of Mr Rubashov's room, and I will make my entrance. The whole thing is conceived as a surprise, you see. And I certainly promise to heed your recommendation: my visit will be brief; a few minutes only, if things go as I hope.'

Overwhelmed by a conviction that the late-night visitor could read her thoughts, Yelena led him through the long corridor to the other wing of the apartment. At the far end, a door was ajar, letting a chink of light shine through. Behind that door was the old man, presumably sitting at his tea table. Yelena hesitated, although she knew nothing of either him or his guest. Rubashov was an ancient man who seldom drew any attention to himself; he was neither exaggeratedly friendly, nor grumpy for that matter; like so many old people, he seemed to live in his memories. She remembered his sighs late at night when sleep deserted him, his way of talking to himself, and the old, yellowed document at which he would sit staring for hours on end, before folding and unfolding it again. He seemed to be waiting for something, the nature of which he had long since forgotten.

She came to a halt. Through a corridor window she caught a glimpse of the street below. A man in chauffeur's uniform was standing on the pavement beside a big black car, which she realised must belong to her visitor. She wondered if he was cold . . .

'You are wrong, Miss Yelena,' said the guest from behind her, 'and remarkably enough, I feel I have used these very words in this apartment once before. My old servant has been in the family for as long as anyone can remember, and he doesn't feel the cold at all. Bringing him up here to warm himself by the radiators would be a little ill considered. The majority of people find him most alarming, and I am sure you would take the same view. What are you waiting for, Miss Yelena? Is my friend not at home?'

The young landlady turned to the midnight guest in the darkness. One doubt was still gnawing at her: perhaps this gentleman wouldn't be a welcome guest in the old man's room. But her indecision evaporated as the visitor assumed for a split-second the appearance of Alexander Sasha Sinoviev in his last moment in war-torn Chechnya, and she knew then that he, the love of her life, had died remembering her.

Resting in the tear-filled eyes of an ikon of the holy virgin of Kazan, Waida the ghost looked out over the kitchen area of widow Orlova's old apartment. *Look at her,* whispered a spectral voice close beside him, *she hasn't got a clue! Who's that chap in the tail-coat, she's wondering, who smells so peculiar and decides to turn up in a chauffeur-driven limousine at twelve o'clock on New Year's Eve; that'll give her something to get her teeth into, don't you agree, batman?*

Waida the ghost twisted wildly to and fro and peered into all the twelve dimensions that death had revealed to him, but nowhere could he locate the speaker. *Don't bother about me,* laughed the voice, *it makes no difference how hard you look, Waida: firstly, I'm not one, but many, I'm a branch on a plural that has in any case been ubiquitous for ever, despite the fact that we have just arrived with our chauffeur and are in all ten rooms of this patrician apartment simultaneously, in legions as they say, in the future, the past and the*

*present; and so, batman, stop straining to see us, it will get you
nowhere; look at the girl instead.*

And Waida saw. Sitting on a stool, her eyes glassy, widow
Orlova's great-granddaughter was pretending to follow the pictures
in something the batman with his hundred years of backwardness
took for an extremely sophisticated kaleidoscope, but which was in
actual fact a Korean television set. On its screen now was the
national President, in a live broadcast from Moscow, with a
champagne glass in his hand and a facial expression intended to
convey confidence in the approaching new millennium. 'In just a
few minutes,' he said solemnly, mopping the perspiration from the
back of his neck with a handkerchief, 'we will sing in the new
millennium together with our national anthem.'

The batman could see that Yelena was paying only cursory
attention to the pictures in the strange kaleidoscope, and that her
thoughts were occupied with very different matters: a tragic love
story that had found its resolution in the transformed face of the
visitor; anxiety about the future, and in particular how she would
make ends meet, having as previously stated invested her last dollar
in a forged baptism certificate and a plane ticket to Berlin.

How will it work out, he heard her thinking, *I don't know a soul in
Germany, but I've got to get away from here, otherwise I'll die, nothing
left but to go on the street, I'd never cope with that, who's the man in
the tail-coat, what are they talking about in that room, can't let it get
too late, I leave tomorrow and Mr Rubashov will have to find lodgings
for the night elsewhere, very strange, his face turned into Sasha's for a
moment, now at least I know he's dead, how will I manage without
money, you can't live on fresh air, long live Russia, long live me . . .*

'Long live the President!' came the echo from the city centre,
where a salvo of rockets was being let off, making the snow-filled
sky look as if it was raining flakes of gold; and under the noise of
the crowd, very faintly, the two voices from the room at the end of
the corridor could be heard.

She won't be able to contain herself much longer, thought Waida,
watching the young girl; *I'd better keep an eye on her so she doesn't
do anything stupid in her human foolishness.*

290

But the curiosity of Waida the batman matched Yelena's own, so when she got up and opened the door to the narrow service corridor that ran parallel to the hall, linking the kitchen with the rooms in the east wing, he decided to go with her. He gripped firmly onto one of her moist eyelashes and let himself be silently transported through the dark corridor with its faint smell of mould and the yearning of newly awoken ghosts to where the contours, the intonation of the two voices began to grow clearer . . .

She stopped in an alcove adjoining the end room. There was a little peephole in the wall. Yelena thought it was from the time of the secret police, but in fact its originator was her great-grandmother Anna Orlova, who at the end of the previous century had had it made so that she could secretly keep an eye on that young rake Rubashov, who was always behind with the rent. Now Yelena held her breath and peeped through it.

It isn't nice to spy on people, whispered a voice from the eyelash next to Waida's, before giving a cackling laugh, *but the girl has only herself to blame, and anyway, how can she possibly tell anybody what she's seen, no one will believe a word. You're mentally ill, they'll say. You need medication! Delirium at your age! Go easy on the booze, young lady!*

And it certainly was a remarkable scene Yelena witnessed that New Year's Eve. For inside the room, by the light of the electric chandelier, at opposite sides of a tea table, sat the ancient Josef Rubashov and his late-night visitor, who now defied any attempt at definition. He was a single, unbroken chain of transmutations, of guises and forms melting ceaselessly in and out of each other. One moment he was an old man with a golden crown on his head, the next a young woman in a veil, deep in prayer with a tame toad on her shoulder. He became a twelve-year-old boy who became a bat wearing a suit, which became a metropolitan, a gryphon, a hydra, a fire, which turned into Waida the batman himself and then young Yelena, suitcase in hand, next becoming a youthful Josef Rubashov, and again an old woman, who transmogrified into a white goose, a black cock, a wild boar with golden tusks, a burning bush, the cutting edge of a sword, a candle flame, a unicorn horn, toneless music, the wind echoing inside an earthenware jug, and finally haberdasher's assistant Andrea Nekrasova in the full flush of her beauty, which aroused the passions of the batman.

Miss Yelena shut her eyes on this bewildering transformative process, but when she opened them again, the visitor was sitting there in his original tail-coated form with his top hat on his head, and on the table in front of him lay his briefcase, full to bursting with pale-blue, hundred-mark notes. He rotated his right ear half a turn, opening a shutter in his top hat, from which he extracted a pack of cards that cut itself as it floated in the air. The young landlady closed her eyes anew in an attempt to save her sanity, and when she opened them for a second time she saw the visitor waving to her from his place by the table, then politely raising his hat to reveal a pink rabbit cropping the luxuriant clover that was growing freely on his head. Only then did her senses fail her, and she fell through darkness . . .

But batman Waida squeezed his elastic ghost body through the little peephole in the alcove wall and abandoned Miss Yelena to her fate, slumped unconscious in the service corridor.

In the light of the New Year fireworks, the room in the east wing was filled with all the souls who had once lived in the old apartment. There were two freed prisoners of war from the Battle of Svensksund, a forgotten romantic poet in a pigtailed wig, and Anna Orlova herself, the major's widow, perched on top of a bookcase, legs dangling as she read from an accounts book for the year 1899, which showed Josef Rubashov still owing three months' rent. From the tap of the samovar peeped the Muscovite dancer with whom the batman had shared a room for his first year in St Petersburg, while under the bed, Zweig the lawyer's clerk was still hunting for his lost chamber pot. By himself at one end of the room stood a lieutenant-colonel of the Cheka who had met his end in a cleaning cupboard, poisoned by a colleague during the purges, with a gleaming party badge on his chest; and in the chaise longue by the tiled stove, wearing a negligee of dew and encircled by nameless spectres, reclined haberdasher's assistant Andrea Nekrasova with a liqueur glass in her hand, waving the batman over to join her.

A dream came true as she permitted him to kiss her dusty hand without resistance. *What a marvellous night!* she whispered softly; *everything is here at the same time, all our lost time and all our dreams, has Resurrection Day come, Waida?*

The batman rested his head in her lap and rejoiced inwardly that she was allowing him to; he listened to the parallel ticking of fourteen different times and had a vision of the desolate marshlands that for a thousand years had dominated the area where St Petersburg was now laid out, before Peter the Great, on horseback, had pointed to the place with his silver sceptre and cried: *From here let the Baltic be ruled!* He kissed the cold brow of the haberdashery assistant and knew he could understand everything without words that night, all the secrets of life and death, all the mysteries of love and time – everything he had ever brooded about was revealed to him in the form of an absolute but inaudible music. He felt it flowing though the room and out across the world, and at the same time he was aware that it was all different for the old man sitting at the tea table opposite the visitor, waiting for the game to begin. *The seconds are ticking down to the new millennium,* said a new ghost voice beside him, *and you're right: seen through Josef Rubashov's eyes, the room looks quite different from the way it looks through, say, yours, because that old man there has still not had the insight of death, and can see neither you nor the old widow rustling her accounts on the bookcase, nor for that matter her husband, Major Orlov, still in the position in which death claimed him in 1864: hanging by a noose from the ceiling after losing his honour as an officer by committing common fraud. And the fact that young Miss Yelena is lying unconscious in the service corridor . . . he's oblivious even to that, deaf, blind and senile as he is.*

If Josef Rubashov could have heard that voice, he would at once have concurred, because for him this was merely a poorly lit rented room in central St Petersburg, where admittedly his fate had once been sealed, and where destiny had once again reunited him with the being who had on that occasion so altered the trajectory of his arrow of fate. He didn't notice the bizarre accumulation of dead people; he watched his guest without expression as the latter, at the table, shuffled the cards in the normal way, and heard him say in an equally normal, human voice, perhaps a little husky from all those cigars:

'You get one chance. We'll play just a single game: double or quits. And for form's sake we must have something tangible to play for. We'll let these banknotes represent the concept of suspense, in this case the potential for total win or total loss, which for you means a lot, in fact everything . . .'

Josef Rubashov was amazed at not being able to summon up any feelings for the being sitting opposite him in top hat and tails. No hatred, no loathing. No surprise that he had offered him a final return match. All he felt was immense fatigue, a longing for sleep, in this last minute of the millennium.

'Let's lay down a couple of simple rules,' said his guest, smiling. 'To make it more exciting, I suggest each player must have at least a pair of jacks to open. Two exchanges are allowed, and discarded cards are to be put down beside your own hand, so they can be checked later. I take it as read that neither of us will cheat.'

The guest fell silent and took out his pocket watch. He wound it and looked at the face with raised eyebrows.

'In thirty seconds a new era will be upon us,' he said hoarsely. 'Allow me, Kolya, to postpone the stroke of midnight until we have finished our game. What does clock time signify on a night like this? And since nothing can be ruled out, I suggest that a flush of four beats two pairs. Are you in?'

Josef Rubashov realised that this whole evening was a dream, filled with inaudible music that explained the enigmas of existence, but he still couldn't perceive it. Tactics and strategies, unused for a century, popped up from his memory. He recalled that you should never raise more than you thought you could afford in relation to your hand, and that you should only stay in a game if a calculation of probability indicated you had the best cards. He remembered the rule that if you bid too high, you run the risk of your opponent folding too soon, so the pot will be smaller, but that conversely if you bid too low, you risk being seen to early and getting a reduced pot for the opposite reason. But these tactical rules, he thought, did not apply tonight, with the unannounced arrival of his former guest, as if his long life of searching had meant nothing. The money in the briefcase was only there as a symbol of what the game represented, all or nothing, and tonight they would only play a single game, with two exchanges, without bidding anything other than the mortality that had been at stake a hundred years before. All this ran through his mind as the guest shuffled the cards one last time and passed them to him to cut.

'Right then, Kolya,' he said, depositing his cigar in the ashtray. 'No point offering you the chance to change your mind. What use would that be? You've everything to win and nothing at all to lose, since the implication of *quits* is all too clear, while logic tells us eternal life can't be doubled. Go on, cut and deal. I've several more appointments tonight. The world is the waiting room of souls.'

And as the roar went up from the celebrating crowds, and the ghosts in their invisible dimension were caught up in the gravity of the moment and gathered round the table in Sadovaya Street in St Petersburg, Josef Rubashov cut the pack and dealt.

'Pray for good luck, Kolya,' said his opponent, receiving the first cards, 'because this is going to be the only chance you get.'

Standing behind Josef Rubashov's back, Waida the ghost peered hopefully at his first hand, which consisted of a pair of queens plus mixed cards of low denominations.

So he's got past the starting limit, whispered Andrea Nekrasova at his side, for everyone in the room had now begun to realise what was at stake in the game, and was watching in great suspense. *He's over the first hurdle, the two jacks. Let's pray to God, Waida, that the game carries on like this for him.*

On the other side of the table, the visitor discarded three cards and asked for the same number of new ones; clearly he had reached the starting limit too. Josef Rubashov also rid himself of his three worst cards, and at a nod from the visitor he dealt again with his trembling, old man's hands.

He put the new cards behind his pair and fanned them out. Again they were low cards.

Still a pair of queens, whispered Waida to the haberdashery assistant, who was now showing her nerves by pinching his arm, *that doesn't bode well, Andrea, the chances of his visitor having a better hand are statistically very great; not that I'm any expert in games of chance, but Rubashov must have reduced his chances by several hundred per cent. Now he's only got one go left.*

The batman laid an invisible hand, intended as a gesture of support, on Josef Rubashov's shoulder, and noted that the visitor wasn't asking for any more cards; clearly he was content. Only Josef Rubashov took fresh ones . . .

Behind him, all the apartment's ghosts were now assembled, murmuring excitedly, and even Mrs Orlova – to whom he was, after all, still in debt – offered up a quick prayer for his good fortune. He fanned out the cards from his last exchange. They were a four of hearts, an eight of clubs and finally a jack of spades. A ripple of disappointment ran through the room, someone swore and there was a ticking as if from a thousand nervous clocks.

Batman Waida's eyes filled with tears as Josef Rubashov, with a hundred years of pain in the action, laid his hand on the table, backs uppermost.

'So you want me to show first,' said his former guest with a smile. 'Why not, Kolya. I feel relatively confident. *Voilà.*'

The guest laid his hand on the table: it was four kings.

'And yours, Kolya? Let's get this over with. I've got to go soon.'

And as all the bells of St Petersburg began ringing in the new millennium, Josef Rubashov turned up his hand and filled the whole apartment with astonishment, for it now comprised four aces, plus a fifth card that was a photograph taken of him in exactly the same room, at exactly the same hour, but a hundred years earlier, with a laughing joker in each corner.

'You let me win,' he said, and his voice was so feeble it was hardly audible. 'You cheated, and let me win . . .'

The visitor got up and took his cape from the back of the chair. He had his pocket watch in his hand again and was staring fixedly at its face.

'Nobody noticed anything,' he mumbled. 'What do human

beings comprehend of the elasticity of time? Suddenly a minute is filled with double the content, but nobody has the wits to work out that the minute itself might actually be twice as long.'

He put his cape over his arm and looked at the cards.

'Oh, and you're right, by the way,' he said. 'I let you win . . . For what reason, you may ask. Pity, perhaps, or possibly everything was decided in advance, or afterwards. But it's true: even creatures like me feel pity.'

The New Year bells were clanging wildly in St Petersburg, and the sky was a single sail of light, but even in all this chaos, all this tumult, the ghosts of Sadovaya Street could hear the question posed by Josef Rubashov as the visitor prepared to leave, the question about what it had all been for.

The visitor looked out of the window.

'Why?' he said ruefully. 'Why a hundred-year life as vicarious victim, as vicarious survivor . . . why just that, Kolya, and why just you?'

He said no more, disappearing from Josef Rubashov's range of vision to be replaced by an inaudible music, a mighty symphony of tones of a frequency so high it was beyond perception and yet, and yet explained every mystery. It was a vast saga in which Josef Rubashov himself was the central character, a story of a survivor and a witness that was now being replayed in the room from beginning to end, a century-old song teeming with lives and destinies, and in that song, in that mighty music, Josef Rubashov understood everything he had ever wondered about, the entire extent of his fate and why he had been condemned to an immortal life. All this he understood without words. He understood that he was himself and everybody else, he was Europe and its people through a century, he was a torrent of events, a wandering seer, a pawn in an illusory game between good and evil; he was a fugitive between the walls, time in a watchmaker's workshop, witness to the Holocaust, the occultists' inspiration, the forgotten victim, the music of the Twenties, life's escape artist, the alchemists' formula, the personal taster of the chosen ones, the assassin of his beloved; he was exalted and degraded, rich and destitute, and the gambler's universe of all or nothing, the game of chance that was existence, the eternal ingredients of human life: profit and loss.

In the room on Sadovaya Street in St Petersburg, time and epochs ran together with a rumble that drowned out the noise of the New Year celebrations, strange colours shone from hidden sources of light, bells rang, water clocks gushed, voices could be heard everywhere and the air was filled with people from Josef Rubashov's documents: the castrato Iliodor with his forged devil's contract, Grigori Rasputin among his women, the chain-smoking Tsar Nikolai II, Paracelsus in the laboratory, Sergeant Feder-Wisch and a tabby cat, Mikhail Rubashov at the moment of his death, Crowley, Houdini, Marinus van der Lubbe, Philip Bouhler and Christian Wirth, Margarete Barsch and a peculiar butler with a spider on his shoulder, the spies Reinecke and Kim Philby, and an archangel by the name of Fanuel. And batman Waida, who now felt his ghost body slowly disintegrating and sleep overpowering him in the form of love for a haberdasher's assistant, realised that they, the disembodied voices that had spoken in the apartment, all belonged to the strange visitor, for he was not one, he was many, he was them, he was everything that human beings could call forth from themselves.

They were singing now, the voices were singing a song about life and the secrets of death, rocking them all to sleep, wearing happy smiles because they had finally attained wordless wisdom. And in that meltdown of light and sound, music and time and ages, Josef Rubashov shut his eyes and felt his consciousness gently thinning, dimming and running out; and finally, before he was aware of it, he was extinguished, for ever, irretrievably gone.

Ten minutes into the new millennium, Yelena the landlady came round on the floor in the darkness of the service corridor. All was quiet in the apartment. The buzz from Nevsky Prospekt was receding as people headed home or to other parts of the city to carry on partying. She got to her feet and brushed the dust from the dress in which she would be leaving the country in fourteen hours' time.

A look through the peephole in the alcove confirmed that her lodger and the curious visitor had vanished.

She went back to the kitchen, and from there along the hall to Josef Rubashov's room. The light was out. The furniture stood in its place. Everything appeared strangely clean and tidy, as if the room had never been inhabited. There was no trace of the two men.

She was suddenly overwhelmed by the sensation that the old man had never existed, that he was a figment of the imagination, dreamed into existence by her or someone else that night. Bewildered by the notion, she crossed in front of the huge wardrobe to the table.

There were some traces of him after all, for she now saw lying on the table his old, yellowed document, the piece of paper he used to sit and stare at in the evenings.

She reached out her hand for it, but at that moment it turned to fine, white ash which was dispersed by an imperceptible draught. She saw the particles twirling in the air and then floating down to the floor, and there, under the table, she found the briefcase the visitor had brought with him.

She clicked open the fastening and looked inside. The case contained fat bundles of pristine hundred-mark notes. Miss Yelena's heart pounded, and she turned instinctively to check she wasn't being watched. *Where's all this money come from,* she thought, *if what I witnessed didn't really happen somehow?*

With the briefcase in her hand, jubilant in the certain knowledge that she would not need to earn a living in the new country for the rest of her life, she went over to the window. The sky was dark. The snow was falling more thickly, laying a forgiving quilt over the city of St Petersburg, its dilapidated buildings and dirty quays, its dreams, hopes and passions, that were now rushing headlong into the new millennium, dead almost before they were born. She looked down into the street where the black car had been, but it was gone. Further along the pavement stood a boy. He was staring up into the sky in amazement.

Miss Yelena opened the window and leaned out. Now, through the white dance of the snowflakes, she too could see:

High in the sky, its headlights casting shimmering beams of a thousand colours, hovered the black car. It was incredible. She watched it circle over the city, over the old tenement blocks of Dekabristov Island, over the glimmering lights of Vasilievsky Island and Bolshoy Prospekt. She saw it rising ever higher, in a softly radiating spiral through space, above the canals and bridges, the River Neva and the city's celebrating crowds. In the end it was no bigger than a distant constellation, winking ever more faintly through the snow until it disappeared high above the white, sleeping dome of St Isaac's Cathedral.